ONLY
FLESH
AND
BONES

ONLY FLESH AND BONES

◇
◇
◇

Sarah Andrews

St. Martin's Press ⚮ New York

ISBN 0-312-18642-8

First Edition: July 1998

10   9   8   7   6   5   4   3   2   1

For Mary Ann,
with love, and:
oγ-oγ-oγ-BOP!

Acknowledgments

My thanks go to Robert B. Kayser, my once-upon-a-time boss at ANGUS Petroleum, now head honcho land baron at the Spur Ranch Company, Douglas, Wyoming, for his depth of insight regarding all sorts of stuff, not least of all range ecology and minerals and ranching economics. My special thanks also to J. David Love, autochthonous geologist, Wyoming State treasure, and sentient being, for his encouragement and detailed review; and Kelley Ragland, editor on the rise, who was tough enough to require the very best of this manuscript.

My unending thanks to Damon Brown, ace pilot and patient husband, for helping this occasional pilot construct the flying scenes herein, and for tolerating yet one more book writing experience with his half-crazy insomniac wife.

Thanks also to: John Perry ("storms move around that valley like rogue buffalo") Barlow for corroboration of flying experiences around Jackson's Little Hole and Hoback Canyon; Susan Gearheart, R.N., M.S., for help with certain unseemly medical details herein; Dave Edwards, manager of the LaBonte Hotel, for an unforgettable tour of everything down to the poker palace in the basement and that "friction fire" between the income and the mortgage; Deborah Dix, Director of Public Relations, the Brown Palace Hotel; and Dr. Baldhard G. Falk, who smoothed out certain details of international trade.

I could not have written this without the excellent and constructive criticisms of: the Golden Machetes—namely, Mary Hallock, Thea Castleman, Jon Gunnar Howe, Kenneth Dalton, and Ruth Wright; Jerretta Kayser, Lise McClintock, Jaqueline Girdner, Robert J. Bowman, and good and always Clint Smith.

ONLY
FLESH
AND
BONES

1

Calving is a cruel season in Wyoming. My father always brought the pregnant cows, in their last weeks, up from the far pastures so he could keep an eye on them in case they needed help, but instinct always moved each cow, in her own time, down to the cover of cottonwood trees by the creek. The rare calf would come by daylight and warm weather, but far too many dropped soaking wet from their hundred-degree mothers into subzero air by the dead of night. The first part to freeze was their ears.

In the morning we'd bring the calf up to the barn, if the coyotes didn't find it first, and do what we could to warm it. I'd hold the frosty fur of its ears between the palms of my wool mittens while Dad weighed it and fussed about where to drive the earring spike that would hold its brightly colored ID tag. Eventually, the dead flesh along the crests of the ear would fall away, and I would try hard not to love the calf, because bad ears meant it almost always grew up to be meat.

Our neighbors thought my father daft. They left their cows in the pastures and slept soundly, figuring that the loss of a few calves was simply Nature's way. Life was tough, after all, and a rancher's love for the land didn't mean he had to get sentimental.

Perhaps it was from holding those calves' ears—and the endless kidding from other ranchers that followed—that I learned a sensitivity for all creatures who get caught by the extremes of life's experiences, beast and human alike, and come to think that they need me. But that may be my ego speaking, and instead, those who face the challenges of life beyond the edge are the strongest. If I hadn't found my own way to the edge, life might have been quite different for me. I might have had what it took to stay on my parents' ranch, or found myself married up to a neighboring spread, instead of heading off into these other lives of mine. Certainly in my girlhood dreams I never imagined I'd become a geologist, and if anyone had told me I'd make a name for myself as a detective, I'd have laughed in his face. But here I am, footloose Em, making my way looking for rocks and other things that lie hidden.

No matter. It's just that all these thoughts get stuck together—those of calving, and of female needs and instincts, and of trying to make it alone and fly in the face of one's fears—when I think of the time I went looking for Miriam Menken.

She was already dead when I started. Had been for eight months, and I knew that, and at first it was not for her sake but for her daughter Cecelia that I took up the search. To me, Miriam's death put Cecelia out in the night air by herself, with the temperature dropping and the coyotes on the hunt, and she'd be lucky to get out of the whole mess with something as metaphorically simple as frozen ears.

2

I'D JUST GOTTEN IN FROM CHECKING ON A NEW CALF OUT IN the corral when Miriam's husband, Cecelia's father, my ex-boss Josiah Carberry Menken himself, phoned to ask me for help. At first, it was easy to ignore his plea: I'd been up half the night with a heifer who wasn't up to dropping a 114-pound bull calf. My mother and I had chased her into the trailer around 3:00 A.M., drawn straws, and, as I got the short one, I had driven the heifer into Wheatland, where a sleepy vet had had me hold various bits of stainless-steel equipment as he carved her open standing up, under local anesthesia, a nice long gash behind her last rib. It's a strange sight, seeing a calf come into the world ahead of its mother's hind legs, but the calf was fine and the cow had stood it like that was all part of the plan, and the vet had sewn her up with a big running blanket stitch, and just a few hours later she was munching hay back out on the ranch, enjoying the April sunrise, the calf bumping at her udder.

But to J.C. Menken I said no. No, I'm a geologist second and a rancher first, damn it, not a detective; can't you get that straight? No, I can't help resolve your wife's death. Sorry.

Then two days later, he turned up at our door.

That was a much grimmer morning. I had stood by ready to assist while Mother reached up inside the hot, moist regions of the last pregnant cow and wrangled her reluctant calf out into the world. She ran strong hands along the calf, checked the afterbirth, and gave the cow a tender pat. Such scenes bring a rise of heart most days, but this last birth meant the end of our labors together, and over breakfast, Mother and I had had a little chat, in which she informed me that, as she now had things pretty well in hand, it was time I moseyed. She said she had appreciated my helping her set the ranch to rights after Father's death, and she knew I'd helped her save at least one cow and fifteen hundred dollars' worth of calves that would otherwise have died, but it was time, she said, for us each to stand on our own respective two feet and either make it or not.

It was the *not* that worried me; if she couldn't make the spread go, then I wanted a try. What did an aging, newly recovering alcoholic think she was doing, trying to run a ranch by herself?

As if she could read minds, Mother added rather baldly that it was *her* inheritance from *her* father that had bought this ranch, and not *my* ranch for *her* to maintain until I was ready to take it over.

So Menken's arrival found me on the phone at *my* father's desk, trying to scare up a lead on a job. Answering the door seemed like a welcome break until I saw who it was, but some mornings life just kicks you in the shorts.

"Emily!" Menken proclaimed, ever-bouyant smile puckering his insipidly pleasant face. It had turned cold again, and his breath formed ghosts.

"J.C., what a surprise," I said mournfully, my words falling from my mouth like little ingots of lead.

With a little wink that suggested that he found my greeting terribly clever, he said, "May I come in, Emily?"

I threw the door wide in defeat. "Mother and I were just sitting down to lunch. You'll join us, won't you?"

His smile bloomed to a grin. "Why, I'd love to. It just happens that I haven't eaten, and I don't believe I've met your mother."

I led the way back through the living room of our log house and into its kitchen. *Rustic* is the quaint term for its decor. There had been days when it looked spiffier, but things had gotten a little run-down in the years Mother was drinking, when Dad was still alive and trying to do everything himself.

Back in the kitchen, Mother was washing lettuce leaves for our baloney sandwiches. I said, "Don't put the fixings away, Ma; we have company."

My mother straightened her patrician spine and turned around, adjusting the tilt of her head to aim the right slice of her trifocals at Menken. She's still a beautiful woman at fifty-nine, austere and slender, a Brahmin recast in western wear. Always a class act whether she's being particularly nice about it or not, she curved her lips hospitably, extended a wet hand, and said, "I'm Leila Hansen. And you are?"

"Joe Menken. I'm afraid Emily still calls me J.C."

I said, "J.C. was president at Blackfeet Oil, before it went down the drain. That's the oil company in Denver where I worked, remember?"

"Ahh." This had become my mother's standard comment of late, and it could mean anything from an uninterested "Isn't that interesting," to a cagey "No, I don't remember, and prefer not to comment on that particular ten years of alcoholic blackout," to a more forward-looking "You filthy four-legged brute, I'll have your balls for that." Withdrawing her hand from Menken's after the precisely correct span of time, Mother extended it now toward the table. "Joe, please sit down. Coffee? I'm afraid it's this morning's, but it's from a decent bean. Em, get those olives out of the refrigerator and put them in a dish. And let's have the last of that extrasharp Pennsylvanian cheddar your Aunt Frances sent, and the rye crackers."

"Coffee would be wonderful." Menken strode across the wooden floor like a general on a goodwill tour of the troops, all tight ass and sucked-in gut. I took advantage of his preoccupation with Mother to check out his attire: Luccesi boots, preabused jeans, and the most conservative of western-style shirts, all straight out of the box. J.C. gone country. I wondered idly how I rated such a break in form; I'd never before seen him in anything but a business suit.

Pulling out one of the mismatched chairs from the table, he sat down and leaned back, spreading his elbows across the backs of adjacent chairs. It was his throne pose, so familiar from the old days in the boardroom at Blackfeet Oil.

"What brings you our way, J.C.?" I asked somewhat facetiously.

"Why, Emily," he crooned, "I've just arrived. Surely even here on the ranch it's considered rude to speak of business so soon. Let's have lunch, and then we'll talk. Besides, I wouldn't want to keep Leila from her fine repast." He beamed up at her.

Mother smiled back, or at least to Menken's eyes she did. He would have had to have known her much better to catch the sarcasm spoken by that subtle lowering of her eyelids.

While I bent myself to the task of building a sandwich for Menken, Mother descended into a chair and took up a line of chat about how very much I'd learned working for Blackfeet Oil. Cussing under my breath, I sawed into the hard, sharp cheese and laid it out on the squashy stuff that passed for bread at the local store. I needed to aim my face where they couldn't see it for a minute or two, while I collected myself; not only did I have deep forebodings about what J.C. Menken wanted from me, but I knew that Mother would make me pay dearly for the last of that Pennsylvanian cheddar.

◈

"I HAVE TO tell you, Emily, it's a bittersweet thing to find myself on a ranch again," Menken confided in me when my mother had ushered us out into the front room after lunch. "I haven't been back in Wyoming since Miriam's death." He sat in the middle of the couch, his arms stretched out across the back and one ankle at ease on the opposite knee. For a moment, he looked pensive.

I perched on the arm of my father's vacant easy chair and stared out the window across the rolling short-grass prairie toward the foothills of the Laramie Range. I hated it when people played on my sympathies. "I really was sorry to hear about all that, J.C.," I muttered. In fact, I would have had to have been deaf not to hear, even though the killing had occurred two hours' drive north of Chugwater, where we lived, on a ranch outside of Douglas. Eight months after the fact, it was still a favorite topic of conversation in cafés and saloons from Cheyenne to Sheridan and Casper to the Nebraska border. It had all the elements of soap opera: big-city woman found dead in her bed on a rented ranch and the daughter roaming the house, out of her mind with grief and terror. No suspects identified. No leads. A murder left unsolved through the long, otherwise uneventful autumn and winter that followed.

"What were they doing on a ranch up there near Douglas?" I asked, immediately wishing I hadn't. It wouldn't do to show my curiosity. It would give him an edge to grab hold of me, drag me in where I definitely did not want to go. Besides, I had already heard the scuttlebutt: Miriam had gone to the ranch with their adolescent daughter, Cecelia, in order to relax away from the city for the summer, enjoy their horses, and, most importantly, remove Cecelia from the influence of some male of the species with big pecs and raging hormones who wanted to teach her some trick riding.

"It was good for them to get away, spend a little time together before Cecelia grew up and flew the nest. And Miriam always had an affection for Wyoming. I had hoped to get up more, but business kept me in Denver entirely too much." Drugstore gossip had Menken cast as the cold, aloof, money-baron husband, staying behind in Denver, glorying in the pursuit of yet another fortune investing other people's money in risky ventures, and seldom showing his face at the ranch. "I made the five-hour drive every weekend I could break away. I'd arrive there late on a Friday evening and return to Denver on Sunday afternoon." He stared at his hands, and with a subdued voice, he added, "Miriam was murdered on a Tuesday."

How quickly news had traveled. I had still been in Denver, living at Elyria Kretzmer's, when she had come home from the office and told me the news that was whizzing like bees through Denver business circles. Now, as Menken maundered onward over the story, I regretted how little I had done by way of condolence to Cecelia. She was, after all, a friend of mine, my adolescent fan club of one, a wanna-be barrel racer, who had frequently asked me up to their place west of Denver to ride the finicky horses that rich folks kept in their stables. I had sent little more than the requisite card. I had meant to send flowers to the memorial service, but by then, my father was dead also, and I had little sympathy to offer anyone. "I kept meaning to visit," I mumbled, "but you see, my father—"

Menken held up a hand. "Say no more; we understood perfectly. Elyria told me everything." He sighed. "What a woman she is. I must admit, when I found myself a widower, I thought of her, but by then she was seeing that Finney fellow, and the next I heard, she had married him! I've met him since," he added abstractedly. "A decent sort, but she could have done better." He shook his head, bemused. Suddenly, as in resolution, he sat up straight, indicating that the moment for action had come. "So I need your help, Emily. It's been eight months, and the matter of my departed wife's murder has still not been resolved. Knowing how talented you are as a detective, I—"

I jumped up from my roost. "Stop right there. Listen to me, J.C.: I've hung up those spurs. The answer is no."

"Now, Emily . . ." His mouth began to widen into one of his most patronizing smiles.

That tore it. Losing control, I blurted, "J.C., just when are you going to get it straight? My name is Em!"

Menken feigned surprise. "Why, if it would help to call you that—"

"No, it would not help." I began to pace. "I'm looking for work, but not that kind of work. I—with respect—do not want to get involved uh . . . this way in your family's dealings." There, it was out. Settled.

Menken leaned his elbows on his knees, stared into space. "Em, I want to know who killed Miriam, but that's not what brings me here. What has brought me so far from Denver is the effect this whole experience has had on Cecelia. She's morose, failing at school. You see, she was there when it happened, and—"

"That's all very sad, but I'm sure very private."

"No, Em, we think of you as a close family friend." He leaned toward me, all amusement at the fun of persuasion dropping from his soft face as he began to plead in earnest. "My daughter is everything to me, Em. She's all I have left of Miriam, all I have left of anything. She was there, but she can't remember anything. It's torturing her, knowing that on some level she knows who killed her mother, yet not knowing. I've had her to the best psychologist I could find, a specialist on these blocked memories, but six months in her care have bought us nothing. I'm asking you not for myself, but for Cecelia."

I hid my face in my hands. This was not my battle to fight; I felt that deeply. And my mother was right: I had a life to get on with, and the sooner the better. Jobs were scarce for geologists, and getting scarcer, and the longer I stayed out of action, the moldier my résumé grew.

As if he could read my thoughts, Menken said, "Even if all you do is talk to her, Em, I would be forever in your debt. And to prove that I know just exactly how to show my appreciation, I will open all the doors I can for you toward finding a new job."

The two of us looked into each others' eyes for a long moment. I saw a man who would not be deterred from his errand. He saw an out-of-work geologist who had just found her price.

I took a deep breath and said, "I suppose I could pay her a call next week sometime. If you really think that my talking to her can help. But you know, all I can offer is just that—talk—and she may not—"

"Good. I'll expect you at the house on Monday for dinner, seven o'clock."

I saw Menken give his denim-encased knee a little swat, a gesture of buisness concluded which I remembered so well from the good old days when he paid me in cash.

3

THE FIRST THING I NEEDED WAS A PLACE TO STAY NEAR DENVER.
If I was going to find a job, I had to be right there sticking my face in the
faces of potential employers, not hiding out on a ranch in the next state.
And it was important to have a place to retreat to, so that Menken couldn't
insist that I stay with them.

I phoned Elyria, who said she knew a woman in Boulder—a Betty
Bloom—who rented a room by the week. She said Betty Bloom didn't
like renting to students, and wasn't fond of long-term rental commitments. Tenants had a way of getting on her nerves after awhile, but a
week or two, or ten, having a new face around the property was something
of a tonic. Betty Bloom sounded like my kind of woman.

I dialed the number Elyria had given me. It rang six times before it was
answered, which told me a little more about Ms. Bloom—namely, that she
did not employ the services of an answering machine. The sounds that
came over the wire when she lifted the receiver told me even more: I
heard the concluding booms of the *1812* Overture and the loud slurping
sound of a washing machine, all but drowned out by a very excited canine
ruckus. "Hel-LO?" she bellowed.

I said, "Ms. Bloom? My name is Em Hansen. Elyria—"

"Wait! Hold on a minute—I can't hear you!" The cannon stopped in
midboom. The machine shifted into a drain cycle. And I heard her utter
more quietly, "Stanley, you son of a bitch, shut up!"

I began again. "My name is Em Hansen. Elyria gave me your—"

"Elyria! Yes, of course. You're the unemployed geologist from Wyoming who moonlights as a detective."

"Well, ah—"

"You got some hot young stud you're gonna move in here, or is it just you?"

I sighed. "Just me." Well, there was Jim Erikson, but he was out in California, and sweet as he was I wasn't so sure if it was smart for me to see him again, and—

"Any friend of Elyria's. The room's a hundred fifty a week—private entrance, hot plate, midget reefer, and a bathroom the size of a suitcase, you shut up by ten P.M., and don't bitch about my dog. When will you be here?"

"Monday okay?"

"Monday? Sure, I'll be here. I'm on Baseline Road above Sixteenth, the stone house with the ugly fence. Come around to the back so Stanley doesn't think you're a mailman. You don't have to knock."

"Stanley will alert you to my presence."

"Yes. If I don't come to the door within five minutes, come back in an hour."

"Okay."

"Don't wear perfume. And try to be here by daylight." The line clicked, and I heard a dial tone.

MOTHER SAW ME off at noon, after one last morning wrestling with fence posts and barbed wire and a lunch of her best can of soup. As we cleared up the dishes she looked kind of sad, but somehow I knew her mood didn't have much to do with the thought that I'd soon be gone. As we walked out across the hard-packed earthen yard to my truck, she said, "Don't make yourself a stranger."

"Okay." I paused, uncertain what else to say. It was being too easy to leave, devoid of emotional tension. What had I expected? The kind of verbal wrangling we used to rope each other into?

My mother stood with one hand on a blue jean–clad hip, the other tracing the ritual of cigarette smokers everywhere, fingers stiffening into a vise as she inhaled, now whipping the little white fetish into a downward arc, now flicking it to free the ash. She was off the alcohol, the addiction that had rendered her incapable of working, but wouldn't this habit kill her just as surely? Squinting at me through a cloud of exhaled smoke, she said succinctly, "It's been nice having you here, dear."

I stared at the ground, worrying a pebble out of the dust with the toe of my boot. "Um . . ."

"It's okay, Emily. It's something of a milestone for us if we've already said what needed saying."

Still I waited. I was waiting, I guess, to see if she would hug me. Or say she loved me. Surely that needed saying, but she said nothing more.

I climbed into the cab and rolled down the window and said good-bye. As I reached up to grasp the wheel, she patted my arm and said, "I'm proud of you." I smiled an acknowledgment of this gesture, the sort of smile that finds its way to your lips out of habit and manners, then fired the engine, put the old beast in gear, and set it to rolling south. I was five miles from the Colorado border before it even occurred to me that I could have initiated something closer than a pat on the arm myself.

THE DRIVE TOOK me down Interstate 25, which parallels the Laramie Range and the Front Range of the Colorado Rockies twenty miles out into the plains. The weather was fair and moving toward hot, and by two o'clock the first cumulus clouds were already darkening into thunderheads over the Arapaho Peaks and spilling out across the plains. I watched them grow with fascination, thinking nostalgically of the mornings and afternoons I'd spent up in the skies overhead, learning to fly a small airplane, getting bounced around on the moist, boiling air that forms such traveling pillows. Or beginning to learn; when I'd lost my job, I'd had to quit. Flying was just plain expensive. But an efficient mode of travel, and beautiful: in the time I'd already spent zigzagging around property lines and making right-angle doglegs and slowing for traffic in this slow-moving truck, I could have flown from the ranch to Boulder and back again. And had a better view.

Perhaps I'll be working soon, I told myself. Then I could afford more lessons, even get on to the big cross-country legs I'd have to fly in order to qualify for a license. And a job might lead to financial stability, and financial stability might lead to—what? Settling down? I laughed at myself, old gypsy Em, vagabond of the western plains. When the trumpets blew, I was likely to be the last single woman standing.

I found myself thinking about Jim Erikson, my sort-of boyfriend out in California; about how I'd tried to tell him how stimulating the weather is in the high plains and the mountains, and how splendid it is when the seasons change. He had listened quietly, no doubt wondering at my taste for drama. I had stared back blankly at him, biting my tongue against the obvious comeback that being an emergency med tech on a volunteer fire department wasn't exactly a way to relax. But he sure was easy to stare at, all six feet three of him. . . .

An hour later, I was still thinking about Jim as I pulled into the alley behind Betty Bloom's stone house on Baseline Road in Boulder. It's named Baseline because it lies along an early survey baseline, and it runs bullet-straight east to west up the ramp of alluvium that forms Boulder's "Hill," that district of older homes and shops that surrounds the University of Colorado. Betty's was a fair-sized house built of red Lyons Sandstone with the most god-awful-looking picket fence I've ever seen. It rose six feet high through three courses of pickets sloppily painted green, mauve, and international orange, and I can't say the boards were laid on with any kind of skill. The house itself looked sound enough, no yawning chinks in its stone armor, no cascading bits of roofing tile or sagging gutters. I shut down the truck, locked the door with a ritual "I'm back in the city" sigh, and pushed my way through the back gate.

Stanley the dog turned out to be a Bouvier des Flandres, an enormous black moving-mop-type dog with a small brain and big devotion to duty. He barked himself silly, lunging at the window by the back door, planting his forepaws again and again like a bad sped-up movie of raucous step aerobics. His nose greased the glass with fresh spinnerets of slobber as hanks of tangly black hair whipped the thin, frail membrane of glass that separated him from me. I took a deep breath and was just muttering a litany against dog defenestration when a hand reached out for his collar and applied an authoritative jerk. Stanley shut up and dropped to the floor. End of demonstration.

The door crunched open, and I got my first look at Betty Bloom, my new landlady.

About fifty, voluminous head of wiry red hair gone mostly to gray. An appealing oval face; pale, amused eyes; skin like milk. She wore canvas shorts and a lavender tunic with no collar, and she had fetched her hair back into a loose elastic covered with bright purple fabric. Her feet were bare. Gauging by their surplus of dirt and calluses, she seldom wore shoes. "Em, come in," she murmured. "Don't mind Stanley; he's just a big baby. So, Elyria tells me you're on another case."

Had I told Elyria that? It wasn't like Elyria to pass on that kind of information, even if I had. Figuring I could handle the dog but not any bullshit, I stated, "She didn't really say that, did she."

Big grin. Flashing spark in the eyes. "No. Just checking. Coffee?"

Smiling back, I said, "Make mine black."

4

Seven o'clock found me winding my way through Genesee, a community of enormous cedar homes built during the oil boom of the late 1970s. After nearly twenty years in place, it still looked like the Martians had just landed the development there yesterday, plunking each behemoth structure down at the end of its perfect strip of black asphalt with an alien disregard for setting. As usual, the homes looked oddly deserted. I steered around quaintly engineered curves until I found the Menkens'.

Cecelia had grown since I'd seen her last, and I was startled to find that she had gotten quite tall. As I parked my truck and walked up the driveway toward where she stood loitering by the three-car garage, she seemed to loom, and I realized that even when I reached her, she would be looking over the top of my head. How long had it been since I'd seen her? A year? I decided that aside from the awkward height she had attained, she still looked a child: no hips, no buns, no tender swelling twixt clavicles and sternum. It had to be hell.

She had herself kitted out in a short black leather skirt, a skintight T-shirt, a voluminous campaign jacket, and a fumbling attempt at eye makeup; an attempt, I was sure, to look sophisticated, but a kid is always a kid, no matter how you package her. She'd gotten her hair under control, at least. Her once-wild medusan mop of dark hair now hung just to her jaw in a chic pageboy.

The look in her eyes made my heart sink. They had taken on a hard, sleep-deprived shadow, and her smear of a mouth dove painfully at the corners. I caught myself sighing, feeling as sorry for myself as I did for her. Where was the confused but cuddling child I had taught to race her quarter horse around the barrels? As she looked up and saw me, the corners of her mouth flicked upward for a moment before giving in once more to the weight of loss and adolescence. "Em," she mumbled, lurching away from the wall of the garage and shambling toward me, hands thrust deep into the pockets of her jacket. "Glad to see you."

"I'm glad to see you, too, Cecelia." And I was. Why is it that any thousand shifty-eyed teenagers glimpsed on the street can be written off as slouching delinquents to be avoided, but when just one of these half-formed creatures turns a hopeful glance our way, we lose all caution and greet her with an undefended heart?

I held out my arms for a hug.

Cecelia contorted her body into a cave-chested twist and looked anywhere but into my eyes as she shuffled closer. A few inches from me, she threw herself onto me like a stevedore discharging a sack of grain onto a waiting cart.

Bracing my feet, I caught her in my arms and squeezed. "You're taller than I am now," I declared, for want of a more inspired opener.

"Mmpf."

"It's been rough, huh?"

She began to sniff.

I ran my hands through her hair, coaxing her sniffling into a bawl, saying, "I've missed you. I feel rotten not coming to see you sooner. Did your dad explain that I've been out of town?"

Head nodding up and down. Hoarse coughing.

"There now. There."

"You never called," she said reproachfully.

"Um, sorry."

"I mean, shit, you—"

I cut her off, a mixture of guilt over not better acknowledging her pain and self-pity arising from my own making me impatient. "Couldn't be helped," I said. She stiffened. I tightened my hug, reaching into her for another dose of importance.

Cecelia abruptly pulled away and stuffed her hands up against her face. "I hate this. My nose gets all red."

"Need a Kleenex?"

"Yeah."

"Well, I don't have one. We're outside, so blow it on the ground like I taught you for skiing."

Cecelia twisted her now-swollen lips in a rueful smile, bent, placed a finger to each side of her nose, and blew. When she had wiped her hand on the tiny scrap of lawn the developer had insisted on planting in this semiarid part of creation, she slung an arm around my shoulders and leaned her head against mine. She had to crane her neck. "Missed you, too," she allowed, approximating a kind of offhanded candor.

"So things have been bad."

"The pits." She rolled her eyes. "Sorry. Haven't lost it like that in months."

"Maybe you need to do it more often."

"No, it sucks. I mean, I'm glad to see you, but you know? I got to go on living. At least, that's what the shrink keeps saying." She shrugged, a sulking gesture of such unappealing awkwardness that no one who had slipped the mighty bonds of adolescence would hope to replicate it. Suddenly, she threw herself against me again and whimpered. "You always understand. You're my best friend in the whole world. You love me better than anyone!"

Embarrassed that I felt so pleased to hear such sentimental nonsense, I said, "Tell me about the shrink."

Cecelia's eyes suddenly widened in terror. "I don't remember a thing!" she blurted.

"I'm not investigating your mother's death; I'm here for *you*. Remember, I never even met your mother."

She nodded, eyeing me with bald suspicion.

"Listen, Celie, life's tough enough when you're sixteen—"

"Almost seventeen!"

"Right, and you've lost your mother the hard way. Not good. Worse yet, your dad says you were there when it happened. When she was murdered," I said, choosing harsh words to cut through the pompous crap she must have been getting from everyone, "so you should be able to finger the person who killed her."

She hung her head.

"But you can't. So help me with this. You just don't remember the incident, or is there a bunch else missing?"

She lifted her head, stared blankly into the air beside my head. "That day, and the whole week after, except bits," she recited. "It happened on a Tuesday, and I can remember from Saturday, waking up back here."

"When did you come down from Wyoming?"

"Friday. Or so I'm told. Dad says it took a few days to get the—um, body released."

"Your dad drove you?"

She looked away. Shrugged. "I guess so." Her voice took on an earnest tone. "It truly sucks, not knowing."

"Because you'd like to know who killed her."

She looked up, confused. "Well, yeah, but also because I usually have such a good memory. I mean, here I was an honor student, you know? And I can't remember what happened in a whole week!"

WE WENT ON talking like that for half an hour or so, getting nowhere, and for longer during dinner. Her reactions to my questions quickly wore a circular groove in the conversation, looping around what should have been her major concerns—the loss of her mother and a desire to avenge her death—and reconnecting again and again to seemingly minor ones. It was like chipping solid frost out of an old-fashioned icebox, lots of effort for frustratingly little gain, and all the time worrying that I'm going to stab the wrong thing with the pick and ruin the mechanism.

The effort to guide Cecelia's train of thought onto a cogent track got worse when her father entered the conversation over dinner. He served grilled venison steaks, which he sliced into with carnivorous glee. "Go ahead, Cecelia dear," he urged, "tell Emily what you *can* remember. You can *trust* her."

Cecelia set her jaw in refusal.

After enormous bowls of double-chocolate ice cream, we moved into the living room and Menken prodded her again. "Really now, Cecelia dear, barring this therapist woman, you've been without the companionship of an older female for over half a year. Let Emily help."

This time, Cecelia gave him a smoldering glare.

The cumulative fatigue of too many miles and too many emotional turns in one day moved me toward the door. "You know, I think it's time for me to call it a day," I said.

"Let me walk you to your truck," Menken said, turning a smile on me that seemed a degree or two too warm.

I grabbed Cecelia by one skinny arm. "Let Cecelia walk me out, J.C.; we got more girl talking to do," and as I backed out through the doorway, I added, "I'll give you a call soon and we'll talk job contacts, okay?"

"Anytime." He beamed.

TAKING ONE LAST stab with the mental ice pick before I climbed into my truck, I asked Cecelia, "So what does this therapist you're seeing think is going on with you? Or have you asked her?"

Shrug.

"I thought so. You just go because you father takes you, right?"

Shrug. "The headmistress said I should go. Dad just agreed."

"So who takes you?"

"I go by bus." She whimpered, craning her neck to lay her head down on my shoulder once again.

I reached up and stroked her hair, stirred by the weight of her need. Stopping to turn toward her, I put my arms around her and held her close, imagining briefly that if she had been my child, I would have taken such good care of her that she would not be needing some hired gun to straighten her out. It wasn't hard to see why this therapy wasn't getting anywhere. It had to be a cold, lonely ride downtown to a psychotherapist's office when you're sixteen, almost seventeen, gawky, your mother is dead, and you don't want to be there in the first place.

Cecelia clung to me like a limpet. "I hate going to her, Em. Why can't I just come live with you?"

So much for maternal fantasies. The truth was I could barely look after myself, and I didn't want to give that fact a whole lot of contemplation. "Do you go at the end of the day?" I asked, keeping the conversation on matters I thought I could handle.

"They let me out of study hall and gym class for it. I go twice a week." Shrug. "It sucks big time. It's this little bitch on spike heels who looks like she wants a cigarette more than she wants to talk to me. And all the other girls at school are jealous that I get off so much."

"Oh, that's great. So your classmates know you're going and everything."

Cecelia hung her head. "I tell them I'm going to the orthodontist." At this, she grimaced, displaying a fine rack of hardware.

"And they're still buying that after how long?"

"Six months. No, they're not. That's part of why I told Daddy it's bullshit to keep going."

I pursed my lips and thought. "When are you supposed to go next?"

"Wednesday afternoon."

"Okay, so you stay at school. I'll just use your next appointment," I heroically concluded, thereby putting myself on the hook for a visit with Melanie Steen, Ph.D.

5

MELANIE STEEN KEPT OFFICES NEAR ST. LUKE'S HOSPITAL, JUST east of downtown Denver. Even though I was not the subject of her services, I felt fully conspicuous as I slid my finger down the building directory and strode purposefully across the lobby toward the elevator, my jaw set in rebellion against the status quo opinion of people who need to see shrinks. Let me tell you, back home in Wyoming persons who ply the psychotheraputic trade are thought to be somewhere between baboons and tax collectors on the chain of evolution.

The elevator dumped me off on the sixth floor, and I sloped down the hall to suite 63, two doors to my left. I let myself in and found myself in an unmanned waiting room. Just me, two stylish overstuffed chairs, an abstract painting, a philodendron, and a magazine rack. No buzzer to press, no sharp-nosed receptionist to get crosswise with, no nothing. I would have knocked on the inner door if I hadn't been ten minutes early.

Instead, I chose a chair and sat in it, and, eschewing *Smithsonian* and *Psychology Today*, took advantage of the chance to indulge in *People* and *Us*. And wondered if I was being observed from the inside office through a hidden peephole or something.

Two minutes into my puerile perusal, the inner door swung open and a dishwater blonde hurried out, reddened eyes carefully averted. I was in the middle of trying to make eye contact to see if there was anything I could do to help the poor thing when it occurred to me that I must be trampling every major tenet of therapist's-office etiquette. Embarrassed, I glanced away.

Right smack on the hour, the door opened again. This time, I was confronted by a very short woman with a ramrod-straight spine and spike heels. Her eyes were too big for her face. In fact, they would have met in the middle if her rather prominent nose hadn't been in the way. As I was clearly not the party she expected to find warming her swanky side chair, she said in a tone that demanded a reply, "I'm Melanie Steen."

"Em Hansen." I stood up and extended a hand.

Melanie Steen reached up (which meant she was *short*, let me tell you, because I barely made five foot seven in the cowboy boots I was wearing) and grasped the tips of my fingers with the tips of hers, one of those "Have you washed your hands?" kind of shakes. Quickly releasing my hand, she waited for me to say something further.

"I'm here for Cecelia," I offered.

She tipped her head a fraction to the left.

"Didn't she call you?"

Melanie Steen's eyebrows rose a notch. They were heavy black things that described very shallow, perfectly matching parabolas.

I lowered my eyelashes a notch and arranged my lips in a not very pleasant smile. "I'll take that as a no. Okay, let me start again. Melanie, I'm a friend of Cecelia Menken's. Her father asked me to give her a hand with things, and I thought the best move would be to come talk to you first."

Her enormous eyes growing even larger, as if I were metamorphosing into a slightly disgusting insect as she watched, Melanie Steen said, "That's very nice, Ms. Hansen, but you of course understand that there is a thing called 'privileged information.' I can tell you nothing without my client's full permission. And as she's a minor—"

"You've already told me one thing. You've confirmed that she's your client."

Ms. Steen's lips tightened. "Ms. Hansen—"

"I'm sorry. You're right, I've gotten into a fencing match with you already, not smart. Listen, as I've come all this way, why don't you call Cecelia at school and get her permission? Please. Or feel free to call her father." When she continued to show marked reluctance to budge from the doorway, I added, "I have both numbers."

I could almost hear the gears in Melanie Steen's mental machinery grinding toward a decision. I wondered if they might benefit from a little oil, and unkindly speculated that extravirgin olive might be her preferred lubricant. Suddenly, she stepped inside her door, pulling it to behind her, intoning, "Wait here," just before the lock clicked shut.

She was back in four minutes. This time, her eyelids were lowered to half-mast, suitable to the mood of having an illicit meeting in a back alley, but her tone was still not friendly: "You may come in, Miss Hansen, although I am afraid there's very little I can tell you. Cecelia Menken is rather a difficult case. We have been working for several months to retrieve her memories of a very traumatic event, and have gotten precisely nowhere. I must conclude that she's not interested in accomplishing any such thing."

And with that frail welcome, I took my first step through the doorway of psychotherapy and into the dark heart of despair.

WHEN I'D SETTLED into the stiff leather chair across the desk from Ms. Steen, I took a moment to collect my thoughts. It was a technique I'd learned in the board-room at Blackfeet Oil: always pause and take time to review what I want to put across, or, in this case, to learn. I'd found that pausing like that also served to put my opponents on edge. At length, I said, "Tell me about this amnesia thing."

"That's a poor term."

I paused again. "And a better one is?"

Melanie Steen slowly shrugged her well-padded shoulders. "Memory loss." Shrug. "Blocked memory."

I leaned back, crossed one boot-clad foot over the opposite knee. Counted to four. "Fine. Tell me about that."

Melanie Steen smiled coolly. "What is it you want to know?"

I made a mental note: a psychologist's office is not the best place to engage in games of psychic poker. The creature had the dealer's advantage.

I threw down my cards and sighed. "My friend is deeply distressed by what happened. I want to support her. I need to understand what's happened to her, and what she's going through now."

Lowering the lids of her enormous eyes a tad, Ms. Steen said, "The human mind is a very complex organ. It must process an endless stream of stimuli, day in and day out. If we were to stop and consider each stimulus, make a conscious decision about how to respond to it, we would be quickly mired in minutiae. Instead, the mind develops defenses, ways of categorizing incoming information and standardized ways of reacting to it."

"Such as deciding ahead of time to step out of the way of oncoming locomotives when you see them coming," I suggested, letting her know I understood.

"Precisely. But what if the locomotive hits us anyway?"

I wasn't sure where she was going with this. "We scream?"

She closed her eyes for a moment, as if in pain. When those twin lamps snapped open again, she said, "Some stimuli, some events, are too shocking to process, or at least not all at once. We register the shock perhaps, and then put the awareness of the event away for a moment, or a day, or longer, while we go about responding to the more immediate stimuli that flow in on top of it. We continue to look after our daily business, keeping ourselves warm and nurtured as best we can. When it's safe to do so, or when the weight of the shock once again outbalances the urgency of more mundane events, we process the deeper layer."

That was a lot to take in. "So how does that work with Cecelia?"

"Cecelia had a terrible shock. She was present in the house when her mother was killed. Perhaps she even saw it happen. Apparently at her mother's direction, she called nine one one, her voice faint with shock and fear, to say that her mother was dying. When the ambulance and sheriff's deputy arrived, she let them in and took them to her mother, then stood by to assist in any way she could, although the woman was by then dead. The point is that Cecelia continued to function, to look after business, if you will."

"Wait. When she called for help, her mother was *dying*? Not already *dead*?"

"Precisely. Her mother's voice could be heard in the background."

"Saying what?"

"Saying? She was screaming with pain."

"Screaming words, or just screaming?"

"Words."

"What words?" I asked, trying to keep my voice level.

"'Help me, Cecelia, he's killing me.' Words to that effect."

"And you know this how?"

"I've heard the tape of the nine-one-one call."

"How interesting. I've heard endless discussion of the circumstances in recent months, and nowhere have I heard that the nine one one tape had been made public."

Melanie Steen's eyelashes dipped briefly. "I requested a copy of the tape to find out if hearing it would trigger Cecelia's memory. The Sheriff's Department in Douglas wouldn't give me one directly, but they sent a copy to the Denver Police Department so that we could play it there, under official supervision."

My mouth sagged open. The image of Cecelia sitting in a police interrogation room listening to a replay of the sounds of her mother's death as strangers watched momentarily stunned me.

Blandly regarding my obvious shock, Melanie Steen said, "Cecelia has not, in fact, heard the tape. I listened to it without her first, and when it became clear that we would not be allowed strict privacy, I decided not to subject her to a hearing. They wanted to film her reaction," she said with acerbity. "Hearing it under such circumstances would more likely have increased her trauma than lessened it."

I exhaled slowly. "Right. Then to summarize: Cecelia remembers nothing."

"Nothing until four days following, when she was safely back home here in Colorado."

"Then is the memory of those days lost?"

Melanie Steen turned her head to stare out the window, giving me a crisp view of her classic profile, like something off a Greek vase. "No, memory is seldom truly lost. It's just in there somewhere, hidden from the rest of her awareness. Locked up for safekeeping. There are soldiers and nurses who served in Vietnam who have no conscious memory of whole months of their tours of duty."

I wondered how many other people had been treated to the drama of this psychologist's pose. "That seems pretty convenient," I said peevishly. "So, case closed: Cecelia can't remember. The vets can't remember. Life goes on. Why bug them about it?"

Profile rotated slowly back to full face, two huge eyes set too close together staring at me like a goldfish trapped in an aquarium. "Perhaps you have trouble understanding this," she said dramatically, "but there is a price paid for hiding."

I didn't like her choice of words, but I remained silent, braced to hear what might come next.

"Simply put, it takes energy to keep the door closed on memory. Energy that might better be used to do one's school work, or to pay strict attention while driving a car. Or think of it like this: if the mind works to suppress extreme pain, such tension attenuates both the lows and the highs, making the mind unavailable for the experience of pleasure." She leaned forward and tapped a long fingernail on her desk. "Just what would you choose?"

For this I wasn't braced. I have one of those nasty uncomplicated minds that instantly moves to answer direct questions by the most candid means possible, making subtle inquiries like, "How are you today?" a workout. As an overly thorough answer featuring a detailed résumé of my life's pains and disappointments sped through my mind, I just sat there, my mouth once again sagging open.

Melanie Steen leaned back again in her chair, head back, chest filled with victory. Tit for tat, she paused a nice long while, then laconically inquired, "Did you have any other questions?"

No I didn't, but I pulled myself together and invented a few, starting with the foolishness of reiterating, "So she has no conscious memory at all of those days."

"Correct."

"What methods have you used to try to tap them?"

"Hypnosis."

Gad, what eyes for that trade. "And no luck."

"She is not a willing subject."

"What does that mean?"

Ms. Steen extended her neck and flared her nostrils ever so slightly, suggesting a measure of defensiveness. "We are dealing with the unconscious mind. The subject must be willing to relax her conscious vigil and let the unconscious arise."

"And if she won't do that with you, what does that mean, in therapeutic terms?"

Now Melanie Steen's lips tightened. "It means she failed to form a relationship of trust."

"Or more simply put, she can't let go with you."

Melanie Steen's face stiffened into a mask.

I wanted to say, Try climbing down off your high horse and make human contact with your client, but thought better of it. I wasn't heartless; it must be hell to spend six months with someone whose heart is bleeding and realize that even with all your best intentions and fancy schooling, you've failed to help her.

6

OUTSIDE, THE SUN WAS SHINING, AND THE SCENT OF CHERRY blossoms wafted from a row of slender trees planted in the few small squares of earth left naked along the sidewalk. As it was getting on for late afternoon, I found my way downtown and sat in the lobby of the Brown Palace Hotel, where I could settle into one of its deep overstuffed couches, order a beer from the tuxedo-clad waiter, and listen to the harpist's soothing notes rise into the serene heights of the hotel's eight-story Italian Renaissance–style atrium. I leaned back into the couch, stared upward at the quiet expanse of antique stained glass high overhead, and wondered if I had gone insane. A healthier woman would have moved to distance herself from a relationship as certain to drag her down as was mine with Cecelia. A woman bent on survival might have phoned the girl's father on the way out of town and told him there was nothing further she could or, in fact, would do for his darling daughter. Instead, here I was, lolling back in the lobby of my favorite old hotel, sucking down a beer while I tried to think up my next move.

Should I scour the Yellow Pages for a new psychotherapist for Cecelia? Surely I could make a better choice than had her school counselor. Or should I go fully overboard, drive up to Wyoming, and pump the sheriff for a shot at that 911 tape in hopes that it would give me greater insight into Cecelia's reactions on that horrible night?

Leaving my beer for a moment, I chose option three (procrastinate), and dialed Menken's office to tell him where I was. When in doubt, report to the chief.

Ten minutes later, the man himself strode in through the revolving glass door off of Tremont Place, his buttocks pulled up tightly, his face shining with well-groomed bonhomie, rolling out a trail of smiles and hellos as he acknowledged the doorman, the desk clerk, and miscellaneous other minions and acquaintances he passed. His actions said, J.C. Menken knows everybody worth knowing in Denver, big and small. J.C. Menken is connected.

As I watched his approach, I remembered briefly the other reason I was in Denver, the other half of our deal. He was supposed to be making me a few contacts, helping me find a job. *Time for the Midas touch, old boy,* I thought as I took another pull from my bottle of beer.

He descended into the soft leather next to me, just close enough that it felt too close, but not so close that I could politely move away. Turning sideways toward me, he draped an arm along the back of the couch, letting his hand come to rest just inches from my shoulder. He was dressed in a lightweight wool in honor of the spring day, a fine brownish gray, and the cool whiteness of his starched shirt collar set off the depth of his ever-present tan. I noticed for the first time that he had lost weight since Miriam's death, that he seemed trimmer, more fit. Seeing my eyes on him, he beamed. "What do you have to report?" he asked.

"Well, for starts I don't like that psychologist," I began. "She's not stupid, not in the least, and I'm sure she's earned her credentials, but as she said herself, the client has to trust the therapist, and having just spent half an hour in her presence, I can tell you all I wanted to do was run for it."

Menken swatted the leather next to my shoulder. "That's why I came to you, Emily! I always could depend on you to bring a woman's intuition to bear on the job. So psychology's out. What shall we do instead?"

"Whoa! Hold your horses. I didn't say all shrinks were out, just this one."

Menken's lips crimped with amusement. "Good! So whom shall we use instead?"

"Well, I—"

"I'll tell you what, Emily. You canvas the local talent; I'll foot the bill for your expenses—you know, parking, gasoline, whatever preliminary meetings you might require to choose a replacement. Then Cecelia can start out fresh, with the benefit of your more informed judgment, not to mention your presence."

"Um, I . . ." I was about to tell him that I might be able to make a few calls—maybe chat with another shrink or two if that was what it would take—but that I'd hoped to move onward with my job hunt, when we were interrupted by the arrival of another man. I looked up. He was short and stocky, indifferently dressed in expensive business attire, and his splotchy scalp shone with perspiration through the threads of his once-yellow hair. He quickly looked me up and down with greasy, bloodshot eyes, then turned his attention toward Menken. "Joe!" he croaked, in a voice that would have made the biggest bullfrog in the pond jealous for its volume and the rumble of its phlegm, "how are ya?" He stuck out a red ham of a hand for Menken to shake, then swung it toward me for a brief tag of fingertips. "Where's a man get a beer around here?"

Menken signaled the waiter and gestured toward the adjacent couch for his friend. "Emily, this is Fred Howard. I wanted you two to meet."

Fred Howard plopped down onto the couch and glanced quickly around the room, a habitual gesture, I supposed, designed to mark the locations of known or potential foes. He said nothing.

Menken prattled onward. "Fred's regional vice president at Boomer Oil. How's business, Fred?"

Fred's face turned red as raw hamburger. "Hell, Joe, same old shit. Say, you see the game last night?"

"Sure. You still following that sorry bunch of losers?"

Fred's eyes bulged with outrage. "Losers! You horse's ass." The two men swapped insults and epithets for a minute until the waiter arrived with Fred's beer. "Ah, here's my medicine," he rasped, and, forgoing the iced glass, took a hard pull straight from the neck of the bottle. As he swung it back down, his head bobbled, as if he'd gotten foam up the back of his nose. He said, "Uhn. Here's Cindey."

A fiftyish woman trying to look thirty was closing on our pair of couches, narrow fingers clamped tightly around a leather purse. She looked overly made up and underintelligent, her tiny pig eyes battling to stay open under the weight of a heavy bank of false eyelashes. The padded shoulders of her silk camp shirt struggled to redefine her collapsing figure, and her skirt, which had been cut short enough for someone with something to show off, unkindly emphasized both her legs, which were shapeless and narrow, and her burgeoning belly, which eclipsed her belt. Glancing back and forth between Menken and me, she extended a damp, limp hand my way. "Hello," she whispered.

"Emily Hansen, this is Cindey Howard," Menken offered cheerfully, rising to his feet to give her a polite peck on the cheek, which she received with a mechanical tilt of her head. She looked expectantly at her husband, as if awaiting permission to sit down.

Fred took another pull on his beer and barked, "Where'd you put the car, Cin?"

"Valet," she breathed, directing her husband's attention toward the uniformed doorman.

"What? That's five bucks for nothing! You—"

Menken cut in. "Emily's the friend who's helping me with Cecelia. Cindey, please sit down. Here, take my seat. Cecelia fairly worships this young woman. doesn't she, Emily?" He smiled broadly. "Of course, I can see why. You're a fine equestrienne, an accomplished geologist, a woman of insight. . . ."

Fred leaned toward me, his slacks binding against his chubby crotch, and squinted at my face. "Ohhh, so that's what this is. Yeah, Joe said he wanted me to meet a lady he knew. And I thought he was starting to date!" Laughter belched from his throat. "Here I was all excited! You looking for a job? We got nothing."

Menken broke in again. "You'd be lucky to get her, Fred. Emily's been out of town for—a year, isn't it?—and yes, she is now available again, should the right position appear, but I doubt you have anything that would interest a geologist of her caliber. I *was* hoping that *she* could interview *you*; you know, pick your brains for ideas about the current business climate, perhaps divine a few leads."

I smiled, tried to look alert and winning.

Fred Howard forced his face into a smile, an effort that made him look like a toad on laughing gas. "Oh, uh-huh. Sure, honey, you call my secretary; she'll set you right up, some day next week. But not now. I never talk shop with a beer in my hand. Might spill!" He roared, delighted with his own joke.

Cindey's shoulders contracted as if she'd been pinched. I sank back into the red leather of my couch and tried to disappear.

"So!" said Menken, "We have a quorum. What say we drive up to Vail for dinner?"

Fred Howard put down his beer. "Now you're talking! You bring the Mercedes, Cin?"

Cindey looked pained. "No, the RX-7."

"Balls! That two-seater ain't worth shit for a road trip. Waiter!"

As Fred hoisted his bottle in the universal "one more" salute, I heaved a sigh of relief that the beleaguered Cindey had brought the wrong car. That meant Menken would drive. He was not usually a heavy drinker, and his Mercedes was the biggest one built, a veritable Sherman tank among automobiles, warranted to withstand high-speed oral sex with a semi. I crossed one leg over the other, preparing to get comfortable while Fred sucked down his second dose of suds, and threw my mind out of gear. It was going to be a long evening.

It hadn't even occurred to me that I could choose not to go. Jobs, or even leads toward jobs, were still too hard to find.

7

As Menken's Mercedes hummed westward along Highway 6 through the western suburbs of Denver, Cindey briefly found something to say. "Freddie dear," she breathed, "I just remembered. I have that early tennis game with Julia in the morning. Why don't we go to The Fort instead?"

Freddie dear coughed around his cigar. "Makes no difference to me."

Menken's face fell a fraction. "Cindey, I'm sure we'll be back by—"

"Oh, please, Joe. You know how I do get nosebleeds at high altitudes."

Menken turned to me. "All the same to you?" he asked doubtfully.

"Fine," I said. The cigar was already starting to get to me, and it didn't matter to me where we ate, as long as someone else was paying. Hence, we wound up at The Fort, a high-end place stuck between two of the hogbacks of rock that rise up against the mountain front west of Denver. The Fort looks from the outside like an old adobe frontier bastion, and it serves buffalo steaks. I ordered mine medium rare.

Having gotten her way, Cindey sat through the meal in silence, her little eyes as glazed as green grapes in aspic and her short spine as stiff as concrete. I got to watching her in fascination. She chewed meditatively, like a cow, and sometimes stopped chewing altogether. I wondered now and then if she had fallen asleep with her eyes half-open, but each time, just when I was almost certain she had, her little hand would raise another forkful of salad to her almost lipless mouth. So lulled was I by this performance that I almost spilled my coffee into my lap when, after dinner, she suddenly snapped awake and insisted that we all go to their house for drinks. Her sudden earnestness stood out like a cow flop on a china plate. Something was up. Where my attention had been drifting, it was now instantly riveted, and I followed quickly on her heels to the car.

The Howards lived in a house that was large even for Genesee, not far from the Menkens. We were hardly in the door at the Howards' when Cindey announced that she was taking me on a tour of the house.

"Women!" her husband roared. "Allus gotta show off. Joe, you and me'll get down to it in the den."

Disappointment showed so baldly in Menken's face that kindness compelled me to give him a wink, one of those "I'm on the job" signals. Menken's eyes ignited with recognition, then warmed with feeling. "You go on your little house tour. I'll be waiting here," he said, and gave my shoulder a little squeeze.

The buffalo steak in my stomach began to stampede in the opposite direction. I blinked, looked again into his eyes, hoping I had imagined what I'd just seen there. It was still there. I walked out from under his hand, following Cindey down the hall.

House tour, hell. Cindey marched me straight to her private sitting room and right into her walk-in closet, where she scrabbled into a stack of boxes. "I hid them in here," she wheezed. She opened one box, another, and another. Her eyes widened in alarm or consternation—I couldn't tell which.

"What are we looking for?" I asked, batting aside a sachet of potpourri that dangled from the light fixture in the middle of the closet.

Cindey's pale hands scratched their way into another box. "When Joe told us you were going to look into Miriam's death, I can't tell you how relieved I was. These things have been sitting here bothering me like you wouldn't believe."

"What things? And I'm not exactly looking into Miriam's death. I'm—"

"Here they are! Now, how are we going to get them past the men? I know, we'll let them get into their little drinks; then you say you're tired and I'll say I'm taking you back to town to pick up your car. We'll take these out to the garage right now and put them in the trunk."

"These *what*?" I insisted, leaning past piles of neatly stacked cashmere sweaters to get a look. Cindey spun and pushed the box abruptly into my arms like it was biting her hands. I wasn't braced, and I dropped it. It crashed to the floor, landing on my feet with a heavy thud that split the cardboard all the way around the bottom. The smell of old paper wafted up from the open flap.

Cindey's little eyes were trained on the box as if it were about to spit snakes. "Her journals," she hissed, whispering beneath her usual whisper.

"Whose?" I hissed back.

"Miriam's."

"Huh?"

"Ever since high school."

"Why do you—"

"Oh, was she ever worried about these things! You should have seen her. Didn't want Joe to see them. Thought he'd get into them and divorce her. So here they sat in *my* closet. God knows, Fred never looks past the liquor cabinet."

"But what could be in here that—"

"That's what *I* wondered. When she gave it to me, the box was all sealed up, and I'm not one to pry, but then when she was *murdered. . . .*" She trailed off suggestively.

"Well, of course that changed things," I said reassuringly. "Why didn't you just turn them over to the police?"

Cindey Howard stared into my face like I'd just sprouted a second head. "The *police*? Are you *raving*?"

"Well—"

She sucked in her breath. "I shouldn't have shown you!"

"No! No, it's okay. They're secret, I can see, and your secret is mine," I added hurriedly. "I just . . . I mean, is there something *in* here?"

Her face went blank. "Well . . . I just read around in them." She looked sideways, discomfort pinching her pudgy face. "Kind of looked over the bits when Cecelia was a baby, see if there was anything that might mean something to her."

"Find anything?"

A bit too quickly, she said, "No, it was the usual stuff, all bitching about the diapers. Real drivel."

I asked questions automatically, a scientist's knee-jerk reaction to incoming data. "Had you known Miriam a long time?"

"Since college."

Speaking before I thought, I said, "But she didn't write anything about you in there."

Cindey Howard stared at the floor. Her lips formed a word she could not speak: *no.*

8

IN BOULDER TWO HOURS LATER, I PULLED MY TRUCK OVER into the off-street parking slip Betty had pointed out to me and rattled the gate so that Stanley the dog would let me know if he was loose. As his answering chorus of barking was muffled through closed doors and windows, I risked the yard, crossing quickly to the outside stairs.

Upstairs in my room, I tiredly dumped the box of journals on the floor, irritated to have them in my possession. During the drive home, I'd had time to think about the responsibility they represented, and I wanted no part of it. They had not been written for my eyes. I had never met Miriam Menken, had not worried about her existence while she was alive, and saw no greater reason to get to know her now that she was dead. I shucked off my boots and placed them on top of the box to keep the flaps firmly shut.

Jeans off, sweater and underwear in a pile at the foot of the bed, I shuffled myself into the shower with the overhead light off and let the water pelt me, the better to wash away the accumulated poisons of the day. I stood in the steaming darkness, letting the waters melt the knots in my shoulders. The steam rose and thickened the air, sealing me in with my thoughts and my loneliness. How strange it had been to be Menken's "date." I wondered again if I had imagined that look he'd given me. Was the old satyr putting the moves on me? I compared him in my mind with Jim Erikson, the man I currently counted as my sexual distraction. The comparison was unfavorable, at least from a physical standpoint. Jim was young and fit, a man who worked with his hands. Menken was—well, it was silly to even look at him in that way. So why was I doing it?

I decided that my imagination had run away with me. Yes, that was it—Menken was only being Menken, urging me on with the job. A little shoulder squeeze here and there wasn't anything unusual coming from an older man. It was a sign of encouragement—at most, affection. I would put it out of my mind.

I shifted, letting the water find the tenderest part of my back. The part Jim had found, that time I let him touch me, let him ease my timidity, my uncertainty, until I was ready for him to kiss my neck, my hands, my face . . . but I had stopped him there. Why did I still resist him? A kinder soul I'd never met, and he didn't lack for looks. He had a steady job, a nice house, and friends who loved him. So what was stopping me? Was it just that tiny fact that he lived so far away? Or was he just not Frank?

Frank! Frank was married now, a father no less; no backing out for that boy, that was for sure. And I'd let Frank go, not the other way around. Why did I long for him now, and not then?

Stop! Quick, think about something safer!

My mind circled back around to Menken.

Crazy old J.C. Menken, alone with his moping daughter in that huge house in Genesee. I thought back to the first time Menken had taken me there, two years before, when I was a newcomer to his now-defunct Blackfeet Oil Company. The two had been alone together even then. She had been a stringy girl of fourteen, wild in her rage and sorrow over her mother's departure. Where was it Miriam had gone? I tried to remember if Cecelia had ever told me. Surely Menken never would have; he'd been bent on pretending she'd never gone. How quickly he had moved to erase the damning limerick Cecelia had scrawled that day on the refrigerator door, begging for her father's attention:

> *Oh, Mommy's up in Aspen snorting coke*
> *She left Friday with a friendly looking dope*
> *Dear old Dad's in the Jacuzzi*

With his brand new buddy Suzie
Trying to see if they can make the bourbon float

It had seemed pretty good doggerel, for an adolescent. I hadn't thought at the time about the implications, beyond the obvious assertion that J.C. had been dumped or cuckolded, but now that I knew him better, I wondered. Would the suburban wife of smooth, conventional old J.C. Menken have been the sort to snort cocaine? And would she have been so obvious about it that her daughter would have known, or, for that matter, would she have let the child know about it if she'd been running off with a dope fiend to a fast town like Aspen? This image of Miriam didn't seem to fit with what I knew of Menken, but then, it was hard to feature any woman living with him for long without losing her grasp on reality.

During Miriam's absence, J.C. had encouraged me to visit Cecelia. I had always met her at the stables, the better to avoid the awkward social contact with my boss. We had gone for rides together on their quarter horses, I on Miriam's gelding, Cecelia on her wonderful chestnut mare. Cecelia had proved an okay kid once she relaxed: bright, capable on horseback, and deeply motivated to improve her barrel-racing skills. We'd set up the oil drums in the arena and ridden the barrels again and again, I schooling the horses and demonstrating the tricks and postures that spun horse and rider around the turns, she doggedly practicing until she began to master them. But I had never met Miriam, even when she quietly returned. She hadn't come to the office, hadn't answered the telephone when I'd called to set up subsequent riding visits with Cecelia. In fact, if Menken's secretary hadn't passed the word to the troops, I'd never have known she was back.

Then in the merry month of May, not quite a year ago, Blackfeet had gone belly-up, and we had all been out of work. I'd looked for other jobs for a while, but quickly ran out of steam as hope dwindled. It was natural that I hadn't thought to call Cecelia to go riding; I had been busy. And then I'd heard that she and Miriam had gone to Wyoming for the summer, and then my father died, and . . .

I hadn't been in touch with much of anyone after that. Autumn followed summer, with winter hard on its heels. And now it was spring again, time for new beginnings.

The shower began to run cold. I turned the cold tap off, but the water only warmed for a minute or so, just long enough to rinse my hair. Bundling out of the water and into some thick towels Betty had left out for me, I settled on the foot of the bed and rubbed my scalp with vigor, trying to shake myself back into feeling warm. I dug out my blow-dryer and let it rip, then pulled on a flannel nightshirt, dove under the down comforter, and crimped my body into the time-honored pose of the fetus.

Why had Miriam come back? The question caught me by surprise, amusing me with its opposite supposition, an understanding that any woman in her right mind would eventually have left J.C. Menken. He was just that strange a man. But then, why had she married him in the first place?

I peeked out from under the comforter. Stared at the box.

Some thoughts are as seductive as chocolate or liquor. This thought— this question, *Why had she married him?*—picked at me, wheedled at me until it finally launched me out of bed and across the floor to that box held shut by the laughable protection of my boots.

I removed my boots and pulled back the cardboard flap. I was confronted with a stack of cheap record books, the kind bound in cardboard that's printed in black and white to look like leather. The bracket on the front of each was neatly lettered, indicating inclusive dates in a tidy, if somewhat looping and naïve, hand.

I carried the first volume back to bed and climbed in. And, with the dreadful sinking of conscience a glutton must feel on the way to the refrigerator, I opened the journal and began to read.

9

THE FIRST ENTRY WAS DATED OCTOBER 17, 1965:

Dear Journal,

It's my fourteenth birthday and Dad gave me this book so I could write things down. He says that keeping a journal is good practice for writing, and I can keep things secret that should be secret. Here goes. Today when I walked home from school Tom Jarret threw a snowball at me. He's real cute. I never thought he'd notice me, but wow!

Miriam Menken's journalistic muse must have arrived slowly, because the next entry was dated weeks later.

December 2
Dear Journal,

Tom Jarret is a pimple head. Today at lunch, he made a *disgusting* noise at me.

The hormone-ridden Tom Jarret continued to make Miriam's fecal roster for several weeks, until a school dance improved his rating with the young journalist:

December 16

Tonight at last was the Christmas Cotillion. Tom Jarret asked me to dance and he's a *great* dancer! Why do I like him when we dance together, but when I see him at school I think he's disgusting?

There was a question for the ages. As Miriam's school year continued to mire in the valleys of scholastic routine and glory atop the poignant peaks of sweaty-palmed socialization, Tom Jarret's reported character continued to fall and rise. With the close of school and the coming of summer, Tom lost out to Hal, and after Hal came Jakey. They appeared to have certain traits in common, foremost among them social ineptitude and acne, but all were compared unfavorably to Tom Jarret when it came to dancing. That Tom must have been something when the rug was rolled up.

I got to skimming, searching for the first mention of Josiah Carberry Menken. I found it in the second volume, halfway through Miriam's first term at college, dated October fifth:

That Joe Menken just won't take a hint. I wish he would quit asking me out.

I flopped back against the pillows with a sigh of exasperation: with this entry, my curiosity was at last confronted by the full ethical prudishness of my puritan soul. Should I read on and have a good laugh at my former employer's expense, or behave myself and leave the social stumblings of the young J.C. Menken to obscurity? I hadn't expected to find this candid a view of dear old J.C., and it jarred me into the awareness that, in spite of the sour and derisive attitude I held toward such things as bosses, I still liked the man and wanted to respect him. Rationalizing that Miriam's opinion of him must have improved somewhat if she'd married him, I read on.

October 10

At the Harvest Dance tonight I met a really great guy everyone calls Chandler. He's blond and has this big handsome face like a *lion*. He's tall and *built*, and a *terrific* dancer. He taught me the Texas two-step. He's such a strong lead it was *easy* to follow him. I hope he asks me out, not that Joe Menken.

October 15

Chandler asked me to go walking with him tonight. I guess that's a date, right? Anyway, we walked around the quadrangle. He wanted to go down by the athletic fields, but I said no, so we turned around. I hope he doesn't think I'm too slow. I really, *really* like him.

October 16

That *dork* Joe Menken asked me out again. As always, I turned him down. I don't know, he's okay looking and all, but he's so *cheerful* all the time, like a camp counselor or something. Julia says he looks like he's trying to hold a stack of quarters up his butt. Pretty gross, huh? But *true*.

October 17

Thinking about Chandler all day today. Does this mean I *want* him?

October 18

Thinking about Chandler.

October 19

Thinking about Chandler. When *will* he call?

October 22

Saw Chandler in the bookstore. It was great! He asked what I like to read, and I showed him some books, and he showed me some he liked. He said I should read his books and he'll read mine and then we can meet and talk about them! I'm glad I showed him the stuff for my lit class and not the drek I read in my dorm room.

October 25

Saw Chandler at the Student Union. He was drinking coffee

with his friends. They're all older, like he is. They all took years off to go to Europe like he did or they're Vets going to college after the service. Chandler's a dream, really tall and *so* good looking. I just love to look into his eyes. They're so *hypnotic.* I said I was reading one of his books and he smiled and said he'd get to one of mine soon. I *hope* so!

October 27

I close my eyes and think about what it would be like to be with Chandler. It's not like I'm a virgin, not after that night with Tim Hodges up at the lake, but there's got to be more to it than *that.* With Chandler, I just know it would be much, *much* better. I keep thinking about how it could be, with him taking me to romantic places, and we fall deeply in love, and then one day, in a secluded place, it just *happens. . . .*

His book is pretty strange, all about this guy Jack Kerouac and the guys he hangs out with, but I guess it doesn't hurt me to read some long hair stuff now and then.

November 1

I'm going to *kill* Joe Menken! I was talking to him by the library—or should I say *he* was talking to *me,*—just when *Chandler* walked by. He'll think I'm dating *Joe*!

November 3

I'm going to live! I saw Chandler and he said we should get together soon! He said how about Sunday afternoon! I said yes!

November 4

Just one more day until Chandler! I have to get together with Julia and find just *the* thing to wear!

November 5

Today's the day! I couldn't eat breakfast. Now it's noon and I'm waiting. I wonder just when "afternoon" means.

Cindey had been right: this was drivel. The only thing that kept me reading was base curiosity over whether the marvelous Chandler really *had* been better than Tim Hodges up at the lake. And a lingering bit of self-delusion that knowing all this, I could somehow help Cecelia. Cecelia, who had leaned her troubled head on my shoulder.

But the next few pages had been taped shut.

And someone had none too carefully peeled back that tape, plundering whatever too-too private entries had been thus protected. I examined the tape closely. Miriam had creased the tape the long way and folded it neatly around the three edges of the pages she wanted to obscure. Whoever had pried it off had tried to do so neatly, peeling it back from just one side of the crease and then neatly tucking the pages back in, but the adhesive had been just strong enough that the paper had come off on the tape. I picked a little at the untampered side, satisfying myself that the adhesive on the nonpeeled side was still strong, not dried to dust, meaning it had been applied fairly recently, and not almost thirty years prior. "Cindey, Cindey, Cindey," I muttered as I followed her down the rabbit's hole, pulling the pages apart again to discover what she must now know about Miriam's torrid past.

November 9

It's taken me until today to be able to write this. I can't even tell Julia. Everything started out so good. He picked me up on his motorcycle and took me to his apartment. I know it sounds silly after all I've been thinking about, but I didn't want to go in, not yet, but he said it was okay, we would only have tea, and that besides, he had a surprise for me. He sure did. Flowers all over the place, on the table, on the desk, on the *bed*. He made tea for me on his hot plate and told me he was looking for a wife, someone like me who was young and innocent but so obviously a woman, and I looked into his eyes and thought how lonely he seemed. Then he read to me for a while and then he was massaging my back and it felt *good*. I'm so stupid—he said he just wanted to *touch* me. He's so big he picked me up like I was a little doll and whirled me about the room, and it was all glorious like dancing, except he put me down on the bed. He said weren't my clothes in the way, didn't I want a better massage? I said I wasn't fast, and he *said* he understood. Then he had my clothes off and *did* it. I felt his penis inside me.

It didn't hurt, not *physically*, but I started to cry. He stopped, and asked why I was crying. I told him I wanted to know him much better first and later would be so much better. He said okay, but he took me back to the dorm. It was awful riding on the back of his motorcycle holding on to him so I wouldn't fall off but feeling sick and afraid it would somehow show and I didn't want anyone to know. I said good night and ran to my room and felt like I was made of ice, and the worst thing is he hasn't called since.

I put down the journal. Closed it. Pushed it away from me as if it had covered my hands with something that would eat slowly through my skin. I jammed them into my armpits, tensing as if I was cold. Something inside of me that I did not want to name felt roused. I wanted to believe I could leave the journal closed, let it go. But I did not. After only seconds had passed, I picked it back up and read on.

November 12

Tonight Chandler was at the campus movie with another girl. Her name is Leslie and she's a real snot from Long Island. I pretended I didn't see. How *could* he! Why hasn't he *called*? Doesn't he want to know me better?

I still want to see him. It makes me feel *dirty.*

November 14

This is so strange I'm just going to write it down and then maybe it will make sense. This afternoon Chandler came by and asked if he could see me in my room for a minute. I said okay but I wasn't sure. I hoped at least that the other girls would see me with him, but nobody did.

When he got to my room, he had this strange look on his face, kind of wild eyed except he always is only this was stranger and he wasn't really looking at me. He got me in this bear hug and groaned and took me down onto my bed with all his clothes on, even this long topcoat he was wearing. He lay on top of me and pushed and breathed hard and got all sweaty and I think he came in his pants. Then he left, looking anywhere but at me. I don't understand. He didn't even kiss me. Later in the evening I saw Leslie and she gave me a look like she hates me. She doesn't even *know* me!

November 17

Today in the Student Union I overheard some of the Leslie snot people talking. They were talking about how Leslie broke up with Hank Arnston to go out with Chandler but that all he gave her was a one-night stand. They laughed and said at least she got a movie out of it. I told Julia about what I'd heard (but not about any of what he did with me!), and she got all scornful and said Chandler is one of those guys who's just racking up a score.

I never felt sorry for anyone like Leslie before. And worse yet, I still want him. I used to think life was so simple.

Carefully tucking the pages back under the tape, I closed the journal, turned out the light, and tried to go to sleep. I felt cruel and dirty myself, as if I had been swilling from a well of tears that should have been left sealed.

As my eyes adjusted to the dark, my rented room took on the nighttime brightness of urban streets, prying open my eyes. After ten minutes staring at the midnight ceiling, I admitted to myself that I was beyond rationality. I turned the light back on and read the next entry. And I felt in some small way redeemed, as it held the beginning to the answer I had originally sought.

November 19

Today I met Joe Menken by the library again. He asked if I'd go to dinner with him Saturday at the Steak & Flounder, and maybe I'm crazy, but I said yes. *Him* I can at least *predict*.

10

Mercifully, the next pages of Miriam's journal held rather boring accounts of ball games and studying, and I was able to calm down enough to get to sleep. I managed to stay that way until nearly ten the next morning, at which time I got up, pulled on a fresh pair of jeans and a turtleneck shirt, and wandered downstairs to see if Betty had any coffee I could mooch. I found my august landlady in the backyard, cussing over the results of a raid by last night's raccoons. "You thieving mongrels!" she was growling to the long-since-departed animals. "Just because I leave food in my car you think you've got to pry your *scrabby* little way in and leave your *scrabby* little footprints all over my lovely seats. I'll fillet you for dinner! That was *my* chocolate, by God!"

"How'd they get in?" I asked.

"Fatherless sons of Satan pried the sunroof open!" she roared. "The nerve. Scratched the paint with their filthy little claws and chewed up the gasket, too! And look here, they left chocolate paw prints on the leather seats. Looks like a bunch of miniature bulimics had a party grabbing the toilet seat or something. *Sham*eless little wretches!"

"Oh. Ah, got any coffee?"

"In the kitchen. And don't leave any paw prints on the counter, y'hear?"

"No, ma'am. Can I use the phone?"

"Why not?" she muttered. "Everybody else does."

I crossed the yard to the kitchen door, where I was confronted by the hair-enshrouded mass of Stanley.

"Morning, mutt," I said, trying to edge past him. He growled, a low, throaty suggestion of where the line was I could not cross. "Betty!" I called.

Still bent to the task of scrubbing at her leather car seats, Betty called, "Stanley! Don't eat this one!"

Stanley ran a quivering wet nose down my arm and into my crotch. As I shouldered the mountain of fur aside, I hollered, "And where's the Yellow Pages?"

From the yard, I heard something that sounded like "Silver-haired bore."

"What?"

"Silverware drawer, goddamn it! And get that carrot out of your ear!"

I shouted back something eloquent—like "I can't hear you! I have the Washington Monument in my ear!"—as I pulled knobs until I found what I was looking for and helped myself to some scratch paper and a pencil. The dog observed all this from close-enough quarters that when his bead of drool finally snapped free, it hit the toe of my boot.

I poured coffee and held it briefly under my eyes to steam them the rest of the way open. Then, taking a first hard pull at the acrid brew, I flipped the phone book open to *P* for psychologists and psychotherapists, Ph.D.

The maze of names took all the zing out of that first sip of coffee. I shook my head with disgust, then told myself that finding a new shrink for Cecelia was just a job, a chore like any other. The key to any chore was to keep it simple. I would devise a plan of attack and get it done, and put Cecelia and her peculiar father and all their problems in the past. Simplicity.

First, I discarded all male shrinks and anyone whose office did not lie within striking distance of either Cecelia's school or Genesee. So far, so good. Thus mentally fortified against anxiety, I worked quickly through the list, rapidly paring the seemingly astronomical list of names down to a less daunting twelve. I called and left voice-mail messages with each. Not one answered her phone in person, a fact that somehow did not comfort me.

When I had thus discharged my obligations, I telephoned Fred Howard's secretary and bullied her into scheduling a half hour of the man's time for what was certain to be a world-beating informational interview. She set me up for Tuesday of the following week. So much for connections.

By noon, I had drunk all of Betty's coffee and had given audience to every little thought that was on her mind that day, which included five pet peeves about her nearest neighbors and some ingenious thoughts concerning how to get even with each, such as showing bulimic raccoons how to access the neighbors' trash cans.

The phone rang at 11:56; it was for me. "It's some probe," Betty purred, handing the thing to me. "Says she's returning your call. Something you haven't told me about your mental state, Em?"

I smiled gleefully. "Yeah. I'm a paranoid schizophrenic insomniac with an itchy trigger finger. I can only sleep soundly after a good kill. Did you know your locks can be picked with a credit card?" Into the phone I said, "Hello?"

There was a pause. "Ms. Hansen?" asked a soothing voice.

"Yeah. Um, yeah, this is Em Hansen speaking."

"This is Geraldine Wharton. You called about making an appointment?"

"Yes. I'm doing a screening for a friend. She's just a kid, so I'm trying to find someone for her. She's having a . . . um, posttraumatic stress reaction," I stuttered, trying to remember the exact words Melanie Steen, Ph.D., had used.

"Yes, I work with that. Can you tell me a bit more?"

"Ah . . ." I looked pointedly at Betty, who just smiled. "Well, she's lost her memory of the event, and her grades have gone into the toilet, and her dad asked me to find someone who could help. The person she's been seeing for the last six months didn't pan out. I wanted to come meet you, and—"

"I'd really have to meet the client," asserted Geraldine. "I charge eighty dollars an hour. I can set something up for her in two weeks."

"No thank you," I replied, then said my good-byes and hung up. Cecelia Menken did not need someone who was bent on cutting her away from what herd she had.

Betty smiled winningly, hopeful that I would talk. I smiled back blandly and asked which way the bathroom was, figuring to return some of the coffee I'd borrowed.

The afternoon ground on. By 7:00 P.M., six psychologists had called back. Their calls always came in a few minutes before the hour, and I quickly became comfortable wandering out of earshot of the phone and helping Betty with yard work between the hour and ten till, when psychologists were apparently busy with their patients. I made appointments to see the ones with nice voices and manners and openings within the next week; others, I discarded.

"How many did you call?" Betty asked.

"A dozen, I think."

"Pretty good batting average," she commented, looking over my shoulder at my list. "Want some dinner?"

"Sure. Why, what would have been a bad batting average?"

"Oh, usually you don't hear from them for days."

I was about to inquire, How do you know? when I caught myself and instead asked, "What's for dinner?"

Betty looked thoughtful, scratched her head a moment, and said: "Raccoon."

11

Contrary to my best resolutions, I continued reading Miriam Menken's journals that evening, when I was next alone in my room under the eaves at Betty's house. I was driven by a potent mixture of prurient interest and what I hoped was a saintly wish to find that the advantage-taking Chandler had met an early demise.

Okay, so the journals called to me like a box of chocolates. The fact was, I'd known a few men like him in my days at Colorado College, and they still held an allure, a have-not's wish for status and, well, debauchery. They were the trust-fund babies, the good-looking boys with lots of charm and little discipline who probed about endlessly for fresh, näive, vulnerable young flesh to exploit. And I? Well, I had been some of that naïve young flesh, but I had been left unexploited. It had been my lot to look on enviously as the wealthy, socially adept girls kept such brightly plumed males of the species circling and pecking at their doors. This Chandler seemed all that and more, not just the cock of the rock but wild, intelligent, entrancing.

Miriam's entries about her first dates with J.C. Menken were sketchy at best, quick notes about where he'd taken her and whom she'd seen there. I laughed out loud at the first mention of Cindey's new date, Fred Howard ("ugly like a toad, and he had the gall to make a pass at me"), but I found myself skimming ahead, looking for any additional mentions of the man/boy she called Chandler. The next mention of him came in the late spring of her freshman year.

May 11

I saw Chandler today at the Student Union. He asked how I was and I said fine and how was he? Just like we were passing acquaintances and nothing had ever happened between us, or that's what anyone watching might think. But he was looking at me very closely. He said he'd gotten married. I pretended this was news to me, but I'd heard that, that he married this really young girl who started college second semester and here he is so much older than even the rest of our class. I guess he really meant it that he wanted to get married, because that wasn't more than three months after he went out with me. People say she was so pretty and bright-eyed but that right away she got to looking really tired all the time and she lost a lot of weight and had to go home to her parents. I'm so glad that one got away.

After that, there was no further mention of Chandler until the spring of her senior year, and only cursory mentions of J.C. Menken; again, where they'd been, whom they'd seen there. I skimmed through the intervening entries. I noted that she seemed to mature, or become more jaded—I wasn't sure which—and that her prose became more interesting, but something eluded me. I had a sense that something was missing, left out by design. When that something finally showed up, it was clear that she'd been keeping a few things back even from herself, things that she now blithely dropped to the imaginary audience of the journal as if they should have been presumed:

May 5

Last night Joe drove down from New York and took me to dinner and proposed to me again, it must be about the 20th time, only this time I said yes. I'm not sure why I said yes this time, but here I am graduating in three weeks and Mother says it's important to have a plan in life, and I don't and Joe does. Besides, we've been sleeping together every Saturday night for almost two years and we never fight, so we must be a good match, right? I hope so. It's just not how I thought it would be, being engaged. I thought I'd feel all this rush of love and excitement, but all I feel is comfortable and a little bit nervous. Maybe the rest will come.

Joe asked why I hadn't said yes before, and I said because he always asked on a Saturday before. He looked kind of perplexed. It was sweet.

May 6

A big day. I took Joe home to see Mother and Daddy again and we stayed for dinner and I told them about our engagement. I think Daddy liked him better this time, at least I hope he did. Mother was all happy and said an August wedding would be just wonderful, but Daddy counseled a long engagement. I wanted to say we've been sleeping together for two years already, so what, but one just doesn't say that at dinner and expect to get dessert. Anyway, I said maybe December. What's the hurry, anyway? Like I said, we've already been to bed, so it's not like I'm curious or anything. It's sure not like in the movies.

May 9

I told Julia and Cindey that I'm marrying Joe and Cindey was mad I hadn't told her first and Julia was mad because she thinks I'm throwing my life away. She had her finger down her throat and everything. I wonder.

May 11

Maybe I've made a mistake. Today I was walking across the quad and the sun was shining and there was a lovely breeze, and it suddenly occurred to me that I was going to be out of here in less than two weeks and I could do anything I want with my life. I could go to Europe or run off to the Southwest and work for an Indian school or be a ski bum for a while. Then I felt scared. It seemed so nice, but so frightening at the same time.

May 13

What's happening to me? Joe came down last night like always and we were making love or having sex or whatever you call it, and I suddenly wanted to do something crazy, like run down the hall naked or something. I said why didn't we go outside and make it under the trees by the athletic fields and he said don't be stupid there are insects. It was a real downer. Now I'm thinking I shouldn't marry him, like this is all I'm going to get for the rest of my life.

Here I found more taped pages that had been stealthily peeled open. The wheezing Cindey had been thorough. I stopped again, asking myself if I really wanted to know what lay hidden. Unfortunately, the answer was yes.

May 18

Now I've gone and done it. Graduation is the 25th, and I've come all this way without running into Chandler again, and then there he was at the next table at the Student Union reading one of his damned books. I tried to ignore him, but he still looks so *good*. I told myself I would ignore him, but when he put down his book and smiled at me, I told myself what does it hurt to be friendly, he can't hurt me here in the Union.

So we got to talking. He asked how life was treating me. I said I was getting married, thinking that's all he needs to know, I'm not available. He looked straight into me with that crazy look of his. It was frightening, but I must admit I'm still thinking about him.

May 21

I met Chandler again this afternoon when I was out walking and we got to talking again and he said let's turn here and suddenly there we were in front of his house off campus. He said why didn't

I come in for a while and I said why not. I guess I was telling myself his wife would be there but she wasn't. He said she wasn't with him anymore because she was sick all the time. I asked if he missed her and he said yes. He asked if I was in love with the man I am marrying and I said I didn't know. The next thing I knew he'd put music on the stereo and his arms were around me and we were dancing and it felt so *good*. Joe can't dance a step. Then his hands were on my shoulders massaging them and I remembered how good he was at *that*, and I decided to *let* him, after all I'm not a child anymore. When he took me to his bed I thought about his poor little wife for just about a half second and then decided something nasty like "she isn't here."

Now what am I going to do? I know better than to love Chandler, that's not the problem, but now I know just how *fantastic* sex can be. He moves like a big cat and touches me in places Joe's never heard of and *roars* when he comes. He got me so hot I didn't care where I was. We did it *three times* before dinnertime.

Now it's two in the morning and I can't sleep for anything. How am I supposed to marry Joe when I know what I'm missing? How am I supposed to *sleep* with him for that matter, when I know he's stopping too soon? I always used to think it was *me*.

12

ABOUT THREE, I QUIT KIDDING MYSELF THAT I HAD AN ETHICAL bone left in my body and just read. I was hooked, and not just by the lip; I had swallowed the bait, and the barb was lodged in my viscera.

Miriam Menken wrote frustratingly little in her journal for the next seven years. Perhaps she was too busy in her new life and status as a married woman, or perhaps she dared not write, lest she find herself contemplating her choice of mate. At least now I had some inkling of why she had chosen to marry J.C. Menken. He was safe, a predictable, dependable man of whom Mom and Dad approved, a good provider, an anchor to the wind. Too bad he bored her to tears.

The other thing I came to know was that I liked Miriam Menken, this woman who had whelped the painfully adolescent Cecelia, of whom I was unaccountably fond; this candid, sensuous woman who had found her passion in one untethered afternoon with a man who radiated more sexual heat than was considered street legal. This admiration came on me by inches, pushing up underneath an unadmitted preference to dislike her. She was, after all, my rival for Cecelia's affection and worship. Slowly, unavoidably, I was letting go of my albeit-sketchy championship of Cecelia and taking up the cause of her dead mother.

When Miriam began to write again, her reunion with journal keeping was precipitated by passion of another kind:

1980

November 17

Dear old journal, you've been a friend to me in the past and I hope it works again. Here I am 30 years old and still no plan, still thinking of leaving Joe, and then today the impossible has happened. . . . I'm pregnant! Good news and bad in the same package, huh? All these years I thought it must be me and now I wonder if it just took this many years for Saturday night to fall on the right phase of the moon! Well, I have something to give thanks for this Thanksgiving. The doctor says the baby is due July 12 of next year.

November 20

Today Joe got home from his business trip to Amsterdam and I told him about the baby. Bless him, he is ecstatic. In fact, I have never seen him like this. It's great, but I wonder what he's been saving it for.

November 22

Thanksgiving with Mother and Daddy. Joe announced the Coming Event. Mother said, "About time." Daddy cried. I threw up clear through dinner. After dessert, Daddy took Joe into his study and they smoked cigars. I threw up *again*. I've always hated cigar smoke, but now it's *awful*.

December 2

I've been thinking of names for the baby. I like Mariah for a girl, but I think I'm going crazy—I want to name the baby Chandler if it's a boy. I just can't see Josiah Carberry Menken, Jr. I'd want *more* for a son. What's wrong with me?

December 7

Last night I dreamt about Chandler. He was sitting on the edge of the bed, and he said, "Don't worry about a thing. It's my baby." I woke up sweating, afraid to waken Joe.

December 24

Joe came home from another trip just in time to decorate the Christmas tree with me and we fought about how much he's gone, how seldom we have sex, and names for the baby. He had the gall to tell me I needed to calm my temper a bit!

Next year this time, we'll have a child with us. Maybe then things will feel closer between us.

1981

January 1

Happy New Year! I hope this year is happy. Maybe Joe's right, I just need to control my temper. I always feel so upset afterward, all humiliated that I got so angry but still angry just the same. My New Year's resolution is to try to look on the bright side of things more.

January 15

I had another dream about C. We were making passionate love and the baby started to be born and I caught her and it was *me*. I looked so *new*.

January 30

More dreams. I told my mother I was having strange dreams and she said it was just the hormones. I hope she's right.

February 20

Joe is staying late at the office more and more. He says he has to win a promotion so he can take care of his baby. He has trips scheduled all spring, and some of them are overseas. I'm not sure I can stand having him gone so far. I see the way my friends get with their small kids all alone, and besides, I feel so *vulnerable* when he's not here.

April 10

Joe has been gone for three weeks now on this trip. Why doesn't his company understand he needs to be home now? He has a *baby* coming! Worse yet, I'm getting to feeling extra horny. I thought that having a baby meant I could put all that aside for a while.

April 14

Joe home. He's afraid to make love, as he thinks it could hurt the baby, and he says he needs to rest from his jet lag and get ready for the next trip. What a bastard!

May 5

I spent the day shopping for baby clothes with Mother. She says Joe's right, it's important to let the baby rest. Don't ask me how we got on *that* subject!

June 1

Joe makes me sit down a lot, even though I want to get up and *do* things. He puts his head against my belly and talks to the baby. I wish he'd talk to me like that sometimes.

June 14

Only four more weeks. The little kid is kicking me hard in the ribs. I'm ready anytime, except Joe's gone again. Maybe he'll be gone when the baby comes. Maybe he should just stay away. That would be easier than constantly getting used to him being gone, then getting used to him being home again.

July 6

All systems ready. I wish the baby would come.

July 12

The day's here, where's the kid?

July 13

Now, damn it!

July 14
    NOW!

July 15

    My waters just broke. I've cleaned myself up and called Joe to
come home from the office and take me to the hospital. It's kind of
nice waiting here in the backyard. I'm trying to keep moving, as it
hurts worse when I stay still. Next time I write, I'll be a mother.

I snuggled down underneath the blankets in my bed, clutching the
journal close. I had enjoyed no close friends to assist through the long wait
of a pregnancy, had no younger siblings, no close cousins to await and welcome into the world, and yes, was at this advanced stage of my child-
bearing years still childless. Until this moment, I had felt none of the
draw to have children. But now Miriam's excitement enveloped me, and
I felt the stirrings of longing, all wrapped up in a tender sense of gratitude that this woman had left this record of her waiting. I quickly turned
the page.

    And found a much later entry. Early motherhood must have kept
Miriam Menken very busy, because she didn't write again for a full year,
and entries remained sparse for years thereafter. She wrote sporadically
and usually when she was having fits, bent as she was on pressing herself
into the mold of perfect mother. Her words focused on the consuming
needs of her growing child, colic and all, but every once in awhile, she
confessed to having screamed at Joe because no one was looking after *hers.*
By the end of Cecelia's first year, Miriam's mind had begun to wander
back to sex:

1982
July 15

    It's Cecelia's first birthday already! Joe gave her a big teddy bear.
Mother gave her a dress. Daddy gave her a savings bond for college.
I whispered in her ear that I'd love to give her a baby brother, but
her daddy will have to *help.*

The next New Year dawned on rocky ground:

1983
January 1

A new year. I resolve to get out more. It's a good thing I'm feeling that way, because we're moving to Denver so that Joe can take a management position at some oil company. Maybe now he'll be home more often.

January 2

Fought with Joe last night worse than ever. I considered leaving him again, but where would I go with a tiny baby? She still cries at every little thing, and still wakes at least five times every night. Sometimes I want to leave *both* of them.

As Miriam's little sprout reached the terrible age of two, the lapses between cheerful entries grew longer and longer. Miriam's depression grew palpable. As Cecelia reached five without learning to sleep through the night and Joe started traveling more and more often, Miriam found her way briefly to a psychotherapist, but she gave up after a few months:

1986
November 1

I've had it with giving another white male control over me. I'm not getting better, and it's not because I don't want to be enjoying sex. I'll just do like my mother says and eat more chocolate. It's certainly cheaper than psychotherapy.

The next years became a trudging recitation of fights with her husband and attempts to deal with her daughter's tantrums. In 1993, Miriam reported the reappearance of Julia, her pal from college. It was only in this context that Miriam mentioned that the whispering Cindey had been there right along:

April 18

Julia Richards moved to Denver this week. Cindey and I met her plane and took her to lunch, kind of a Hooray We're All Together Again. Then we drove out to Green Mountain to see her settled into her new home. The moving van wasn't there yet, *of course*, but she seemed to like the house empty just fine. She roamed from room to room kind of dancing on the carpets and hardwood and linoleum and sat down cross-legged here and there and closed her eyes and made humming sounds. She sure has changed her act since college, but it's still the same old Julia underneath, full of opinions.

May 8

Julia took me driving in the mountains. We got to talking about *things*, and I opened my big mouth and told her how it is with Joe, and she said why did I put up with that? I had to admit of course that I don't *know* why. Not really. Here's Julia on her own and she seems so much happier and more at ease than when she was with Charlie. She says she doesn't have as much money, but she doesn't need as much because she doesn't have as much need to cheer herself up with trips to the spa and lots of clothes and other indulgences. I wonder what my life would be like on my own.

It seemed that Julia had a way of stirring things up:

July 12

Julia has been taking one of her *workshops* again. Last time it was Guru somebody teaching her meditation. This time I think it was Goddess worship. I don't know *what* to think. Each time she comes back, she says that whatever she just learned or experienced is *the* answer, as if all of them could be *the*. She does have a certain *glow* about her, though.

August 12

Today I signed up for a weekend retreat with Julia. We're going to a place in Steamboat Springs. There will be no one there but women, and we're supposed to learn to love ourselves more. It's worth a try. Maybe I can learn to like what my life is like.

I turned the page, eager to learn what Miriam learned from her weekend away, but it was the last page of the journal, and as with previous volumes, it was filled with undecipherable notes and what looked like miscellaneous phone numbers. I slid out from under the covers and dug down through the cardboard box, only to find that I had just finished reading the last volume there.

13

FRIDAY MORNING, I PUT A CALL THROUGH TO CINDEY HOWARD just as early as I thought was decent. "Are you sure you gave me all of Miriam's journals?" I asked, barging past the obvious question, which was: Had I been reading them? I was damned if I was going to feel guilty around someone who had pried open those taped pages before I did. Besides, addicts prefer not to confess.

"Yes," she whispered. Pause. "Why?"

"The last entry is dated years ago. And there's a closing date printed on the cover of that book, which leads me to believe she at least started another."

Pause. "No, that was all there was in that box. I'm sure of it." Pause. Then, in an even more whispery tone meant to convey either conspiracy or scathing judgment—I wasn't sure which—she said, "What did you think?"

"Of what?"

Silence.

Cindey's little games were beginning to annoy me. I spitefully decided to ignore her. Instead, I asked, "When did she store those with you exactly?"

Pause. "Just before she went away one time."

"You mean the time in September a couple years ago, when she took off for a while?"

"Yes."

It was my turn to pause as I tried to figure out to whom Miriam might have entrusted subsequent volumes. "Does Julia Richards still live in Denver?"

"Yes. . . ."

From between clenched teeth, I said, "Would you give me her phone number . . . please?"

I could hear Cindey breathing, either as she thought or as she sifted quietly through papers or perhaps a Rolodex on her desk. Presently, she read the number off, very clearly and slowly, to make sure I'd gotten every number right. Then she said good-bye and hung up, never asking why I wanted to know. Which left me wanting to call her back to find out what she wasn't telling me. Fuming at the ease with which Cindey seemed to manipulate me, I dialed Miriam's other college friend instead.

Julia Richards answered on the third ring, the classic American anti-technology "catch it before the answering machine" reflex. Her hello was brusque and throaty. I identified myself, wading into her private waters as smoothly as I could. "J.C. Menken asked me to look into this whole situation on Cecelia's behalf. I was wondering if I could meet with you. I don't like to pry into your life or Miriam's," I said, lying to myself as much as to her, "but I'm not sure how to help the daughter without knowing the mother better."

Julia's response was swift but noncommittal: "Joe said you might be calling."

"Ah, good. Well, I understand you were one of her closest friends, and I was wondering if—"

"Why haven't you asked Joe about her?" she asked with a heavy note of irritation.

That rocked me back on my heels. Why hadn't I? And how did she know I hadn't?

Julia answered her own question. "Because he didn't know her, that's why. You knew that intuitively. They *never* know us as we know ourselves," she said, putting a spin on the conversation that lost me entirely.

"I suppose you're right. What I was thinking was—"

"Oh, I suppose we could meet. But really, I'm not sure how it could help."

"Well . . ." I drawled, stalling while I thought up a justification for our meeting, having temporarily lost the thread of reasoning that had prompted my call. "For instance, I understand that she kept a journal. As her closest friend, you—"

"*Did* she? Where would it *be*?" Julia's tone had shifted. It held sarcasm now.

She has a missing volume, I thought. *But only one? And why the rancor?* "Um, could I—"

"I'm off for the weekend, but hell, I see no reason you shouldn't have a look at it, if you think it would help Cecelia. I mean, she's dead now, isn't she, and all things come to light. She was silly, you know, always hiding things, thinking she could shove the genie back in the bottle."

"Have you shown it to the police?"

"The who? Why? What business does the Patriarchy have in the heart of a woman?"

The what? Trying to keep up mentally with the merry chase Julia was leading, I suggested, "Well, being as how it's an unsolved murder and all . . ."

Her rancor turned to outright hostility. "Oh. Right. The Patriarchy kills her, so I'm supposed to let them paw through her things. Sure. Maybe I'll withdraw my offer."

"Well, I—"

Her voice terse with exasperation, Julia said, "Listen, you want to know something about Miriam? Then meet me at a public place, so I can get a look at you first. I don't like the sound of all this."

I counted to ten. "I understand. Or at least I think I do. Whatever you say. What's convenient?"

Julia named a bistro in downtown Denver. Eleven-thirty Monday, for lunch, she informed me, and not a moment later: Julia Richards was not going to be kept waiting while any jive business rats slurped their soup onto their neckties, no way no how. With that, she rang off, leaving me to sort out the etiquette of "doing" lunch with a law-unto-herself feminist who hides her friends' secrets in plain sight.

I put down the phone and sighed. This still left me with nothing to do until Monday, a situation I find very hard to weather in city or suburbs. I made a few calls to old oil-patch chums, trying to hook a lunch date for a little impromptu job-hunt networking, but no dice. Everyone was out of town, staring at a deadline, or already booked. So I decided to do a little early spring fishing up Boulder Creek, and if that didn't settle me down, well, maybe I'd drive up to Douglas, Wyoming, the place where Miriam Menken had rented a ranch and met her fate. I told myself it would help me help Cecelia if I first did a little reconnaissance.

❖

I TOLD BETTY I'd be gone until Sunday or Monday. "What if some more of the shrinks call back?" she asked.

"Would you ask them to call back on Monday, please?"

"Why don't I screen them for you, and make you some dates?" she suggested, a little glint lighting her eyes. "Just tell me what you're looking for."

I grinned. "You're a good judge of character; just listen to them talk, and if you don't like them, tell them they must have a wrong number. If you like them and they'll see me within the week, make a date. But leave the rest to me."

Betty feigned a pout, but shoved the coffeepot across the breakfast table so I could tank up for the drive, and with decided vim scribbled down the paltry few dates and times I would not be available to meet with psychotherapists. Thanking her, I took a last swill of coffee, went out the parking slip, and turned the truck's nose toward Boulder Creek.

After a few hours thwacking a dry fly into a creek that was way too cloudy with runoff for a fish to see bait smaller than your average terrier, I quit kidding myself and headed toward the highway and the wide-open splendor of Wyoming. Besides, it was a splendid day, just right for a road trip. In my old bomb of a truck, the Boulder-to-Douglas run would occupy about four and a half hours of down-home AM radio.

Sunlight danced along the spine of the Rockies to the west as I rolled northward over the undulating plains, humming past town after town that seemed bent on consuming what remained of the cropland that separated each from the next. I passed Longmont and Loveland, Greeley and Fort Collins, zipping past highway exits that hadn't been there when I was a kid. Fort Collins had a Budweiser brewery north of town that wasn't there when I was a college student, and it seemed to have spawned another suburb. Where farmers had once grown corn and winter wheat, pregnant mothers now wheeled strollers full of tomorrow's voters down clean new sidewalks. I wondered idly what folks would do for food when every last inch of farmland was tilled under to make way for split-level houses, asphalt, and strip malls. I wondered also, as the rate of doubling of the human population on this planet accelerated faster than the BMW that careened off an entrance ramp past my laboring pickup, if I would get my answer in the next decade, the next year, or even the next week. My grip tightened on the steering wheel.

But as I breached the border between Colorado and Wyoming, I felt the muscles along my neck and shoulders relax. The land still opens wider there, and the number of cars and trucks on the road dropped abruptly, thinning even further as the road unrolled its asphalt tongue past the capital, Cheyenne, which lay barely within the state's borders. On that early spring day, the clouds spun eastward all wispy like a horse's mane over the Laramie Range, trailing to gossamer tendrils half a county short of Nebraska. Cirrus clouds heralded a change of weather within twenty-four hours or so. Always colder than Colorado, the plains of Wyoming might yet see a return to winter, even a spring blizzard. My rancher's brain recorded this evidence of weather automatically, remapping possible futures based on the constraints and stresses it would bring. Time to check the cattle and the feed, bring in the last few pregnant cows . . .

I continued northward over the rolling short-grass prairie past Chugwater, where I nodded silently to the west toward the ranch my mother now ran without my father. A muscle tightened in my chest. I switched channels on my faltering old AM radio, dredging up the stock report to occupy my mind and hasten my wheels onward toward Wheatland and

Glendo, where wheat and sugar beets engulfed those minds that didn't dwell on beef. Just before the "blink and you'll miss it" metropolis of Orin, the highway crossed over the braided channels of the North Platte, which flows north and then east as it rounds the nose of the Laramie Range. Gradually, the road bent westward around this obstacle also, and soon I was approaching Douglas.

I arrived with three or four hours of daylight to spare. I took the second Douglas exit and stopped at the V/1 Gas for Less filling station on the right, across the road from McDonald's. A full tank is a necessity in ranching country; one doesn't leave town for a tour of the ranch roads without topping up. If one does, one can find oneself walking a long way.

After presenting a credit card on which to float the price of a fill-up and a jumbo bag of Fritos, I ever so casually got to chatting with the woman behind the counter. She was a tired-looking sort with thin blond hair lying long and straight as straw over cushiony shoulders that melted downward into a tremendous girth. Her eyes moved from my credit-card slip to the signature on the back of my card and then to my face with enough certainty to suggest intelligence, however buried it might be beneath whatever circumstances goaded her to eat. "Where's the sheriff's office in this town?" I asked, knowing full well where it was.

She told me, elevating one great sloshing arm to aim her words. Her eyes fixed on me, a tacit question.

I smiled. "I need to talk to him about that woman who was murdered out at that ranch last summer. I'm a friend of her daughter's," I said, as if tossing of a bit of chat for the sake of companionship. "I'm Em Hansen, from Chugwater. Don't I know you from barrel racing, back in high school?"

The woman gave me an "in your dreams" chuckle. "Since when do I sit on anything that don't have a motor?" she drawled. "I used to *attend* the rodeos, though. Chugwater? You *Clyde* Hansen's daughter?"

"Yeah," I said, surprised. Surely she didn't recognize me. I was far too great a wallflower to have caught anyone's notice, much less be remembered by someone I didn't recognize myself. Or would I have known her without the weight? "You knew my father?" I asked, still uncomfortable speaking of him in the past tense.

"My dad did. Sorry to hear 'bout his passing."

I averted my eyes. She leaned onto the counter and gazed into space. I sighed, said, "Thanks," and let a moment pass, releasing myself into the familiar, slower pacing of ranch conversations, where there's nothing and everything to say and no time and forever in which to say it.

The woman stared out the plate-glass window beyond the racks of snack food. "My dad said your dad was a good man," she offered kindly.

"Mmm." The conversation seemed headed down a track I didn't want to travel.

"Your ma's running the ranch now, I hear."

"Mm-hmm." This topic I definitely did not want to discuss.

"Yeah, well, times is tough," she said, apropos of nothing and everything. She continued to stare out the window.

"Hmm." I stared at the credit-card machine.

The woman seemed to notice me again, out of the corner of one eye. "You say you know the daughter?"

"Yeah."

"Hmm." Her eyes focussed back on inner space.

"Yeah, Cecelia's a nice kid. A little wild-looking, but she rides a horse okay." I gave her a knowing look, as if this was all that really mattered.

"'At's what I hear."

"She's still pretty darned upset. Flunking out of school." I shook my head dolefully.

This bit of melodrama proved a sufficient offering to start the gossip pumps. My informant straightened up and regarded her long shell pink fingernails. "Yeah, sheriff couldn't get no sense outta her when it happened, you know. Poor kid," she intoned, now folding her hands into her enormous armpits and feigning total absorption in the scene outside the station window, which I daresay had not changed in the decade since high school had dumped her out the far portal of her educational journey.

"Mmm?"

"Yeah, clean outta her head, way I hear it. She better now?"

"Well, that's why I'm here, actually. Like I say, flunking out of school. Seems she can't get past it. Imagine witnessing something like that."

"Oh, uh-huh," she agreed, nodding her head. Two of her chins eclipsed and reappeared several times. "That's how they go." Her eyes met mine with a desolate frankness she likely did not intend.

"Yeah, so I said I'd come up here and look around a little. You know, kind of scare the ghosts away for her." I lowered my gaze in modesty. "Sweet kid. Trusts me." All of which was true, I hoped.

"Mmm."

"Thought if I could find out a little more of . . . how it happened, you know, she could get her memory back and all. Maybe we can figure out who did it, set her mind to rest."

The woman grew suddenly mute.

"Well, thanks for the directions," I said, snapping up the receipt and turning slowly toward the door. When twenty seconds had passed and the woman still had not moved or even shifted her gaze my way, I wandered back out to my truck. As I gave the truck door a good yank to slam it shut against the noncooperation of its aging hinges, it occurred to me that the woman's final silence had spoken volumes. It meant that she knew something about the killing, or at least had an opinion she was disinclined to express, and that meant there was more she *could* have said, but wouldn't say it to an outsider, even one about whose father she had heard good things.

I turned the key, put the truck in gear, and pulled back onto the road.

Munching happily at my junk food, I passed the state fair grounds, where I had done my time in 4-H competitions and ridden my share of races. Always before, I had come to this town as a ranch child, a member of the greater Wyoming community, but this time, it was clear, I walked the thin line between insider (friend) and inquisitor (foe). I wasn't sure I felt comfortable in either role. But as I nodded to the giant jackalope statue that graces the edge of downtown Douglas, my mind ever so quietly slipped into its inquisitive groove, and it came to me that the woman at the V/1 Gas for Less had not told me her name when I told her mine, even though she knew of my father.

That meant that in gossiping terms, I had been worked over by a real pro. She was not only a pro but a pro who did not want to go quoted by name as not having said what she had so carefully not said. But a pro also exults in having information, and can't help but flaunt it, even if that means in some small way passing it on.

I smiled, my heart rising to the challenge of interpreting whatever message she had left hidden in plain sight.

14

THE SHERIFF OF CONVERSE COUNTY WAS NOT IN HIS OFFICE when I arrived. "Gone down to the drugstore for some salve," the dispatcher offered, speaking to me via a microphone from her lair, which lay beyond a bulletproof glass window and a cramped secretarial layout replete with wandering philodendron. "Secretary's out for a minute," she garbled through the microphone, managing to indicate that her absence was more keenly felt than the sheriff's.

I tried to make eye contact with the dispatcher, but the glare on the glass prohibited such niceties. I could just discern the hunch of her shoulders and the glint of fluorescent lighting on her glasses, both unnervingly steady as she added, "Have a seat. He can't be long." She indicated my choice of three yellow vinyl lounge chairs that shared the tiny waiting room with an enormous red Coke machine. A fourth chair was occupied by a dried-out little man with faded hair who seemed to be decaying into a puddle formed by his oversized pair of jeans.

The dispatcher was right. Sheriff Elwin Duluth skulked into the building before I'd gotten even halfway through the can of belly wash I wrestled out of the vending machine to wash down the Fritos. I jumped out of the bright yellow lounge chair I had selected and offered him my hand to shake.

The sheriff momentarily froze. He was a tall, wiry man who carried himself with his arms tensed and elbows out, as if he feared an electric shock from his Sam Browne belt, or thought that at any moment someone might challenge him to a draw. I supposed this posture was meant to look imposing, but it led me instead to the impression that he suffered from some horrid rash in his armpits, a supposition that fit with the salve he'd just gone out to purchase.

The sheriff looked me up and down as if I were an impudent teenager he'd just caught necking behind the high school.

I let my hand drop, unmet. "Sheriff Duluth? My name's Em Hansen. J.C. Menken—you know, the husband of the woman as was murdered here last summer—asked me to help him out a bit with his daughter. Terrible thing. Got a minute?" All this I spat out pretty fast, before the mental machinery behind those cold, arrogant eyes could figure out a way to get rid of me.

The sheriff grimaced. "I suppose." Ever so gingerly, he grasped the leather of his heavy belt between thumbs and index fingers.

I glanced backward at the little guy who was still sitting quietly in the fourth yellow lounge chair, so near in that tiny room that his knees almost pressed into the backs of mine. Then I looked pointedly at the locked door that led into the inner sanctum of the offices and said, "In private, sir?"

Duluth worked his lips viciously.

The man in the chair smiled attentively. His smile greased Duluth with unctuous friendliness.

Bristling with anger, Duluth buzzed the dispatcher to let us through the door and stormed down a congested hallway past more tiny offices, an equipment vault, and a heavily armored door. When he'd gotten inside his office and put the protection of his desk between us, he eased himself slowly into his swivel chair, taking the last inch with teeth-clenching foreboding. Then he asked, "What exactly's on your mind, miss?" His last word came out as a hiss, like from a snake.

Miss? Gagh. I hadn't been called anything but Ms. in years. *Welcome home,* I thought, Julia Richards's wrath against patriarchal shitheadedness echoing through my head. Revising my notion concerning the whereabouts of his rash, I took a deep breath to calm my stomach and leaned back in my chair to indicate that I was in no hurry. During the drive up, I had considered as an opening line something warm and cozy, like, *I'm trying to get a feeling for how things looked the night of the murder,* but clearly such sensitivity would be lost on the likes of Sheriff Elwin Duluth. So instead, I just said, "Cecelia Menken can't remember what happened from that night until the following weekend. Could you tell me what you found when you went out there? You know, like how she behaved? I'm trying to get a handle on this memory blank of hers, try and understand what set it off." I spread out in my chair as far as possible to indicate that I was not some compliant little cookie he could push around.

The sheriff leaned stiffly back in his swivel chair. He read the ceiling with his eyes, knit his brow into a fully theatrical frown, and drawled, "Oh, she was sorta dazed."

"You think she was drugged?"

His eyes locked on mine. "No. Why?"

"I don't know, just a thought." Where had it come from? "She dialed the emergency number herself?"

"Right."

"And when you got there, you were the only ones there—except for Miriam's body—until when?"

Duluth snarled, "Just what are you trying to get at, Miss—"

I hooked my right foot over the opposite knee and returned his glare. "Hansen. Emily Hansen. My father was Clyde Hansen, down in Chugwater. I'm a friend of Cecelia Menken's, and I'm trying to learn what I can about her mother's murder so I can help restore that girl's mind to balance."

"I don't think you'll find folks very talkative around here," Duluth sneered.

"Why not?"

The skin around his eyes tensed with anger, as if he found my question impudent.

"Well then," I continued, "who else came to assist you that night?"

"Lissen here, you're talking about an unsolved murder. I can't go handing out any information—"

I held up a hand. "I understand that. Believe me. I've worked with crime-scene investigations before, and trust me, I don't really want to get more than so involved with this one. I'm just trying to help the kid."

"You saying you're with law enforcement?"

"Huh? No, I'm a geologist by training. Well, you see, geologists are pretty good at sleuthing things out, too, but we usually prefer to work on mysteries involving rocks and minerals and hundreds of millions of years of missing evidence."

Duluth narrowed his eyes in obstinate nonunderstanding.

"Erosion," I said cryptically. "Wipes out more data than you'd want to believe. But getting back to Cecelia—"

"What crime scene, then?" he challenged.

Suspecting that he was about to laugh, I said, "Well, one up in the Big Horn near Meeteetse, and then one down in Denver. Here," I said, pulling out one of my business cards, which held the now-defunct number of dear old Blackfeet Oil, "this is me. This is the oil company Mr. Menken was president of. Husband of the deceased. And this," I said as I started to scribble on the back of the card, "is the number for Sergeant Carlos Ortega of the Denver Police Department, Homicide." I pushed it across the desk toward him.

Duluth looked thoughtfully at the card, his face still drawn down in the guard of contempt. Then, dragging the telephone to him so he wouldn't have to adjust the position of his hind end, he picked up the receiver and dialed. I could hear a voice connect at the other end. "This is Sheriff Elwin Duluth, Converse County Sheriff's Office, up here in Wyoming," he said suspiciously. "I got an Emily B. Hansen here," he continued, reading from the card. "Says she knows you."

I heard more chatter over the phone.

The sheriff's eyebrows rose a half notch. He handed me the phone. "He wants to talk to you."

I heard Carlos Ortega's cheerful voice. "Emily," he sang, "what you up to? And who you giving my desk number out to?"

"He's legit, Carlos."

"You didn't answer my first question."

"I'll come see you when I get back in town—nice of you to ask."

"You better. I've been lonesome for the sight of your face. I told the sheriff you were okay, but you play nicely with the lawman, you hear? Now give me back to him, please."

Duluth took the phone back and scowled, said "Uh-huh" about five times, nodded his head, then asked, "You know this fellah Menken? I see. Oh, uh-huh. Well, I'll hold on to this number, then. Okay. Uh-huh." Then he hung up and turned his scowl back at me. "I say again: you're asking me about an open murder investigation. I can tell you only that I went to the scene and that your friend was dazed and upset."

"So whom else could I talk to?" I asked sweetly.

He stared for a while longer, then said, "County coroner, but he's similarly sworn."

"Whose name is?"

"Fenton Wilder."

"And?"

"Ambulance crew from the hospital here."

"Names?" I had to fight back irritation. Given who he was and what he did, he would know every emergency health professional in this underpopulated part of the universe by their names—first, last, middle, and nick.

He shook his head.

I pulled a small pad of paper and a pen out of my jacket pocket and made a show of making notes. "Men? Women?"

"Couple guys."

My patience was growing thin, and I fought to control my mouth. Okay, so he wasn't going to tell me anything about the crime scene, but he was at least going to save me a trip to the county assessor's office. Calming my voice as best I could, I said, "Well then, maybe you can tell me who owns the ranch Mrs. Menken had leased. You know, the one where she was murdered."

At this, Sheriff Duluth's hard lips suddenly stretched into a nasty grin. "Sure I can," he crooned. "That'd be Po Bradley. You just go talk to ol' Po;

he'll set you straight." The grin widened even farther. "Sure, you're a smart one, ain't cha? Yeah, you go talk to Po. *You'll* figger it out." And with that, Sheriff Elwin Duluth rose and none too politely showed me to the waiting room's door, which he quickly slammed against the adoring gaze of the little man in the baggy blue jeans.

15

So I needed to find a man named Po Bradley. An obvious place to start would have been the telephone book, although it was unlikely that the average rancher might be near a phone at this hour of the afternoon, but Lady Luck had the UPS truck idling by the front of the building. In rural Wyoming, delivery drivers learn to recognize each rural resident and the vehicles they drive, so that if they have the good fortune to spot them in town on the day their new long johns arrive from JCPenney, the driver can save what might be an hour's round-trip by simply flagging the rancher down. Or by dropping the package into the bed of the pickup, if its occupant is away from the vehicle. I hurried around to the driver's side of the UPS truck and asked how to find Po Bradley's place.

The driver glanced up from her electronic notebook. "Out the Cold Springs Road about twelve miles on your right, along La Prele Creek. Can't miss it; it's the Broken Spoke Ranch, big sign over the entry road. You lookin for Po?"

"Yeah." I smiled. "Em Hansen."

"Oh yeah, I heard you were about. Ginger Henley," she said, introducing herself. "You're driving that old beige Dodge pickup over there, right? Well, if you want to talk to Po, you can probably find him over at the Moose before long."

"The Moose?"

"Moose Hall. About watering time, ain't it?" She pointed over her shoulder in a general way. "He drives a Ford F-250 with a club cab. Brand-new. Silver. Plates say, 'Po.' But then, he'll stop first at the LaBonte. Makes the rounds, our Po. Turn left at Walnut there."

I nodded my thanks, made a mental note of the speed at which my arrival was being transmitted along the jungle telegraph, and turned left at the Converse County Bank onto Walnut Street.

WALNUT STREET RUNS along the northern edge of the old part of downtown Douglas, a town that time has left unmolested. Douglas has stayed solvent and dignified (give or take a statue or two or three honoring the noble jackalope, that infamous cross between a jackrabbit and a pronghorn antelope that sings to lonesome cowpokes by the full moon), neither growing too fast nor dying of population drain. Douglas exists mostly for its own sake, neither bloating on the oil boom of the 1980s like Casper did nor identifying with state and federal government like Cheyenne. It has not lain down with rich folks like Jackson or Pinedale or Saratoga, nor tarted itself up as a Wild West tourist town, like Dubois or Cody. Douglas just *is*: a small, quiet city settled by Scots and Germans who labored long and hard and held on to their land.

The LaBonte Inn is a three-story turn-of-the-century railroad hotel built of red brick. I pulled my truck around the corner onto Second Street and parked, then sat in the cab for a moment, briefly surveying my surroundings: big brick post office to the south. Anthony's clothing store to the west. Row of shops catercorner. On down Walnut, the old railroad station itself, now a video rental emporium. Not a single silver F-250 with vanity plates in sight.

I've seen grander hotels than the LaBonte Inn. Denver has the excellent Brown Palace and Cody has the atmospheric Irma, both of which were created with fancier trimmings which they've had the good sense to conserve. The LaBonte has a solid sense of itself none the less, right down to the five-foot-tall jackalope over the main entrance. I wandered past the coffee shop, a booth and counter affair with plate-glass windows (one embellished with a cowboy shouting and kicking his horse, which had its forelegs raised in victory over having just roped a calf; caption: GET LOST

YA DURN GLORY SEEKER!), and ducked into a narrow hall that led under a plywood-faced marquee rimmed with twenty-watt lightbulbs. I found myself in a lobby that had as yet evaded the remodeler's sledgehammer. It was graced by an old glassed-in registration desk, a lot of dark wood, and a lovely patterned tile floor. Yet one more jackalope peered jauntily at me from a glass case set into one wall. Several square wooden pillars gave way at hip level to tapering white plaster cylinders, and I could see in a wooden archway the remains of a fine old main entryway, beyond which now lay a banquet room full of spit-polished businessmen, one of whom was rousing the rabble from a lectern.

I turned toward the man who sat at the registration desk. "Help you?" he asked, without looking up from his paperwork.

"Ah, yeah. What's a room cost here?"

"Range upward from thirty-three a night. Fix you right up."

I hesitated. The current state of my finances wouldn't cover many nights on the road, even at those rates. I smiled sheepishly and said something about scoping the possibilities, figuring I'd better give Menken a call before I started running a tab. "Which way to the bar?" I added, completing the impression that I must be a down-on-her-luck drifter. The man pointed to his left, smiled, and went back to his work.

The ceiling in the saloon had been lowered to give it that cozy feeling. I crossed the room past the Bud and Miller neons and the electronic dartboards and took a seat at the bar. As I passed, nobody in the room except the bartender looked directly at me, but my arrival was surely noted by every primate in the place. *A stranger breaches the sanctity of the deep jungle. A hush falls through the treetops. Chatter and grooming cease as the newcomer is evaluated. Gender? Female. Bearing? Guarded, yet friendly. The alpha chimpanzee, a giant male, makes a show of ignoring the intruder, picks at a flea, scratches as if bored. The local females shift in their branches. The low-status males stare openly. . . .*

It's unusual for an unknown woman of any age to wander alone into a saloon in Wyoming, whether she's a wanna-be detective investigating the local cause célèbre or not. I looked around. There were three men and a woman sitting in low chairs at one of the little faux-wood Formica-topped tables, a pair of weatherworn old men at another, and one lone man sitting three stools away at the bar. A typical turnout, I supposed, for a Friday afternoon.

Having been taught some manners, I addressed myself to the bartender, a middle-aged woman whose long suit in life was clearly patience. I ordered a beer to nurse and asked, "What's in those bottles?" pointing at two large square vessels full of vile-colored liquids. One was labeled AFTER SHOCK, and the other, AVALANCHE. It was an idle question, meant to illicit a response like "Bourbon" or "Whiskey," a kind of conversation opener.

"Oh, they're terrible," she said bluntly. "That one tastes like mouthwash, and the other one'll make you sick."

"Oh." My eye traveled down the bar toward a row of bottles that were swathed to the neck in brown paper bags. A sign below them read $1 UN- LESS YOU CAN GUESS WHAT IT IS. THEN IT'S FREE!!! So much for promotional gimmicks. I took a sip of my beer and said, "I'm looking for a man named Po Bradley. You know him?"

The woman raised one eyebrow half a notch, as much as to inquire, Doth a bear void himself in the sylvan wilderness? "Not here yet," she said. "You seen him, Fred?"

The man sitting at the bar cleared his throat. He was fiftyish, and he wore brown twill Sears work trousers, an insulated denim jacket, and a King Ropes gimme cap. His pendulous yellow mustaches quivered as he spoke: "Po Bradley?"

"Yeah."

He was silent for a while, making a display of looking thoughtful. He ran one gnarled hand down his cheeks, a gesture that ended in a ritualistic smoothing of his mustaches. "No, ain't seen him."

Beta chimp wimps out. I took a sip of my beer. "Know who has?" I inquired.

He glanced involuntarily at one of the men seated at the table, a guy with enough flesh to build two men, with spare grease left over for a third. "Nope, sorry ma'am, can't help ya."

"Shall I ask him?" I suggested.

At my question, a bass voice boomed from the middle of the big man. "Ask me what?" he rumbled, without looking up from the plate of french fries he was consuming. He was one of those guys built to challenge the snaps on the biggest-sized cowboy shirt ever made, and on closer inspection, he wasn't just fat. As he looked up, turning his enormous head and throat to regard me, my busy little brain quickly shifted metaphors. Jungle be damned: I was facing off with a bull in his private pasture, with no fence or red cape between us.

He chewed rhythmically. His eyes reflected a passing interest but held no fear toward a puny little varmint like myself. I half-expected to see a tasseled tail whip up to clear flies from his back.

My beer and I picked our way gingerly toward his table. *Nice bull; just want to read the markings on your ear tag . . .* Stopping a few feet farther out than I usually would in approaching a stranger in a public place, I nodded a greeting and said, "Hi. I'm Em Hansen."

"Hi back at ya," he boomed. He flexed his lips briefly into a smile, a motion that set a shock wave through the stubble on his fully inflated jaws. "Henry Clough," he announced, then hooked one sausage-sized thumb over his shoulder, indicating a narrow woman with thick glasses and thin gray hair sitting next to him. "The wife, Beverly." Next he pointed in turn at each of his other two companions, wind-wizened men in their early fifties with hat hair and deep creases about their eyes and mouths. "Win Downey. Jim Tretheway."

"Hi. Pleased to meet you all," I said, looking each one in the eye, then planting my gaze back on Henry Clough. It took an effort of will not to feel intimidated. I told him where I was from and all, the full formal version with my begats.

"I knew your pa," he said. "I liked Clyde. The Stockgrowers' Association's the less for his passing."

"Thanks," I said, and let the requisite moment of mournful silence pass between us before I said anything more. "So you heard what I was asking at the bar."

He lowered his eyelids briefly.

"Actually, see, I'm here on the behalf of the family of the woman from Denver who was killed out there at Mr. Bradley's place last summer. I used to work for the deceased's husband. Daughter's a little pal of mine."

Henry Clough shifted his bulk incrementally back in his chair and rearranged his gargantuan arms, resting his chins in one hand and cradling the elbow with the other. And waited.

"I'm trying to help the family out," I explained. "I'm told the girl was there at the time, but she remembers nothing." I rolled my eyes a bit, suggesting that I was from here and the Menkens were from there, and what could you expect? "So I'm told this Po Bradley owns the house, and—"

"Oh." Henry returned to his original posture and hoisted another bunch of french fries to his lips. He thought about what I'd said. He was in no hurry; men his size don't have to be. At length, he leaned onto the spindly little table and cleared his throat, an effort that started somewhere down beyond his knees and moved upward, ending with an elastic flexing of his lips. Then he informed me, as a teacher to a student, "Well, first you want to understand what happened didn't happen at Po's house. You want the *old* homestead. The home ranch. That's what was leased to your friend's mother. The Bradleys built a new place farther up—*way* up—the road years ago on another spread they got, better heating and all that, but them city folk seem to love the old houses, especially in the summertime."

"I see." This was typical. To survive and prosper, most ranches acquired further land as it became available, and sometimes the parcels did not adjoin.

"Yep, Po was up beyond. Mizz Menken was at the old place. Horse pasture and so forth. She brought her own, and all."

"Aha."

"So it wa'n't *at* Po Bradley's place a-tall."

"Of course." *And Po wasn't there. And you want to make sure I get that straight.* "Right. I spoke to Sheriff Duluth. He said I should talk to Po."

Henry Clough dropped a hand onto the pitiful little table with a thud. "Now don't it just figger? That boy—"

Beverly Clough leaned forward and spied me with bright eyes from around her husband's far side. "He was after her, you see."

"The sheriff?" I asked. "After Miriam Menken?"

Mrs. Clough nodded, screwed her eyes into knowing little dots. "He was boastful. Said he was going to nail her."

Henry put the back of one hand against his wife's shoulder. "Now, Beverly, don't you go filling this young lady's ears full of such notions."

She brushed the enormous hand away as if it were a fly. "It's the truth, Henry."

I pondered this. "You mean, the sheriff saw this city woman sitting out there all lonesome at the ranch, and thought . . ."

"But he doesn't have Po's charm, now *does* he? Two of them been competin' over women like that since high school." She fixed her eyes on me again. "You a friend of the dead woman's, you say?"

"Yeah. Well, no, I never met her, actually. I worked for the husband down in Denver for a while, and taught the daughter some barrel racing. Nice horse she's got."

Beverly nodded, her face stretched out long as if to say, *Yeah, with enough money you can get most anything.*

Money, a sore subject in Wyoming. Anyone who owns a ranch is worth millions on a balance sheet, but all the assets are tied up in land, livestock, and machinery. Cash is a rare commodity, and the lavish spending of it is conspicuous.

I took a sip of my beer and spoke directly to Beverly, retracing ground to see if she'd offer more than her husband had. "Well, I was just wanting to see the place, you see. It's Cecelia I really care about—she's not been the same and all, since the—you know . . . it was a big shock for her, to say the least. Her dad asked me to talk to her about things, see if she can let it go, kind of move on with her life, you know? But like I say, the problem is she can't remember anything of what's bothering her so much. I just thought if I saw the place where it happened . . ."

The tension lapsed from Henry's face. "Well, if *that's* all. But maybe you'd just as like to see Po's wife. She has a set of keys, and she's right here in town." He swiveled his jowls around to Win Downey. "Right, Win?"

Win closed his eyes and opened them again. "Yeah, she's in town. That's the person to see."

Henry looked back at me. "Right, that's who you need to see. Gwen Bradley. Nice lady. She'll help you out."

And that way I don't meet Po Bradley, whom your sheriff would like to charge with this murder. Because he might have done it, you don't know for sure. But either way you don't want someone from outside—even some little old cowgirl from the next county—upsetting the local hay wagon. I understand, that's just not good manners. Well, fine, if you like, I'll start with the wife. But trust me, folks, if your boy did it, he should and will pay for it. I smiled equitably. "Okay then, Gwen Bradley. She likely to make an appearance tonight?"

Henry looked a mite embarrassed. "Gwen? Well, y'see—"

Henry was interrupted by the arrival of one more man in the bar. I saw him out of the corner of my eye, and at the same time saw the skin around Henry Clough's rubber lips tighten. The new man was also a vessel in his fifties, but as slim and lithe as Henry Clough was overfleshed and stiff. I turned and measured him with my eyes. He was no longer in his prime of form and function, but there was something about him that registered as if he was; a liveliness about him, something in the spark of his eyes and the bounce of his step that said he was ready to play. His lips were already stretched in a friendly welcome, but when he saw me, the smile warmed up extraspecial.

I smiled back. "Po Bradley?" I said.

"The same."

Henry opened his mouth to reassert control of the conversation, but I cut him off, saying, "I'm Em Hansen from Chugwater, and I was wondering if I could visit your old homestead."

"Sure, no problem," Po said, whipping two chairs around from the adjoining table. As he lowered himself into one chair, he slid the other expertly up to the backs of my knees, saying, "What's a matter with you old sheep herds, don't none of you never offer a chair to a lady?"

16

WELL, I MADE A DATE TO MEET PO THE NEXT MORNING AT THE place where Miriam and Cecelia had gone to pass the previous summer, but I never got another word out of him or anyone else about *the* topic that night. Henry Clough and his friends need not have worried, if their fear was that I'd find out anything untoward about their charming friend; he was a pro at dissembling, a master at redirecting a conversation, making the whole performance so entertaining that I almost forgot to care that I was being put off.

Before the evening was out, I'd been ushered down the street to the Moose and had met almost everyone else in Douglas. Douglas might be the county seat and the jackalope capital of the universe, but it's still a small town, each and every soul well tuned to the local hum. I could almost hear the telephones ringing with the news of my arrival echoing through the kitchens and living rooms of the farthest ranches out from town before I'd emptied my last beer.

As Henry Clough took his leave at the end of the evening, he shifted his dark, ursine eyes back and forth between me and Po a few times. He began to turn toward the door, but then turned back, took my hand in his in a fatherly way, and said, "Now, you watch yourself, young lady. Any daughter of Clyde Hansen's deserves a little warning about our Mr. Po. Just don't you get drawn in by that smile of his, y'hear?"

I laughed and made a "Go on with you" gesture, thinking, *Po's old enough to be my father.* Perhaps it was the beer thinking for me.

Henry tipped his enormous head anxiously to one side, said, "You be careful on all accounts, okay?" And with that he left, herding his wiry little wife ahead of him.

❖

I SPENT THE night stretched out in my old goose-down sleeping bag in the bed of my truck under a tent formed by the drape of a tarp, tucked out of sight behind a little butte off the road above La Prele Creek. After the cloying experience of being ogled by half the county, I didn't feel like booking into a room at the LaBonte by myself, and besides, the night sky always calms my soul.

I snuggled the edges of the bag up around my face, fighting off the deep chill that had ridden in with the westerly winds, thankful that the front hadn't come from the south and brought a dump of freezing moisture from the Gulf Coast. I might see a sifting of fine westerly ice snow before morning, but the tarp would keep it off me and spare me a night folded up on the short bench seat in the cab of the truck.

I needed time to think. If I'd been honest, I would have admitted to myself long before then that I wasn't really on a mission to help Cecelia, much as my heart ached for her. No, I had turned my searchlights onto Miriam. As I'd read the first volumes of her journals, I had thought her boring and naïve, but soon her words had begun to speak to me, or to something deep inside of me. I had come to know her by accident, through a candor few people share, and I found that for all her normalcy and plainness of thought, I liked her. I had consumed her simple words, wondering with her as she wondered, and griping with her as she griped.

I had begun to compare her experiences with the mysterious Chandler with a few of my own, lining her sexual adventures up against my best moments with dear old Frank Barnes, the man I let get away. Even though Frank was married now and a father, I found that I kept on thinking of him, even as his new commitments sealed him away from me forever. But even now, as I lay out underneath the cold Wyoming sky, a feeling of sexual warmth flowed into me at the thought of him.

And then there was shy but steady Jim Erikson, the man in California who kept on writing even though I seldom wrote him back. Did the mixture of feelings I held for him portend as much frustration as had Miriam's for J.C. Menken? Or was there something important I needed to learn about the nice stable guys that I'd been too restless to learn before?

When Miriam's words had run out with the last volume in the box, I had felt a terrible letdown. I wanted to know more about her, and know her better, so much so that here I was, chasing like a bloodhound to the last place where she'd drawn breath. I suppose I was hoping I'd find a final volume of her journal resting by the bed where she'd slept, closed over her pen to mark the last entry. I wanted that entry to sound a note of resolution, completing a life I had come to care about. I knew this was foolish: Whoever had killed her had probably stolen those last words from her, tearing her from this life before the pen had cooled from the touch of her hand.

Feelings of hope and resignation chased each another back and forth in my mind until I finally admitted to myself, under the privacy of the cloudy, wind-bitten sky, that this early ending to Miriam Menken's story felt to me like theft, and the fact was that I wanted, deep in my guts, to know who had killed her.

Losses. My father dead, and my mother firmly in charge of the ranch, and Frank was gone from my life. My father I could not bring back, but why had I let Frank go while he was still living? Frank had never sought to chain me; he had always understood, always let me roam as far as my crazy spirit led me. What in hell had I been thinking, roaming so far that he gave up hope of my return? Or was I kidding myself that I cared, safely investing my foolish grief in the man I could no longer have? And finally, why did I have to follow such a solitary path in this life?

I rolled restlessly onto my back and traced the constellations that now shone through a parting in the drifting clouds. Orion. Hercules. Perseus. Greek heroes striding over Wyoming, journeying outward to embrace adventure, returning home to share with their tribes the wisdom gained through trial. Miriam had led a mundane life until her early forties, had run wild into the mountains with an unnamed man, and had returned. If she'd lived, could she have told me what might lie beyond the cramped perspective of my own thirty years?

The breeze freshened, sealing up the rift in the clouds. I shifted into the lee of the upwind wall of the truck bed and tugged at the tarp to make sure the clips were holding. At length, my eyelids grew heavy, the clouds blurred into the soft underparts of my dreams, and I slid into the warm arms of sleep.

17

THE FIRST THOUGHT IN MY HEAD ON WAKING WAS THAT I HAD made the right choice in not driving right out to the ranch with Po the evening before, as he had none too subtly suggested. "You can stay at the house," he'd said. "You'll be snug as a bug in a rug with me. No problem. You don't need to worry about no ghosts, neither, Emmy dear. Your friend's mama's gone away where she ain't comin' back."

Had I heard sadness in his tone, or an attempt at getting sympathy? My mind didn't have to rummage far, in the relative clarity of daylight, reduced state of fatigue, and dissipating beer buzz, to realize that Po Bradley had found Miriam Menken more than a bit attractive. Of course he had; if he found me worth smiling at, then a lively woman spending the summer off the leash would have caught his attention in the blink of a gnat's eyelash. Had he pursued her? Maybe. Won her? *Nah,* I thought, *Miriam liked her men—*

No, wait, Po can dance—

Yes. He had turned me around the dance floor nicely. And among other returning memories of the previous evening was the image of Po, his lean backbone swaying with the music, dancing Beverly Clough across the floor at the Moose, his eyes locked on her as if he'd found heaven in her soft gray peepers. She had held her spine primly away, but she hadn't otherwise fought him. Yes, Po could dance. I made a mental note to ask him if he had ever danced with Miriam Menken.

❖

THE ROAD IN to Po Bradley's new ranch house was marked by a rough-hewn timber arch that spelled out BROKEN SPOKE RANCH in tall, proud letters. My truck rolled off asphalt and onto dirt twenty feet off the county road, then jounced over the horizontal bars of a cattle guard as I crossed the line of a barbed-wire fence. I paused and looked around, aghast. As I'd crossed this boundary, I'd moved from a good strong stand of grass into a mixed scrub of sage, squaw brush, and the dispirited remnants of grass, all chewed down to nothing. Even the previous year's growth on the sage was bitten off, a sure sign that whatever cow had foraged there had been hard up for dinner. Even under the half inch of fine snow that had collected during the night, the range looked sad and forlorn.

I sighed. Po Bradley was no kind of rancher, or at least no custodian of the grass, which was saying about the same thing. Any cattleman worth his salt knew what he was really doing was keeping the range healthy first and worrying about the cows second. Perhaps Po was too busy dancing to worry at all.

Before putting the truck back into gear, I noticed that the mailbox was a navy blue job with white letters that crisply read A. BRADLEY. I continued half a mile in off the pavement before I found Po's house. "What's the *A* for?" I asked, as he met me at the door.

He smiled a cheerful good morning and handed me a cup of coffee. "Huh?"

"On your mailbox. Was *A* your daddy's first initial or something?"

Po grinned ear to ear, ready to tell me something cute about himself. "*A* for Arapaho, my full given name. My older sister couldn't say it right, or so the story goes; she called me 'Apapapo.' Got shortened pretty quick. Folks never gave me no middle name; guess they figgered Apapapo was enough name for one little guy."

"Ah. What's your sister's name? Cheyenne?"

"Nope, just Annie. As in Oakley. 'Cause she ain't shy. Ma didn't give up cowboys for Indians until I came along."

I sipped my coffee, grateful as ever to the magic of the sacred bean as it shook awake the far timbers of my brain. Yep, Po Bradley sure was an engaging sort of fellow. I watched him as he moved about his living room, picking up his boots and socks where they'd been tossed off the night before, and wondered if there could be anything in the sheriff's apparent notion that this man had killed Miriam Menken. He sure didn't look like a murderer to me: no shifty eyes, no furtive movements, no smoking gun; but then, of the three murderers I'd already met in my short career, only one of them had fit that stereotype, and it was the two I hadn't spotted who made the lasting stuff of nightmares.

And, I told myself firmly, there was the little matter of motivation. I couldn't imagine why Po Bradley or any other rancher would want to kill a woman who was paying good money to rent the old homestead of his ranch; it wasn't practical, and practicality goes a long way toward making up people's minds in Wyoming. And it wasn't just financial expediency that had to be considered. There was the fact that, sentimental matters aside, women in Wyoming still ranked in value somewhere between the new John Deere tractor and the prize bull, for all a man would want to risk going to jail over killing one. And, like the tractor and the bull, a woman served a function on a ranch, and a man wouldn't want to have to go around getting a new one if he could avoid it.

Po paused in his efforts to straighten up his unkempt bachelor lair to offer me some breakfast. "Got some eggs and bacon, real easy. . . ."

"No thanks," I lied, as my stomach rumbled to the tune of frying bacon. I didn't want to get any cozier with this man out here where there wasn't a Henry Clough to watch out for me.

"Let's go, then," he said, stepping into his boots and shrugging on his western-cut down jacket. "We can take my truck."

"Thanks anyway," I answered smoothly, "but I'll just follow you. That way, I can head straight on out from there to my next appointment." I was proud of this little subterfuge: if Po did prove to be a wrong-o, it supplied me with my own way off the premises, one I could use as a two-ton weapon if need be, and at the same time gave him the impression I was expected somewhere else at a known time later that morning, so he would think twice about detaining me by force.

He smiled and nodded in reply. Everything in creation seemed just fine with Po Bradley.

We headed back down the road toward town and a mile or so later turned onto the dirt road that lead to the old homestead of the ranch. Ours were the first tracks in the newly fallen snow for a quarter mile. We turned in under another arch, this one formed of lodgepole timbers turned gray with age. The track bent around the flank of a step in the river terrace, then opened up to a fabulous view: sweeping vistas of the north end of the Laramie Range, beautifully tended irrigated hay fields, a winding line of cottonwoods and willows marking a perennial tributary to La Prele Creek, and, tucked in there among the trees, a fine old log homestead complete with barns and corrals. I got out of my truck in front of the low chain-link fence that separated the dooryard from the open range and gaped. The contrast between this well-kept spread and Po's overgrazed acres was stunning. "Beautiful," I cooed.

Po raised his shoulders and dropped them. "Oh, I suppose."

"The grass is sure—" I caught myself, quickly before I could say what was on my mind: *You sure take better care of this place than up around your new house.* "You keep this part just for the hay? I don't see any livestock here."

Po put a hand on each hip and arched his back, working out a kink. "Sister Annie inherited this little part here when our folks passed on, and she won't let me put no cows on it."

"She live here, then?" I asked, looking about to see if there was a second structure where the not so shy Annie might be hiding.

"No, she moved to Denver couple years ago. Had to be near her doctors." He shrugged. "Don't know whether she's grateful or not that I found her a tenant." He shrugged again. "Course, the tenant gone and got herself killed, poor lady." He shook his head.

I regarded him askance. Was this an act for my benefit? "But you got the main part of the ranch." *And your wife lives in town . . . ?*

He sighed. "Yeah, I got it okay."

I began to drool, even as I acknowledged that eighty acres, even irrigated, were not enough to support a separate ranching operation in the arid lands of Wyoming. "She looking to sell this place?"

"House and eighty, yours for the low low price of four hundred thousand."

"Oh, then she doesn't want to sell."

"Hey, that's all irrigated land. You could have a fine little horse-breeding operation here, or build on and make her a bed-and-breakfast."

"Sure, if I had enough capital going in to buy some breeding stock, nurse the mortgage, and eat for five or six years while I came up to speed. Then I got to pray the price of beef comes out of the cellar."

Po looked at me appraisingly. "You understand this stuff."

"Ranch-bred myself, remember?" I said with some heat. There are few things more obnoxious to me than a man who thinks all women incompetent. The judgment just has a way of bouncing off womankind and sticking to the man like glue. Reigning in my temper, I changed the subject back to his sister's spread. "Still, she's not exactly giving it away."

"Folks from Hollywood seem to feel differently."

I sighed. This was the problem: the weekend hobby ranchers with their passing whims and lack of economic imperative were running the price of land up out of reach of young hopefuls like me. What I couldn't afford to get started with was a tax write-off to them. There were three economic realities that rode on the backs of the true ranchers: the need to nurse debt (the mortgage), pay operating costs (equipment purchases and upkeep, feed supplements, and wages to the hired help), and make a living (profit). The way things were, on a given year a typical rancher could hope to meet two out of three. The older family ranches often did the best, as there was less debt and the multigenerational intimate knowledge of the spread and its climatic environment made for the most efficient management of resources; but in those cases, the family's wealth was tied up in the land, and if a rancher wanted to retire or withdraw capital to nurse declining health, the grim reality of debt came back to haunt him, and he had less to leave his offspring. It was ironic that the central part of the ranch I'd grown up on had been purchased with money inherited from my mother's father, a banker back east. Even with that leg up, my dad had had to beg more help from my mother's family in the lean years, a constant source of friction among the disapproving easterners, my rebellious mother, and my embarrassed father.

I gazed out across the eighty beautiful acres of irrigated hay fields that lay before me. It was an easy guess that the Broken Spoke Ranch had originally been comprised of at least six to ten square miles of grazing lands, with long-term leases to additional grazing on extensive Bureau of Land Management acreage, as well. It was typical in local society that the son or sons inherited the bulk of the lands, but this choice little bit with the original homestead had been left to the daughter. An odd arrangement. And then Annie Oakley Bradley had moved down to Denver to be near her doctors. Declining health or a chronic condition? "How long ago did your folks pass away, Po?" I asked.

"Oh, four years or more."

I shook my head in empathy. Even with the one time tax exemptions allowed with inheritance, the current appraised value of the Broken Spoke Ranch would have made the U.S. government his 40 percent partner. Mortgage time again, just to buy out the inheritance taxes. Was that why Po was grazing his grass down to a nub? I thought a while, trying to come up with a polite way to ask, and as I thought, I remembered that he was driving a brand-new truck and that his wife lived in a house in town. Not small capital expenditures. "Times are tough, aren't they?" I finally said, as suggestively as I could. I gave him a winsome smile.

Po tipped his head to one side. "Oh, I'm doing okay," he replied. And then, snapping up my bait, he added, "Course, I'll be doing even better when the oil well's drilled."

"Oil?" I said, appalled. Everyone knew the chance of hitting oil south of the Platte River in this county was like trying to find ice in hell. Or at least every oil geologist knew that. Ranchers still hankered after the dream. It was a cash crop they didn't even have to tend, if they held the mineral rights to their own lands. All they had to do was cuss out the degradation of their land as the pump jacks went in, then cash the checks.

Po assumed a knowing stance, jaw slightly thrust out. "Yeah, I got a deal going with an oil company out of Denver. Gonna drill a well over that way a couple sections, over beyond where the shoulder of that hill comes around." He gestured toward the west. "Got the tin shed in and graded themselves a road and everything. Just a little holdup on the schedule."

"Shed?"

"Where they store the drilling mud."

"They built a shed for the drilling mud?" I asked.

Po turned his look of appraisal back on me. "You know something about drilling?"

I thought a moment. It wouldn't do to show off and give him my full résumé as a petroleum geologist; that might make him quiet up on me. Instead, I opted for the more blue-collar part of my background: "I used to sit wells as a mudlogger," I said. "You know, the monkey that stays out at the well and pulls the drill cuttings out of the return mud and samples the works for oil and gas."

Po gave me a vague look, but nodded his head. "Well, then you know how they use that mud to drill the well. It's real important."

"Oh, yeah. Real important," I agreed, wondering just what in hell an oil company was doing grading a location and building a special shed just to store the sacks of unmixed mud. It came powdered, in hundred-pound bags, like unmixed Portland cement. The roughnecks add water and toss it into the system as needed. Every few feet deeper into the hole takes another sack of mud. It's pumped continuously down the hole through the drill pipe, out the center of the bit, back up the annular space between the outside of the pipe and the borehole walls, and into a storage pit beside the rig. The stuff lubricates the drilling, flushes the drilling cuttings to surface, and counterpressures any gas or oil that might want to come up to see you out of control. The sacks of dried powdered mud—bentonite, a swelling clay, to be exact—are brought onto the site on a flatbed truck, then stored in a little portable shed that the drilling contractor brings out with the massive rig. And sometimes, the mud is brought out premixed, in a big truck. From companies like Wyoming Mud, just an hour's drive away in Casper. *So why build a special shed?* I wondered. "So they built you a nice tin shed," I said, like I was really impressed.

"Yep. Brought a 'dozer in, made 'emselves a nice road, and built me a shed."

"When they doing to spud?"

"Spud?"

"Start drilling."

Po frowned. "Well, like I said, there's been a slight delay. But they're gonna do it. Already brought the mud in and everything."

"Oh."

"Where's your folks' ranch?" Po asked, pointedly changing the subject.

"Oh, down by Chugwater."

Po's eyebrows shot up with interest. "Your brother running the place, then?" he asked slyly. "I hear your pa passed on last summer. Dreadful sorry."

"Ma's running it," I said simply, thinking that would end discussion of that uncomfortable topic. I knew he would refrain from asking about the size of her holdings, just as I would never ask why in hell he was over-grazing his; either question would be unspeakably rude. One simply did not ask the size of a rancher's spread; it was like asking how much money a person had in the bank. "So. How long this place been in your family?"

"My granddaddy homesteaded here back in 1888. Built the front room, wintered over, then went back to Illinois and got hisself a wife. She raised him a good brood, and they added on to the back. Got to be so many, they built a nice big Victorian house over on that rise, but that burned down when I was a kid, and my folks moved us back in here, put a big LP gas furnace in the living room. Suited me fine until my wife got to natterin' at me 'bout needin' a little privacy. So we moved up the way here to the other house."

And then she outright left you, you lascivious old fool, I wanted to add. *And where'd you dig up the money for the mortgage on your wife's house in town, and a nice new truck?* I glanced at his hands, which looked used, but not any too recently. The callouses were clean and none too thick, and there was a fineness to them I don't generally see in the hands of a man who's just come from bucking bales and digging holes for fence posts.

Po opened the gate in the dooryard fence and let me in, then preceded me to the front door of the house, which he unlocked with a key he kept on a chain in his pocket. The inside of the house was as nice as the outside. The original small room, which now served as an open hall closet and mudroom, gave onto a nice-sized living room, with kitchen to the left and bedrooms beyond. The living room was cozy yet spacious, graced with old-fashioned log furniture and even an antler chair, and the kitchen, while not exactly modern, was well equipped with gas range, a large refrigerator-freezer, and even a dishwasher, for heaven's sake.

Po stood staring fixedly at the left-hand door of three that led off the back of the living room. "That's where it happened?" I asked.

He nodded.

I took a breath, paused, then marched resolutely across the room and opened the door.

❖

DEATH IS A mysterious ending to something as noteworthy as life. I'm not satisfied as to what happens next, if anything, but when some people die, they do seem to linger for a while around the portal through which they made their exit. Not so Miriam. She was simply gone.

When I pushed open that door, I saw nothing but a bare bed frame, a bureau, an open armoire, and a bedside table. Her clothes and all personal objects were gone from the hangers and bureau just like she'd checked out of a hotel, taking every scrap of habitation with her. No last exhaled breath, no comb, no loose hair, not even a slip of paper in a wastebasket waited in that room.

"Why no mattress?" I asked.

When I got no answer, I turned and looked at Po, who was hovering in the doorway, trying to settle himself against the frame as if for moral support. He glanced nervously at the bed frame and thrust his left hand into the pocket of his jeans as if to anchor it, but his right hand kept moving, touching his head, the back of his neck, his upper chest, the opposite arm. "There was . . . you know, a mess."

"Oh."

Po's voice came out tiny, tightened by embarrassment and grief. "Sheriff said they needed it for evidence."

"Um, stains."

"Yeah."

"Po, how did she die?"

He didn't say anything for a while, then: "They said . . . well, they found she'd had some kind of poison."

Poison? "Any way it was suicide?"

"No, that was the funny thing. It was some kind of dose, but I saw the boys lookin' about. They couldn't find the bottle it come in."

I knit my brow. "She die quietly, Po?"

"Oh, no . . . well, no. There were . . . signs of a struggle, and, well . . ."

"What?"

Po's face tightened into a wince as he continued to stare at the bed frame. "Well, don't you suppose that you *would* kind of writhe around a bit if something like a poison was takin' you? I mean, come on . . ."

I moved Po Bradley off my mental list of possible murderers. No way a man that squeamish over death could have caused it. Unless, of course, he was one hell of an actor. "Po, can I ask you a personal question?"

"Sure."

"You and the sheriff not get along or something?"

"Huh?"

To distract him from feeling self-conscious, I moved farther into the room, eyed the old black telephone sitting on a bedside table, began pulling out the drawers of a bureau that stood under a window that looked south toward the mountains. In the months since Miriam's death, spiders had built great fortresses between the curtains and the window frame, and the yellow dust kicked up from the road and pastures beyond had settled on the top of the dresser. There was nothing in the drawers. "Well, I saw the sheriff yesterday, and—"

"What're you lookin' for?" Po asked.

"Books," I said, without considering my words.

"Like that one she used to write in?"

I turned. "Yes. Black, with a marbly white pattern on the cover, like they're pretending to be leather."

Po smiled into the internal space of memory. "Yeah, she had one of them. I'd find her settin' out on the front porch writin'. Real serious she was about all that. Wore her glasses for it, and always snapped it shut when anyone approached." The smile grew even warmer, wider, as he remembered. "I'd tease her I was going to sneak up one day and read over her shoulder, but she said, 'Po Bradley, you stay out of a woman's business.' Feisty, she was."

"You liked her."

"What wasn't there to like?" Po's eyes shifted onto me with a gleam, his social appetites suddenly rekindled and ready to shift into the present tense.

"Good dancer?" I asked slyly.

"*Great* dancer. *How* that woman could move."

I decided that it was time to get the hell out of the bedroom, mattress or no. I had to brush past his shoulder to get out, as this man of fancy manners did not move to give me room.

Taking a deep breath, I strode around to the second door, opened it, only leaned rather than taking a step inside, so I wouldn't get cornered again. I found myself looking into a bathroom. Next door gave onto a short hallway with two other doors. I sprinted down and opened one, then the other. Both were bedrooms. "Which one was Cecelia's?" I asked, my voice coming out half a pitch high. I told myself to calm down, not let this man worry me, reminded myself that he was a rake who preferred to ooze into position and let his charm and the heat of his body do the work for him, rather than force his luck. Vain old rooster that he was.

I turned and found him once again leaning against the door frame behind me, this time lounging, his posture clearly seductive. "Room on the right," he said. "Bed's still made in there. . . ."

I took a perfunctory glance, noted the position of the bed, the armoire, the telephone, and the bureau, said, "How nice," slammed the door, and bustled back past him. And through the living room. And out the door into the yard. And was in my truck buckling the seat belt before he caught up to me, somehow managing to look like he hadn't sped up the rate of his saunter. "Well, thanks, Mr. Bradley," I said abruptly, closing the door and rolling down the window, rather than having to leave the door open to talk to him. Nothing like a quarter inch of steel to limit a man's ability to grope.

"Po. You can call me Po, you know that."

"Sure. Well, gotta get to that next appointment of mine."

"Sure, sweetie." He reached in through the open window and grasped my near hand.

I narrowed my eyes and stared, fury leaping into my heart. "Mr. Bradley, sir, I'm not being feisty; I'm just plain not interested."

Po jerked back in surprise, the creases in his face popping so wide open that their absence of tanning made them glow like a spider's web catching the sun.

Po was not half so surprised as I was. It was not like me to be so blunt. It just made me mad that a man my father's age would, well . . .

"Fine," he said. His face relaxed back into its perennial smile. "Well, if I can help you any more, you just say. Anything a-tall. I'd like to see this thing put to rest, you know."

Recovering myself, I said, "Fine. You know what happened to that journal she was writing in?"

He shook his head. "Didn't that go back to Denver with the rest of her things?"

"Oh. Okay, you see or hear anything that night it happened?"

"No, ol' Sheriff Elwin sure asked me that, too." He shrugged charmingly, slipped his hat off and scratched his head in a considered parody of giving my question greater thought. "Well, lessee. I seem to recall a friend of hers dropped by earlier that afternoon."

"Friend?"

"Yeah, big buck with a fancy car."

When my mouth began to sag open, Po continued. "Yellerish-haired guy, looks like he coulda played football in school, only he seemed more the type 'at was into intramural sports, if you know what I mean."

Screw your come-ons, I thought impatiently. "You catch his name?"

He grinned. "Nope."

Ignoring the mischief in his eyes, I said, "This was someone her age, right? Not a suitor for the daughter."

"Nope, plenty of gray in that there mustache."

Big brawny guy, graying blond with a mustache. "What kind of car you say it was?"

"Gold BMW 'at needs a tune-up."

"Out-of-state tags?"

"Nope, Wyoming." Po furrowed his brow in a mockery of great seriousness as he added, "I told that there sheriff all of this."

I dug around with another ten or twelve questions, but Po couldn't or wouldn't tell me any more about the unnamed caller, and I ran out of new angles for jogging his increasingly selective memory.

Tired and aggravated, I turned the wheels of my truck toward town and the breakfast for which my stomach was beginning to scream, wondering just how deep the game between Po Bradley and the sheriff ran.

18

THE JACKALOPE SPECIAL AT THE LABONTE INN COFFEE SHOP CON-
sisted of one egg, one pancake, and my choice of two pieces of bacon or
sausage links for $2.95. The coffee was hot and the water cold, both fea-
tures that are necessary to shroud the strong, rather soapy taste that comes
out of the taps in Wyoming.

I struck up a conversation with the waitress at the counter, but while
she was plenty interested in the topic, she didn't know anything about
Miriam's death I hadn't already heard, and her opinion of Po Bradley was
something she kept to herself, beyond a suggestive smile. After eating, I
browsed around town a bit, finding a fine bookshop in the R-D Drugstore on the main drag. I scoped out the library, the post office, and the
county offices, then tried to reach the county coroner, but was told he was
out. A call to the hospital got me no closer to talking to the ambulance
crew. I soon got restless, which is to say, people were getting a whole lot
more out of ogling me than I was out of questioning them. It seemed that
Saturday was a day to get ranch chores done, and what the hell was I doing
hanging around expecting someone to hand me my answers on a silver
platter?

I phoned my uncle Skinny up in Kaycee to see if he wanted a visit, but
got no answer. Which meant that I was officially at loose ends. Which
meant what? Go back to Boulder and sit on my butt the rest of the weekend? Not a pleasant idea. Then I got to thinking about the peculiar

matter of the drilling mud out on the Broken Spoke Ranch. While it had nothing to do with Miriam, I was sure, it had a lot to do with petroleum, and, well . . . I got into my truck and started driving back out the Cold Springs Road, figuring I'd just take a peek.

It wasn't difficult to find the shed, if you knew what you were looking for. Cat drivers that do subcontract work for oil companies have a certain style to the roads they blade in. They just drop that slab of metal and shove, drawing as straight and wide and flat a run as they can out to the location. The gate built for access—another dead giveaway that something was going on there, a cut in the barbed wire with extra sturdy new posts put in before a new wire fence was constructed—was a bit unorthodox. Usually a cattle guard is placed across the road, a trough topped with iron rails that spans the opening between the new fence posts, instead of a wire gate. Cattle stay away from the rails, not wanting to get their hooves caught in between them, but trucks can drive right over them, making a characteristic thrumming sound. Heaven knows, no oil-field workers want to be bothered opening and closing any gates, but perhaps the people who had built the well location just hadn't gotten as far as putting in the guard, and had just strung up some wire to keep Po's half-starved cattle in.

The gate was secured with a heavy padlock, another irregularity. Locked gates are considered somewhat rude in Wyoming. Figuring the builders could screw their bad manners, I parked my truck outside the gate, climbed over it, and marched on in to inspect the shed. It was not far from the fence, but situated around behind the shoulder of the hill, just as Po had described it. A very strange place for a drilling location, when there was all that nice flat land farther away from the shoulder of the hill. Why hug topography?

I cast my mudlogger's eye about the site. A pad had been bladed in, and a preliminary gouge cut where the lined mud pond would sit. Not very big. Was this to be a shallow well, or were the drillers going to bring in tanks to hold the overflow mud? And that shed—it wasn't any bigger than usual, but it sure was fancy. And it sure was locked. Why, to protect a few hundred dollars' worth of clay? I walked right up to it and squinted in through the crack between the door and the jamb. Nothing was there.

"Nice, huh?" said a voice behind me.

I jumped sideways, spun around. "Po!"

"Emily," he purred, eyes going all sleepy on me, like a cat does while it's digging its claws into your lap.

"Hey, nice location!" I said stupidly.

"Real nice," he replied, advancing on me, his thumbs hooked into his belt.

"Hey, sorry, just got curious," I prattled, circling around him toward my truck. How in hell had this man sneaked up on me? I looked down at his feet, which he moved slowly, artfully, like the smooth dancer he was. "Okay, hell, I owe you an apology, skulking onto your land like this. But you know, I just wondered about how these guys said they were going to drill you a well and then didn't." The words spewed out of my mouth, an idiotic jumble of excuses trying to sound like reasons.

But it worked. Po stopped, thought. "You think there's something funny about this?" he asked. His eyes had gone hard.

I kept walking toward my truck, and he followed me, matching my pace.

"Speak," he said.

"I dunno, Po, but it seems damned weird to me to grade you a location and put you up a shed and then there's nothing in it and you got a gate but no cattle guard. I mean, when they gonna get the rig in here, anyway?"

"Like I say—"

"No, I mean really. Shit, Po, there're a lot of guys in the oil business as don't mind takin' advantage of a man," I said in my best down-home Wyoming us-versus-them talk. "So who's drilling this hole, for starts?"

Po was quiet for a moment. Then he opened his mouth and said just two words: "Boomer Oil."

19

BOOMER OIL? THAT WAS FRED HOWARD'S COMPANY! AS I RE-
call, I said something stupid to Po, like "Oh, Boomer? Sure, I heard
of Boomer," then kind of hurried the rest of the way to my truck and gave
him a cheery wave and started driving. Fast. I just didn't like the way
things seemed to be so close and familylike. But then, perhaps Miriam had
known about Po's sister's ranch for rent because Boomer was working in
the area, or Boomer had known about Po because of Miriam, or—

But it still didn't make sense. Why drill a wildcat south of the Platte
River when no one was making a nickel in more likely places?

I told myself I'd ask J.C. Menken. Maybe. I wasn't sure I wanted to
know if they were all mixed up in a doomed-to-be-duster rank wildcat
project. It was unseemly. It stank of tax dodging and money laundering.

Back in Douglas, I stopped at the McDonald's for a burger and use of
the telephone, and called information. I asked for the number for an old
friend of mine named Nick, who lived in Casper and knew the mud
business. Second generation. If it was a drilling location this side of the
Tetons, Nick would know it. I found him in. Which was not unusual, considering how slow the oil business had been of late. "Emmy! What can I
do you for?" he drawled in his soft little voice.

"You know anything about a wildcat location Boomer Oil's got going
southwest of Douglas?"

"*South*west?" he said, appalled. "No, can't say as I do. You're kidding me,
right?"

"Nope. Not according to what the landowner says. I figured you'd know about it. They already brought in the mud, according to him."

"Didn't buy it from us," Nick replied. "You sure? Whose ranch?"

"Po Bradley's. Broken Spoke."

"Oh, I heard about that daydream."

"Daydream?"

"Yeah. He talks that up to everyone, big show-off. But that well was never even permitted."

"Not permitted? They bladed a location."

"The hell."

"Yeah, they did. Well, the whole thing's screwy, so why am I surprised it was never permitted?"

"Got me there. Yeah, we all figured it had to do with that murder out there on the ranch."

"Huh?"

"Yeah, well, ol' Po was talking the well up real big up to the time that lady was killed, and then alla sudden that was the last we heard."

I thought about this. Why would a murder on the ranch scare off a drilling deal?

Nick was talking. "You say they got mud stored in a shed?"

"Well, no," I replied, realizing I was spouting Po's line rather than what I'd observed with my own eyes. "But there's a shed."

"Funny."

"Yeah."

"Oh, well . . ." Nick said, letting his voice rise and trail off to express with tone what words can only approximate.

I thanked him and got back on the road to Denver, telling myself I'd stop by my, er . . . mother's ranch to see if she maybe needed a hand with things, as long as I was passing by. Better to think and identify with the ranching side of the equation rather than the oily side. At the moment, it had more dignity.

◆

TWO HOURS LATER, I rolled to a stop in the familiar ruts of the dooryard of the ranch, climbed out of the truck, and wandered inside. I found Mother writing out the bills. She looked up over her glasses and before I even said anything, she growled, "Everything's under control, thank you."

"Well, I was just passing through, and—"

Mother snatched her glasses off her face and dropped them onto the desktop. "Damn it, Emily, you're always just passing through this way or that. When are you going to quit that wandering and start living your damned life?"

I just stood there, staring at her, my heart turning to dust. As cruel as she had sometimes been to me while she was drinking, I'd always been able to write it off to just that, drinking.

She turned her head and stared out the window, took a deep breath, clenched her teeth, and said, "I'm sorry."

I decided that she didn't mean her apology, that she was just running through the ritual of her Alcoholics Anonymous form. I said nothing. She could damned well live with what she had said.

Still staring out the window, she said, "You'll find sandwich makings and some mail in the kitchen," and bent back over her checkbook.

I suppose most people would have left, but so much of me was so used to this kind of parley with her that I went out to that kitchen, made a cheese toasty sandwich, and sat down to consume it and some milk that I soon discovered had gone sour. Replacing the milk with cold coffee from that morning's pot, I settled in to read my mail. Which amounted to an alumni begging letter from my college, two pieces of junk trying to look like something I'd want to open right away, a credit-card bill, and a letter from Jim Erikson.

Jim. A welcome distraction. I glanced back out at my mother to make sure she wasn't watching. What would this be, another of his shy notes asking when I was coming to California again? Why couldn't he just phone me, and we could maybe get to know each other a little more, and then . . . but then, I hadn't exactly phoned him either, had I?

I ran a thumb over the plain, practical little stamp he had selected to carry his missive on its way. Jim was a genuinely *nice guy*, the kind you dream of taking home and showing off, if you don't have a mother that might bite him; polite, a team player, tall, good-looking, employed. And it had been a while. Why wasn't I more interested?

I opened up the note to find yes, a very short note and a photograph of the sun setting over the Pacific. Very dreamy surf with dark angular rocks offshore. I remembered the scene: it was Goat Rock State Beach, a place he'd taken me on our one honest-to-gosh date. A hint, right? I gazed at the photograph for a while, trying to catch the allure of endless ocean, trying to believe I could make it substitute for the vastness of the prairie I loved.

The note was short and sweet:

Dear Em,

Seems I have to be in Denver next week Friday on family business, closing my great-aunt Joline's estate. So unless I hear otherwise from you, I'm going to come and see you.

Jim

He'd written his phone number across the bottom, just in case I'd lost it.

Friday? I looked at the postmark. This *coming* Friday, just seven days hence? I was surprised to find that my pulse had quickened. Was it that Jim had just shown a little grit to go with his dogged persistence? Or was it the thought that he was going to appear in my scenery, instead of requiring that I melt into his? I smiled, suddenly glad at the thought of looking into those bright blue eyes of his. And maybe running a hand through his mane of golden curls. Hmmm.

I hopped up and grabbed the phone off its cradle on the wall and dialed. After four rings, I got his answering machine. "Ah, this is Jim Erikson, ah, please leave a message," it began shyly, and then, as always, revving up at the shift from private to public self, his voice continued quite strongly: "If this is an emergency, please dial nine-one-one or call the firehouse directly at . . ."

That's my boy, I thought, *once a volunteer fireman, always a volunteer fireman.* I was surprised to find myself wondering if he could be as happy in a firehouse right here in Wyoming. My mother wanted me to get a life? I'd show her what a life could truly be.

Laughing scornfully at the direction my mind was taking, I left a message saying where I was staying, gave Betty Bloom's number in Boulder, pocketed the credit-card bill, shuffled my remaining mail into the circular file, and nodded good-bye to my mother's back. Outside, I headed into the barn, pulled my dad's old spin casting rod off its hooks on the wall in the tack room, and headed south to the Cache la Poudre River in Colorado, where the spring runoff was farther progressed and the fish might just be turning their crafty minds toward food.

20

AFTER A GOOD HALF HOUR'S CONSIDERATION OF WHAT TO WEAR
to my meeting with Julia Richards, I decided to go as myself, and put on
jeans. Which was part of why I felt so out of place as I hiked from the
parking lot down Seventeenth Street, passing all the young slicks in their
well-tailored suits and tight shoes. I shoved my hands into my pockets and
trudged onward down the bottom of that canyon made of office build-
ings, turned right at Champa, and soon hove onto Eighteenth.

The Rocky Mountain Diner is a nice, trendy little joint stuffed into an
ornate three-story Victorian office block that has miraculously escaped the
hungry wrecker's ball of Denver's skyscraper-happy 1980s. The legend GET
IN HERE graces its genteel front door, and its menu admonishes patrons to
"Check your guns at the bar," and suggests that you "Don't squat with
your spurs on." Its interior designers managed to maintain an anachronis-
tic atmosphere while satisfying the modern taste in seating, and its cooks
know their ways around buffalo meat loaf and Rocky Mountain oysters.
I was in the middle of scowling at the menu, wondering why I was in such
a lousy mood if my near future held a ration of their wonderful mashed
potatoes with brown onion gravy, when I heard my name spoken.

I looked up, to find myself eyeball-to-eyeball with a very electric
woman.

Julia Richards. She didn't top my five foot five, but she tallied in mentally as a very tall person. Present. Erect. Assertive. In charge. She had an

attractive face with wide cheekbones and a tousle of dark curls that left her neck naked but tagged the tops of a pair of those large-framed glasses that seem to say, *I'm fine with wearing glasses, what's your problem?* Behind them, her eyes were sharply blue. Her lips were wide, her cheeks a well-scrubbed pink. She wore a dark suit of a soft wool and a crisp white blouse open wide at the collar. Beyond that, it was no makeup, no jewelry, and definitely no bullshit.

I extended a hand. "Hi, you must be Julia."

She pumped my hand and looked deep into my eyes. "Let's sit."

She commandeered a booth for us at the far end of the room, ordered a green salad and herb tea without opening the menu, told me which soups and salads were worth having, and folded her hands on the tabletop to indicate to me and to the waiter that the clock was ticking. I muttered something about having the same, then called the waiter back and added a cheeseburger deluxe, medium rare. And black coffee. *None of this lily-livered tea stuff for old iron-guts Hansen.*

I had about a second and a half to wish I could get past being a reactionary dip before Julia called the meeting to order: "You want to know about Miriam Menken."

"Yes."

"Why?"

Oh my God, the third degree. I truly wasn't up to this. Not now, not here, in downtown Denver, where my mind was riled by the raw stench of business maneuverings. If confronted when in such a mood, I was sure to pull a sulk and sound as shallow as the suit-encased businessheads all around us sounded to me. I took a breath and let it out in a long sigh. And I reached for the truth, wondering what it might be. "I'm not sure," I said.

Julia Richards relaxed a notch. "At least you're honest."

"I try to be."

"You sound like Miriam, you know that?"

"How? What was she like, I mean to talk to?" I tried to keep the note of longing out of my voice, but failed.

"You never met her?"

"No."

For a moment, Julia looked away, the activities of the street reflecting on the lenses of her glasses. "She was a very vulnerable person."

I was just opening my mouth to ask, *In what way*, when Julia looked back at me and asserted, "That's a compliment, in case you don't know."

I closed my mouth. The conversation was going to go wherever Julia wanted to take it, and that was that. I waited until she spoke again, watching her, trying to divine from her posture, her gestures, and her tone of voice how she felt about her departed friend. At the time, I thought: impatient. Now, I think: sad and lonesome.

"You're young yet," she said. "Early thirties? Yes? And I'm guessing you've never married."

"How do you know?"

"It's not a matter of clairvoyance; you don't wear a ring on the third finger of your left hand, and while you don't seem very confident, you don't look like you've been rendered that way by a man. There are signs. I could list them, but I won't. I don't have time, and you're young enough to deny it even if you understood."

Defending myself against I knew not what, I said, "I haven't had children, either, but I care about Cecelia."

Julia closed her eyes and opened them again, very slowly. "Point to you. It's an unpopular decision not to have children. But they do deserve our love," she said, her voice a few decibels quieter. "Well. Suffice it to say that Miriam was a rather naïve woman who gave up a lot of her power to her husband. You don't know what that means, because you haven't made that mistake yet. It means you're always frustrated, waiting for this man to be the prince charming you've read about, wondering what you've done wrong that you've got a mate but still aren't happy. With Miriam, it took on the character of making her pout. It wasn't attractive, not to men and not to women. It made her seem remote and uninterested in other people, so needless to say she spent a lot of time alone."

" 'Alone,' " I repeated, evaluating the word. It seemed to fit that the woman who had entrusted so much of herself to her journals might have been too solitary, at least on an emotional level, for her own happiness.

"Yes, too much time alone. Not a good thing when you're as ignorant as Miriam was."

"Ah," I said, politely agreeing rather than be caught denying her declaration of reality. I mentally compared the woman sitting across from me to the portrait Miriam had painted of her in her journal. Hadn't she described Julia as being lusciously at ease, dancing from room to room in her new home and her new freedom? I wondered what had happened over the intervening years to leave her so abrupt and—I reached into my heart for the resonance I was picking up from her, trying to place it—disappointed?

"Yes, Miriam was bright, but not smart." Julia crunched onward through her indictment of her departed friend, laying out her judgments as an impatient gardener turns over last year's soil and weed stalks with a spade. "Or perhaps the word is *shrewd*. She was not shrewd. I often wondered why I spent so much time with her, but I'd known her forever, and there's a lot of value in being around someone you've known that long. She was a touchstone, a link to the past. Let me know how far I'd come. And she had a good heart," she added, almost as a consolation prize.

No, not disappointed. Despairing? I stared at Julia's hard blue eyes, trying to plumb their depths as she had mine. And yes, found that small despair that eats at people who expect more of themselves. With a jolt, I realized that her crushing judgments were an attempt to assign her pain to Miriam.

As if reading my thoughts, Julia stiffened. The little muscles along the lower lids of her eyes tightened, telegraphing a warning.

I slouched down submissively and stared into my water glass. "I guess you're right. I've never been married, not even lived with a guy for very long. I—"

Julia interrupted. "Did you have any substantive questions to ask me, or are you just fishing?"

I smiled bleakly. "Just fishing."

Our salads arrived.

Julia picked up her fork and put it down again. "You know, I really am on a tight schedule today. I'm going to take my salad to go. If you insist on looking through Miriam's rather sophomoric attempt at immortality,

you can come back to my office and read it there. But you must understand that what you read stays with you and doesn't go any farther.
Miriam's wish was that Joe never see her writings, ever. As custodian of
her journal, I insist that you use the information only in your efforts to
help Cecelia, and never repeat any of it to anyone. And you must promise
to keep an open mind. And an open heart." Having delivered this edict,
she added in a smaller voice, "There are things waiting for you down the
road of life you can't see from where you're sitting."

21

THE JOURNAL THAT MIRIAM MENKEN HAD STORED WITH JULIA picked up where the previous one had left off. Apparently the women's retreat Miriam had attended with Julia stressed positive visualization, as there was a spate of entries that said things like "I am happy and enjoying the best years of my life," written twenty times over. After a few weeks' worth of such hopeful platitudes, the journal lapsed back into unadulterated bitching. By Christmas, she seemed sick of her own irritability, and announced a New Year's resolution to think about something else for a while. For the next six months, she recorded mundane events, but in July, her resolve collapsed back into a black rage. The first entry that month said it all:

> July 3
>
> Tonight I really lost my temper with Joe, worse than ever. He just stared at me like I was something mildly boring on TV. No wonder I'm a bitch, it's six months since we even *tried*. He says why don't I take a vacation and get some rest, like my problem is I'm *tired*! You bet I'm tired. I'm tired of his never listening to me, never even trying to give me what I want, and I don't just mean sex.
>
> I suppose most other women would be happy just having a man who always comes home and brings a fat paycheck, but when I lie there next to him at night, I just want to scream, or scratch his

thighs and make him bleed. Am I tired? No, I am depressed, and there seems no way out of it. Maybe he's right, I need a nice *long* rest.

I keep wondering if he'd mind if I had an affair. Or if he'd even notice.

July 15

Cecelia's birthday. She's twelve years old today and may as well be twenty. Her sulking has gotten much worse, and all she wants to do is be with her horse. Soon she'll be a teenager, and then she'll be off. Then what will I do with myself?

On such desperate notes, the journal continued through the end of December. Then the first month of the new year brought a jolt that was somehow no surprise:

January 18

I saw *Chandler* today. I thought I was *dreaming*. I was coming out of the Brown Palace Hotel after lunch with Julia, and he was just crossing the street. I stopped in the doorway and Julia banged into me, and she wanted to know what had made me stop. Of course, I didn't tell her.

Maybe I *was* dreaming. Chandler Jennings happened to me over twenty years ago and a thousand miles from here. And he wouldn't look like that anymore, would he? Not *that* good! But this man *moved* like him.

January 20

It *was* him. Tonight when I met Joe for dinner at the brew pub on Wyncoop, he was sitting two tables away with some men. Luckily, Joe was seated with his back to him, but then, maybe he wouldn't know him anyway.

I couldn't eat. I tried not to stare, but finally he looked up and saw me. I don't think he knew me right away. He got up and left the table for a while, and just then Joe got up and went to say hi to the men he'd been sitting with. I had to go to the women's room, and it's downstairs and along a narrow hallway, and when I came back out, he was there, blocking the way. He came right up to me and stood close to me and said, "You're Miriam Benner, right? I thought that was you." He gave me that smile I remember, and it took me right back.

All right, I'll be more honest with myself: I got weak in the knees, just like I did the first time I ever saw him, only this time it was almost frightening. But delicious, too.

It was automatic after all these years as Mrs. J.C. Menken to just say hi and walk on by, but he stopped me. He put a hand on my shoulder and kind of squeezed it and said, "You look wonderful," and his eyes were glowing with that *hunger* of his. How long has it been since Joe spoke to me that way? I was so sure I'd lost my looks.

Chandler asked if I was living here, and all of a sudden I couldn't stand to tell him that yes, I'm a housewife right here in Metro Denver and that's my brain-dead husband I was sitting with. So I just kind of smiled and nodded and he said great, we should get together. Then he squeezed my shoulder again and he was gone.

All the rest of the evening all I wanted to do was get home so I could write this all down because it felt so good, but now all I want to do is cry.

February 17

Today at last I saw Chandler again, and this time I was ready. I was skiing up at Vail with Julia, and thankfully I had on that really great outfit that shows off my legs, or what's left of them. I'd quit skiing before Julia and was waiting in the lodge and there he was talking to someone in the bar. He's kept his hair, a real thick ruff, though the gold is shot with gray now. His face still has that boyish grin, really devastating with a few more lines in his face, and those eyes still have that wild shine. All these years I've remembered that face and dreamed of it when I wanted to have orgasms, and here it was almost unchanged. It was almost scary, like that kind of face and spirit aren't supposed to be on the face of a man past forty. I don't know how to describe that any better—it's just that he seemed oddly sad, even though he was looking so lively, like he'd left something important in his life undone. He wasn't dressed for skiing, just those nice heavy corduroy slacks and a thick turtleneck sweater and casual shoes. But he made quick work of checking out my outfit and he did pause at my thighs and smile.

I get to dream, right?

February 23

I had words with Joe again tonight. Just that: *I* had words with *him*. He hardly said anything, except, "Now Miriam, I know it must be hard when I'm gone so much. But you'll do fine, you always have, right?" And then he gave me one of those little pats on the knee he's so good at.

The next six weeks of entries held an outpouring of dreams and fears that she had indeed lost her looks. And her mind. Spring found Miriam fighting her way out of a serious depression and into an attempt at hope:

April 5

Back to life, damn it!

Joe is up in Wyoming, something about a death on one of the drilling rigs, and Cecelia is on a school trip. Tonight I'm going to do something *fun!*

April 6

I dressed in jeans and a bulky sweater and went down to Denver to a little jazz club called El Chapultepec. It has a cactus in neon out front and another sign that's an arrow that says "EAT." The music was terrific!

April 8

Went to El Chapultepec again. It was wonderful! Just for starts, the bartender recognized me and gave me a nice smile, but then I saw *Chandler.*

He was sitting at a booth with some other people. A woman was next to him. I couldn't tell if she was with *him*, but when he saw me, he gave me that *look*!!!

I can't sleep for thinking about him. I can't stop thinking about Chandler's beautiful bristly mustache, how it would feel brushing against me as he kisses me here and there and here again. . . .

I have to stop thinking like this.

April 9

Joe is home but I told him I was meeting Julia and had him stay home with Cecelia.

I went to El Chapultepec.

He was there again. This time, it was as if we had planned to meet. He was alone at the same booth, and when he saw me, he gave me his slowest smile and slid over to make room for me, leaving his arm on the top of the seat. Later, when the band played a slow number, we stood up and danced. There wasn't much room between the booths and the bar, so we had to stay close.

Now what do I do? He never said anything out of line. We sat down again and just talked about this and that, but I could still feel his warmth, as if he was still touching me. Before I knew it, I had had too many beers to drive home to Genesee, so we had to walk around town for a while. He took me to the Fairmont and we had coffee in a far corner of the lobby, back where no one could see. Then it was late and he said he'd better run me back to my car as he had an early business date, even though tomorrow's Saturday.

Where is he staying? Is he still married? I didn't even ask. But I did give him my number.

April 20

He called. At first he said he was just thinking of me and then said why didn't we have lunch? I said sure, telling myself that I get to have friends that are men, and it was lovely. We met at a little café in Evergreen where there was water running from a fountain making enough sound that people couldn't overhear us, and we talked and talked and talked.

Then we realized that it was almost three and I had to go get Cecelia from school. Parting in the lot he gave me a little hug and said we had to stay in touch.

April 28

I haven't heard from him. I hope everything is okay.

Joe just sits at the dinner table reading the *Wall Street Journal* and talking about how incensed he is about this industry or that commodities price. I want to slap him!

May 5

He called! He said he'd try to make time when we could be together later in the week and "just talk." How I wish it could be more!

May 8

I'll just tell it straight. He called and came to the house. Said why spend the money at a restaurant when all he wanted was to look into my eyes and see me smile. I left one of the garage doors open and he drove right in and closed the door behind him, just as if we'd planned it. Then he came inside and we went straight to the daybed in my sitting room and it was just like twenty years had never happened. He hit every nerve just like before, and we were hot and sweating and right there in the middle of the rug on the dark gray sheepskin just like I've tried so many times to interest Joe, but he never would. The fleece felt like velvet against my back.

May 10

I can't think of anything but Chandler. Thoughts of him fill me up so much that I can't even think how I really feel about what I did. Am I a bad woman? I'm not in love with him. He's just a friend, but he gives me something Joe never has. All these years I thought Joe was just keeping it from me, but now when I line the two men up in my mind for an instant, it's like they're two separate species, and I think that of course Joe is capable of being sexual, but Chandler is different. He's *sensual.*

Joe thinks I must have the flu or something. I told him yes, that I'm a little under the weather. Cecelia sits over in the corner of the kitchen and watches me, like she knows *exactly* what's going on. I tell myself I'm being paranoid.

May 19

Chandler hasn't *called*!

May 21

Just when I was losing my mind, he called and came up here at lunchtime and suddenly it was three again. I feel delicious and relaxed and scared and slightly sick all at the same time.

I am a very bad woman.

June 14

He visits me often now, sometimes two and three times a week. I'm in a trance. The sex always seems like it's going to be so wonderful, such an extravagant, secret thing to do, but then afterward I feel half sick. I try to put it out of my mind, but then the next day I find myself watching the phone, as if I can make it ring. What am I going to do when school's out and Cecelia's home all the time?

July 6

Cecelia is being awful. She mopes around watching TV, and won't leave the house. Stares at me a lot. I tell myself she can't know. Can she? How I wish she'd just go visit a friend, maybe ride her horse. When Chandler calls, I have to say that Cecelia is home, but to try later.

July 25

Today I saw Chandler's car go by on the road. Cecelia saw it too, and turned around and *looked* at me.

July 31

She *does* know. I overheard her talking to her friend Heather Wentworth, whispering about how "the man with the gold BMW was here again." How could I be so stupid? Heather lives right up the street and her mother just sits around all day drinking, staring out the front window. Where did I ever get the idea that just because I feel so alone here, nobody notices me? What if it gets back to Joe? Do I want that to happen? And how could I have thought this so important I could let it get between me and my daughter?

I was jolted from my reading by Julia's sudden entry into the conference room across from her office, where she had installed me with my lunch and the journal. Julia, who glanced at the journal with such indifference that I knew she hadn't read it. But then, Miriam hadn't even bothered to tape these incriminating pages shut. Miriam had known she could trust Julia's disinterest. "I have to leave for a meeting," she announced.

My buffalo burger sat half-eaten on the plate. I glanced at my watch: 1:30. Betty Bloom had scheduled an interview with a shrink for two. "Um, I do, too," I muttered. "Why don't I take this with me and bring it back later?"

"No way. You can come back if you must, but it will have to be another day."

"When?"

"Not until Friday at the soonest. I'm going out of town."

No! "But your secretary could watch me, or—"

"No. N-O. I may not think much of Miriam's literary compulsion, but she was a friend of mine, and I will not chance that her innermost angst will be scrutinized by the public."

I groaned, closed the journal, and stood up. "Let me walk you to the street."

Julia shrugged. "If you insist."

We took the stairs down five flights just as we had come up, no doubt a health regime that the indomitable Julia had devised to ward off weakness and the grim specter of anyone thinking her conventional. "I'm guessing you haven't read that journal," I said, not certain how to dive into the topic.

Julia turned her head toward me. "Of course not. I have a life, dearie."

That stung. "But—"

"I'm in a hurry." She was getting ahead of me, almost jogging down the stairs, the soft lapels of her jacket starting to flap. The curls on her head bounced like a hundred dogged soldiers marching double time quickstep.

"But there was someone she mentioned in there. I was wondering if you knew him. It could be important."

"Who?"

"Chandler—ah, I forget his last name." Had Miriam mentioned it?

She shot me a look of openmouthed surprise, then turned her face back toward the stairs and quickened her step.

"Miriam met him in college. Tall, good-looking guy with a mustache."

Julia spun on me with a look of fury. Checked herself. Seemed frozen, caught in a moment of uncertainty. Then as we reached the street, she said, "I have to go," jumped into a cab, and went.

22

As I marched up Eighteenth Street toward my next appointment, I decided with appropriate fury that Julia had been wrong, that Miriam Menken had in fact been a very intelligent woman. Case in point, she had known exactly where to hide her journals and with whom.

With these thoughts and the disturbing revelations of the journal teeming in my mind, I burst into the waiting room of the second psychologist on my list, Mary Ann Fielding. Her inner door was closed. I picked up a magazine and took a seat. Flipped pages impatiently. Jiggled my foot. Fretted.

Had Miriam run off to Aspen with Chandler, leaving Cecelia to write frantic limericks? And if so, why had Miriam come back? I wanted to know. I needed to know. So stricken was I by this need that it never even occurred to me to wonder why it seemed so important.

Mary Ann Fielding swept into her offices at five minutes before the hour carrying a shopping bag from Macy's, glanced briefly at me, let herself into the inner office, and closed the door behind her. Precisely at two, she reopened the inner door and silently beckoned me to enter.

Quiet room. One desk, two chairs, a sofa, floor-to-ceiling bookcase with books that looked unread. Fern. Shopping bag out of sight. She gestured for me to sit down in the chair opposite the desk, then lowered herself into the one facing it, expertly hiding her legs from view.

I sat. Waited.

"What brings you here?" she asked, her voice consumed by the sound-proofed air.

"I'm looking for the right person to help a friend of mine. She's a teenager whose mother was murdered. Cecelia was there at the time, but remembers nothing. She's a bright girl who always did well in school before, but now she's flunking out." *Had her grades begun to slide earlier,* I found myself wondering, *after she and Heather began to see the gold BMW?*

"I see."

I snapped my mind back into the room. "Cecelia's been seeing someone else, someone who was trying to help her retrieve her memories, but so far no luck. I spoke with this person myself and, er, thought it better to see who else might be available to assist her." I squirmed in my seat, my mind straying back to the information I had just read in Miriam's journal.

"Mmm."

"Oh, so I'm wondering if you can help."

"Tell me a little bit more, please."

"More?"

"Tell me about this girl's relationship with her mother."

"Oh. Well, the mother. Ah . . . well, she'd been gone for a while, you see, but had come back. I'm—this meeting is confidential, right?"

"Of course."

"Right, so the mother was having this affair—maybe only I know about this, so this goes no further, right?—with a man who . . . well, you see, her husband's not much to write home about as a lover." What had Miriam said? Sexual, but not sensual? "I mean, she said as much, or wrote about it, but even *I* wouldn't—couldn't—*imagine*, but maybe that's beside the point. You see, Cecelia dotes on him, and he on her, and I don't know the mother except from her journals."

"Her journals?"

"Yeah." I was getting balled up, uncertain which parts of the story were important—or at least to Cecelia, or to this psychologist—and which weren't.

"Mmm?" she prompted.

"Well, I mean, can you work with this kind of stuff?"

The psychologist leaned forward, put her elbows on her desk. "This doesn't sound to me as difficult or as confusing as it may seem to you at this time. Such feelings are not so uncommon as you may think. Of course, you'd need to see me for several months, working on perhaps the simpler aspects of these matters before we could hope to get into your core issues."

"My what?"

"It takes a while for the therapeutic relationship to become established."

"What? Oh. No, no, no, you don't understand. This isn't for *me*; it's for this *girl*. Cecelia."

The psychologist smiled encouragingly. "Certainly."

"No, *really*."

The smile spread. I could see teeth now, but the eyes were distant. "No problem. We'll just talk about Cecelia. I can make time for you on Tuesdays."

I hoisted myself from my seat. Waved bye-bye as I passed through the door. And closed it behind me. Tightly.

AFTER THAT LITTLE tour of the land of fantasy, I needed to speak with someone I knew would listen to reason. As luck would have it, Sergeant Carlos Ortega was in his office at the Denver Police Department's homicide squad.

I found him leaning back in his chair, adding a carnitas burrito to his already ample girth. He smiled as he consumed it, dark eyes caressing it with love and gratitude. "Em," he murmured. "Sorry, this is the only one I got, but there are chips." He placed a paper sack with big round grease stains on top of a stack of papers on his desk. "Please, help yourself."

I pulled what was left of my buffalo burger out of the bag I was carrying. "Got you covered. There a microwave around here?"

He gestured toward a hall to his left. "Third door. Hurry back—it's been much too long since I've seen you, friend."

Once ensconced with a revitalized burger, I told Ortega about Miriam's murder and Cecelia's slow decline, about the ranch where it happened, my visits with Julia, Cindey, and J.C. Menken himself. The parts about the journal, I left out.

Ortega listened intently, his round brown face alert, his short fingers carefully managing the soft sides of the shortening burrito so that not a drop of its precious juices would be lost. When I was done, he said, "Oh, so that's what you were doing talking to that sheriff."

"Yeah, well, the Menkens are friends of mine, and you know . . ."

He nodded. "Mm-hm. I know about you. Curiosity is like a drug to you."

"You're one to talk."

Ortega smiled. "They still not found out who did it?"

"Right."

"Some kind of poison, you say?"

"That's what I hear on the grapevine."

"Lab work should have told them a lot. But they don't have the same setup we have here. They may not know exactly."

"I see."

"So you talked to the sheriff, and you've been poking about the town, too, right? No, don't answer that. I know you, Em. When your curiosity gets the better of you, you are a force of nature." He gazed levelly into my eyes.

I returned his gaze. "The sheriff thinks this Po Bradley guy did it, so maybe he isn't looking far enough. And now I maybe know something that maybe the sheriff does not."

Ortega waited.

"Well, you remember when we were working on the case at Blackfeet Oil," I began.

Ortega's eyes twinkled again. "We? Oh yes, that's right, you were my boss for that investigation," he chided.

I wrinkled my nose at him. "And a damn good one. Well, this is that same Menken family. J.C. was the president of the company, remember? Only now the company's folded and he's on his own, putting together investment deals for wildcatting and so forth." As I said this, the image of the drill site on Po's ranch slid across my mind.

Ortega nodded. Gently pressed the last morsel of his burrito between his lips. Sighed with gastronomic gratification.

"You'll remember that his wife, Miriam, now the deceased, was gone during that time. Well, Cecelia thought she'd run away with some other man, but J.C. kind of behaved like it wasn't happening."

"He's good at that."

"Right. And she came back and nobody said boo."

"Oh. Mmm."

"But now I've found out that she did have an affair, for certain."

Ortega looked suitably pained at the news that the Menken marriage had been sullied by infidelity.

"No, really, I think it's important."

Ortega arranged his face in a mask of polite interest.

I knew this act. This was his way of getting me to spill everything while he told me nothing. Fine, two could play this game; I'd tell him just a little bit more, but certainly not everything. "This guy up in Douglas who rented them the house where it happened saw the guy the same day it happened," I announced, seeing a possible flaw in my logic even as I spoke: how did I know for certain that the big, mustached Chandler that Miriam had described in her journal was the same mustached man with the ailing gold BMW that Po Bradley had seen the afternoon before the murder? But then again, how likely was it that it could be someone else? Cars of that description were more than unusual in ranch country, and the likelihood that both car and driver would fit the description that closely was near to nil.

My bullet had hit its mark. Ortega's face had lost its glow of humor. "Okay," he said quietly.

"So what should I do?"

"How do you know this?"

"I . . . know this."

Ortega sighed and folded his hands meekly in his lap, his long-suffering saint posture. "Em Hansen, you're going to get me in trouble again, aren't you? *And* yourself."

"Could you just give me your opinion? Truth be known, I'd just as soon stay out of this myself."

Ortega snorted. "Sure, that's why you already drove all the way to Wyoming. Okay, so you have evidence and you have your reasons to keep it to yourself. But you want to figure this out, or get someone else to figure it out for you. Okay. My opinion? You should turn over your evidence, my friend."

"I don't have it."

Ortega cocked his head, a gesture that gave him the air of an inquisitive chickadee. "Okay, so this is material evidence that you have seen but don't control. Interesting. You want me to play twenty questions with you?"

"No."

"You want me to get hooked, too?"

"No. No, in fact I want to get unhooked. I want to know how to get done with it, get out, go home, and mind my own business. I want—"

Ortega hung his head and smiled. "Em Hansen, you will never be the one to go home. You are one of those *locos* that wanders through this life with the burden of questions that don't have answers weighing on your heart. It's as if you thought your mortal soul was in peril." He touched his shirt above his own *corazon*. "In Mexico, someone would build a shrine to you, and all the local peasants would come to ask for miracles, but here in *Norte* America, everyone is much more sane and rational: they just hand you an expense account and ask a favor that might get you killed. But okay, so I'll look into this and see what I can learn." He raised his head and looked at me, shook a round finger. "But you must promise this time to *try* to keep at least your *physical* self safe."

23

I FOUND AN ANNIE OAKLEY BRADLEY IN THE TELEPHONE BOOK, which led me to a care home in Arvada, a suburb not far from Lafayette. She was resting in a wheelchair with her eyes closed, breathing shallowly from a plastic tube strapped underneath her nose. She looked older than Po, much older, but it was probably her illness that made her so gray. She opened her eyes when I said her name. "Who are you, dear?" she asked.

"Em Hansen. I'm from Chugwater. I . . . I'm looking into the death of the woman who rented your ranch last summer."

Annie's eyes fluttered closed again. "Oh."

"Po said the spread belongs to you. It's beautiful."

Her eyes opened again, clearer this time, and a smile spread across her face. "Yes."

"I'm sorry something so awful had to go and happen there."

Annie shifted in her chair. "That's life, I guess. Or should I say that's death." She laughed thinly at her own joke.

"I'm wondering if you wouldn't mind telling me a few things about your brother."

Her pale blue eyes focused sharply on mine. "Oh? Well, why not? You can't take it with you. The information, I mean."

"Right. Well, here it is: I'm trying to figure out why he hasn't taken better care of his part of the ranch."

The pale eyes closed again. "Po is a dim bulb."

"Oh."

"Always has been. Not lazy exactly, just not half-smart. Course, he was the boy, so the folks left the wad to him, but he didn't take much to ranching, never did. Just thought he could sit back and lease the land, live on that. Stupid kid."

"Your land looks much healthier," I said, immediately sorry for my choice of words.

"Hah. Of course it does. I was the one who knew how to manage the irrigation works. It takes a lifetime to know a bit of land, several lifetimes, even. My pa and his pa both worked those ditches, knew how to catch the runoff, steer it here and there, soak it through the ground, pick it up again downhill and use it again. Po didn't grasp any of that." She coughed, stopped to breathe more oxygen from her tube. "Guess Pa couldn't stand to see it go to nothing, so that part, at least, he left to me."

"Who's running it now? It still looks good."

"Nephew." Cough. "Good kid. I taught him what I could."

"Why not leave the acreage to him?"

"Nah, he's going off to the military soon's he's old enough. Can't make it on eighty anyway. Time to sell it. Bygones be bygones."

"Yeah." I paused, thought for a while. "You happen to know about the oil company that approached Po to drill the wildcat on his land?"

"Oil? Yeah. Po told me about that. Bunch of nutheads from Saratoga. There's no oil our side of the Platte. Up north is where they got oil."

Saratoga. "Think they'll drill it?"

"No. Couldn't of wanted that oil too badly, could they? Bunch of gamblers was a dumb as Po. Guess Po got a free shed out of it, though."

"Wouldn't he have gotten a little more than that?" I asked, knowing I was really pushing past the point of bad manners. But Annie didn't seem to care.

"What d'you mean?"

"Well, money. Leasehold agreement?"

Annie made a pshaw gesture with one hand. "Two cents. You're wanting to know if it was enough to buy that wife of his another house." Her dry lips spread slightly with mirth as I started to color. "Wasn't. God only knows where he came up with that cash."

I DROVE BACK to Boulder and sat, fresh out of ideas of what to do with myself. Time is not always my friend. That evening, it hung about my shoulders like a shackle and chains, holding me in the irritation of the present moment. I had nowhere to go. I had nothing to do. The few friends I'd kept contact with in Denver all lead busy lives, and were not, therefore, available to distract me from my growing restlessness. Even my new landlady had plans for the evening. Stanley the dog snubbed me more bluntly, directing at me doggy sniffs that suggested I smelled foul even by canine standards before retiring to the far corner of the yard.

There was a message for me on the kitchen counter in purple ink advising me that Cecelia Menken had called. For some reason, I couldn't handle returning the call. Instead, I just slunk upstairs to my room and lay down on the bed. The needs of young girls would have to wait.

◈

BETTY BLOOM LEFT early the next morning for a rousing spate of exercise at some spa, her wild corona of reddish hair billowing out over a dark green sweat suit and a collar formed of a mint-colored towel. "Don't forget you have two shrink appointments today," she called cheerily as she dashed out the back door. "Your hat size ought to be about a five by the time you come home tonight."

"Ta," I grunted as I lurched toward the counter to set down my coffee and retrieve an English muffin from the toaster.

"Ta yourself," she called. "You've got Renata DuBois at eleven. Address on the calendar." I heard Stanley whine pitifully as the door closed behind her.

I burned my tongue on the muffin. My still-sleepy fingers spasmed, fumbling my coffee mug, sluicing scalding liquid across three magazines and a pile of unpaid bills. I grabbed a stack of tea towels and mopped away, but the contrariness of the universe being what it is, by the time I had them downgraded from sopping to simply damp, my muffin had grown cold as a tomb.

I poured a second cup of coffee and sat down to wait for the jolt of caffeine I prayed would come, wondering how I could hope to readjust to an eight-to-five workday even if I got a job. Somehow it was no problem getting up in the morning, or the middle of the night, for that matter, when I was doing ranch work, or any other kind of work that took me out-of-doors, but the prospect of struggling into business clothes and plunking myself behind a desk for eight hours a day just made me want to dive farther under the covers.

Pah. And here I was trying to get myself up for a nonjob interview with Fred Howard, just the kind of good ol' boy creep I wanted to work for least. I laughed wearily into my coffee mug, wondering if the time I'd spent hanging out with het up feminists like Julia Richards was starting to poison me against working inside the patriarchal system which so grated on their nerves. Or was it some virus of discontent caught while reading Miriam's journals that had me snarling at the thought of even talking to Fred Howard?

Putting off the inevitability of finding a real job in favor of playing detective, I telephoned J.C. Menken, telling myself I should report in and maybe hit him up for some expense money. After all, the trip to Douglas had cost me a fortune in gasoline, and I was beginning to run up parking fees as I maneuvered around Denver.

Menken had already left for work, but a sulking Cecelia was there, awaiting her ride to school. "Oh. Cecelia," I said, caught short at finding her still home. "Hi."

Cecelia read my awkwardness like it was written in neon.

"Oh, it's you, Em. Well. I'll tell Daddy you called."

"Well, ah, actually I need to talk to you, too," I said, with a wave of guilt. "I'm ah . . . returning your call," I lied, wishing I knew even an ounce of guile when it truly mattered.

"Me?" she said with a bitterness that skewered me to the bone. "Why would anyone want to talk to *me*?"

Impatience bloomed into irritation. "Cut it out, Cecelia. I wanted you to know that I agree with you. That Melanie Steen person isn't anyone I'd want to open up to, either."

Cecelia made a noncommittal sound somewhere between a clearing of her throat and a melodramatic grunt.

"So your dad and I talked and he agreed I should find you someone better. So I am."

"Whatever."

"No, really, I think it's a good idea to give it a try with someone else, so I'm sort of screening some candidates for you."

"Huh."

"So meanwhile, I was wondering . . . well, there you were in the middle of nowhere with your mother, and this guy Po Bradley—"

"Oh, *that* asshole."

"Asshole? What did Mr. Bradley do that pissed you off, Cecelia?"

"Oh, forget it!"

"No," I snapped. "This is all about *remembering*, Cecelia."

"I don't want to," she spat.

"Well, I do," I said, trying to adjust the note of irritation in my voice to one of pleading. "Talk to me, Celie."

"Okay. Okay! You want to know? He thinks he's like God's gift, you know? Always coming around and seeing if Ma *needed* something. A real *anus.*"

"And *did* she need anything?"

Cecelia began to shriek. "Jesus CHRIST! What the hell do you *mean*?"

I mentally slapped my own wrist for my insensitivity, took a deep breath, and jumped into the middle of what was really on my mind: "Celie, honey, I know your mother went away for a while and then came back. Remember? It was when we first met. . . ." *It was back when you were more like a kid,* I thought bitterly. *Back when you still listened to me, and came to me with what mattered to you; back before you learned to hold each and every citizen of this earth over the age of twenty-one in absolute contempt.*

Silence.

My head rushing with guilt over shucking her off for her mother, I said, "Cecelia, I'm trying to piece together what was happening in her life, so I can understand this picture better. So I can help."

More silence.

Rushing onward with the next wave of irritation that hit me, I said, "When she went away, you thought she'd left with a man. You wrote that in a limerick on the refrigerator, remember? And now you're all upset about Po Bradley. So tell me, Cecelia, was your mother doing things—you know, behaving in a way that made you feel bad about her?"

More silence, and then, "No. I thought she went away with that man, but it turned out she didn't."

"Wasn't with him?"

"No." It was a whisper.

"How do you know?"

With a raw edge of defiance, she blurted, "Because he came to see me while she was gone, *that's* why!"

"Chandler came to see *you*, Cecelia?"

The voice that answered that question hissed with anger. *"Yes!"* A moment later, Cecelia spoke again, this time wobbly and uncertain: "Why?"

I rummaged wildly through my brain for any question to ask other than the one that crowded my mind, but there it was, unavoidable. "Um, Cecelia, did he—"

"Oh, right! You think I'd let him *touch* me?"

"Well, that wasn't exactly what I was going to . . ." I trailed off, because yes, that was exactly what I had been going to ask. And because I didn't want to admit even to myself just how badly I wanted to know what this guy was really like. Finally, I said, "Well, tell me about him, Cecelia. Was he, ah, nice to you?"

A pause. "What do you mean?"

"Well, how did he approach you?"

Cecelia's voice shifted into an elaborately vague tone, which I took to mean that she knew she was onto something important and wanted to play it for all it was worth. "Oh, he'd call me up sometimes, just to see how I was." But then, after a masterfully brief pause, she delivered her coup de grâce: "No one *else* did that."

I thought about that one for a while. All I could think to say was, "You're right, Cecelia, people have left you on your own way too much."

24

THE PAINFUL TENOR OF CECELIA'S WORDS STILL CROWDED MY head as I waited in the offices of Renata DuBois, M.S.W. I had found Chandler disturbing enough as he sauntered through Miriam's journals— no, let me be honest: disturbingly alluring—but now he had sprung from those pages into the life of an underaged girl. What had he been doing, visiting Cecelia after her mother had left? I could only suppose that he had visited with her alone, without the protection of her father, as what father would allow such a man to pay calls on his daughter?

Renata DuBois was a dishwater blonde with preoccupied eyes. As she beckoned me into her consulting room and indicated a chair, those eyes inspected the four walls, the floor, the ceiling, and the top of her desk, but never looked directly at me. "Tell me why you are here," she began, apparently addressing her folded hands.

I sighed. So much for screening these creatures over the telephone, where such habits as lack of eye contact went undetected. But I jumped on in, figuring that as long as I was there, I might as well give the woman a full screening. "I've been authorized to find a therapist for a young friend of mine," I began, watching her for any reaction that might indicate that, like her predecessor, she thought I was hiding some festering neurosis behind a fantasy friend. Renata remained impassive. So far so good. I uncrossed my panty hose–plastered legs and recrossed them the other way. I was decked out à la corporate interview, as I had Fred Howard to visit next. "She's a teenager who's had a terrible trauma and has reacted by blocking the memory of that trauma. I'm a family friend, and I hope to help her by finding someone she might feel comfortable talking to. I mean, clearly her problem is a bit out of my scope. I'm a geologist," I found myself saying. Having followed the social custom of looking away from my audience as I spoke, I looked up at Renata DuBois to gauge her reaction. I found that she was staring intently at me, but the instant she saw my eyes focus on her, she averted her gaze to a spot on the ceiling without tipping back her head or raising her eyebrows. I looked up, startled. There was nothing up there that could have attracted her attention so suddenly, only plain white paint on ordinary drywall texturing.

"Please continue," she said.

"Well, I understand that blocked memory is not uncommon, but I'm wondering if maybe you have some special experience with it."

"Please tell me about your friend's trauma," she instructed the ceiling.

I took a deep breath and plunged in. "Well, this is a teenaged girl whose mother had been gone for a while in some sort of rebellion from her marriage. I don't know the particulars, but the mother came back and then later took the girl with her to a remote ranch a ways north of here for the summer, to get her away from the advances of some boy." I looked up. Renata DuBois's dark blue eyes bored into me for a split second longer before twitching toward the ceiling.

"Um-hum."

"Um, and, well, the trauma—" My mind stalled again, rethinking just what Cecelia's trauma had entailed. "Her trauma was that while on this ranch, her mother was murdered." I glanced quickly at the psychotherapist, trying to catch her eyes before she looked away. *Boing,* up to the ceiling again.

"Murdered?" she said.

"Yes. Some man murdered her. The local authorities have no leads on the killing, and the daughter, who was presumably fully conscious at the time, can remember nothing from the morning preceding the murder until some days afterward, when her father brought her back to Denver." Glance. *Boing.* "So she probably saw it happen. In fact, her mother could be heard, um, dying in the background when the girl phoned for help."

By this point, I was staring at Renata DuBois the entire time I was talking, waiting for her to peel her eyes off the ceiling. I was past auditioning her as a possible counselor for Cecelia—there was no way a sulking teenager was going to put up with this kind of optical gymnastics—but for my own part, I wanted to know just how long I could keep this woman staring at the ceiling. Quite a while, as I was to discover.

After forty or fifty seconds, I couldn't stand the suspense. "Hey!" I shouted. "Are you with me?"

"You were saying," said Renata DuBois.

"Hey! Every time I look at you, you get your eyes stuck up under your eyebrows. I . . . I'll be blunt. I find that very disconcerting."

"Oh. I look away so I won't interfere with your process."

"My what?"

"Process. My gaze is very intense, because I'm concentrating very carefully and fully on every word you say, the tone of your voice, your incidental gestures. So when you look at me, I look away so my attention doesn't intrude on what you need to do here. Please proceed," she told the ceiling.

I leaned forward and rubbed my own eyes. How had I thought this would be a simple task? I said, "I've taken too much of your time already," and began to collect my jacket and keys.

"As you wish," said Renata DuBois. "That will be ninety dollars."

"Ninety *what*?"

"As I explained over the phone, my time is valuable to me. I charge ninety dollars per hour, or any portion thereof. You may write a check if you prefer."

I MOVED FROM that unfortunate interview on to the one at Boomer Oil, which I presumed would be equally galling.

Fred Howard was in a meeting when I arrived, and did not make himself available to me at the scheduled time. His secretary smoothly apologized to me, saying that he was being held over in another meeting and would probably receive me ten or fifteen minutes later than expected. That gave me plenty of time to fail at picking anything substantive from her brains, stoke up on free coffee from the coffee room down the hall, and wonder whether I should ask him about the wildcat on Po's property. If I really wanted a job, it was exactly the wrong sort of thing to talk about. On the other hand, if I wanted a job, I had might better look for one with a company that had better ideas about where to drill wells.

Half an hour into Fred's ten- or fifteen-minute delay, I got to reading the company prospectus. "Boomer Oil Corporation, a wholly owned subsidiary of Van der Vliet N.V., Amsterdam," the glossy pages announced. Well, it was news to me that the Dutchies owned Boomer, but what I didn't know about any specific corporate entity anywhere up or down Seventeenth Street would fill a great many books. I stared only briefly at the financial sheet (such cold and no doubt elaborately shuffled reckonings of numbers never having been my cup of tea), then thumbed lazily through the stiff, slick pages, which featured photographs geared to impress me that Boomer Oil was truly booming: low-angle photo of big rig thrusting its muscular derrick skyward somewhere in the western United States; white men in hard hats and blue coveralls fondling drill pipe in foreground. White man in white lab coat staring wisely into test tube, clever, mood-inducing lineup of shadows in face and reflections in protective eyewear. White men in clean hard hats and thousand-dollar business suits applauding as one of their brethren puts three-hundred-dollar shoe to the shovel to break ground for new industrial compound. Same white men in suits baring teeth in semblances of friendly grimaces as they shake hands with big black man in regal caftan and pillbox cap.

Boomer was doing deals overseas? I'd always known it as a purely domestic company, even in the years when everyone who could get a passport was trying to get the hell out of the United States to make a buck. I flipped back to the introductory page again, reread the bit about Dutch ownership. Ah, the Dutch had acquired Boomer in just the past year or so; that explained it. So the hand-shaking pose was indeed Boomer's virgin (and Dutch-financed) venture overseas, but to where? I flipped back again. Western Africa, an offshore test slated. Black guy in caftan very happy indeed. More gold crowns for that guy's teeth.

I'd heard about such tests: millions of dollars to get in and get out, leaving the test hole plugged because hey, it was only a test. I didn't understand such activities, but such was apparently the wisdom of doing business with "emerging" nations.

I turned my head toward the efficient-looking woman who sat between me and Fred Howard's office. As I opened my mouth to speak, she neither looked up nor skipped a beat with her typing, but stated smoothly, "I'm certain Mr. Howard will be with you any time now."

I smiled, happy to be thus informed that being kept waiting for forty-five minutes in this office was such a routine occurrence that this woman had perfected the art of mollification. "How do you like working for the Dutch?" I asked her.

"Oh, it's no difference that I can tell," she said. "Well, there's the odd fax or phone call overseas, but aside from learning how to dial internationally, it's been no trouble at all."

I pondered this summation of the difference between isolationism and emergence into the multinational economy. "But it looks like you're getting some different projects. Like this one in Africa."

"Oh, that. I don't handle the business with the travel agent; Lily down the hall does that."

"How about this chemical concern?"

"Hmm?"

"There's a picture of a man here with a test tube."

"Oh. Mmm. You mean the plant in Colombia."

"South America?" I looked back at the prospectus. La Plata Mineral and Chemical, Bogotá, Colombia, a subsidiary of Boomer Oil. "Has Boomer owned it long?" I asked, wondering what the connection might be.

"Oh, just a year or two."

"Oh. Does Mr. Howard travel overseas much?"

The woman leaned her well-tailored self forward and put her finger on the screen of her computer. "Ohhh. Um," she murmured pointedly, narrowing her eyes to an attack on the mysteries of binary civilization.

"Where does Mr. Howard go when he goes? Has he been to Africa?"

"Will you excuse me?" she intoned. "I have to get this out before lunch."

"Sure." Five minutes later, the door to Fred Howard's office finally swung open and two men shuffled out. One of them was Fred Howard.

The tall, paunchy man with him was saying, "So get yourself up to Saratoga this weekend, Fred. And leave Cindey at home this time, eh?" He clapped Fred on the shoulder and laughed, his own unique mixture of phlegm and bass rumble, with subtle overtones of squeaking hinge.

Fred wrinkled up his piggy nose and snorted, swatting the bigger man with one of his stiff, piggy-thick hands, then used the appendage to guide him toward the elevator bank.

When the tall man was safely packed away behind closed elevator doors, Fred turned around, and only then noticed me. His eyes grew wider briefly, then collapsed back to their usual tininess. He stared at me blankly for a moment and then hurried back into his office.

The phone on his secretary's desk buzzed. She picked it up, said, "Yes, Mr. Howard? Oh, mm-hmm," put it down, stood up, and said to me, "Mr. Howard will be just a few minutes more. Why don't you come with me a moment? I'll show you around."

I climbed to my feet and followed her. When we were about ninety seconds into the tour, just out of sight of Fred Howard's office, I began to lag behind, and when she turned a corner, I gave her the slip and hurried back down the hall toward the waiting area.

I was just in time to see Fred Howard leading a third man out of his office. This man he did not put on an elevator. This man he showed to the stairs. That struck me as mighty odd, as we were six stories up. I ducked into the coffee room and peered around the doorjamb at them.

As Fred pushed open the fire door that led to the staircase, the third man lingered for a moment, digging through his jacket pockets. He was not a young man. The ravages of perhaps sixty years of hard living had stiffened his shoulders and hands, and only threads of his once-black hair still clung to his oily scalp. His hands shook ever so slightly as he produced a fine silver case, selected a cigarette, and maneuvered it to his lips. As he stepped toward the fire door, he bent forward and lit the cigarette, cuddling the lighter as if he were in a high wind, closing his eyes in satisfaction. As he bent, he turned slightly, instinctively checking what was behind him, and I saw more of his face. His sallow, sunken cheeks writhed between the flaring nares of his arching nose as he drew in the ritual relief of the first drag. He looked straight at me, with eyes as sharp as needles.

I grabbed a coffee mug off the counter next to the door and brought it to my lips as if drinking, and watched.

There was no way this man was taking the stairs for the exercise. I knew at a glance that he did not belong in this office, and the fact that he was being smuggled out via the fire stairs was only my first clue. The oil patch was still, twenty years into equal-opportunity employment, a white, northern European—decent boys' game, and this man did not fit that description. Moreover, his suit jacket had just a bit too much style and silk.

The third man's needle eyes flicked left and right, taking in the details of the room, flicking back to me, fixing my position with the precision of a field gunner adding to a list of potential targets. And as he fixed me, I measured him. He was fundamentally different from the shoulder-clapper from Saratoga, not a good ol' anything, and neither was he a corporate suit boy or a pink-faced moneyman from Holland. He was the product of a rougher neighborhood, a place where people get physical about their arguments.

Fred Howard turned, saw me, scowled. It was the kind of quick contraction of facial muscles one sees on a man who habitually substitutes anger for fear.

The secretary rushed up behind me, panting. "Oh, ah, there you are! Ah, please, step this way." She grasped my arm and pulled. Hard. I thought I heard an edge of panic in her voice, and as Fred Howard's glare shifted from me to her, I could see why.

All this happened in an instant. The third man straightened, raked a look across Fred Howard's face that must have burned. I could almost smell the bacon frying. Then he clicked his lighter closed, strolled past Fred with the ponderous ease and power of a tank maneuvering between obstacles, and disappeared into the stairwell.

I let the secretary lead me away.

FIVE MINUTES LATER, the secretary took me back into the waiting room and without saying bye-bye, scooted back behind her desk.

"Well, thanks for the tour," I said. "Most interesting."

"Mr. Howard will be with you in a few minutes," she said idiotically, her eyes fused to the computer screen.

I leaned back to watch her. She was, after all, a stunning example of the see no evil, hear no evil, speak no evil secretary. I bet she drew top dollar, and I hoped I had not just cost her her annual bonus. As I watched, I saw one of the lights on her telephone bank blink off, then come on again. It stayed on for two or three minutes. Twenty seconds after it went off again, the phone buzzed. The secretary lifted it to her ear, said, "Yes, Mr. Howard," stood up, faced me as if I were a firing squad, and informed me that I could now enter his office.

I lurched to my feet and wandered toward his door. It did not follow that someone like Fred Howard, and especially someone at his stratum of the corporate world, would place any of his own telephone calls. It didn't therefore take a wizard to suppose that he had been placing a call he didn't want witnessed.

The secretary followed the path of my gaze nervously. "Uh, Mr. Howard's a very busy man," she squeaked, urging me along.

"I can see that," I said as I followed her direction into his lair.

IT WAS THE kind of cave most corporate officers lurk in: big, imposing, stylistically forgettable. Fred sat in an enormous leather swivel chair behind the broad mahogany desk, looking as magisterial as any man the size and shape of a pig can. As I took Fred and the room in, a rather nervous voice in the back of my mind moved to remind me just how dangerous it can be to encounter a wild boar on his own turf.

Fred did not rise as I entered the room. I installed myself in one of the smaller, upholstered chairs that faced the throne, then said, "Thank you for meeting with me today, Fred."

He waved a pudgy hand and squeezed his chubby cheeks into a smile.

I watched him, unsmiling, waiting for him to speak.

His smile congealed into a toothy grimace, and I lost sight of his tiny eyes. Even as ugly as he was, I might have been taken in by the display of joviality if his skin hadn't been the color of a day-old corpse. "S'nothing," he said expansively. "Any friend of Joe's. But like I told ya, we got no work here, and I don't know shit about anyone else up and down this street. But it's your nickel." He stopped talking, dropped the pretense of the smile, and returned my gaze.

The hair began to stand up on the back of my neck. He was watching me, the pig staring at me from the scant cover of the shadows at the edge of the forest, measuring me to see how much I had seen of his position and his territory. It occurred to me, just a little bit late, that in my infinite wisdom I must have witnessed something I might have been better off not witnessing.

"Well, fine," I said, trying to look and act and smell like the hapless chick who wants the job, and not an enemy to be gored. "Hey, nice office you got here." I shifted gears, grinding into interview mode. *Sound knowledgeable. Ask questions about the growth potential of the company.* "Well, I got to reading your corporate slick sheets while I was waiting out there. You got bought out by overseas money, I see." I knew as soon as I'd said this that my tone had been a little too much like: so, you got bent over a stump, sucker.

Fred Howard's little eyes came the rest of the way back out into view, focused sharply on me for an instant, then were again eclipsed by his cheeks. "Yeah. Yeah, new money. Great, great."

"Good money, though?" I asked recklessly.

Fred stared a moment longer. "We gotta take it where we can get it."

"Oh." *And spend it in dumb places,* I thought, *like setting up to drill dusters on the Broken Spoke Ranch?* "So what's it like working for the Dutch?"

Another look. He waited.

I made my eyes a little rounder, a little stupider.

He seemed to relax a bit, but grew instantly more morose. "So whaddaya wanna know?" he asked irritably. "I got maybe five minutes to give ya. Boomer's midsized and growing. Foreign money's taking all of us over, one by one, all up and down the street. You got a problem with that?"

Startled, I smiled prettily. "Sorry, I've been out of town for most of a year, as J.C. told you, and I'm trying to catch up, is all. All this influx of foreign money is kind of interesting. I mean, I'm just an old ranch girl from Wyoming. I go back to the days when we were all a bunch of cowboys and girls drilling holes on back acres and getting lucky, so I guess we're all in this foreign takeover basket together. Right, Fred?"

"Wyoming. Huh."

I nodded. It was getting harder and harder to play dumb. The man's manner was pissing me off so thoroughly that I wanted to clobber him with everything I knew and suspected about him and all the low-life, self-serving swine he ate slops at the corporate trough with. Why in hell couldn't he just wise up and line up a little talent—like me—with a job, and see something happen?

As if reading my mind, Fred said, "Trouble is with cowgirls like you, you think knowing where some oil is is all it takes to make a deal. It's a brand-new world out there."

Shifting gears, I said, "I guess making the deal is your job. But finding the oil is mine."

Fred's lips drew up like a little purse. "You mean the job you'd *like* to have," he said nastily.

I caught myself leaning forward in my chair, like a supplicant. I tried to lean back and relax but managed only to cave downward. As I did so, Fred's skin began to return to its normal blotchy pink, and I began to see how he'd gotten as far as he had in the high-stakes poker world of the oil patch.

He said, "Now, if we're done here, I got several other meetings to go to." As he spoke, he leaned forward onto the desk, and I noted that his chair was jacked way up to what must have been its highest setting above the floor. He stood up and moved to the side of his desk to indicate that it was time for me to go. He had to bend his arm slightly to rest his hand on the top of his desk. Oh, the misery of a short man in corporate America, where everyone the hell else is exactly five foot nine and a quarter.

From the depths of my own bitterness, I began to smile. "So you're going offshore in Africa," I said, staying seated.

"S'outta another office."

"Okay, how's domestic production coming along? I saw a picture of a rig out there doing what rigs do. Where was that?"

Fred Howard began to curl and uncurl his stubby fingers. He remained standing, willing me to rise before he began to look stupid or out of control. "Infill drilling. The engineers do that." Suddenly, he fixed me with a leering grin and asked, "So, how you and J.C. getting along?"

My mouth sagged open.

"Oh, come on, you know he's got an eye for you. He's not dead yet, ya know. Yeah, he's a vital guy. And lotsa bucks. Young woman like you oughta jump at a chance like that."

I could feel the blood coursing into my head. "I'm sure you are mistaken."

"No, really, you two got so much in common. That East Coast tweedy stink to ya both."

Rising abruptly from my seat, I said, "I'm sure I've taken too much of your time already."

"S'nuthin. Naw, really; I heard Joe talk about you. He—"

I gave him the flat of my palm in a "that's enough, stop it right *now*" salute, said an abrupt "See ya," and marched out the door. And closed it. Firmly. And crossed to the elevator. And got the hell gone.

As the elevator doors closed, I thought I heard the secretary sigh audibly with relief.

25

"SURE, YOU CAN BUY LUNCH," I INFORMED J.C. MENKEN AS WE hurried down the sidewalk. He moved in a fast saunter, I in a still-fuming stomp. "You owe it to me, after what I just went through with your pal Fred. I'll be candid with you. I find his sense of humor a bit lacking."

Menken's cheeks were rosy in the noonday April sunshine. "Oh, now, Emily, I'm surprised at you. I thought you knew how to handle yourself in the corporate jungle. Or have you gotten rusty during your sabbatical?"

Had I? "Well—"

"What could he possibly have said to you that's gotten you into such a state?"

"Well . . . oh, forget it." No, I wasn't going to give my former boss turned eligible widower an opening like that.

"No, tell me," he insisted, his eyes dancing in smug delight.

"Here's our restaurant," I said, steering him into the Rocky Mountain Diner. *Might as well kill two birds with one stone,* I told myself, *see if Julia really went out of town.*

"Oh, this place. A charming little bistro. I hear they have roast duck enchiladas here, but I have to watch my figure, you know. Did you make reservations? This is a popular place, and I'd say there was little chance of finding a table free at this hour."

Julia was there all right, huddled over a plate of greens across the table from a woman I didn't know. When she saw me, or perhaps when she saw

Menken, or saw me *with* Menken—I couldn't tell exactly which—Julia's eyes widened, first in alarm and then in embarrassment.

"Julia!" I called as we swept up to her table. "I thought you'd be gone until Friday."

Her shoulders tensed. She introduced us to her companion, who shook my hand with a grip that went with sensible shoes, plenty of exercise, and enough glasses of water per day.

Menken gave the two women a grin that went clear back to his second molars. He spread his hands in benediction. "Why, what luck finding you here. May we join you?" He put a hand on Julia's shoulder and sat down in the empty chair next to her.

Julia lunged to her feet, grappling her handbag by midstrap like she meant to use it as a weapon. "No, Joe, we were just leaving. Lydia, give me the check." To me, she said, "I'll see *you* another time, I'm sure," and, snatching the check off the table, hurried away toward the cashier.

The startled Lydia hoisted herself to her feet, grabbed a last chunk of bread out of the basket, nodded good-bye, and followed her friend toward the door.

While I stood there hoping flies didn't land in my open mouth, Menken calmly pulled Julia's abandoned napkin over his lap and broke a crust of bread out of the basket. "Sit down, Emily," he said. "Tables can be hard to come by during the lunch rush." As a flabbergasted waitress arrived too late to avert Menken's maneuver, he informed her, "Our friends had to leave. We wanted separate checks anyway. I'm ready to order now, aren't you, Emily?"

OVER BABY BACK ribs, coleslaw, and fries (I ordered the most expensive thing on the menu, angry as I was over the debacle with Fred Howard), I laid out my demands to J.C. Menken. "I need you to make some more contacts for me with your CEO friends up and down the street here. And smart ones this time," I grumbled. "Like guys who know better than to drill wildcats south of the Platte River up there by Douglas."

Menken's eyes sharpened. "What do you mean?"

"Like the one they were going to drill on the Broken Spoke Ranch."

Menken looked blank, so I added, "Isn't that how you knew about Po Bradley's place?"

"Why no. Miriam made that contact." His eyes saddened for an instant, then recovered. As if by an act of will, he smiled, and teased, "So you didn't enjoy your visit with Fred?"

"Fred was . . . not much help, but at least I see now what to ask in these interviews. There's foreign money coming into the oil patch now, and that appeals to me," I said, turning the conversation toward more neutral topics. "I've never been overseas, not even to Europe. Perhaps you know someone who's got a project going in Africa, or somewhere interesting like that. I saw where Boomer has an agreement going there, at least, and there have to be more."

"Done," J.C. said, nibbling a bit of unbuttered bread. "I'll have my secretary make you some appointments. No, don't worry," he said, raising a hand as if I was about to protest. "You need your energies for our other project. And how's that been going?" he asked cheerfully.

I let my shoulders drop. "Hard at it. You're into me for ninety dollars." I presented Ms. DuBois's receipt for the check I'd written earlier that morning. "This could get pricey, you know."

"No cost too high for my Cecelia."

"None?" I said, speaking before I'd thought.

"Certainly not. Why, what other expenses have you incurred?"

"Well, I meant to tell you that I took a drive up to Douglas this weekend, just to poke around, see if I could find anything out that might help, ah . . . Cecelia. And, well, I didn't run up a hotel bill or anything, but—"

Menken beamed. "You just bring me your receipts," he said. "And you drove? Why, that's a long way to go, Emily, and what if you have to go again before we're done? I think you should consider flying next time, catch the evening hop up to Casper and rent a car. Saves two hours at least. Here, why don't I just give you some money in advance?" He whipped out a checkbook and scribbled happily. "A thousand dollars seem about right? There. Now, about dessert," he said happily, replacing his checkbook and plucking the menu back up from the table. "How about a slice of the mile high chocolate cake? Young, healthy figure like yours can certainly take a few calories. Or here, the Grand Teton hot fudge ice cream sundae."

Much as chocolate has always sung its siren song to me, my mind was anywhere but on dessert. I was already halfway back to the Wyoming border, but I wasn't flying commercially: I was three thousand feet off the deck in a single-engine plane, watching the shadows of the foothills grow longer as I pushed the craft at a 120 knots toward the high, wide horizon through the freedom of the skies.

26

POSSIBLE EXCUSES TO RETURN TO DOUGLAS CROWDED MY HEAD AS I hurried down the street to my bank to deposit Menken's check. As with all links into small airports, the price of flying commercially from Denver to anywhere near Douglas (namely Casper, the only airport in the area with scheduled flights) on short notice is steep. I was certain I could about justify the hourly rental cost of flying there myself, thereby gaining two major cross-country flying legs for my pilot's license. Accepting Menken's money obligated me to do more for him, of course, but hell, I wanted to help Cecelia, and . . . and what?

I stopped in the middle of the sidewalk, wondering at how easily Menken had reeled me in, the thousand-dollar windfall dragging at my pocket like a brick. *Give it back,* an exhausted little voice in my head pleaded. *Give it back and stay independent.*

Right, stay out of a trouble I couldn't quite name but knew must be waiting for me.

Give back all of it? another voice countered. *He does owe you for the ninety-dollar shrink fee, after all, and your good old truck sure drank a lot of gas on the way to Douglas and back. . . .*

I started to walk again, promising myself that I'd sit down and do the math when I got home to Betty Bloom's, figure out what Menken really owed me, and return the difference. *And what if some of these other shrinks want cash on the barrel head? Speaking of which . . .*

I picked up my feet and began to move. My next interview was only a few minutes away.

◈

THAT APPOINTMENT WAS another disappointment. While it was not as negative as the others, I found a lack of positives that was just as damning. The woman had a noisy problem with her adenoids, and looked anxious for a smoke, just the kind of authority figure a teenager could easily disregard. In her favor, she gave me half an hour of her time for free. After twenty minutes, I excused myself and left, figuring she could keep the change.

Next, I took myself back down to Sergeant Ortega's office at the Denver Police Department. Once again, I found him eating, this time a takeout order of Mexican pastries. He looked up, deep-fried dough pocket running with honey halfway to his lips, and said doubtfully, "Sopaipilla?"

"Thank you, no," I answered kindly. "I just dropped by to see if you'd had any luck with my little bag of excitement up in Wyoming."

Ortega closed his mouth over his sopaipilla and chewed. "Em Hansen, you are like the dog who thinks sheep herding is too slow so he starts herding the other dogs. You are always snapping at my heels. You're thinking the Denver Police Department has nothing better to do than chase some loco Wyoming *lobos* for you."

"Sorry."

"Well, you are a lucky person, because in fact I do have something for you." He set down his pastry and pulled open a drawer, produced a single sheet of paper, and smoothed it across his desktop with a greasy thumb. "Your lady died of a drug overdose."

I just sat there, stunned.

Ortega shrugged his shoulders sympathetically and picked up another sopaipilla.

"But everyone says she was murdered," I said numbly. I was not ready to find out that Miriam of the journals, this friend I'd never met, had been a reckless dope fiend. Well, okay, she might have been a reckless lover, but dope was another matter. Or was it?

"She *was* murdered."

I knit my brow. "Quit playing with me, Carlos."

Ortega looked up meekly and took another bite. *"Mil disculpas,"* he said softly. "It is a bad habit in my profession to be playful where we can. I thought you didn't know this woman."

"Yeah, well, I *didn't* know her, but I'm kind of *getting* to know her."

Ortega cocked his head, waited.

Oh, what the hell. "I've got her journals."

His eyes closed. "Ah."

"Or some of them. This other woman has the most recent ones in her office and won't let me at them, or at least not since I opened my big mouth and asked her about a man who's in them." I heaved a sigh. "I told you Miriam had been having an affair, and that a man was seen visiting at the ranch the day she died."

Ortega opened another desk drawer, deposited the bag with the remaining sopaipillas into it, wiped his hands on a paper napkin, and pulled a pad and pen to the center of his desk. "She *was* murdered, Em. This lab report says she was dosed with unusually pure cocaine. I suggest it was not her choice, because there were signs of a struggle, and the woman tried to vomit it up. And yes, we can hear that struggle on the nine-one-one tape, and hear the woman calling for help, and hear her beg her daughter to run away from the man who was doing this to her."

I put my hands over my face. A violent struggle. So this was part of the shock Cecilia had experienced. "Who in hell murders with cocaine?" I asked.

"Who indeed."

"Not a common occurrence in Converse County, Wyoming," I said feebly.

"No, I'd say not."

"So that's why there's been no arrest. It's not a local."

Ortega shrugged his rounded shoulders. "The sheriff believes a local man named Arapaho Bradley killed her, just as you told me."

"But how would Po Bradley get hold of pure cocaine?"

"Sheriff Duluth told me this Po Bradley keeps fast company. He told me he spends his weekends in Saratoga, like that should mean something to me. Where's that?"

Saratoga. I was beginning to hear that town named too often. "It's a town south of Rawlins. Used to be a sleepy little ranching community like all the rest, but in recent years the rich boys have moved in with their hobby ranches and golf clubs. They've bought up a bunch of the land just to keep their favorite trout streams to themselves."

"Hobby ranch?"

"It's the Wyoming nickname for a rich boy's ranch. They buy an old family spread for a huge load of dollars so they can use it as a weekend get-away. They put up a cushy new 'ranch' mansion, install a rent-a-cowboy in the tumbledown old hut, run a small herd of Herefords across the place, and call it a tax dodge."

"You sound like you don't approve of such use of land," Ortega said dryly.

I shook my head. "No. They aren't dependent on the income from the property, but they like the tax write-off, so when it comes time to market the beef, they'll take low dollar. That drives the price down for everyone else. Which in turn drives old Wyoming families to give up and sell to city boys with lots of dollars."

"And this cuts to your bones."

I looked up into Carlos's dark eyes and suddenly wanted to bawl. "Oh, Carlos, here I am trying to find a job because I don't have a ranch myself to run, and this morning I did a so-called information interview with this shithead who'd rather eat road apples than give this little cowgirl a job. There he sits making probably mid six figures, with bonuses every time he lays someone off, and I'm not even asking mid five. And just to put the cherry on the sundae, he keeps me waiting most of an hour before he chases me off, and who's he in there wasting my time with? More of those six-figure Charlies who're all clapping him on his back and telling him to 'Come on up to Saratoga.' "

Ortega blinked.

I hadn't realized until I said all this just how much the whole episode had bothered me. As it was happening, I'd been too busy trying to make a legitimate interview out of a mercy chat to notice exactly how rotten it had felt to have my begging bowl out. "Well, that's where and what Saratoga is," I said miserably.

"Ah." Ortega had averted his eyes to his page of notes, studiously leaving me a shred of pride as I pulled myself back together. "Okay. So would these 'hobby ranchers' include maybe a drug dealer or two?"

My mouth sagged open as I quickly computed possible connections involving grim-looking hawk-faced characters who conferred with unhappy corporate executives who were close friends of men whose wives had been killed on rental ranches in Wyoming that belonged to playboy ranchers who spent weekends in Saratoga with corporate executives who kept time with hawk-faced characters. The world sure had a way of shrinking when you connected all the dots. "It could indeed. I take it I never heard what you just told me."

Ortega nodded. "*Es correcto.* I never said it to you. But I do say this: cocaine is not a nice substance. Such pure cocaine suggests a dealer, or even a direct line to the overseas distributor. Whoever brought it into that house and forced it into that woman is not running in polite circles. I recommend with all my heart you drop this case right now."

This seemed eminently reasonable. Hand back Menken's check. Wave bye-bye. *Wait.* "What about Cecelia? If she was there, doesn't this mean she's in danger?" *Perhaps she remembers, but is afraid . . .*

"I don't know. I got a transcript of the tape, and I'm thinking that whoever did this may not have known that Cecelia was in the house, or thought she was asleep. She's a smart girl, right? Was there a phone in her room, so she could stay hidden?"

"I think so." I thought of the layout of the house. Would a struggle in her mother's room have been heard over a phone in Cecelia's? Or had Miriam's phone been off the hook? Or had there been a third phone in the kitchen? I couldn't recall. "If only we knew," I said, my interest in finding the right psychologist increasing. Just how much had Cecelia seen?

"It is not ours to know this much about this case."

"Let me see the transcript."

"No."

"Carlos!"

Ortega's eyes went as deep as wells. "Em, I apologize. I have indulged myself in talking to you about all of this. But it is not my case, and not my jurisdiction. And you are my friend whom I want to keep safe. I know the stupidest thing I can do is challenge you, but please, *please*, this time stay out of trouble, okay? This is not your fight. Leave it to men—people—who are trained to deal with this kind of stuff. Go on and get a job. Have a good life. Start saving for your retirement. Who knows, maybe you can make a lot of money and buy your own place under the sky."

I sagged back in my chair. Ortega was right, this wasn't my fight, and it was time I began trying to have a future. I spread my hands in submission and said, "Okay."

Ortega eyed me carefully, pulling at his lower lip. "Good. So why not meet me back here about six. We'll have dinner, keep you busy while you get used to this new Em Hansen," he said. "And while we eat, you can tell me what you know from these journals. Get it off your chest. I'll see that the information is treated as kindly as possible."

I sighed and nodded. "Fine."

BUT IT WASN'T fine. There had been no mention of drug taking in Miriam's journals. I had three hours to kill before Ortega went off duty, and Miriam's unread journals called to me like the siren of the rocks. And he'd asked to know what was in them, right?

I called Julia's office and was told that she was out. So I phoned Cindey Howard. It was a gamble to go to her for information; she might have spoken with her husband since he had run me out of his office, and it wouldn't do to seem like I was still snooping around his questionable doings.

Cindey's voice came on whispery and hoarse, as if she was answering a clandestine call. "Oh. Em. What do you want?"

"I want to ask you some more questions about Miriam."

"What about her?"

"Well, really about a man she knew in college."

Cindey didn't say anything right away, but I could almost hear the wheels in her brain turning, slowly, cagily deciding what she would say in reply. When she spoke again, her voice was almost seductive. "Why don't you come over?" she said. "Say in half an hour or so?"

I thought, *You want me in your house for some reason?* I pondered this, decided that she must not have spoken to Fred, as he had definitely given me the bum's rush and would not, therefore, be asking his wife to invite me over for a social call. So it was okay to go, and if she even mentioned to him that I had dropped by—which seemed unlikely, given the little that she had to say to anybody—she would report the truth, that I was only asking about Miriam. Besides, I wanted to know what she wanted from me.

Forty-five minutes of thrashing through afternoon traffic later, I pulled into her driveway. Cindey answered the door wearing gray leggings and a velour tunic that featured white snowflakes on a field of maroon. The ensemble would have looked great on someone more Cecelia's age.

"So Emily," she whispered, peering at me through her unreadable little eyes, "what brings you to my door?" As if she hadn't asked me to come.

I stepped in out of the cover of the imposing front entrance to the chill spaciousness of her front hallway. "I was hoping you could help me know a little more about your friend."

"Miriam?"

"Yes. There are some gaps I need to fill in."

"Hmm." Cindey led me into the vast cavern of her living room. We seated ourselves on opposite ends of a mauve leather-covered couch laden with throw cushions, facing each other. "So you're beginning to *find out* about her, aren't you," she stated, her voice taking on that seductive purr again.

"What do you mean?"

"Oh, you know, beginning to knock the princess off her pedestal a bit."

I leaned back and looked at her appraisingly. "If you have something to tell me, why don't you just spit it out?"

Cindey busied herself with an examination of her fingernails. They were long and narrow, and projected from the tips of her chubby fingers like talons from a hawk's toes.

I tried again, something more mollifying. "You know, of course, that I'm really only doing this for Cecelia. After all, I never even met Miriam."

"Yes, poor Cecelia."

"What was their relationship like?"

"Oh . . . it had its ups and downs."

Cindey's act was beginning to grate on my nerves. "Tell me about the downs," I said, playing along in spite of my irritation.

"Well you know, Cecelia has never been a very popular girl."

"And?" This was like pulling teeth. Only I wasn't quite sure whose teeth were being pulled.

"Oh, it just infuriated Miriam. She had no sympathy for it."

"Really. And just how was this expressed?"

"Oh, she was always trying to drag the poor dear off for a haircut, or to buy clothes. It was shocking."

That's the pot calling the kettle black, I thought. Something about this didn't fit. Cecelia really had been an unkempt mess until fairly recently. She'd needed all the help she could get. So why was Cindey taking this tack? Just to get some digs in at Miriam? It was time to steer the conversation somewhere that would give me more hard facts and less innuendo. "I remember that a couple years ago, Miriam went away for a while. Do you know where she went?"

"No."

"Or with whom?"

She shook her head, but gave me a look I suppose was meant to be coy.

I found it annoying. "You don't know," I pointed out, meaning it to sting just a bit. "But you two spent a lot of time together. What did you do with all that time? Shop? Go to the spa?"

Cindey shot me a heated look. Recovering herself, she offered me a cigarette, and when I refused, she lit one herself. "My one vice," she said. Had she asked my opinion, I could have suggested a few others to add to her self-awareness. After breathing in the smoke, her voice came out even more hushed, a hiss from the grave. "To answer your question, Miriam and I had a long-standing habit of lunching together." She leaned her head back and tried to make a theatrical gesture with the cigarette, arching it through the air, but her body was so stiff and tight that the movement was short and spastic.

"How long was long-standing?" I coughed as the smoke curled past my face.

Cindey ignored my hint. "It started clear back in college, when we were in classes together. We'd go straight from history to lunch. It was on the way back to the dorm," she added, as if I might think she cared whether she had lunch with Miriam or not. "But Miriam didn't confide in me very much. I won't say she was secretive, exactly, just didn't seem to have much to say." Cindey pulled her feet up underneath herself, pointing her toes to make her feet look more elegant.

"I see. So you knew everyone she knew in college, then."

"I suppose so."

"Even this Chandler guy." I tried to make it sound like a casual question, but I failed miserably.

"Chandler?" she asked, her voice all innocence.

Okay, I thought, *if that's the way you want to play this.* "The man in her journal. Big guy, older than the rest of the class. Good dancer."

"Oh, *him.*" Her eyes glittered.

"Yes, *him.*"

Cindey shot me a more shrouded look, took another drag on her cigarette, then studied the smoke at leisure. "I'd say we were acquainted, nothing more."

"What was he like?" Now it was my turn to feign innocence.

A long pause, during which time Cindey looked straight into my eyes, as if gauging her next move. "Kind of wild."

"Wild how? Like an animal? Like a bad boy?"

"Oh, I hear he ran with a rather fast crowd."

"Drugs?"

A shorter pause. "Ye-e-es, lots of people did drugs back then. It was the era."

"Ah. Have you seen Chandler since college?"

Pause. One heartbeat, two . . . "I'd *heard* he was in Denver."

I felt like I was doing dental surgery with tiny tools on a large, slow-moving animal, all the time dimly aware that I was leaning too far into the creature's mouth for safety. Cindey continued to stare at me. I sat up and leaned forward, put my feet flat on the floor, trying to indicate that I was ready to leave if she didn't cut with the sleepwalking act. "Would you know how to get in touch with him?"

Cindey's eyes glowed with unkind pleasure, looking right into me, as she shook her head.

"Well, then why don't you put me in touch with your college alumni office?"

"I'm not sure they'd have an address."

"Why?"

She shrugged her shoulders. "He was something of a rolling stone."

"Then show me your college yearbook. That'll give me clues."

My request clearly startled her. She glanced around as if surprised to be caught at an illicit act, like a teenager found smoking behind the barn. I was perhaps not supposed to know that she still had that yearbook, still kept it somewhere close, where she could easily retrieve it. But she got up, took another stylized drag on her cigarette, and shuffled off down a hall-way. When she returned, she was holding a large, heavy book bound with a faux-leather cover in maroon with white letters. She held it open, flip-ping back and forth through the pages, her eyes scanning nervously, as if checking certain pages to make sure it was okay to show them to me. Even from across the room, I could see that the edges of certain groups of pages had grown dark from excessive contact with the oil of her fingers. "The senior portraits are in the middle," she said as she handed me the volume, opened to the page where her own highly romanticized pose had been recorded among seven others. "Cindey Ann Shwartzer, Beaver, Pennsyl-vania; French," it read.

I flipped back several pages to *M* for Menken, but of course J.C. had been in an earlier class, and Miriam hadn't yet taken his name. "What was Miriam's maiden name?" I asked.

"Benner."

Yes, there it was, a few pages before Cindey's. I stared into the eyes of a softly lovely young thing with dark hair worn long and straight and parted down the middle, the uniform of the times. She had an oval face, with the kind of eyes that arch at the top but are straight across at the bot-tom, a plain, straight nose, and a look of hopeful surprise. "Miriam Jane Benner, Pleasantville, New York; History," the caption stated. History? Surely she hadn't read up on the raids of the Vikings and the triumph of the agrarian class. And wait, there was Julia, also done up in long, straight hair, a look of challenge and youthful arrogance stiffening her face. "Julia Joyce Richards, Northbrook, Illinois; Political Science." "What about Chandler?" I asked. "What was his last name?"

Cindey lit another cigarette, said, "I don't know."

I reached the length of the couch and placed the book on her lap. "You can just flip around until you find it."

Cindey began to turn pages with all the affect of someone killing time over a magazine in a doctor's office. She squinted at two or three pages, paused, passed the book back to me. "I'm not sure I'd recognize him."

I stood the book on its spine and let it fall open, certain it would find her favorite page. Sure enough, it flopped open not on her page, nor on Miriam's nor Julia's, but on another. One portrait immediately caught my eye. A husky god of a man in his mid-twenties, better-than-average good-looking in a rough-hewn, heavy-boned sort of way, but it was the eyes that arrested me. They were simply dazzling, but at the same time disconcerting. Wide-set, dark for a blonde, and of an unusual shape. And he held them wide, as if he'd been caught in a candid shot, shooting a challenge of surprised curiosity into the camera. It was the sort of look one sees in the eyes of a man crazed with poetry who lives on the streets. Even in this tightly posed portrait, he held his shoulders forward, raw and animalistic, a hunter about to spring forward onto its prey. The name captioned beneath the photograph was Edward Jennings. No middle name. It read, "Camden, Maine; American Studies."

I spun the book around until the page faced Cindey. "That him?" I asked dryly.

"Oh," she said. "Hmm. Yes, I think so."

I shivered on behalf of the fallen Miriam, uninformed girl from Pleasantville. Shivered again for myself. "Edward?"

"I suppose Chandler was a nickname. People called him that. 'The Chandler.' "

I took a slip of paper out of my pocket and wrote down the name and town, and asked, between my teeth, "Did he rape a lot of the women at your college?"

Cindey stiffened, a subtle movement in one already so rigidly posed. "Rape? What rape?"

I looked up from my note taking. Cindey's eyes had gone black with fury.

I said, "Come on, Miriam wrote about it in her journal. Your freshman year. Chandler took her to his digs and forced himself on her. You remember, it was in those pages that she taped shut. You—" I stopped myself, mentally slapped my own wrist. I had not come here to engage in warfare with this woman.

But it was too late. Cindey narrowed her tiny eyes. "That was no *rape*. There was no *force*. Miriam knew *exactly* what was going on!"

My mind raced as a jumble of feelings jammed in my chest. I groped for the words that could stem the heavy tide of her thinking, reached for some unassailable logic that could inform the sanctimonious Cindeys of the world, pierce their armor of denial and shake them into an instant of understanding. Very softly, I said, "Miriam was young. She was naïve. She said no not yet. That should have been enough."

"Oh, *bull*shit! Miriam *wanted* it."

My voice rising again, I spat, "What's *that* got to do with what *he* did? Wanting it and asking for it are two different things!"

"Well, she *asked* for it. Everybody knew about him. Did he have to drag her into that apartment? Hell, no; she walked in there on her own two feet! She's the horniest woman I know."

"The hell. She didn't know him. They ran in entirely different crowds," I said, and then, realizing that I was falling into the trap of arguing on Cindey's terms rather than my own, I asserted, "He told her he was only taking her inside for a cup of tea. She said no not this time and that was her right. He took advantage of her innocence. Besides, *nothing* Miriam might have done justified what *he* did. Don't you believe in holding men responsible for their actions?" And as I said all this, choosing my words with precision, I became aware that for a moment, Cindey had chosen words that suggested that to her, Miriam was still very much alive.

Cindey's eyes went down to slits, a viper getting ready to spit. "I get so sick of women who want everybody to feel sorry for them after they've had their fun. They want to blame it on the man. They—"

"No, *you're* the one who's blaming. You're blaming the victim."

"Miriam was no victim! She *flaunted* her little proclivity. You should have *seen* the way she flirted! I mean, my God, you get her at a party and just one little drink, and—" Cindey broke off, sputtering, her mouth working like a fish on the bank. "The men *fawned* over her. It was disgusting!"

I was spellbound, awash in the potent poison of Cindey's envy, slowly losing my grip, uncertain now just whether black truly were white. . . . "I suppose you think she killed her*self*, too, that there never was a murderer, that all this hue and cry searching for the man who did it is just a wretched scheme to make some decent man look bad."

Pause. "Exactly." Cindey's eyes flashed with the cold glint of victory.

I sat perfectly still, stunned, my scientist's mind already taking this new theory and running with it, testing it, turning it this way and that to see if it might hold a grain of truth. *What if Chandler was a dealer, and he supplied Miriam with the pure stuff, and in a fit of despair, she . . . and Cecelia watched her mother do it, stood by in horror as her mother gave her the ultimate rejection? . . . But everyone keeps saying there was a man in that house, and . . .* I took one more long look into the eyes of the woman who sat across from me, and said, "I think it's time for me to leave."

Cindey followed me to the door. As I strode through it, she said, "Just don't take those journals for gospel, you hear me? Miriam left a few things *out*."

27

From a pay booth at a 7-Eleven store near an exit off of Interstate 70, I called the alumni office at Miriam's college and asked to know the whereabouts of an Edward "Chandler" Jennings. I rationalized that I had a lead and had to follow it fast, before the trail grew cold.

The voice that answered the line at the alumni office gave me a very polite brush-off. The old alma mater, it seemed, did not give out personal information about its graduates, but it was regally certain all efforts would be made to forward a note to a graduate if I cared to send one in care of the office.

Round two, I called information for Camden, Maine. Several Jenningses listed, but no Edward. Which number did I want? I asked for two at random, had to call back for the third. One was an old coot who shouted at me to speak up three times and then slammed down the phone. The second was a young man with a nasal accent who informed me that he'd just moved to Maine from New Jersey to start a business making wooden toys, all natural wood with no toxic finishes, and developmentally correct. Hadn't met any other Jenningses yet, but hey, the winters here were unbelievable!

Number three was pay dirt, of a sort. "Edward? You mean my cousin, maybe?" asked a baritone with a Down East drawl. "He scrammed out of here back in the sixties. En't thought of him in decades. Kind of wild, as I recall, but he was a lot older than I was. Ay-yup. He was an only child, don'tcha know, got sent to all them nice preppy schools and so on. Ay-yup. His folks died years ago, left the house to him. He come back and tried to make a go of it here, don'tcha know, but I don't recall it much. I think Ma had him over to dinner once, but I was out that evening somewheres or other. Had my mind on other things, girls and such. Never saw him to talk to or nothin'. My folks said you can't come home again; that's why I never left, y'see? Ay-yup, Cousin Edward sold the house and left—lock, stock, and Beemer."

"A BMW, you say."

"Gold, even. Ay-yup, puttin' on airs."

"Oh, I see."

"Ay-yup."

"Mm-hm."

"Went overseas, I heard."

"Overseas?"

"Ayuh, somewheres in South America. Workin' in the oil fields."

"Colombia?" I asked, making a wild try at a connection with Boomer Oil.

"Coulda been. Don't know."

"Would your folks know anything more?"

"Well, my pa's dead, and if you can get sense out of my ma, you'd be doing better than anyone over at the nursing home's done in years."

I thanked him and rang off. Stood there at the pay phone, with traffic whizzing by and a couple of zit-faced kids arguing over who got the chunk of cardboard with some athlete's blurry fizz on it out of a packet of bubble gum. The wind started to pick up. I itched for that final connection that would make sense out of the picture. Colombia twice in one day, or at least South America and oil fields, and also Saratoga again and again, and old family ranches near Douglas. And people who knew one another in college somewhere else entirely.

I dialed information for Douglas and got the UPS station number and asked for Ginger Henley. "She's on a delivery run, but could someone else help you?" asked a brusque-sounding voice.

"I want to ask her about some shipments up the Cold Springs Road," I said.

"Who to? You got a tracking number?"

"Well, I don't believe this shipment would have gone in by your carrier."

"Oh . . ." said the voice.

"More like, did you notice who did deliver, or from where? I'm talking about a number of sacks of powdered bentonite, sent out to that new tin shed Po Bradley has, and like maybe the same shipper came and got them back again. It wasn't anyone from Casper—I know that already."

I heard a thoughtful humming. "You call back later," she said. "I'll ask."

FOR OLD TIME'S sake, Sergeant Ortega and I picked up burritos at Chubby's, a place out on Thirty-eighth Street, and took them over to his mother's house to eat. Mrs. Ortega fussed all around us in her cramped kitchen, smiling her welcome, bringing us chips and salsa and cold *cervezas* to go with our spicy treats. Still telling myself I was going to quit the investigation, I spilled the whole story about Miriam's frustrating marriage and her strange affair with the disappearing Chandler. "So there you have it," I concluded, after the second half of my burrito had long since gone cold on my plate. I can usually best a Chubby's burrito no sweat, but this evening my stomach was too tense, no match for *carnitas* and *salsa picante*. "I'm asked to help the child through her grief and I get all balled up in the life of the mother."

Carlos closed his eyes in meditation. "I've never been married myself. I don't understand these things."

"Well, that makes two of us," I said, but in part, I was lying. I'd never been married, but I was raised on the same stew of confused thoughts and values that Miriam had been, and even though I had entered college fifteen years or more later, after date rape and a handful of related ills had been given a name and officially struck down by the laws of the land, I had still learned what little I knew about love and sex the hard way. And just because the national so-called consciousness had been raised, and no was supposed forevermore to mean no, didn't mean that girls and even women had quit having hopeful fantasies about whatever charming prince they had just met at the dance. Or at the grocery store. Or at the office.

Or that said amoral prince had quit taking advantage of hope, fantasy, and ignorance.

So here I was hiding the sore truth about my own bits of bad luck from my dear friend Carlos Ortega, blithely pretending I was interested in Miriam's story only from an intellectual standpoint. "So I'm wondering what this guy Chandler did for a living, when he wasn't busy seducing suburban housewives. And I'm wondering what kind of a game Cindey Howard is playing with me."

Carlos opened his eyes and looked at me. "Why?"

I smiled. Yes, Carlos Ortega, old war *caballo* that he was, was just as caught up in this maze of questions as I was. "Well, my take is that she had some kind of an agenda in giving me those journals in the first place. More than just getting them out of her closet, I mean. And then today, she was playing real coy, but if she didn't have any further interest in the matter, why get me up to her house? It's like she was trying to reel me in to ask her something. And she checked that yearbook over pretty carefully before she let me see it, then acted like she didn't know Chandler's real name or what page he was on. My guess at the time was that she was checking to make sure he hadn't written anything embarrassing on it."

"Had he?"

"No. Nothing at all. But the book flops open to that page."

"Hm. And she thinks Miriam committed suicide."

"So she says."

Ortega took another pull on his beer. "So tell me this: was this Cindey a good friend to Miriam Menken?"

"Not hardly."

"Why do you think not?"

"The old green-eyed devil."

Very soberly, he said, "Ah, *tiene celos.*"

"*¿Qué?*"

Ortega looked up and twisted his lips wryly. "*La mujer es en celos,*" he said, lifting his index finger with a flourish.

My Spanish was getting too rusty. "Huh?"

Ortega shook his head in apology and made a circular gesture with one hand, a kind of "keep talking" prompt.

I said, "Well, see, here's this unattractive middle-aged woman who's obviously not ready to give up on attracting people, witness the ensembles and the posturing. Her husband's a pig—sorry, there's no kinder word, and I mean no offense in terms of the other uses of that epithet—who contemplates using the investors' money to drill guaranteed dusters, and likes to go off for weekends with the kind of boys who like to leave their wives at home. I may not know much about marriage, but it doesn't take much imagination to guess what it must feel like to have that guy keep your dance card full. If I was married to him, big house or no, I'd be looking around myself and seeing greener grass on the other side of every fence I had."

Carlos nearly choked on his burrito trying not to laugh.

"And she called Miriam a flirt," I said. "That could mean anything from she *was* a flirt to 'Pig, I wanted Chandler myself,' to maybe Miriam was the object of some of Freddie's prurient grunting."

"But Mrs. Howard stays with Mr. Howard."

"She's the type who would," I found myself saying. "The old-fashioned chickenhearted female who takes crap from her husband for fifty years and dances on his grave, if she doesn't die first from gargling all that bile."

"Why not leave him?"

"She hasn't got the guts. And she probably thinks she couldn't hold her head up in church if she did."

"You think she goes to church?"

"Let's say the country club. Yeah, that's more to the point: she's into power, or being married to power, and Fred's got it."

"What kind?"

"Well, he's regional vice president of an oil company," I said, immediately seeing the flaws in my reasoning. Certainly, Fred Howard had power over a lot of people right here in Denver, but life in the oil patch had been one long litany of hard times for the last decade and a half, with people losing their shirts or their companies left and right. Even now, as things were beginning to look a little more hopeful again, Boomer Oil had been bought out by foreign investors, and at best, Fred's upward mobility had just been capped. Things like that had a way of eating at little piggies like

Fred Howard who counted their self-worth by their material worth and position. For the nth time, I wondered just what kind of business he was doing with the men I'd seen in his office that day. Surely not something he wanted the Dutch to know about, or he wouldn't have taken the trouble to place his calls himself. I shared my thoughts with Sergeant Ortega, and finished off by saying, "But maybe he was doing some other kind of business on company time."

Ortega smiled tiredly, got up from the table, and gave his mama a hug. When he turned to me, he said, "For you to wonder, Em, because you're dropping this, remember? Come on, I'll take you to your truck."

THAT NIGHT, I slept relatively soundly, having convinced myself, however briefly, that I had given up the chase.

First thing Wednesday morning, I suited up and got back on the turnpike from Boulder to Denver, but this time, I made an intermediate stop. Jeffco Airport, the place where I'd been taking flying lessons, was a quick detour to the south.

Driving straight to the flying club that kept a line of Cessnas and Piper aircraft gassed up and ready for rental, I reactivated my membership and stopped off to see my instructor, Peggy Jones. Peggy was a thin, wiry little woman who reminded me of a pretzel. She wasn't shaped like one, just made of the same ingredients: equal parts salt and crust. "Oh, you're here," she said, not getting up from the overstuffed chair where I found her lounging. "You ever gonna finish your ticket?"

"That's what I'm here for," I said. "I got a little money finally, and I want to knock off my cross-countries."

"Pshaw," said Peggy. "I can't see you flyin' nowhere. There's rust on your wings so thick, you look like you're wearing a fur coat. I ain't signing your logbook less you do a little dual first."

"Then I expect we'll have to do something about that." I grinned. "You got time this afternoon?"

Peggy stared out the window in mock resignation. "Oh, I s'pose so. Call it two o'clock."

"Done."

❖

MY NEXT STOP was the office of candidate shrink number four, one Jane Hooker, M.S.W. I thought the name had promise, but my hopes were not rewarded.

"I'll tell you straight, your friend needs strong guidelines and someone to teach her some discipline," she declared, knitting her grizzled eyebrows ferociously. "I'd be doing her no favor if I kept her in here month after month, letting her sulk. Life is tough, yes, and it deals you some terrible blows, but then you move on." She took a drag on her cigarette, blew it out through her nostrils.

"Well, but what about this memory blockage, or whatever you call it?"

"Yes, some people block things out for years, but then, others don't, so what makes the difference?"

"I was about to ask you."

"For a diagnosis? Why, I haven't examined her yet, but I'd say we're talking about an hysteric personality here. Probably borderline, as well."

"What's a borderline personality?" I asked, feeling like I'd just been fed a shit sandwich.

"They're annoying to deal with. You have to corner them, even pick a fight to clinch the diagnosis. If they come back fighting, you know you're dealing with a borderline. Children who are raised in abusive, deprivational situations often have deep trust issues, never fully form as a personality. Empty people, just as you describe. She won't respond to the authority of her current therapist. Wants to hide."

"I don't think Cecelia's been abused," I replied, feeling tempted to hide from this authority myself.

Jane Hooker looked at me out of the corners of her eyes, took another drag. "How do you know? Abuse often occurs when no one's looking. It happens in even the nicest families. And it can happen without anyone even laying a hand on her. Perhaps mommy chewed her out a lot, called her names. She have a temper?"

"Well, I—"

"Or she ignored her. Or daddy was always gone. Or there was some deep sexual dysfunction that no one wanted to talk about."

There was nothing I cared to say in reply. Slinging labels at the ingrained pains and difficulties of the Menken family seemed more a part of the problem than part of the solution. So I just sat still and tried to look serene, as if a smooth exterior could protect my friends.

Jane Hooker stubbed out her cigarette. "Now about you—what's your involvement in all of this? Why haven't you brought her in here to talk to me herself? You playing surrogate mother or something?"

I was so angry so fast that I couldn't control my tongue. "No, ma'am," I said. "I'm just another busybody like yourself, who can't keep her nose out of the family melodrama."

She pointed the coal of her cigarette at me. "Touché. But I ask again: what's your connection?"

"I used to work for her daddy, and yes, I still have trouble telling the old boy no."

"So you're everybody's pushover."

"Must be."

Ms. Hooker worked her brows up and down a few times more to see if I'd budge. When I didn't, she said, "Smart kid, huh."

"I hope so, because this one's a good old-fashioned mess, and I'm in it up past my neckerchief. Gonna need all the smarts I can get."

"Why do you care?"

I smiled. What was the alternative? To not give a shit? "Why? Here's a common garden-variety housewife, college-educated, well-off, who's got a healthy-sized appetite for sex and a husband who keeps her on short rations. Back in college, she was date-raped by—" I tried to think of an economical way to describe what I knew of Chandler "—by a sexual predator. At forty-something, she has a fling with the same guy. Then she disappears. Then she comes back. Then she gets killed. Sorry, ma'am, but I can't quite put the novel down."

Jane Hooker M.S.W. squinted her steely eyes at me. "Women feel ashamed of their desires."

"Excuse me?"

"They get to fearing them. She married the man who'd regulate her appetites for her, then got herself seduced, telling herself she wasn't responsible."

"What are you saying?"

"She's frigid."

"Like hell," I said, no longer able to avoid curling a lip at her.

Jane Hooker lit another cigarette. "The woman couldn't relax. You asked my interpretation."

"So you don't think she was raped."

"I think she *participated* in the rape, made herself available," she asserted, moving her cigarette in a tight arc.

"Oh. Then you don't hold him responsible for his actions?" I checked myself again, furious to hear the timbre of my voice rising.

"Yes, of course. But let's also look at what her need to reenact the victim archetype got her."

Now she had totally lost me. "But this man might be the one who killed her. Are you saying she asked for *that*?"

Jane Hooker squinted at me as she considered my question, much as a chess player might do before a particularly complex move. "No, I don't think he would kill her," she said at last, "any more than a cat would miss the chance to play with the mouse it catches."

THE NEXT PSYCHOTHERAPIST I visited at least seemed possible. Her name was Ernestine Schwartz ("Call me Tina"), and she was kind enough to take my part in the proceedings at face value. "Let's get a cup of tea while we talk," she said, and, putting on her coat, led me down the street to a small café. "I like this place because it has a nice courtyard out back, and hey! it's open today. Let's take our drinks out there."

So we sat in the balmy sunlight of a Colorado spring morning, and I laid out my tale for the umpteenth time. When I was done, all Tina had to say was, "I've never dealt with anyone who's been traumatized in this way."

"But do you think you can help her?" I asked, trying to keep the anxiety out of my voice. This was the first halfway human therapist I'd talked to, and I didn't want her bowing out without a trial.

Tina raised her shoulders a notch as she sipped at her cup of Orange Zinger. "Don't know 'til I try," she said matter-of-factly. "I have an intake opening available tomorrow afternoon. Why don't you bring her by then, and see if she feels comfortable with me?"

◈

I STOPPED INTO an electronics store to buy an answering machine for Betty's house, then killed the next hour in at a stockbroker's office reading up on Boomer Oil in *Standard and Poor's*. I found that Boomer had been nearly busted before the Dutch bailed it out.

Next, I met with the final psychotherapist on the list. She was a very plain woman about my age who was kitted out in aviator glasses, a loosely-fitting man's oxford button-down shirt, and chino pants. Her shoes had heavy-lugged soles, her hair was cut in a short, shapeless, wash-and-wear butch, and she was about thirty pounds overweight. Her name was Mary Pinetree, although from her gray eyes and dishwater blond hair I sensed not a drop of Indian blood in her. She gave me her card, which read: "New Dawn Rape Crisis Center, Mary Pinetree, Assistant."

"This explains why I don't remember getting your name out of the telephone book," I said. "You're somebody's assistant. And why am I not speaking with that somebody?"

"I am the designated assistant assigned to screen you" was all she said in reply. She sat down on one of the battered sofas that crowded the bare wooden floor of the front room of the old Victorian house that comprised the New Dawn Rape Crisis Center and picked up a clipboard. On it, I could see a long form with lots of blanks to be filled in. She indicated another sofa on which I should sit.

I sat. "So what kind of a program do you have for kids with memory blanks?"

"We'll get to that later," Mary Pinetree said, flipping down two or three sheets on her clipboard and making a quick notation. "Now, when did the rape occur?" the woman asked.

"Rape? There was no rape."

Mary Pinetree looked up at me and smiled knowingly.

I took a deep breath and counted to ten, or at least to five. "I reiterate, I am here on an errand for a friend. She has no memory of a very traumatic event, but that event, to the best of my knowledge, did not include rape. I took the name of one of your psychologists out of the phone book because she listed a specialty in helping adolescents in crisis."

Mary Pinetree scribbled something, gave me another look, this one slightly superior. "All right, then when did this 'traumatic event' occur?"

"Last summer. Her mother was murdered."

Mary Pinetree scribbled diligently. I stared across the room, through a double-hung French door, into what looked like the central office of the center. Two women dressed almost identically to Mary Pinetree moved about with martial bearing, collating papers and smacking them together with a stapler. "Ms. Pinetree," I said, "I suppose you weren't fully advised before I came in here regarding the nature of my errand, but we need to get something straight. With all respect, I have no interest in speaking with you further until you start to give me a little bit of information—like whether you have a certified professional here with adequate grounding in assisting a teenager with a memory block."

Mary Pinetree managed to come out with one more knowing look. "I have three years' experience here, the best hands-on training. And yes, I deal with women all day long who can't remember whole years of their lives, even whole decades. Rape does that to women."

But not to men, is that what you're saying? "Are you telling me that you do some of the counseling here, too?"

Mary Pinetree's expression remained smugly opaque, except that her eyes seemed to narrow a bit back there beyond the reflections in her Gloria Steinem glasses. "Yes, I do group therapy. Under the guidance of an M.S.W., of course."

"Is that M.S.W. present during your sessions?"

"No." As in, *Why should she be?* She looked back at her clipboard. "Now—"

"And how long do you usually grill your prospective clients with that form of yours before you offer them any help?"

"Sometimes it takes two sessions. Sometimes more. We like to be thorough."

"And let me guess: you charge them for this time."

"On a sliding scale, of course. And then, if the rape is prosecuted, the victim can apply for assistance through the county."

"Then you expect me to pay for this screening session."

"Yes."

"How much?" I asked, pulling my checkbook out of my jacket pocket.

"I'm sixty dollars an hour, unless you can verify that you are a low-income—"

"Don't worry," I told her hotly, "daddy has deep pockets. But I'm writing this check for thirty, because I won't be staying." I handed her the check, said, "You can keep the change," got up, and turned my back on Mary Pinetree as I left the room. I said nothing further to her, figuring she hadn't let us get well enough acquainted that I owed her the basic civilities. But as I headed down the sidewalk through the warming spring air, I said out loud, "That one was for you, Miriam. We don't pay no one to have control over your baby."

28

THE SKY WAS WIDE AND CLEAR, AND THE HIGH MOUNTAINS GLIS-
tened with a late mantle of snow. The voice in my headphones said,
"Seven seven bravo, cleared for takeoff." I taxied the final ten yards, lined
up on the runway, came in with the power. The propeller spun into a pale
blur, gobbling up the air, pulling the little airplane faster and faster down
the runway. I pulled back the yoke. The little plane lifted, and we were
away.

"Give me a standard turn to the left as soon as you've got your thousand," Peggy barked through the headphones as she tapped the altimeter.
"Then take us up to Tri-County Airport for a couple touch-and-gos."

"Right."

One thousand feet above the elevation of the runway, I rolled the yoke
to the left and applied left rudder, pushing on the left pedal, coordinating
the turn, luxuriating in the pleasure of skills remembered. The little airplane climbed smoothly, now passing 7,000 feet, now 7,500. The foothills
began to shrink, and the towering flatirons of Lyons Sandstone that flanked
the rampart beyond Boulder became but a necklace as the wide vista of
the Rocky Mountains opened up. Cars on the Denver-Boulder turnpike
dwindled into ants scurrying to and fro, ephemeral specks on a landscape
sculpted over tens of millions of years by wind and ice and water as
billion-year-old rocks rose to greet the heavens. At eight thousand feet, the
bottom of a clear wave of air off the mountain front grabbed us and gave

us a good bump. We were but a bubble of humanity, a mite in the eye of an enormous God of grandeur. All the psychologists, potential employers, suffering teenagers, and lost lovers in the universe were as waves on a sea of infinite power and grace.

At Tri-County Airport, I made three landings; the first pretty ragged, the second somewhat better, and the third smooth as silk. Then we rose again, taking to the high air over the cornfields east of Longmont, and practiced stalls and spins and approaches to a soft-field landing. Returning an hour and a half after our takeoff to Jeffco, Peggy called for current runway information, then tried to make a call to the tower. She got no answer. Giving the radio a good thump, she growled, "Damned thing, worked on the ATIS frequency just then, so what's this shit it won't get me the tower?" She switched the dial back and forth, trying to catch a signal. Finally, we heard a call from the tower, ushering a twin-engined Cessna into the pattern. Peggy called our location and intentions, got us cleared, and then switched back to the intercom. "Em, what I tell you about relying on radios?"

"That you can't."

"Right. What's the jingle?"

"Aviate, navigate, *then* worry about trying to communicate."

"That's my girl. And always believe the seat of your own pants before you let some yahoo in the tower tell you how to fly. Got it? Some of them think they can fly, but most of 'em can't. They'll ask you to do all sorts of things your plane can't abide with."

"Right."

"So, where you want to take this bucket for your cross-countries?"

"I was thinking of Converse County Airport up in Wyoming for the first leg."

"Up there by Douglas? Why so far?"

"I got someone I want to visit."

"You know you can't carry passengers until you get your license. And you can't charge money for flying until you get a commercial rating past that."

"No, but I can fly to somewhere where I got some work to do, right?"

Peggy shrugged. "Your nickel. Then where? How about Scottsbluff?"

"No, I was thinking about Saratoga."

"Shively Field? You nuts? You can't go over the Laramie Range between Douglas and Shively, much less over the Medicine Bows between Shively and here. Ain't I taught you no respect for mountain flying?"

"Yeah, you didn't spare the rod on that one. I know, it's not for beginners. I was thinking of running doglegs around the mountains. It'll work."

"And tire you out. There's a reason they don't make you fly to hell and gone for these student cross-countries. You need more experience before you start putting in that many hours in one day."

"I mean to spend the night in Douglas."

"What, curled up in the seat of this backbreaker?"

"No, in the local hotel. It ain't fancy, but it's clean."

"Long time since you've had any?" Peggy snorted.

Blushing, I pressed the radio switch on the control wheel and called in my approach to Jeffco Tower, then switched back to the internal intercom to answer Peggy. "You ask too many questions," I said simply. "So you going to sign me off or not?"

"Not to Saratoga I'm not."

"To Douglas, then."

"Is that where this buck is?"

"Peggy, there's no buck!"

"So you say. I got two teenaged daughters. I know a 'There's this guy I gotta see' when I smell one."

My knuckles turned white around the control wheel. I just needed to find Chandler to find out what—but of course, on some level, she was exactly right. "Okay, I'm looking for a lead on this guy, see, but he's not my boyfriend. He's—"

"Sure, ace, it's your nickel. Just so long as you're willing to find an airport if you get tired or the weather goes bad on you."

I nodded and said, "Don't worry," foolishly thinking that the weather would be the least of my problems.

29

THAT EVENING, I PHONED CECELIA TO LET HER KNOW ABOUT OUR appointment with Tina Schwartz. "She seems nice," I told her. "I think you'll like her."

To this, Cecelia didn't reply.

"Really," I urged, turning on the old pep-rally spirit. "I liked her, and I don't like shrinks. Not that I'd ever even spoken to one before last week," I added, unconsciously assuring her that a date with a psychologist was indeed something over which to be embarrassed.

A heavy sigh came over the line.

"What is it, Celie? I'll be there with you. It'll be okay."

Finally, on the verge of tears, she spoke. "Em, can't it be *just* you? I mean, we've always gotten along pretty well, right?"

The frailty and longing in her tone etched slowly and deeply into my heart. "Yes," I whispered. "Yes, you know I care. But Celie—"

"Then why can't I just, like, hang out with you?"

"Well, you can," I replied, immediately weighed down by the obviousness of this lie. "Okay, you're right, I haven't been around much for you in ages. I—" I what? I can't seem to get my life sorted out? I can't handle being that close? I miss the little girl you were and don't know what to say to the young woman you are becoming?

"Please," she whimpered.

Tears stung the edges of my closed eyelids. "I'm trying to find you a good person to help you."

Her voice came as a faint breath: "I'll try, Em. But I can't talk to anyone like I talk to you."

I spent Thursday morning getting my ducks in a row for the cross-country flight. I had to figure time and distance, rate of fuel consumption, airspeed at various presumed wind speeds, adjusting for the crosswind I expected, and factor in allowances for extra time and fuel should I have to land somewhere other than planned. I was, after all, limited to VFR—visual flight rules—planning, in which I could fly only under skies clear enough to see where the hell I was going.

I worked with air charts and flight computer, checking my route for obstacles such as mountains and mesas over which my Piper could not fly. Saratoga looked like it would be a little complicated, as it sat in a wide notch between two mountain ranges, but there appeared to be safe passage in and out, with plenty of room for turning.

At noon, I broke for lunch. I found Betty downstairs speaking into the telephone at full roar, instructing Boulder's city planners where to put their fencing setback regulations. "Such foolish people," she said sweetly as she hung up the phone. "They think I shouldn't be allowed the basic privacy and noise abatement afforded by a good old six-foot-tall fence along the Baseline Road side of my property. When I bought this place, it had a prim little three-foot picket job along the sidewalk, as quaint as a chipmunk's tonsils. Now, I was so foolish as to check with the Planning Department before tearing it down and replacing it with a proper six-footer, and they had the temerity to inform me that I could not tear down and replace taller, as I must in such cases observe a greater setback from the sidewalk. 'Oh,' quoth I, 'but may I instead repair the existing fence?' 'Certainly,' they said, 'thy fence is thine to repair.' Repair it I did. Six feet tall. Now it seems someone has registered a complaint regarding its sculptural qualities. Heavens, their taste must be in their mouth."

I glanced out the front window at the weird agglomeration of three-, four-, and six-foot pickets that graced the edge of the lawn. "I was wondering about that," I said, "but now tell me about your artistic selection of colors for said fence. I like what you did with the blaze orange and the fuchsia, but I'm not sure about the pea green and the chartreuse. And the barn red, isn't that a bit retro?"

"Why Em," said Betty Bloom, smiling her prettiest, "I just wanted the city to know how much I appreciated their regulations. And besides, what redhead is fully at home without such subtle hues?"

"Of course," said I. "What was I thinking?"

We put together a lunch of kippers, whole-wheat bread, and mayonnaise (my contribution), and hummus, tabouli, and crisp fresh greens (hers) while Stanley chased cattle through the vast pastures of his dreams.

At 3:30, I pulled into the parking lot in front of the main building of Cecelia's chic girl's prep school. As it was another splendid spring day and school had just let out, the front steps of the building were awash with adolescent females, most clothed and brushed and primped within a gnat's eyelash of looking like they were preparing for a photo shoot for some fashion magazine. As I mentally calculated the expense some of these creatures had gone to to turn themselves out for school, I began to understand why Cecelia had spent so much time, once her tears had dried, in telling me what I should wear to this event.

Some of the girls were bright-eyed and lively, others proud and haughty, still others painfully depressed. My charge fell in the latter category, I decided, as I moved into the throng.

I didn't see Cecelia anywhere along the steps, which was the place we had agreed to meet. Stopping a smooth-faced blonde with half-lowered eyelids, I asked if she had seen her. "Oh, *her*? I don't keep track of *her*."

I tried another girl, an athletic-looking sort with a glisteningly oily face and nice manners, and another, a plump asthmatic with braces, but no one had seen Cecelia. "We're just waiting for our mothers," a redhead in pea green leggings offered, as if that should be all the information I needed. I found a seat on a stone bench at one end of the steps and prepared to wait.

As I waited, a long procession of BMWs, Volvo station wagons, and Mercedes coupes found their way down the long drive and circled in front of the steps, and girl after girl peeled out to be wafted away in her carriage. It was great theater, as each deb came up with her own variant on studied boredom while she dropped lazily into the waiting cushions of her parents' forty- or fifty-thousand-dollar runabout. Before long, my eyes glazed with the ostentatiousness of the displays and I found myself eavesdropping on the conversations.

"Who's she?" one six-foot-and-rail-skinny type asked the blonde with the drooping eyelids as she eyed me suspiciously.

"Oh, just someone looking for that Cecelia slut."

"Oh," said the rail.

A second blonde turned and joined the discussion, saying, "Oh, Heather, you're just fascinated with sex yourself."

"Am not."

"Are."

"Slut."

"Whore."

"Just where do you get off, Lily? I hear you're doing it with that Jamison pig. Don't his zits pop all over you when he *comes*?"

"You're just jealous."

"Oh, *sure.*"

Fascinated as I was by the verbal sophistication of their repartee, I got up and began to pace. Where was Cecelia? Had she forgotten the timing of our plans?

Just then, one of the enormous glass doors at the top of the steps crashed open, and all those jaded eyes involuntarily turned to see who had thrown it open. There, triumphant in a cloak of haughtiness a deeper shade of blue-black than any other present there that day, stood Cecelia Menken, my charge. I had the good sense not to call out, *Get a move on, Celie, or we'll be late for our appointment with that shrink!*

Seeing me, Cecelia began to pick her way down through the mass of gawking onlookers, carrying herself in a fair parody of the regent allowing her subjects to observe her. I played along with things a little, meeting her in halfway up the staircase with a gentle kiss and a half hug. Nodding gravely, Cecelia acknowledged me. "The outfit's pretty good," she whispered, "but did you have to bring that *truck*?"

"Hang in there," I whispered back, and then, loudly enough so that every pair of ears could hear me, I said, "Sorry, Cecelia, but my Jaguar is in the shop today getting the leather seats oiled, and my man took my Cherokee to A Basin, so I had to bring the truck I use to haul compost for my herb garden. But perhaps you'd like to drive it, as practice. You know, for when your dad gets you a new truck so you can trailer you horse to the shows."

Cecelia's eyes lighted up. "Sure," she chirped.

After we'd loaded up and Cecelia had treated me to a neck-snapping job of gearshifting that miraculously shot us through the gate and a mile down the road without backfiring the engine, I told her to pull over. "Enough practice for today," I said evenly. "And besides, we're late. Gotta put old Bessie here to the mistress's hand."

"Thanks, Em" was all Cecelia had to say, as she settled back into her usual depressed glower.

"Did you like driving it?"

"No, it sucked. Why don't you trade this in for something with an automatic? Coulda broken my shoulder trying to shift this thing."

We argued the comparative merits of automatic versus standard shifts the rest of the way into Denver, where I stowed the reviled pickup in a lot and goosed Cecelia up the steps to Tina Schwartz's second-story counseling rooms. Tina met us at the door and gave Cecelia a greeting that was full of gentle smiles. "Why don't you sit wherever you feel comfortable," she said.

I looked around the large room and saw a few padded swivel chairs and a broad camelback couch, but there were also piles of soft, inviting cushions in other corners of the room, should anyone feel more comfortable on the floor. A wide table was decked with modeling clay and stacks of craft paper and marking crayons, and there were weird creative output of very upset clients all along the walls and on the bookcases.

Cecelia dumped herself at one end of the couch and glared suspiciously around the room.

"I'll just sit on one of these swivel chairs, Cecelia," Tina said, "and Em, you sit wherever you'd like. Maybe Cecelia would like you to sit with her on the couch, to keep her company."

I sat, and Tina got Cecelia talking enough to ask about the paints and drawing supplies on the table. Tina explained that many of her clients found it helpful to put their feelings into pictures. Cecelia looked doubtful but interested. In a few minutes, we moved to the topic that had brought us through the door: Cecelia's trauma. "It must be awful to lose your mother, and lose her in that way, Cecelia," Tina said. "Em tells me you can't remember the event."

Cecelia began to pick viciously at her cuticles. "No," she mumbled. "But it's behind me, you know? I don't like to talk about it."

Tina nodded respectfully. "Your call. Is there anything else on your mind you'd like to talk about? How about school, or your friends?"

Cecelia drew in her shoulders, looked furtively around the room. "Who cares about those bitches?" she said.

"They were really something," I said.

Cecelia shot me a look of warning or thanks—I was not sure which.

I kept talking. "I mean, Tina, I went to pick her up and there were all these stuck-up babes with expensive haircuts, all standing around accusing one another of being interested in sex, like that's something sick or abnormal. How's an adolescent girl with a reasonably healthy endocrine system supposed to have anything else on her mind?"

Tina nodded. "I know, it's a tough age."

Cecelia began to search her hair for split ends, making a great show of ignoring us, but she had shrunk even farther down into the couch, and the one long, skinny leg she had slung over the other was now hooked tightly back behind the other heel like she was trying to twist herself into a knot.

Tina said, "Cecelia, you're here to find out if you want us to work together. What do you need to know about me?"

Cecelia stared at the floor, said, "I got to go to the bathroom."

Tina rose and showed her to the door. "It's right down the hall to the left," she said.

When Cecelia was well out of earshot, I said, "Tina, I brought that up to try to get Cecelia talking, but those girls really horrified me. Why do they call each other names like 'whore' and 'slut'? Okay, some of them looked like they were on the way down to Colfax Avenue for an afternoon of soliciting, but that's just the style, right?"

Tina shook her head. "The good old double standard's still alive and well. We don't treat girls with a whole lot of respect as they become women, don't say, 'Hey, you're a woman now; congratulations!' Instead, we say, 'Now, don't you get in trouble.' We give girls such confused, devaluating messages. Where are our positive role models? Can't think of many other than a chaste Madonna, eh? Next stop: Mother Teresa. Most children's books that show someone being clever or adventuresome or leading others are about boys, so what does that tell us?"

"But why are women nasty to women?"

"Well, as we move toward middle age, women usually do start being more supportive of each other. We all know the punch line by then, know the joke was on us. But when we're young, we're really, honestly competing for the male of the species. And what's the image we aspire to? We're supposed to be pure and giving, but also drop-dead sexually attractive. When we grow old, we fear we'll be castoffs. My uncle used to have a joke that went, 'When your aunt gets to be fifty, I'm going to trade her in on two twenty-fives.' "

I laughed in spite of myself.

Tina continued. "We're so upset about growing old in a society that has no use for old women that we project hatred and distrust on the young. That would piss anyone off."

"But Miriam didn't feel that way about Cecelia. At least I don't think she did. Hell, she was out having an affair. . . ." My words trailed off as I tried to fit this piece into the puzzle Miriam had left behind.

Tina said, "Miriam didn't have to feel that way, but if she didn't actively campaign to give her daughter another outlook, the negative message was right there waiting to take over. I'll bet Cecelia has the normal stack of videos in her home collection. Look at the story of Snow White: the jealous old queen who casts her out. What does that tell us? And her name's Snow White, for heaven's sake."

"Yeah, not Horny Young Babe Looking for Experience," I said.

Tina grinned. "Right, so what does Snow White do? She goes to live with seven little midgets with personality flaws, cleaning up after them without even being asked. In my business, we call that codependency. What kind of self-esteem or fulfillment do we see there? Then the queen tracks her down and really gets nasty. She appears as this ugly old hag and talks her into eating an apple, just so we don't go around thinking old can really be beautiful, and with that apple motif, we're back to the Bible, for heaven's sake, blaming women for original sin."

"Knowledge is evil," I said, wondering again what Miriam had learned in her flight from the proscribed narrow path of decency.

Tina was warming to her story. "Okay, so the queen shows up as the hag and KO's Snow White, but hang on to your hat: the only thing that will save her is love's first kiss. Get the image? She needs a *man* to save her, but she's got to be a cherry, or she's got to stay in the glass coffin! God help her she should have experimented with anyone else!"

"But voilà, here comes the handsome prince," I said.

Tina opened her hands skyward. "And that's the end of the story, girls! He gives her a little peck, loads her on his horse, and they're out of there. You remember the last words on the screen in the Disney version?"

"Wasn't it, 'And they lived happily ever after'?"

"In Gothic script, no less!"

"Like that's the end of a woman's story," I said, thinking wryly of my lonely bed in a rented room. I tried to put Jim Erikson into that picture, but my overheated brain handed me the image of Chandler Jennings instead, smiling at me, turning the bed's cold sheets into warm, soft sheepskin. Shaking the image from my mind, I tried to preoccupy myself with wondering just how long Cecelia was going to hide in that bathroom.

Laughing, Tina was saying, "So here's the message, girls: keep house for emotionally stunted slobs and someday a prince will come save us!"

"Save us from what?" I asked.

Tina shrugged. "From having to grow up, perhaps?"

30

As my laboring truck hauled us up the grade toward the point where Interstate 70 slices into the mountain front, I asked Cecelia what she thought of Tina Schwartz.

In reply, she mumbled something acidic, like "Psychologists suck."

"You seemed pretty amenable to making a second appointment with her."

"Do I get a choice?"

"Yes, damn it!"

Cecelia shot a hurt look at me, and I realized that I had in fact shouted at her. Why, because she wasn't thrilled with my attempts at passing her off to someone else? *Maybe it doesn't suit her to get well,* I thought. *Then I'd be gone again.* "I'm sorry," I said. "All you need is one more person telling you to pull yourself together, and then running off somewhere. Would it help if I promised to stay in better touch?"

Cecelia's eyes slid briefly toward me, then back to the road in front of us. Her posture was caved in, a slack monument to noncommunication.

I tried to make my voice soft and solicitous. "You know, it's a long, hard life you got ahead of you."

The truck ground steadily up the interstate. The landscape rolled by in a chaotic flow as we climbed through the towering earth-guts road cuts of Mount Vernon Canyon, a jumble of Precambrian migmatites that looked like God had stepped on her toothpaste tube with the cap off. So wild and beautiful were these squiggles of mashed earth history that they always caught my eye, but Cecelia looked neither left nor right.

"I've been reading your mother's journals," I said. "She seemed a complicated woman. Had a temper, huh? I'll bet it felt like shit when she took off on you like that," I added, kind of wallowing around in my own muddle of guilt and imperfect intentions. "I'll bet—"

Cecelia wheeled on me. "Do me a favor," she spat, her eyes wide with fear and rage. "Get out of my life!"

"Listen, Celie, maybe your memory's not really lost. Like, maybe it's just sitting there by the road behind you, like you kind of left it there because it was too heavy to carry."

"Get out! Get out! GET OUT!" Cecelia screamed, so loudly that my ears began to ring. Her face went purple, a writhing mass of pain and anger.

I forced myself to look at the road, to remember that I was guiding a ton of metal up a hard surface at high speed. *Okay, then, I'll get out,* I told myself. *I don't need this. Clearly, I am not welcome. Those are fighting words, and I see no tears coming out of those eyes. I will have a short chat with her father, in which I will tell him that I think we have a therapist who might get somewhere with the problem—his guess is as good as mine.*

And then what? Thanks very much, I'll be sending a final accounting sometime next week, and how about those job contacts?

Well, not exactly. . . . I'd perhaps add that I intend to take another spin up into Wyoming to cross my T's and dot my I's. . . .

But it didn't go quite that way.

I parked the truck in Menken's driveway and followed Cecelia into the Menkens' big, impersonal house, chasing along behind her to make certain she did not slam the door between us, forcing me to wait on the front doorstep until her father came home and relieved me of the duty of "watching" her.

Cecelia careened into the kitchen and made for the pantry and a very large bag of jalapeño potato chips. She was obviously not going to offer me some, so I took my own turn in the pantry, reemerging with a bag of taco chips. I chewed hard, trying. Having something to chew would help me to calm down, to remember that I cared about this girl.

The better to ignore my presence, Cecelia punched the message button on the answering machine. "Hi, Cecelia," a recorded voice said unpleasantly, as if the name tasted foul in her mouth, "I need a ride to school tomorrow. You can pick me up at the usual time. Bye. Oh, this is Heather." Heather, the blasé blonde from the steps of Cecelia's school? Was she the "friend" Miriam named in her journal, the girl she overheard Cecelia talking to about Chandler?

"Bite me," Cecelia screamed at the machine, her shoulders beginning to shake. She almost dropped her bag of chips.

The machine beeped and went on with a second message. "Hi, sweetheart, this is your dad. I'm on my way home, so please keep Em there with you until I get there. I need to speak with her. Thank you, darling, and see you soon."

The machine gave a time trace for each call, and I calculated the time when we'd see J.C.'s Mercedes swing into the driveway. I didn't have much time. I said, "Who's this Heather creature, and why's she bugging you for rides to school if she's so blessed antisocial?"

"Fuck her."

"I'm asking for a specific reason, Cecelia. Her last name wouldn't be Wentworth, would it?"

Cecelia stared morosely into her bag of potato chips. "Yeah. Why?"

"You and Heather used to be closer?"

"Maybe."

"What changed that?"

"She's a snot."

"I was looking for something a little more specific than that. Like, did you have a falling-out?"

Cecelia knit her brows more tightly and stuffed a full handful of chips into her mouth.

Waiting politely for her to chew and swallow, I said, "She still calls you for rides to school."

Cecelia fixed me with a virulent stare. "Yeah, well, she has to, doesn't she? Her ma's in the hospital for doing too many drugs, and her dad goes out of town at the drop of a hat."

I felt a sudden sense of stillness, as if a missing arc in a circle had just dropped into place. "Drugs? Exactly what drug did Heather's mom take?"

Cecelia took a noisy breath and let it out. "Cocaine."

"So she's in a rehab center."

"Yeah."

"Do you know which one?"

"Betty Ford," she muttered. "But she's getting home tomorrow. So that means Heather's father's going to find some reason to be gone again, so the Heather bitch has to hit *me* for another ride."

"Cocaine's a nasty drug, Celie."

"I *know*!"

"Who told you about it? Your mom?"

"No, Mrs. Howard. *Mom* was too busy—"

The heavy purr of the Mercedes's motor sounded in the driveway. Cecelia quickly stuffed the bag of potato chips back into the pantry, closed the door, and rushed to wash her hands at the sink.

Aloud, I thought, *"Cindey?"* I couldn't imagine such a conversation.

The front door opened and J.C. Menken strode in. Cecelia ducked her head furtively, as if we'd been discussing something illicit. Her father caught her by the arm as she tried to slip past him, and he planted a kiss on the top of her head. She stiffened, then leaned against him like a dog. He patted her on the shoulder, a gesture indeed more appropriate for a dog than for one's daughter. Releasing her, he beamed at me. "Emily, I'm so glad you're still here. How did things go?"

Taking her chance, Cecelia slipped out of his arms and disappeared down the hall to her room.

"Oh, I'd say pretty well," I began, preparing myself for what I presumed would be a long chat.

"Splendid! Now, you'll join me for dinner tonight, yes? The Howards have invited us over, and I'm sure Cecelia would prefer to study. Cindey doesn't like to cook, but Fred fries a passable steak when motivated."

I tried to speak, but the very idea of eating with that pair again had made me suck in my breath so fast that a chunk of taco chips had become lodged in my windpipe.

J.C. grinned expansively. "Excellent! I'll just freshen up and we can go!"

◈

ON OPENING HER door and finding me standing there with J.C., the mask of Cindey Howard's features shifted ever so slightly from blankness to shock to repellency to a cagey welcome. She glanced uncertainly into the house before opening the door the rest of the way to let us pass through.

I walked through the broad archway into that vast living room and stopped short. Over by a far window stood the hawk-faced man from Fred Howard's office.

He turned, fixed his needle eyes on me, frowned. To Fred, he said, "Who's this?" He didn't speak loudly enough that I could hear him, but I could see his lips move around the words.

Fred made a gesture that said, I'll handle this, and hurried toward us as if readying himself to tackle an advancing line of footballers.

I was damned if I was going to be handled. I marched across the room and presented my hand to be shaken. "Em Hansen," I said fixing my strongest gaze on that disturbing face. "I don't believe we've met."

The man looked not at me but at Fred. His hand rose to pull the cigarette out of his mouth, but I caught it in a handshake. It was as cold as refrigerated meat. His eyes began to burn with anger, looking a threat at his host.

"Em!" Fred squealed in a bad approximation of jollity, "we didn't know you were *coming*. What a *pleasure*." He grasped my arm and tried to steer me toward a wet bar that stood along one side of the room. "What'll you have?"

I held my ground, fury feeding my rebellion. *You want to push me around? Well, you had the drop on me in your office, but now I am a guest in your home, and you will treat me with respect!* "A proper introduction would do nicely," I said, sweetness hissing past my teeth.

"I'm afraid Cindey hasn't set enough places, and we only have five filets, J.C. Maybe another night."

"No matter," I replied, answering for Menken. "Cecelia decided to stay home and get up-to-date on her homework. Big test in the morning, Fred. So who's your friend?"

I caught a glimpse of Menken out of the corner of my eye. He was smiling, but he kept his lips tightly shut, letting Fred twist on whatever rope he had strung up for himself.

The entire dinner went like that. I kept trying for an introduction to the anomalous dinner guest, but Fred kept dodging me. Cindey sat at her end of the table, drinking a lot of wine while eating almost no food, looking back and forth between me and Menken. Fred made inane small talk, which Menken parried with ease. The mystery guest said nothing. Hardly anyone ate anything at all. Each course seemed to appear and disappear at the speed of a sleight-of-hand artist, and before I could say "Gotcha," the dessert dishes were being whisked from the table. Fred all but ordered me to help Cindey hustle the spent dishes into the kitchen, but I stuck to my "date" like glue and followed the men into Fred's den, a swank, low-slung room with another wet bar, this one done up in Black Watch plaid and leather. All the while, the dark-eyed man's complexion grew darker and darker, like a cloud filling with rain and the threat of thunder. Fred served up snifters of brandy to himself, Menken, and the unnamed man, but ignored me. Smiling, Menken handed his to me and presented himself to Fred for another. As he sipped his brandy, the hawk-faced man, watched me closely from under his eyebrows, like a rat watching his enemies as he sucks filth at a sewer, but said nothing.

"Nice brandy," I said, not having the slightest idea what I was talking about. "So what do we not talk about now? Maybe drilling rank wildcats on the Broken Spoke Ranch?"

Fred had his back to me, pouring another dash of the brown liquid into his snifter when I spoke. His shoulders shot up and I heard the bottle hit the counter abruptly. The unnamed man's eyes turned dark as flint as his head swiveled toward his host. I fantasized them so sharp that they could carve through his fatted flesh.

"Em," Menken said equitably, "this is a social occasion. I'm sure Fred doesn't want to talk shop just now."

Fred turned and faced him. A look of mutual reappraisal flowed between them.

The conversation settled back into inane utterances, the one man still silent. I sipped carefully at my brandy, not wanting to let the alcohol have me. After ten minutes of tense civility, Menken announced cheerily, "I'd better get Em back to the house so she can head home. She has a big day of job hunting tomorrow. Fred, thanks for a fine meal, as always. Good to see you, too, Al." And he steered me out of the house.

Ten feet down the driveway, I said, "Al who?"

Menken began to laugh. "Emily, you were superb! You worked instinctively, killed them with good manners! I didn't have to tell you a thing. Why, if I played bridge, I'd want you as my partner."

I said, "Marvelous. I get treated like a day-old cow pie and you want me to be your bridge partner. Mind letting me in on the gag?"

"Gag?"

"Yeah, damn it, who was that guy, and why didn't you want to talk to him?"

"Oh, no, no, no, Emily; what you don't know can't hurt you, right?"

I stopped abruptly. "In fact, what I don't know *can* hurt me. Who *was* that man, why didn't you want to talk to him, and why in hell wouldn't Fred introduce him to me?"

"This is precisely what I mean. You knew instinctively that I didn't want to speak privately with him, so you forced your way into the brandy and cigars ritual in the den. You were magnificent!" He had stopped walking, too, and stood facing me, hands in his pockets, grinning. His white, white teeth and the silvery thatch of his hair shone eerily in the light from the moon, which had momentarily broken free of a bank of clouds. He began to rock back and forth, heel-to-toe, heel-to-toe.

I spoke quietly, earnestly. "J.C., this is not a laughing matter. You asked me to help your daughter, and I'm finding that I have to look into your wife's past to do so. Well, her past connects her to Cindey Howard, who has a grudge against her—I say *has*, not *had*, because she's still pretty het up about something, and she's trying to draw me into an agenda she isn't being so kind as to spell out to me. Now you drag me over to her house and there's a man there who isn't glad to see me. No big deal, except I saw him at Fred's office, sneaking down the fire stairs, so I can only suppose he isn't into any kind of business I'd like to be involved in. He wants to talk to you, but you don't want to talk to him. Fine, point in your favor, but don't go around thinking that this doesn't put me in harm's way, Joe, because it sure as hell might."

J.C. Menken brought his hands up out of his pockets. "Joe? You called me Joe!"

"Damn it, *listen* to me! This isn't a social meeting; this is—"

Menken's grin widened. "Sure, I understand."

I didn't like the look of that grin. I started walking again, hugging my arms around my chest as if I was cold. We had a quarter mile to go to his house and my truck and a fast retreat to Boulder. I lengthened my stride and began to hustle.

Menken easily matched my stride with his long legs. "I haven't walked in the moonlight like this in a long time," he said. "I used to walk with Miriam like this, on summer evenings."

I would have broken into a run if I hadn't been afraid of looking foolish. "Fine. Let's talk about Miriam," I parried, adding bluntly, "I've been reading her journals. She seemed kind of depressed."

"Miriam?" He tipped his head to one side, considering this thought. "She had her down moments, I suppose, but more of the time, she seemed angry. She had a healthy temper."

"What do you mean, healthy?"

"I mean she'd yell. Yell and throw things. I'd have to leave the room, and it rather frightened Cecelia when she'd get like that."

"What?" I stared at Menken, trying to match what he was saying to what I had read, both about him and about what I'd learned about her. Miriam's journals painted a picture of life with a man so self-involved and inattentive to her feelings that she was half the time ready to brain him. A healthy temper indeed: was this the good old business executive Menken, putting the entrepreneurial positive spin on a bad situation? Or was this the social Menken, being candid with a family friend?

I stopped walking and looked at him again, really studying him this time. There he stood, a man nearing fifty, still upright and physically strong. Relaxed and at ease, he lounged now with his hands again in his pockets, his weight on one hip. His hair was almost fully gone to silver, but it was still thick, even if his hairline lay higher up his forehead than it used to. I could barely see his eyes, lost as they were in the warm gray shadows of the night, but with his face relaxed and contemplative like this, they seemed infinitely softer and more kind than the armored orbs he had always shown on the battlefield of the boardroom. And with his head cocked slightly to one side, his face seemed almost dear.

"Please tell me more about Miriam," I asked.

"She was everything to me," he replied simply. "Whenever things got tough at work, I'd think of Miriam and our child waiting for me at home, and I'd happily redouble my efforts, just to keep them safe and cared for."

My brain skidded off this reckoning of his side of the story. Hadn't he ever noticed that redoubling his efforts was keeping him away from home too much? "I . . . I get the feeling from her journals that she was something of a restless person," I offered diplomatically.

"You're talking about the time she went away."

"Yes, and—"

Still looking straight at me, he said, "Miriam was a very interesting woman, Emily; almost a girl still when I first met her, but then, I was hardly more than a boy myself. A woman grows in thirty years, or if she doesn't . . . well, one winds up with someone one can hardly call alive. Miriam was very much alive. Vibrantly alive. But sometimes, people that alive are . . . well, let me say this, Em: she could go off half-cocked."

And all those years, Miriam had thought this man had been ignoring her. Sadness seeped into my bones. "So you knew."

"Knew? No one ever really knows another person, even if they live with them all their lives, but yes, I knew she was restless, in a great many ways. Sometimes it was me she couldn't stand anymore. Sometimes it was Cecelia. They fought, you know. She'd run off to see her parents, or to take a class, or—But after every departure, big or small, she always found her way home again, ready to try again; and for that, I loved her."

I looked into Menken's shadowed face, trying to limn greater assurance that we were both talking about the same events. It seemed too rude to look this man in the eyes and say, *I read all about how angry she felt toward you, and about how little she thought of you as a lover, and about the man she preferred. . . .* So all I said was, "I'm so sorry you lost her."

"So am I, Emily. So am I."

I began to feel cold and awkward. It was time to change the subject. "Well, getting back to that man at the Howards'," I said, beginning to turn back toward the path home.

Menken didn't move.

I turned back one more time to face him.

He said, "Em, his name is Al Rosenblatt, and he keeps company with men who ought to be in jail. He's got Fred going on some deal, I think, and they invited me to dinner tonight to try to involve me in it. My answer is no, and you helped me say that tonight. But enough of that." He closed the distance between us, placed his hands on my shoulders, and kissed me on the lips.

31

An hour later, I sat in Betty Bloom's kitchen on Baseline Road in Boulder, spilling my guts. It was weakness to tell her anything, but shit, I had to tell *some*one.

"So he gives you a big wet one, and then you did what?" she was saying as she tried to pump me even further up by serving me the concentrated residue of the day's coffee.

"Not *wet*, damn it! He's a . . . a . . . *gentleman!*" I pushed the coffee mug away in disgust. Already I was sorry I'd told her anything. How could I even begin to explain what it was like when a control freak like Menken finally shows his tender undersides to someone? It was like being handed a confidence, and here I'd gone and betrayed it to the very next person I had met.

"So you ran for it."

"I—" No, I had not run, just walked—very quickly. And Menken had fallen into step beside me, hurrying along with his hands in his pockets, trying to behave like he did this sort of thing every night. I was only too aware that I was probably the first woman he had kissed since his wife had been killed, and if he had been more faithful to her than she had to him, I was his first taste of someone new in twenty-five years. And yes, I was running away; you betcha.

"Then what happened?" Betty demanded. "Come on, you're dragging this out. He go for another one?"

"No, I got to my truck, and that was it. I drove here. Bam. End of story." Or something like that. There had been an awkward moment at the truck where he'd looked like he might be on the point of apologizing or something, so I'd quickly said something like, "I'll call you," and he'd said—I couldn't remember what he'd said. Had I even been so kind as to listen? And when did I become the keeper of the feelings of a man nearly twenty years my senior?

"Well, I tell you," Betty Bloom was saying, "Elyria *told* me about this Menken guy, but she never said he had *that* kind of trick up his sleeve."

"You will *not* tell Elyria about this," I said emphatically.

"Oh, so he did get to you. Hmm, a little 'love among the ruins' action."

"Go to hell."

"Save you a seat by the fire."

"Please, Betty."

"Aww . . ."

"Quit jerking my chain!"

"Quit being a sap."

I straightened up like I'd been slapped. "Just what in hell you mean by *that*?"

"You say this fellah's hired you to help him help his daughter, because his wife was murdered. Well, either he's using the daughter and the dead wife routine to get you in bed, or he's using you to get at whoever he thinks killed her. Either way, he's playing the sympathy card, which I say stinks on ice."

I considered her words. That was the trouble with dealing with a rationalist like Menken: just when I thought I had him figured out, he got all complicated on me, and just when I thought he was being complicated, the situation was in fact foolishly simple. The tough part was figuring out which was which.

"I'm going to bed," I said resignedly. I got up and began to stagger out toward the stairs to my room.

"Sure. Sleep tight, Cinderella. Oh, and you got a couple calls while you were out," she added. "On your answering machine." She batted her eyelashes, letting me know what she thought of my contribution to the household's electronics.

I turned and stared at her.

"Someone named Julia Richards and someone—a very *nice*-sounding someone—named Jim Erikson. Oh, and a regular call. Someone who said she worked for the UPS. It's a Wyoming area code—I looked it up—and she said you could catch her tomorrow morning between eight and eight-fifteen. I told her I didn't know when you'd be in but that I was certain you'd call back in the morning." She lifted a slip of lavender-colored notepaper off the counter by the phone and smiled.

I snatched the slip of paper out of her hand and began to dial. Julia could wait; Jim wouldn't. He answered on the third ring. "It's Em," I said. "What's the plan?"

Jim's shy voice was barely audible over the sound of a diesel engine echoing in the tight confines of a garage; he must have forwarded his calls over to the firehouse. "My flight gets in tomorrow at twelve-fifteen. I was wondering if—"

"You need me to fetch you at the airport?" I asked a bit too abruptly. If Betty had leaned any closer to the phone, she would have fallen into my lap.

"No, ah, no . . . I'm going to rent a car. I was thinking I could see you sometime in the afternoon. I have to talk to my aunt's lawyers and so forth, and—"

"Sure. Where are their offices? I can meet you there." As in, Don't come here; my landlady will leave us no privacy.

Jim gave me an address in Lafayette, a small town not far from Boulder.

"What time's your appointment?" I asked.

"Two-thirty."

"Okay, let's say they take an hour or so. I can be there at four."

"Fine. And Em—"

"What, Jim?"

"I'm ah—"

"Me, too, Jim," I said, not the least bit sure what he had been about to say. "Gotta go now. I have a redheaded carnivore here sizing me up for the frying pan."

"You what?"

"Four o'clock tomorrow."

"Sure."

I pushed a forefinger down on the phone button to break the connection and dialed Julia's number. I caught her just turning in for bed. Without preamble, she said, "I've decided that if you're so interested in those damned journals, you should just come get them. My office, two o'clock tomorrow, and don't be late."

"No problem," I told her, mentally reckoning the time it would take me to drive from Denver to Lafayette. I could make it. I said good night and hung up the phone. And smiled back sweetly at Betty the lioness Bloom. And went to bed.

◆

I DREAMT ALL night about a baleen whale as big as the universe that was trying to kiss me, which seemed all right, except that its kiss sucked me perilously close to its vast filtration system, and I didn't want to become food.

The next morning, I stumbled down the outside stairs from my room at about 7:30 and found Betty already up, dressed, and setting out what looked like a tea party in the backyard. She had a nice damask tablecloth right down on the ground, and on top of it she had placed a plate of half-chewed doughnuts, a jug of coffee, and her nicest cups and saucers. She began to pour. "What the hell are you doing?" I asked.

Still pouring, she said, "My friends the raccoons got into my car again last night and ate half my doughnuts. I just thought they might like a little coffee with them, you know? Kind of dip them, with their scraggy little pinkies in the air?"

Taking advantage of Betty's removal to the backyard, I hurried inside and telephoned Sergeant Ortega, who was already in his office. "Al Rosenblatt," I told him.

"Who?"

"The man who was in Fred Howard's office when I interviewed. His name is Al Rosenblatt. You know anything about him? He was at dinner at the Howards' last night. Menken took me. Something about a deal Menken didn't want to become involved in."

Ortega made a *hmm-hmm-hmm* noise, which meant, *I'm thinking about this.* "You meet me here for lunch, okay?" was all he said.

"Sure, what time?"

"Noon okay?"

"Noon it is."

Next I dialed Ginger Henley at the UPS in Douglas. "Oh, Em," she said. "Hey, Laurie here says you wanted to know who's been shipping sacks of drilling mud in and out of here. I thought that was kind of strange, too, so I talked to the guys who drove them in. They came from Canada."

"Canada?"

"Yeah, Edmonton. There's oil up there, isn't there?"

Canada. I thanked her and put down the phone, wondering why in hell anyone would import drilling mud from Canada when it could be had sixty miles away.

No sooner had I laid the phone to rest in its cradle than it rang again. Betty was still outside, now reciting her ritual curses at the raccoons, so I answered it. "Miss Hansen?" a woman's voice asked. It was a familiar voice, one I'd heard recently, but I couldn't place it at first.

"Speaking."

"Please hold for Mr. Howard."

"Mr. who?" I began, but I'd been put on hold.

A moment later, Fred Howard's uncouth voice came over the line. "This Hansen?"

"Yeah."

"Okay, we got a job for you. You report immediately."

I stared blankly at Stanley, who had a moment earlier ambled in the door, taken a very messy swill of water from his stainless-steel dish, and flopped onto the kitchen floor. Stanley stared back, clearly affronted.

"You there?" said Fred Howard. He sounded anxious.

"Yeah, yeah, I'm here. Just how soon is immediately?"

"Today. This morning. Your flight leaves this afternoon."

"Where are you sending me?"

"Africa."

"Well, I don't know. . . ."

"Hey, you sounded so interested," Fred said boisterously. "And just this morning, y'see, one of our well-site guys had to take this emergency leave."

I glanced at the black plastic kitty-cat clock on the wall in Betty Bloom's kitchen, trying to make sense of what I was hearing. The kitty cat's tail and eyes switched back and forth to tick the seconds away, *ticktock, ticktock*. "Well, Mr. Howard," I said, idiotically slipping into employee-boss formality, "you got to understand, I don't even have a passport."

"Right. Right—that's why we gotta get started early! Got a full day for you."

"You haven't even said what you're going to pay me."

"Pay you? Oh, of course, of course. Yeah, well, I'll match whatever Menken was paying you. Plus ten percent. Full housing benefits for overseas duty, of course. And a servant. Food. All that stuff. You'll make out."

Ticktock, ticktock. It was 7:50. At ten o'clock, I could be at Boomer Oil to find out what was going on; noon at the Police Department, to assure Carlos Ortega that I was still alive; two at Julia Richards's office, to get the journal; four in Lafayette. It was going to be a full day. "See you at ten," I said, and headed for the shower.

Fred Howard's secretary handed me a mound of papers to sign and assigned a "helper" to walk me through the process of getting a passport in a tearing hurry. This "helper" was big and male and shadowed my every move. When he followed me to the bathroom and waited outside while I peed, I decided it was time to terminate my employment with Boomer Oil. I told him I'd need to get a copy of my birth certificate, which was still in storage with a box of important papers in Elyria Kretzmer Finney's basement. He said he'd drive me over there. I used the hide-a-key to get in, fumbled around for a minute or so looking through my boxes, then allowed as how I had to use the bathroom again. The upstairs bathroom at Elyria's house has this neat window that looks like it doesn't open, but does.

I'll wager I was climbing onto the number 32 bus headed back downtown before the big guy figured it out, and I would have a little explaining to do with Elyria if he got mad and tumbled the place before letting himself out, but there you have it. Nevertheless, I was fifteen minutes late for lunch with Sergeant Ortega.

When I got to his office, I found he had company: two men in dark suits, cooling their heels, waiting for me. They goose-stepped me down a hall and sat me in an interrogation room, opened a folder, turned on the recording machines, and showed me a black-and-white glossy of Al Rosenblatt, a grainy candid blown up from a negative that had held a much larger image. "That him?" one of them said.

"Yes, that's him." There was no doubt; I'd know those needle eyes anywhere.

One of the suits slapped the folder shut. The other walked me through the story of where I'd seen him and what he'd been doing. "Now you tell me why you want to know," I said when I was done spilling what paltry little information I had.

Ortega closed his eyes and shook his head, a barely perceptible jiggle: the gesture said, Don't ask. Let it drop.

I sighed. "Well, if it's so hush-hush, Carlos, then you'll probably also want to know that Fred Howard phoned me up this morning first thing and offered me a job."

The suits rotated their heads toward me with an audible *click*.

"Starting immediately," I said. "In fact, that's why I was late. He's goosing me through a passport application so I can be on a plane for Africa this afternoon, complete with heavy-weight escort."

"Don't go," Ortega said.

"I have no intention of going," I answered. "You think I'm nuts? I'm sure West Africa is lovely to visit this time of year, but there's nothing wrong with my nose. I know rotten fish when I smell it." Okay, so I'd allowed myself the fantasy during the hour it had taken me to drive into Denver and park the truck. I would have loved to go to Africa; it was just that I also wanted to make sure I came home again, and in good shape. I would have been more stupid than naïve if I had deluded myself that there weren't at least twenty men on Fred Howard's Rolodex he would have called before me if his offer had been legitimate. No, it was clear that Fred Howard simply wanted me out of town. *Way* out of town. I had simply played along to see what I could learn, and to see if I could get a free passport.

The boys in suits had another twenty questions for me. I filled them in on what I knew of Fred Howard's business dealings, finishing off with a thumbnail summation of the state of the oil business. "Foreign money's buying out some of the midsized to small oil companies," I said. "These are privately held corporations, so the buyout is absolute. I can only imagine what that does to boys like Fred Howard, who go from being biggish fish in the local pond to little guppies in the holding corporation ocean. Maybe he's even looking down the barrel of a forced early retirement with reduced upside."

The suits looked pensive for a moment, then excused themselves. Ortega said, "They've been tracking Al Rosenblatt for years."

"Who are 'they'? FBI? DEA?"

"Don't ask."

"Carlos—"

He waved a hand at me. "Em, you know I can't talk about this stuff."

"Then they're narcs."

"Please, Em, you stay here with me awhile, okay?"

"But I've already told you everything I know."

Ortega closed his eyes, said, "Even if they know that, there's such a thing as revenge." When he opened his eyes again, they shone with moisture.

I think it was about then that I began to realize exactly how much trouble I was in.

JULIA MET ME in the waiting room by her secretary's desk and all but threw the journal into my lap. "There. Now it's your problem," she said.

"You read it, didn't you?"

Julia set her jaw in anger. "You want to know who Chandler Jennings is? I'll tell you who Chandler Jennings is. He's a drug dealer, pure and simple. You wanted coke back in college, who'd you go to? Our boy Chandler. You want to know how he got that nickname? Chandler means a candle maker. 'Go to the Chandler,' they'd say, 'he'll light you up.' "

I hadn't even gotten up from where I sat in the depths of yet one more swank overstuffed waiting room chair, so sudden had been her appearance and assault with the book, so I just sat there and stared.

Chandler. Drugs. Colombia. Oil. Miriam. I was finally beginning to connect the dots.

Julia stood in the middle of the waiting room. She stared not at me but at the book on my lap, and now that the strength of her anger had drained away, I saw at last the pain that dwelled beneath it. So Chandler had gotten through to Julia, too. What had it been, a lost weekend of experimentation with drugs and sex? Or had she found the experience pleasant but too short? And now she had read Miriam's journal.

"Do you think he lit Miriam up?" I asked gently.

She shook her head. "Miriam? No. She was a cheap drunk. Hypersensitive even to aspirin, and she didn't like the feeling of being high, or at least not on chemicals. Wouldn't touch drugs with a barge pole." A moment later, she turned and started back into her office.

"Wait. Do you know how I can get in touch with him?" I asked.

She let out her breath soundlessly, her shoulders falling, and only then did I know she had been holding it. "No," she said tiredly. "Men like Chandler don't leave a forwarding address."

I TOOK THE journal to the privacy of the cab of my truck and opened it, my hands scurrying ahead of my sight. The whole case was flying open now; seemingly unrelated pieces of the puzzle were connecting. But here in my hands lay the beating heart of the mystery.

I found Miriam in a fugue:

August 2

Cecelia just *watches* me. I have to tell him it's over, and then I'll tell her not to worry, and somehow let her know that he won't be coming again.

August 5

Chandler came again today and I tried to tell him that he couldn't come here anymore, but every time I opened my mouth, nothing came out. I couldn't stand the thought that I would never feel his touch again. Then when he came to me and put his arms around me, it was like he *knew*. He walked out the door with a look on his face that was *spooky*. I didn't even have time to feel relieved before the longing set in.

As disgusting as I feel about my deceit with Joe, Chandler's been a friend to me, and I didn't want to hurt him. I keep staring at the telephone, willing him to call, so I can explain. But I must care more for Joe, or I would have left with Chandler. Or maybe it's just what I've always known, ever since that time senior year: I don't love Chandler.

I don't know who I am anymore. I look out the window and wonder where I am, because I *am* that girl I was and I'd so much prefer that this present time and place hasn't happened yet.

August 21

I've tried to tell myself again and again that it isn't *him* I need; it's the *sex*. But sex smells like him now. Feels like him. Sounds like him. My body even smells like him. Belongs to him. And yet I don't love him. I can't find it in myself even to weep.

There was a break of several weeks. When Miriam started to write again, it was from another location. If I had to guess, I'd say it was Aspen, that ski resort in the high Rockies where the rich and famous try to look swell on skis. That's where Cecelia's refrigerator-door limerick had sent her, anyway. Except that wherever Miriam was, she was not there with "a friendly looking dope."

September 30

There's no beginning or end to this, so the middle is as good a place to start as any. I've been here over a week now, and the therapy is helping, I think. Julia said that this woman could help with whatever was bothering me, and at least it's a relief to be away from home. I thought I was going to have to talk in a straight line, but that's not how things happen around here.

Joe doesn't know where I am. What a strange feeling. In all the years we've been together, I have always been right where he knew how to find me. Right where he'd left me. I guess he'll know where I am when the bank statement ~~arrives. I'm not so ignorant~~ that I'd do this on a credit card. God knows, Joe knows how to track something as transparent as that a whole lot faster. I even paid cash for the gas to drive here so he wouldn't know for just once in his life even which direction I took off to. I just hope he takes good care of Cecelia, and reads her note to him, or the parts that would be okay for her to see.

October 22

The therapist says I should write. What an irony. I'm the one who's kept a journal since I was how old? and I can't figure out anything to say.

October 30

Write something. What? Five days a week, I sit with this therapist, and words tumble out of my mouth, but I don't seem to have anything to *say*. She says I'm depressed. She's offered medication for it. I think I'd rather feel the pain for a while.

She's asked about my parents and all that stuff, and we talk about it, but I'm beginning to get angry. Sure, my life as a little girl wasn't perfect, and sure, there were jerks who didn't understand me and all that stuff, but damn it, I've made a mistake and I feel *sick* about it! Can't she understand that? I want to take the pain of it and ram it through my hand like a thorn so I'll keep on feeling it and never stop. She asks if I think Joe or Cecelia were really hurt by it. I can't understand that logic.

November 6

I'm supposed to write down my dreams. I don't remember the dreams I have at night, never have. She says that if I keep paying attention to them and write, write, write, I'll likely start to remember them. Bullshit.

November 7
    I hate this.

November 8
    I hate *her.*

Miriam had moved in her grieving from numbness into anger, and its strength was beginning to push matters to a head. How I wished she'd written more in those days, left greater detail of her flight into depression, and hiding, and psychotherapy. I hadn't yet met the emotional beasts that stared at her from the edge of her campfire, and I knew nothing of the process she used to chase them away. But I kept on reading for the parts I could understand, looking for that strength that had helped her grow. Had that strength, ironically, been Chandler?

I read carefully, sifting her words for evidence, for any lead that would tell me what had brought about her death, and who had killed her. Experience had taught me that seldom was one person wholly responsible for a murder. One person might strike the killing blow, but it took often many to build the maze of loss and confusion that brought such moments into being. Certainly Chandler's name was inscribed on every path that led to or from her, and it seemed more and more likely to me that he had been the vector of the killing dose. And yet I couldn't see him feeding it to her, couldn't see this man who had lain down with her on softest fleece and listened to her words with such tenderness rising up against her with killing vengeance. Certainly he had forced himself on her in college, not once but twice, first in his rooms and then days later in hers, pressing desperately against her for relief, but would a man like that kill the single thing that released him?

February 21
    I'm going back. I thought for a while, how easy to just stay gone. I told myself that after all I've been gone five months, and that hasn't hurt much, so why not just extend it indefinitely? But she says I need to confront things as they are, otherwise I'd probably just pick

up where I left off in a new relationship. I suppose that's true. Truth seems hard to identify anymore.

I wanted to think that what led me to Chandler was some universal need or truth or suffering, but she says I need to look first at just me and my one marriage, and try to leave the rest of the universe out of it for now. I asked her if she had a better perspective on it, and she says that I'm trying to cut myself off from feeling my needs. I guess that's right. All I feel just now is sad. Sad that I can't seem to have what I need. With Joe, I have all the security in the world, but no passion. With Chandler, it was the opposite. I try to push this need for passion away from me, but it keeps coming back, seeping into my dreams, both when I'm asleep and when I'm awake. What are my needs? I need to be touched. I need to feel that one special body next to mine. And I need to love the man inside that body. Is the man I need just a phantom from my imagination?

It isn't just sex I want. I had sex with Joe, but it never filled me. I want my senses. Joe loves me, or at least as well as he knows how, but he has no sense of touch. Chandler knows how to touch me, but I've never kidded myself that he knows how to love. He's not a man, he's a ghost.

Phantoms and ghosts. I'll have to learn to tell them apart.

February 22

Home tomorrow. She says I need to remember that it's okay to have needs, even if they can't be met. What a novel thought.

So Miriam was going home. Suddenly, I remembered another homecoming; Heather's mother, the addict who was due home that afternoon from the Betty Ford Clinic. It could not be mere coincidence that this woman had succumbed to cocaine addiction just as Chandler had appeared in the neighborhood. She must know him. Might know where to find him. I looked at my watch: 2:45. If I made all the lights just right, I could be in Genesee by 3:15 and question the woman quickly before her daughter came home from school. I would have to be careful, make certain that Cindey Howard did not see me or my truck pass through the neighborhood, and it would make me a little late meeting Jim in Lafayette by four, but surely the lawyers would keep him waiting, and his aunt's will had to be more complex than he had thought.

I can make it, I told myself as I put the key in the ignition and turned the truck toward Genesee.

❖

I FOUND HEATHER Wentworth's mother sitting in a wrought-iron chair with gaily colored chintz cushions. She had placed it in the middle of the otherwise-empty back deck of her sprawling cedar house, and she was leaning back, tipping the front legs up off the thick wooden planking, sipping at a glass of plain water as she beheld a stand of ponderosa pines and the mountains beyond.

I introduced myself and explained my presence. "I'm a friend of Cecelia Menken's," I began. "Her dad asked me to help her move past her mother's death, and . . . well, that brings me, among other places here. I'm thinking you might know a little about a man named Chandler Jennings."

Mrs. Wentworth hurled her glass of water into the grass beyond the deck and began to cry.

I felt deeply embarrassed.

Presently, she began to talk, her words thick with tears. "He *used* me, you know. Oh, at first I thought it was the real thing, that he truly cared about me, but that was a load of bull. Okay, I was drinking, and I did that part on my own, I *know* that, but *he* got me on the coke. Turned me onto it for sex, at first, like it would be so much more fun if we were high, but then it was coke first and the sex maybe, and then just the coke. You want to know about Chandler Jennings? He's a *monster!*"

"How'd you meet him?"

Mrs. Wentworth looked up at me like I'd only just appeared, kind of surprised. Her eyes and lips had swollen with the tears, making her middle-aged face seem almost young again, if infinitely tired. "Cindey Howard introduced us. Why?"

"Where? When?"

"Up in Saratoga some weekend, a couple years ago."

I worked with her awhile, sharpening her recollection. She admitted to some haziness ("The drink, you know. . . . I have to just deal with that now, be an adult"), but I was able to deduce that Chandler had appeared in her life not long after he had reappeared in Miriam's. As precisely as I could get her to reckon, he had taken up with her about when Miriam had over-heard Cecelia talking with Heather.

And Miriam had thought Cecelia knew. But had she known? Had they been talking about Heather's mother, and not Cecelia's?

"Do you know if he was seeing other people in the area?" I asked.

"Chandler? Shit, he was probably fucking half the women in this de-velopment." She rolled her head in misery and let it hang, as if it were no longer of use to her.

"I have just one more question for you. Those weekends in Saratoga—was there a man named Al Rosenblatt there, too?"

"Rosenblatt? I don't know. There were lots of people up there. Could have been."

I described him.

"Oh, that one. Yeah, there was a man like that at dinner with the Howards once. And I saw him at the golf course once, only he didn't play."

"Did he ever speak with you, or your husband?"

"With Hector? Maybe. Yeah, I seem to recall he did, only I'll be damned if I was invited to join in the conversation."

"You say Chandler used you. Do you mean to meet other people, or to make a sale of drugs?"

She shook her head lethargically. "Sale? Hell, he gave them to me free."

"Then what—"

"He wanted information. I can see it all now. I was so *stupid*!"

"What kind of information?"

"What my husband's company was doing. That sort of thing. It's been takeover city out there. The asshole was just pimping for information. Get me high, screw my brains out, and then pump me for information. What a dumb shit I am!"

"What kind of information?"

"Who was making it, who wasn't."

"You mean whose company was doing okay, and who was on the skids?"

"Yeah, tender little nothings like that."

"And how *is* your husband's company doing?"

"Okay now."

"Meaning?"

"His sales record was slipping, but my, he's busy now. Always gone. Can't even be here for my triumphant return."

"What does your husband sell?" I asked.

"Mud."

Of course. "Drilling mud."

"Yes."

"Does your husband happen to work overseas at all?" I asked, playing a hunch that was beginning to feel more like a certainty.

Mrs. Wentworth waved a limp hand. "Sure. Venezuela, mostly. Colombia, once in a while."

"And Canada. Edmonton perhaps."

"Of course."

"Not to mention Wyoming."

"Why not."

"And his company's had hard times lately."

"Haven't they all?"

"But the happy news is he's got a new client who's going to drill a test hole in offshore Africa."

She opened one bloodshot eye. "How'd you know? Hey, what's this all about, anyway?"

I PHONED SERGEANT Ortega from the first pay booth I came to. "Rosenblatt's smuggling cocaine in bags of drilling mud," I said.

"Where are you, Em? I'll send a car."

"You know, the funny thing is, he didn't even need Wentworth's mud company to do it."

"Wentworth?" I could hear his pencil tap down hard as he began to scribble notes. "First name?"

"Lives in Genesee. Next door to the Menkens. Look him up."

"Name of company?"

"I don't know. Try the phone book. But the thing is, there are clay deposits in Colombia. Barite, much purer than our domestic bentonite. There's even a pharmaceutical application for it, and it's white—a nice pure white, just like cocaine. They could have used Boomer's chemical company down there in Colombia. Or maybe they're doing that, too. Diversification, you know; it's good for business. Spreads the risks."

Ortega spoke quickly, keeping his voice low. "Em, you're way too close now. It's not just one man on an operation like this; it's many. And you don't know who the rest of them are or what they look like and neither do we. Please come to my office right now. *Now*, Em!"

All the pieces were going together smoothly. "They could have used the pure barite and just swapped half the containers for cocaine, but no, they had to get complicated and use bags of American mud being returned from drilling jobs in Venezuela. They brought them in through Canada. Why? I suppose Canadian customs wouldn't check as closely as ours. Then once it's in Canada, they have only to ship it across to Edmonton, a nice oil capital, so it looks like a normal oil-field transit from there. Sure, bring it down into nice wide-open Wyoming, and store it in that shed on the Broken Spoke Ranch; just tell that old moron Po they're going to drill him a wildcat and make him rich—nobody'll believe a braggart like him anyway. Fred Howard they need for the African jobs, so they could launder the profits through what look like legitimate investments offshore. Why, I'll bet they even meant to drill that hole for Po. One-stop shopping: drug storage and money laundering all in one. Problem was, there was a murder on that ranch—lady died of a cocaine overdose—and they thought they'd better not attract any more notice."

"Em . . ."

"I wonder what they wanted J.C. for. Shit, they should know they can't put that boy in harness; he's too crazy by half."

"Please."

"Oh, don't worry about me, Carlos. I have to go to Lafayette to see a friend. A boyfriend, goddamn it, and no, it has nothing to do with any of this. To hell with my little life, anyway."

❖

I WAS LATE, an hour and thirty-five minutes, to be exact; I hit commuter traffic going up the back way via Rocky Flats to Boulder, and then got stuck behind an accident on the turnpike trying to get to Lafayette. And then I'd gotten lost.

I found Jim Erikson leaning against his rental car in the parking lot outside the lawyer's office. He looked as stiff as a cigar store Indian, and about as animated.

"I'm sorry, Jim," I began. I considered lying to him, even made up a quick story about a cement truck and a school bus as I crossed the final ten feet of pavement between us, but that wooden look on Jim's face told me that no amount of apologizing or fabrication was going to make a difference.

I leaned into him and gave him a kiss, which he did not receive with a discernable welcome. Flesh hit flesh, but that was all. I felt an urge to shake him. Chaotic thoughts spilled about inside me, setting off a rebellion I didn't know I possessed: I wanted him to thrill me, damn it! What was I supposed to do, fall for some guy like Menken and go stark raving nuts like Miriam? With an angry edge to my voice, I said, "Listen, Jim, it's been one of those days. I got offered a job at about eight-fifteen this morning, and had to be there like immediately. My next appointment was at noon, to which I was fifteen minutes late, and the one after that at two. And I can't even begin to tell you how strange each of these meetings has been. I—"

"Well, I suppose it can't be helped, then," he said nonsensically, his face stiff with indignation. "Where do we go from here? You free for dinner, or do I need to get back in line?"

Fury rose up and shot words out of my mouth before I could control their tone. "No, I'm *not* free for dinner. Like I've been trying to tell you, I'm in the middle of a really weird day, and—"

"Later then?" he said, eyes flaring.

I paused, my gears fully jammed. Later? What, were we supposed to go to bed? To bed with a man who had just rendered a kiss into sawdust? I briefly considered taking him to Betty Bloom's house. What would she think of him? Would she laugh? "Well, I'm staying with this woman who doesn't like me to bring men . . . ah, guests home, and—"

"Fine, then. I'll send a card when I get home."

"Listen to me! I've got the Denver Police and the FBI or something telling me to lie low. I've got a landlady who doesn't like men. I've got a half-finished case hanging over my head. I've got—"

Jim squeezed his eyes shut. "Oh, so that's how it is. Didn't you learn *anything* out there in California, nearly getting killed? Do you go *looking* for this kind of trouble?" To himself, he muttered, "What were you thinking of, Jim? She didn't want this to happen, and you knew it."

Never argue with a wounded man, I told myself. *Try apologizing.* But when I looked down inside myself, I found not regret, but anger. Anger that he didn't care what I had been doing with my time. Anger that he was angry with me rather than worried. And yet I was too uncertain of myself to simply walk away. I took a deep breath, tried to sound upbeat. "Listen, you're going to be here several days. Can't we get together—" I stopped, realizing that of course I would be gone. Flying. I had scheduled that cross-country flight for first thing the next morning, and no one knew about that plan but me and Peggy. Yes, I had to go, what safer place could Carlos Ortega ask me to be? Wide-open space was the safest place for a ranch-bred woman like me. Out in the back of nowhere, or down the creek hidden among the cottonwoods. . . .

Jim's eyes were open again. As he read the abstraction in mine, his face went slack with resignation. He opened his mouth and spoke his mind: "Woman, you are as slippery as a cake of soap." He climbed into his rental car and rolled down the window. "If you wake up in the middle of the night and find you're a leopard with a new set of spots, I'll be at my aunt's house in Broomfield, going through her papers. Her name was Priscilla, same last name as mine, because she never married, just like you."

I stepped back and swept one arm out magnanimously, indicating that he could pass.

❖

THERE WAS NO time to grieve.

Back in Boulder, I telephoned Sergeant Ortega to tell him where I was.

"They'll know you didn't make your flight by now," he said sadly. "They'll be looking for you. Come meet me at my mother's house. You'll be safe there."

"Thanks," I said, "but I have another plan."

I heard Ortega sigh deeply. "Stay in touch?"

"Don't worry about me, Carlos. Like I say, I've got a plan."

Betty was watching me, eavesdropping from the living room. When I hung up the phone, she came into the kitchen and planted herself between me and the door that led to my room. "What's up, Sherlock?"

"Nothing. All right, something, but I think it best if I don't tell you about it."

"Have it your way."

"Anyone call?"

"I don't know," she said. "I've been out."

"No messages?"

"Not the way that thing's looking." She lifted the trash can and pointed inside at what was left of the answering machine. It was in five pieces, two large and three small, all sporting prominent fang marks. The message tape was in shreds. "Men," she commented, staring daggers out the back window at Stanley. "They're all alike, human or canine. Can't tell technology from a chew toy. Now, you know why I didn't have one."

I stared desolately at these mute remains. Had Fred Howard called again, angrily, or perhaps desperately wanting to know where I was? "Betty, what was the greeting message like that you put on there?"

"Oh, something like 'You have reached the home of Betty Bloom; now fuck off.'"

"No, seriously."

"It just said, 'You have reached Betty's machine. You know what to do.'"

That seemed uninformative enough. But had I told J.C. Menken where I was staying, and would he tell Fred if Fred asked him? I was sure I had written a spurious address on the forms I had filled out that morning, but had I given the real one at any time? I strained to remember. Couldn't. *Hell.* "Betty, I'm sorry to tell you this, but I've got to . . . um, get gone for just now. Um, there are some men who might come looking for me, and, um, it's best if they not find me. Or you." I smiled weakly.

Betty gave me a look that could fell a raccoon at twenty yards. "Well, darling, you know my opinion of men."

"I can't say you're wrong this time."

"Safety in numbers?"

"Stanley coming?"

"Sounds like a plan."

"I think we should hide my truck somewhere and take your car."

Betty began to smile. "Getaway driver. I like that."

"I'll teach you a little escape-and-evasion driving."

"Better and better." Betty pulled back her wild red hair, gathering it into an elastic ribbon to ready herself for action. "I favor a little camping, myself. The air's been so pleasant, and there's supposed to be a nice moon tonight."

I watched her move methodically about the kitchen, picking up her keys, readying a few delicacies to snack on, and a thermos of coffee. I had known her only a short while, and yet her gestures were already familiar. I took comfort, trying not to notice that the similarity lay in a self-sufficiency born of female bachelorhood. I said, "Just so long as you can get me to Jeffco Airport at dawn."

32

THE SOUND OF BETTY'S DEEP, RHYTHMIC WAS ALL BUT DROWNED out by Stanley's heavy snores. I sat in the front seat of Betty's Volvo, trying to read Miriam's journal by the thin light that shone form the open glove compartment. I'd run out of food, my back was getting stiff, and I felt stupid and alone, even with Betty and her enormous beast laid out behind me. I'd stuck my nose in a hornet's nest for sure this time, and blown my chances of building something with Jim in the process. With nowhere to be going and nothing to be doing until dawn, I needed desperately to escape the pain of losing Jim and fear of the men who wanted me gone. I needed a distraction as big as Miriam could offer. She did not disappoint me.

March 10

Joe and I are fighting already, or should I say *I'm* fighting? He just gives me that crimped-up smile of his. Didn't he even notice that I was gone for five months? Can't he move forward with me, even an inch? I try to detach and acknowledge what is, but it just gets under my skin that he doesn't seem to listen to me, and I blow up and start screaming. I try to keep it together until the appointments I have with the therapist I'm supposed to work with down here, but then the new therapist urges me not to stuff my feelings like that. She's assigned a book for me to read, which says that blowing up is just one thing I can do with anger. It says that anger is like a signal that something needs changing, but also an energy I can use to make the change happen. I have a choice: I can blow up, and just dissipate the energy (in which case, nothing changes), I can save it until later (time to think things over and decide what I want), I can decide to live with things the way they are (fat chance!), or I can use it like fuel to pull myself together and assert my needs. And thoughts. And desires.

April 5

I awoke this morning from a dream about Chandler. In the dream, he was old, and dressed in white robes. I was thanking him for everything he had taught me. I must be getting better if I can see the good along with the bad.

Cecelia's not glad to have me back. At least she's being reasonably pleasant, but she seems to have a private joke she's not telling me about. She's growing up at last, primping a little and wanting new clothes, something more than just another pair of jeans to wear while riding her horse. Life does go on. I took her to Denver to shop. The poor little dear is growing breasts!

I read on until two in the morning, following Miriam through her continuing visits to her therapist, over the hills and down into the valleys of her negotiations with her husband, and around to the autumn before the summer she died. There, the journal stopped. I closed the book and examined the cover, wondering why I hadn't checked it earlier. Sure enough, there were both starting and ending dates, just as with all the previous volumes. I opened again to the back page, looking for more of her cryptic notes. The only one I could make out said simply, "Rambling Rose." I shook my head. It could mean anything. Such as the state of her heart, or the prickliness of her mind. Or did it refer to Chandler, the man who made even Julia Richards sigh? Either way, I had one more volume to find, and I had a strong notion who had it.

33

BETTY DROPPED ME AT THE AIRPORT AS THE SUN ROSE OVER THE eastern horizon, spreading tendrils of light out across the undulating plains. As I watched Betty's Volvo disappear along the road that led back out onto Wadsworth Boulevard and her quick retreat into parts unknown, I stretched, working out the kinks born of trying to sleep spread across its front bucket seats and parking brake. My mind was a jumble of excitement over the coming flight and jitters over the search for the final volume of Miriam's journal. I longed to know what she had learned in her final year of life. The last entries left her on the verge of discovery, faithfully recording each step on her rise from rage and depression to a life of self-direction.

Just to make certain no one knew where to find me, I switched planes at the last moment, and when I telephoned Flight Service to lay in my flight plan for Douglas, I gave them a false name. Then, moving briskly out onto the tarmac, I did my pilot's walk-around, checking flaps, airframe, and fuel tanks, pitot tubes, and oil. All was in order: tanks topped off and tires inflated, no nicks or dings in the wings, fuselage, or propeller, no bird's nests in the air inlets. Satisfied that she was airworthy, I unchained the wings and tail from the tie-downs and climbed aboard.

After adjusting my seat and seat belt, I turned off the avionics and carburetor heat, set the master switch and fuel pump at the on position, primed the throttle and set it at one-quarter open, and adjusted the fuel mixture to full rich. Popping open the side window, I observed the ritual of calling, "Clear prop!" even though no one was around, and fired the engine. It burst into life instantly, filling my ears with a satisfying roar that sounded extraloud, as I lacked the protection of Peggy's excellent headphones. Sadly, the phones came and went with her and not the plane. For this flight, I would have to depend on the speaker and microphones that were mounted on the dashboard and just use my imagination to fill in the holes that engine noise and inferior speakers would bite in my communications.

Next, I moved through the final details of engine check, checking oil pressure, throttle, right and left carburetors, and the carburetor heater, switched the fuel pump off, turned on the anticollision light, the landing light, and the radios, set the transponder at standby, checked the settings on my instruments, and tipped the control wheel left and right and stepped on the rudder pedals to make sure the elevators and rudders were working.

Once the two radios were on, I set the top one to the local Air Traffic Information System frequency (126.25) and caught "Information Beta," the current update. Beta told me the current wind speed and direction (light and variable), active runway (two-niner right), and the barometric pressure (a nice high-pressure day for a bright, sunny flight). I dialed the pressure setting into the control panel and reset the altitude to the runway elevation, 5,670 feet above sea level. Flipping to frequency 121.7, I unhitched the microphone from its cradle on the instrument panel and depressed the switch. "Jeffco Ground, this is Piper two two six two foxtrot at the Air Center with 'Information Beta.' Request taxi to two-niner right."

"Six two foxtrot, okay to taxi beta, turn left onto alpha, hold short at A-one. Contact tower on one one eight point six."

"Six two foxtrot," I replied, glad that the radio was working. It was more difficult to hear the calls without Peggy's headphones, but the course I was flying would not require that I communicate all that much anyway.

I taxied slowly down the taxiway, excitement kicking the butterflies in my stomach into a maelstrom. It had been many moons since I'd flown solo, and here I was flying clear to Douglas in one hop, a distance of nearly two hundred miles. I comforted myself that for all that distance, I had to make only one landing. Chugging along aloft is the easy part of flying; it's that little interface between being airborne and becoming a three-wheeled landcraft that gives people problems.

I pulled the airplane to a stop and did my final run-up just short of the end of runway 29 left. When all proved to be in order, I picked up the microphone again, switched the radio setting to 118.6, and said, "Jeffco Tower, this is Piper two two six two foxtrot. Request permission to take off, straight-out departure."

"Six two foxtrot, permission granted."

"Six two foxtrot." My heart swelling with the rush of adventure, I taxied the final thirty feet onto the runway, rammed the throttle to the dashboard, and headed for the sky.

TWO AND A half hours later, I put the little airplane down relatively smoothly on the sainted soil of Wyoming. Landing in Douglas was almost anticlimactic after skimming along over the plains and past the mountains I had seen every day during my childhood. The Converse County Airport is fairly new, a long strip of neatly laid tarmac along the north bank of the Platte River. I had radioed the airport's unicom for advisory, was told by a bored and garbled voice that the current runway was 28, made sure I was lining up on the new airport north of town and not the old one, which had been turned into a drag strip, and set up my landing. I squitched down at 8:30 A.M. to a welcoming committee of grazing antelope and scattering jackrabbits and taxied to the ramp. I had my choice of tie-downs. Mine was, in fact, the only plane there.

All was prim and proper and lovely. There was a small truck ready to fuel the plane. There was in fact very little else in sight, just one large blue hangar building and a tired old yellow tractor, which served both to plow the runway in the winter and mow the grass in the summer. Converse County Airport was my kind of airport.

After phoning the rental-car agency (Gubbels Ford/Chrysler, actually;

Charlie Burris said he would be out from town to pick me up in a nice new Taurus in just a few minutes, first hundred miles free), I put through a call to Sergeant Ortega. "I'm in Douglas," I said into the mouthpiece. "I've got a rental car. Camouflage. No one will know me without my truck."

"Oh, Em, that's you. Okay, good. Listen, no one but you and I know where you are, so why don't we keep it that way?"

"I'm just going to make a few visits here. Nothing risky, just a casual chat with a few ordinary citizens."

"Em, I been on the phone all morning. Those nice gentlemen you met here yesterday agree with me you need to be in protective custody. You can't trust anybody out there. Please, Em, you'd be safer back here in Denver. You can stay with my mother, okay?"

"Jesus, Carlos, what do you take me for, a moron?"

Sergeant Ortega said nothing.

Filling the silence, I said, "Ha, ha, ha. Fine, so I jump the gun sometimes. This time, I am being a good girl. I want to live long and be happy."

"By flying straight to the scene of the crime. *Estás loca, amiga.* I don't like it. Who are you seeing? Not Mr. Bradley?"

"I'm going to talk to a nice law-abiding sheriff, if he'll see me. Would you please call him and see if he'll let me hear that nine-one-one tape?"

"Em Hansen, you play with fire."

"I'm doing the best I can, Carlos."

Pain squeezed his voice into a whisper as he said, "Check in again soon, please."

"Sure."

"And Em . . ." he began again but stalled out.

"What?"

"Sorry about your boyfriend."

"How did you know about that?" I squealed.

"I'm a detective, remember?"

"Betty—"

"Ms. Bloom is sitting across the desk from me right now. *She* is enjoying a nice safe cup of coffee and eating a nice ordinary doughnut. I find her very sane and charming, and her dog is a wonder among beasts."

Now it was my turn to sigh. It was a beautiful brisk morning in Douglas, but yet the warmth and clutter of Sergeant Ortega's office called to me. No, I wanted—just what did I want? I wanted Carlos to be my friend and not ask. I wanted not to feel foolish or guilty, and not dwell on the fact that I could have phoned the lawyer's office to tell Jim I'd be late but hadn't. What was I worrying about? The loss of possibilities didn't even hurt much yet; I was too certain I didn't want to wind up in a sexually suffocating marriage like Miriam's. But did that mean I had to step over the edge and go looking for a man who was guaranteed to hurt me? "I'll check in at noon," I said, and hung up the phone.

I GUESS I lied to Carlos, at least if you count errors of omission. I didn't go first to the sheriff's office. I went to see Po Bradley's estranged wife, Gwen, in her nice house down by the Douglas Community Club. I was willing to bet that she didn't talk to Po a whole lot anymore, and I was right.

We had settled in her kitchen, I swinging nervously back and forth on a stool by the breakfast bar, she inhaling deeply from a cigarette, leaning on the counter as she squinted at me through the smoke, when I next called Denver. "Carlos," I said into the mouthpiece, "I'm at Gwen Bradley's house here in town. We're having a nice chat. Were you able to arrange my next, ah, appointment okay?"

"Yes," he said mournfully. "He says he'll see you at two o'clock. But that's it, Em. You give yourself into his protection or there's no more help from me."

"So you think he's safe?" I asked wryly.

In reply, I heard some Spanish phrases that were new to me.

As I hung up the phone, Gwen Bradley handed me a freshly brewed cup of coffee and lit another cigarette off the butt of the last. "So where were we? You're trying to find out who killed that woman," she said gruffly.

"No. Well, as I said, I'm trying to help—"

"Oh hogwash. That daughter of hers was a fright; I wouldn't drive five minutes out of my way for her, let alone come all the way up here from Denver twice."

"As you wish." I shrugged my shoulders. There was no merit in arguing with the Gwen Bradleys of the world.

"So you're thinking Po might of done it."

I shrugged again. "Did he?"

"Aw, hell, I got no use for the man, but he ain't no murderer. Too busy running around stickin' his pecker where it don't belong to kill anyone. And let me tell you, missy, as you like to know already being raised in these parts, a man don't go killing anybody less he's got a good reason to. It's just too wasteful of his Godalmighty freedom if he gets caught. Not that no one would get all that upset about it 'cept old Elwin."

"Tell me about the sheriff. What's he got against your husband?"

"Aw, Po swiped his girlfriend back senior year, just for sport. Don't reflect well on me that I married him anyway when he was done with her, does it? 'Cept he had me pumped up already."

"So Po's cast his charms around right along."

"Po's a horse's butt end. Swiping women out from under Elwin's nose is a lifelong hobby for that boy. It gets Elwin so riled, see."

"Just for sport."

"Just for sport."

"Then he and Elwin competed for Miriam Menken's attention, too?"

"Of course."

"Funny, I didn't get the impression Duluth had personal feelings for the deceased."

"Feelings? You mean like emotions? He ain't got but the one, and hatred's got nothing to do with affection, let me tell you." Her hard eyes glittered.

"How'd he get elected, then? Seems to me we usually get someone up for sheriff we can at least respect."

"Oh, we did. Took early retirement for a heart attack. Ol' Elwin's just finishing out his term for him. But he'll probably get reelected; we're used to him now."

"You think he does a good job?"

"I think he does an average job. But let's get back to the meat of this here chat. I don't think either one of them Don Juans scored with that one. She had a little self-respect, Lord love her." A nasty grin spread across Gwen's smoke-furrowed face, revealing a line of dentistry that spoke of too little care and too many cigarettes. "Wouldn't bow to the level of no local cowboy types."

I was beginning to have a hard time telling who Gwen Bradley held in the greatest contempt: her husband, the sheriff, men in general, or everyone ever born. "Did she get to know anyone in town before it happened?"

"Nope, just lallygagged out there on that ranch. Had everything delivered."

But Po knew that Miriam could dance. "She ever come down to the Moose?"

"Not that I heard. Course, I don't frequent the place, myself," she said loftily.

No, you just hide out here licking your abscesses, but your stooges are down there each and every Friday night, aren't they.

Gwen lit another cigarette off the butt of the last. "Course, that husband of hers showed up every weekend, sure as death and taxes. You could set your watch by seeing that Mercedes-Benz roll onto the Cold Springs Road off the interstate."

"He always drove?"

"How else you gonna get anywhere in these parts? Ride a horse?" She laughed at her own joke, a long, rasping, rhythmic cough.

I was about to reply, No, you can fly into Casper and rent a car, as he suggested I do, but instead I said, "Yeah, well, J.C. Menken is something of a creature of habit."

"In Friday evening, out Sunday afternoon. Good doggy." She laughed again.

"You were telling me about Po's attentions to Miriam. The bad doggy."

Gwen almost hacked herself unconscious with bitter mirth. "Yep, he paid her court all right. Made every excuse to show up at that homestead, I hear.

"Po liked to play the big man," she continued cuttingly, "pretending he had a spread the size of Texas with a hundred thousand cows eating grass as green as Astroturf. Even started to carouse with them rattlesnake jet-setters up there in Saratoga, he did."

"Oh?"

Gwen picked at a bit of tobacco from her unflitered cigarette that had gotten stuck to the tip of her tongue. "Well, that's how it is when you inherit a ranch but you ain't got the talent to work it. Lazy old good-for-nothing leases the land out to anyone or their brother, lets them graze it to sagebrush, and they *know* that." To her cigarette, she added, "Never would work an hour if he could spend two figuring out how to avoid it."

I decided the time was right to cut a bit deeper. "That how he got involved with those high rollers down in Saratoga?"

Gwen looked at me askance, thought a while before answering. Making her mind up, she flicked her cigarette in disgust and said, "Yeah, when that started, that's when I got out, made him buy this house in cash quick, before he put us both out on the street."

"You mean before he sucked the ranch up his nose." *In cash?*

Gwen's eyes closed. "Oh, you know about that, huh?" When her eyes opened, she spoke quickly, more easily, obviously relieved to have his little secret out. "Oh, yeah, that boy likes to think he can play like the big dogs. Keeps his old tail wagging, y'see." She shook her head, willing her bitterness to consume her sorrow.

I set down my coffee mug and rubbed both hands over my face. "I don't suppose when he's down in Saratoga he keeps company with a man named Al Rosenblatt, does he?"

Gwen scowled fiercely. "I stay out of that business." She looked sharply at me. "This Rosenbap ain't the big blondie in the BMW, is he? Naw, blondie don't look even half Jewish."

I wanted to laugh at the boneheadedness of her stereotype, except that it wasn't funny. Even less funny was the realization that Po knew damned well who Chandler was, and had known all along. So he'd been playing me, and successfully. "No, the man in the BMW would be Chandler Jennings, I think."

"Oh, yeah, I heard that name once or twice."

"And you've seen him."

"Well, yeah, he started coming around two, three years back. Hah. Comes in over the back road like so much bad weather."

"Over the mountains?"

Gwen gestured tiredly out her kitchen window toward the ramparts of the Laramie Range. "Yep. Comes in over the Esterbrook Road with his little deliveries from Saratoga. *Damn* Po. We was doin' fine. I could of run that spread without him, let him fool around all he wants, but no, he's got to go and get hitched up with that crowd. Wildcat oil wells, indeed!"

"You got this house out of it," I said, half to comfort and half to confirm my suspicions.

Gwen's eyes turned hard again. "I'd rather have my dignity."

I looked deep into her eyes, mapping the damage. Chandler had barely met this woman, yet here was his mark. Miriam. Julia. Mrs. Wentworth. Heather. Cecelia. Why did I want to meet him? Was I *una loca*, as Sergeant Ortega said? Or did I just want to map the rest of this wreckage with my own eyes, then decide for myself just how much of him was devil and how much prince? "Gwen, would you have any idea how to reach this guy?"

She looked at me askance. "You looking for what he's selling?"

"No. I'm just trying to find out—aw, hell, wouldn't you like to get Po's connection behind bars? Think: did he talk to him on the phone ever? You might have an old phone bill, or . . ."

Gwen examined me narrowly as she took a last drag off the short end of her current cigarette and groped for another. "Wait here a minute," she said, and left the room. She was gone for perhaps five minutes, and I could hear her rummaging around through closets at the other end of the house. When she returned, she was carrying a packet of phone bills, all stuffed back into their envelopes and held together with a blue elastic band. Still holding her precious cigarette between her first two fingers, she picked through the stack with her thumb and finally selected one. "This ought to have it," she said. She pulled the pages out of the envelope and began to read, holding the sheets at arm's length to get them in focus. "Here, this call's to Saratoga, and this one, too. Same number both times. Try that."

"Let me write it down," I said, pulling my notepad out of my pocket.

Gwen was talking again. "Course, I don't think blondie is the kingpin of that gang. He's strikes me more as the delivery boy. Or the scout."

"How do you figure?"

"I hear cocaine costs a bundle, but we wound up with more, not less."

"And?"

"And he was always asking questions. Cocaine for information, that's the way it seemed. I never did figure out what the money was for."

"What about the oil lease?"

"Oh, sure, that was the way they packaged it."

"And then Miriam's dead, and they change their minds."

Gwen's sharp little eyes riveted on mine again. "Yeah."

I put the notepad back in my pocket. "Gwen, just one woman to another? I suggest you go on not liking it and go on keeping your nose out of it."

"Mum's the word."

"You ever tell any of this to Sheriff Duluth?"

Gwen Bradley reeled back her head like I'd just made a bad smell. "Why would I want to go and do that?" she inquired as she lined the cigarette up with her narrow lips one more time.

PARKING THE RENTAL car by the towering jackalope statue that graces the main drag of Douglas, I walked until I found a public pay booth and dialed the number Gwen Bradley had dug out of her husband's telephone bills. A deep male voice answered. "Hello?"

"Oh, hi. May I please speak with Chandler?"

"Chandler?" the voice said, sounding annoyed. I heard the soft rumbling of a hand being placed over the receiver, but the cover was so sloppy that I heard, "Where's loverboy gotten to these days? Oh, back up there with the movie stars and the big tits, huh? You ever figure out where his hidey-hole is up there?" The muffling went away, and the voice said, "He's not here. Who should I tell him called?"

"Oh, just . . . um . . . a friend." I tried to sound nervous, like I was a bat-brained female looking for sex or drugs, or both.

"Sure, lady. Well, he's not here, so I can't help you." I could hear male tittering in the background.

"Thank you." Movie stars with big tits. Was Chandler in Los Angeles? No, movie stars *and* big tits. I rang off and dialed information. "Jackson," I said, when asked what city. It was the only place in Wyoming that had movie stars as a regular diet, and it was world-famous for the mountains known as Les Grands Tetons, bigger than anything Hollywood could ever produce with mere silicon.

"Go ahead."

"Do you list an Edward Jennings?" It was worth a try.

"No, I'm sorry."

I hung up the phone and thought a while. Jackson, Wyoming, a nice little town that had been eaten alive by tourists. *Why would Chandler hide there?* Even as I asked myself the question, I had the answer: *Because he would blend right in. The old boy knows the fine art of hiding in plain sight!*

I lifted the phone back off the hook and dialed Jackson information again. "Do you list a place called the Rambling Rose?"

Pause. "Here's your number," said the operator, and clicked me off onto an automatic number server. I held my breath, punching the numbers into the phone before I could forget them. The phone rang once, twice. Clicked. "Rambling Rose Bed-and-Breakfast," a hearty female voice told me.

"Oh, hi," I said winningly. "I'm looking for my friend Chandler Jennings. Is he staying there?"

There was a slight pause. "He's not here just now," she said, curiosity giving her tone a lilt. "May I take a message?"

"Do you expect him later?"

Another pause, this time with rustling of paper. "He'll be back tomorrow afternoon. Whom may I say is calling?"

"Thanks, that's all I wanted to know." I hung up quickly, before she could ask again.

SHERIFF ELWIN DULUTH seemed as irritated by my presence as he had the week before. "So you want to hear the tape," he muttered as he loaded a cassette into a machine. "Hold on to your hat." The machine began to fight him. He punched buttons, swore.

"Is that the original?" I asked.

"No way. We keep that locked up. This is a copy we made to send to Denver for that psychiatrist lady." At last, he figured out which button made the tape play and punched it.

I heard a squawk and a bunch of static, and then the dispatcher's voice, barely intelligible over the tinny noise of the recording equipment: "Sheriff's Department." The voice was answered by a commotion and the roaring of the equipment, but no voices. The dispatcher's voice came on again. "State your name and your emergency, please."

In the background, I heard a woman scream: a long, harrowing sound descending into a groan, coming from some distance from the telephone. "Help me!" the woman pleaded. "Please." There was weeping, and the sounds of more struggle. "Oh, God, please *stop* him!"

The dispatcher's voice came again: "State your name, please."

The phone was dropped, picked up again. "Cecelia." This voice was close to the telephone, barely above a whisper. I wouldn't have understood what had been said if I hadn't known the voice.

"Who?"

"Cecelia Menken." A crash in the background.

"Do you require assistance?" the dispatcher's monotonous voice inquired.

"Um, yes. My mother—" Another crash, and heavy footfalls. Hysterical screaming began anew.

"Do you require an ambulance?"

"Um, yes. Anything."

"State your location, please."

"Um, the ranch."

"You at Po Bradley's old homestead?" the dispatcher said, interpreting the display on her instrument.

"Yes. And, um, can you hurry?"

"We have a cruiser on the way, dear, and the ambulance will follow. Make sure your gates and doors are unlocked so they can get in. Can you do that safely?"

"Um . . ." This last sound quavered with fear. The crashes were getting louder now.

"Who's in the house with you?" the dispatcher asked.

"Please, *God!*" the voice in the background wailed.

The line clicked dead.

34

DESPERATELY NEEDING A FRIEND TO TALK TO, I FOUND MY WAY back to the telephone. I began to dial Ortega's number. I wanted to tell him what I had heard, that she had died in agony, that she had sounded not just frightened and in pain but also incredibly *sad*. But I couldn't bear to hear him worry about me again.

I hung and fussed through the phone book for a moment, looking for the county listings. Dialed. A woman's voice said, "County coroner."

"Mr. Wilder, please."

"Oh, he's down at the drugstore," the woman said. "Getting some salve."

I thanked her and headed down the sidewalk along Center Street toward the R-D Drugstore, wondering abstractedly just what kind of skin affliction was going around among public employees. As I neared the doorway, a slight man with a washed-out mustache, wire-rimmed glasses, and a classic old palamino-colored Stetson hat was just walking rather stiffly out the door, carrying a small paper sack. "Mr. Wilder?" I called.

He turned. Waited expectantly.

I introduced myself. "You've probably heard about me by now. I'm trying to help Cecelia Menken."

He nodded and blinked, his eyelids coming to rest a bit lower than they had been, as if on guard.

"I was wondering if I could ask you a few questions about the deceased."

"I can't talk about that," he answered.

"Well, I know this is a murder case, and as yet unresolved, but—"

"And I'm a sworn servant of this county. Now, if you don't mind," he said, bending stiffly forward in preparation for his continued transit up the sidewalk.

"Was she badly bruised?" I asked.

Fenton Wilder brought himself up with a start and squinted at me from behind his glasses. He may not have been willing to use his voice, but his body English spoke volumes; it said, *Now, how would you know about that?* Recovering himself, he said, "Good day, miss," headed along to his Carry-All, climbed in, and drove away.

AS THE GATE to the old homestead of the Broken Spoke Ranch was locked, I parked the rental car by the side of the road outside the cattle guard and climbed over it, closing the final two-tenths of a mile to the old Bradley homestead on foot. The air was brisk but clear, bringing the distant backdrop of the mountains into a sharp, pale float beyond the ranch house. No dust kicked up around my boots; the winter's snows had left the hard, dry ground packed as firm as asphalt. As I walked, I studied the bumps and ruts beneath my feet, then checked to see if my boots had left tracks. They had not, or at least no markings your average white-boy sheriff might notice. I wondered what condition the earth had been in the night Miriam had been murdered.

I made a complete circuit around the house, looking in at each window. Nothing had changed in the week since I'd seen it. Through one window, I could see both the kitchen telephone Cecelia must have called from and the passageway through to the bedrooms. There were bare wooden floors and plastered walls between the kitchen and that hallway. The sound must have amplified as in a drum.

I shook my head. No wonder Cecelia had blocked the memory.

"That's where they found the girl," a voice said behind me.

I spun around. Po Bradley stood not twenty feet behind me, one foot up on the outside of the split-rail fence that kept livestock out of the dooryard. Po, the one man in Douglas I did not want to see or have see me. "Nice to see you again," he said.

I glanced quickly around, alarmed that I hadn't heard him approach. I couldn't see his truck. I looked back at him, scanned his hips and hands to make certain he wasn't armed. "Where'd you come from?" I asked, trying to make the question sound friendly, which it wasn't.

"Oh, an old hand has his ways of getting around," he said slyly.

I could see my car up by the entrance road, where I'd left it carefully tucked out of sight of the road. It stood alone. I looked to the paddock by the barns. No truck.

"No, I didn't come from the barn, either," he said, now clearly enjoying himself. "Come on now; don't you think I know my way around the place I grew up on?"

I scanned the surrounding territory: the hay fields, the line of as-yet-leafless cottonwoods that followed the banks of the stream. I followed the trees to the junction with the irrigation ditch that watered the hay fields, and caught a glint of chrome behind a budding willow, just beyond the requisite strands of barbed wire that would keep the livestock away from this steep-sided approach to life-giving water.

Po chuckled. "That's right, the irrigation ditch. Now, a fellah wanted to get onto this place and not leave no tracks, what would he do?"

I didn't like the way this was going. He was right: all a man had to do was walk in along the dry ditch, do his dirty deed, retrace his steps, and lift the floodgate. *Whoosh,* his tracks would be erased. I almost asked, Is that how it happened? but caught myself in time.

Very carefully, I started wandering toward the gate that led out through the rail fence. Po matched my pace. I continued walking toward my car, glancing at him only as if I was really thinking about something else, casually checking to make certain he was not armed.

"Didn't expect to see you back here so soon," he crooned. "Though, I must say it's a nice sight, a young thing like you around the old place again."

"Thanks," I muttered. I kept on walking and talking, moving toward my car. "It's a nice place. Don't see many like it anymore. Just wanted another look."

"Sure, sure," Po said, swinging his near shoulder closer and closer to me with each stride. "Just a little visit to admire the scenery."

I was halfway to the car now, and if need be, I was certain I could out-run him. I picked up the pace.

"You're a little late for lunch," Po continued, "but you can come on up to my place anyways. I don't mind an early dinner."

As my mind worked to decode the threat behind his words, part of it reeled at the thought that this line of palaver was enough to rouse the local women. *Winters must be pretty boring here in Converse County,* I thought. *But wait, everyone except his wife holds this guy in affectionate esteem, and they distrust the Sheriff. They think Duluth wants to stick him with a murder he didn't commit. Or for which they don't want to see him hang.* I shot Po a sidelong glance. Was I making him nervous? "Well, here's my car," I said, quickly jumping in and slamming the door. Then, not to seem spooked by his behavior, I rolled down the window and casually let my arm drape across the lock button, dropping it home. Maybe he'd forget he'd seen me. Maybe he didn't even know the men from Saratoga were looking for me. Maybe pigs had wings.

Po leaned his elbows onto the window frame. "Maybe you want to clear things up, where our old sheriff does not," he drawled.

"Maybe I do."

"Think on it. The irrigation ditch." And with that, he straightened up, turned, and started to walk away.

I leaned out of the window and called after him. "Wait! Po, why don't you just come out with it? Come on, tell me what you're thinking!" I now had my hand on the ignition. If he tried anything, I could run for it. "Tell me about Saratoga, damn it!"

Po turned back. "Saratoga?"

"Yes, Saratoga. How did Miriam know to rent this place? Did you meet her there?"

Po looked at me appraisingly. "Well, I suppose you could say I did."

"Where? Maybe at a dance?"

Po smiled saucily, bounced his head around with an effort at charm. "Well, now—"

"Or did maybe Chandler Jennings make the connection?"

Po let his face hang. He seemed to age ten years in an instant. "Oh, you know him, huh?"

"Never met the guy. But you have. You described him to me last Saturday as if he was a total stranger, which he is not."

Po spread out one hand in a gesture of dismissal. "Can't blame a fella for trying."

"Trying what?"

Po leveled his brow, tried to look dignified. "Trying to bring him to the law's attention. Hell, I didn't want anyone to know about that other stuff, though."

"The drugs he brought you."

Po tipped his head coyly. "Liniment."

"You don't shove liniment up your nose."

Po set his lower lip in a pout.

"I won't tell the town about the coke, Po, but you'd better start talking."

Po straightened up and let out his breath. Looked around quickly. "Well, okay, I went up to Saratoga a couple times."

"And met this man Chandler. You meet him through some other men, or you meet him directly?"

"No, just him, at least at first. I met him in a bar. Seemed a nice-enough sort."

"But then he offered you cocaine, and got real friendly. Asked you a lot of questions about your ranch."

"How'd you know?"

"So he starts coming out to the ranch, kind of has his self a look around. Says he has a friend wants to drill a test on your ranch, and he'll pay good money for the lease, right?"

"Right. I figger what the hell, I don't have to tell him there's no oil down these parts."

"So they front you the money. What was the name the investors used?"

"The who?"

"Whose name was on the check?"

"Oh. Island Research Group."

"And what bank was it drawn on?"

"Now, that was real interesting: it was from some bank down in the Caribbean. I figured that was where the island stuff come from. The money was good, though."

"But they stopped moving forward on the plans to drill when Miriam was killed."

Po considered this. "About then, yeah. I was real disappointed. Not to have no hole in my ranch, mind you, but they was going to send me to that island of theirs while the drilling was going on, just so I wouldn't have to be bothered by all the noise."

"I'll bet," I said dryly, wondering just how dumb he thought I was. "The rental of your sister's place, the old homestead—how'd you make that connection?"

"One day, he's making a visit and he says, 'I know this woman as like to rent a place for the summer.' "

"*Chandler's* visiting."

Po looked at me quickly, as if he was afraid he'd suddenly given away too much. Shrugged. Went on. "Yeah. He says, 'She needs a place to stay where they can keep horses. You know a place like that?' And I say, 'Sure.' Well, I told Annie I'd take the money and put it in her bank account, see."

"With a nice little management fee for you."

Po looked hurt. "Of course."

My mind was going a mile a minute. "Did he say who had him looking for a ranch? Was it Miriam asked him to look?"

Po thought, then gave me a look like he really had it figured. "No, I don't think so, because after she came and he dropped in on her, she didn't seem a-tall glad to see him. Sent him away. Told him, 'Buzz off and stay away from my daughter.' "

"You saw and heard this all."

"Yes—or no, I er . . . dropped by later on, and she told me then."

No, you were downwind behind the cover of those willows, right where the air would carry their words to you. "Of course. So after Sheriff Duluth and the others left the scene that night, you thought you'd better cut the water into the irrigation ditch to cover your eavesdropping old tracks."

Po twisted his face up and began to scratch the back of his head.

I fired the engine, but before I drove off, I said, "No wonder ol' Elwin thinks you did it."

BACK IN TOWN, I dialed Sergeant Ortega, reaching him this time at his mother's, where he'd gone for dinner. "Carlos, I'll be hiding out in the car tonight and then heading due west tomorrow. It'll be a long flight, but I'll check in with you as soon's I get there, and you can pull rank and track me though the FAA's Flight Following Service, if you insist. But you can help me even more by getting into the records for commercial flights from Denver to Casper and back on the night of the murder. Here's why. J.C. was the one who put the idea in my head to fly here, like he'd done it a hundred times, and he even knew the flight times. But Gwen Bradley says he always arrived by car. And I got to believe that for the night of the murder, his whereabouts have already been checked, meaning he wasn't out of sight long enough to have driven up here and back himself. But what if he flew? Just to be thorough, you could check the airport records for private landings and takeoffs into Casper. A person could land here in Douglas without being noticed, perhaps, except then he'd have to have a car waiting, which would defeat the process of slipping in and out anonymously by air. It's a long shot, but y'know?"

Then I phoned J.C. himself. He sounded puzzled. "Em? Where are you? I heard from Fred Howard this morning. He asked if I knew where you were. He said he offered you a job and—"

"Never mind that. Please. I was just wondering—who was it found that ranch for Miriam to rent anyway?"

I was surprised by Menken's answer. "Cindey Howard. Why?"

35

I PLANNED THE FLIGHT TO JACKSON OVER THE SMALL COUNTER OF the service window at the airport. The smooth surface lent itself to the job of marking out the long overland route on the air charts. I would need two charts to make the crossing, both the Cheyenne sectional and the Salt Lake City sectional. Both faces of each chart gave a detailed view of landmarks, flight obstructions, and airports over a strip of land eight degrees of longitude east to west and two and a half north to south, or about 400 miles by 120. Like an atlas, the charts showed ground elevations by contours, slices of color, and by shaded relief. The airstrip at Douglas rested at 4,929 feet. Most of the ground I would cover between there and Jackson would be higher. I would be flying a plane the size of a two-seater Volkswagen with only a 100-horsepower engine and an unpressurized cabin. I figured I had an effective ceiling on a cool day of about twelve thousand feet. On a hot day, I would be lucky to make ten.

I laid out my course carefully, dodging well to one side or another of the mountains that lay between me and Jackson. It would be a small matter to swing north of Casper Mountain, avoiding the northern end of the Laramie Range, and from there I had a fairly clear shot two hundred miles westward along the Sweetwater River drainage to South Pass, the low point on the Continental Divide, over which the emigrants had climbed on the Oregon Trail. But South Pass was as far north as I could go: north of that lay the formidable barrier of the Wind River Range, a one-hundred-mile-long rampart of wilderness peaks soaring to twelve and thirteen thousand feet. From South Pass, I would fly northwestward up a valley past Big Piney and Pinedale, between the Wind Rivers and the Wyoming Range. The valley was high in elevation, replete with mesas rising to 7,500 feet, but it boasted several airports should I need to abort the trip, and it was plenty wide, so I would have plenty of room to maneuver. At the north end of the valley, where the mountain ranges met, I would need to turn west into the narrow confines of Hoback Canyon. Hoback was only a few miles wide, and I would need to make a few shallow dogleg turns to dodge minor kinks in the canyon and then turn ninety degrees to the north fifteen miles in, but I could stay below nine thousand feet all the way to Jackson Hole. All told, I would cover about 320 miles.

The only alternative route would take me to the north end of the Wind River Range, past Riverton and Dubois and over Togwotee Pass, then southwest into Jackson Hole along the Snake River. This seemed a less good idea. Togwotee Pass lay at 9,658 feet, between peaks that soared thousands of feet higher. With the minimal ceiling the Piper could reach, I could barely skim the top of the pass, and I'd have little effective room to turn if turbulence or a downdraft was waiting for me at the top. Peggy was right: I wanted no part of mountain flying.

I laid down my pencil and rubbed my eyes. Even on a nice day, I would face a head wind flying west, perhaps ten or fifteen knots. At full bore, the Piper could cruise at one hundred knots, or nautical miles, per hour. Subtract fifteen, and I would peak at eighty-five knots. Three hundred and twenty statute miles was 280 nautical miles. The math wasn't pretty: three and a half hours—a long, buffeting, tiring ride for a beginner.

The man behind the counter let me use his phone to call the Casper Flight Service station for a weather briefing. Casper forecast clear skies with a five- to ten-knot westerly wind until early the next afternoon, at which time the weather was going to deteriorate steadily toward evening, when storms were possible across the western half of the state.

I then called a rental-car agency and arranged to pick up a car at the Jackson Hole Airport at 11:00 A.M. I was able to choose among four rental car agencies: serving two major national parks, a skier's paradise, and a fly fisherman's nirvana, Jackson Hole's was the busiest airport in the state.

I reached for my figures. Three and a half hours' flying would get me into Jackson well ahead of the weather, as long as I was in the air by 8:30. For safety, I'd make that seven, or earlier even. The sun would be up by 6:30 and shining along my tail, not into my eyes. Not a problem.

Satisfied, I made notes of the radio frequencies I would need during the trip. Then I folded up my charts and nodded to the man who stood whistling behind the counter.

"Heading out in the morning?" he asked.

My heart skipped a beat. He had overheard my call. I was slipping. Sure, he looked like a nice paternal sort of guy, and I was up home in my own territory, but this was not a vacation trip I was on. Trying to look unperturbed, I said, "Yes. I'd like to pay my bill now, please."

"You going to leave your rental car here for Charlie Burris to pick up, or do you need a lift back from town in the morning? I'll be going home soon, and no one'll be out here all night." He looked kind of concerned about me.

That was the one wrinkle I hadn't smoothed out. I had thought of turning in the car and sleeping in the sleeping bag I had in the plane, but that would mean two nights in a row sitting up, and I was already feeling the fatigue. Besides, Po knew the car now, would have figured out where I'd gotten it, and would know I had come by air. Turning in the car would be a signal that I was leaving town, and as mine was the only plane there, I would be easy to trace. "I was thinking of leaving it here tomorrow. I won't be gone long," I said, hoping that, at worst, this man would gossip around town that I was just going up for a spin and would be back soon.

"No problem. Where you staying?"

I didn't answer fast enough.

The man smiled kindly. "Camping out, huh? I couldn't help but notice the gear you had in the plane. Listen, I got a daughter your age, so I know the score. Why not pull your car into the hangar here for the night? You'll be a lot more comfortable inside. I'll be back by seven tomorrow morning. Got to fly down to Denver."

I nodded. As he turned to leave, I said, "You mind not letting anyone know I'm out here? I'd feel safer that way."

He gave me a thumbs-up and headed toward the adjoining hangar to open the overhead door.

◈

I DREAMED I was running from a airplane, a fast twin-engine job with a long snout and propellers that wanted to chew me to pieces. It grew closer and closer, the sound of its engines eating up the sky. I sat up abruptly in the car inside the hangar beside the airstrip, suddenly awake and aware that the sound, at least, was real.

It was pitch-dark.

Who's coming in for a landing in the middle of the night? I wondered as the sound of the engines faded, turned, turned again, and began to increase in volume once again. Someone was flying a nice neat landing pattern in a fast airplane.

I climbed out of my sleeping bag and out of the car, wandered out of the hangar area and into the darkened lounge that faced the runway. I was just in time to see the twin-engine Beechcraft roll up on the tie-down apron. It was a hot little plane, with enough windows down the side to suggest that it had seats for six or eight passengers. It came to a stop, and a door opened. Instinctively, I pulled back into the shadows at the edge of the row of windows. Even as my mind caught up with my reflexes, I knew that I had seen the man who now stood silhouetted in the doorway of the plane: Al Rosenblatt, the man who preferred not to be seen.

The cold of the night air cut into me like a knife.

A man stepped out of the shadows beside the building and walked toward the plane. Po Bradley. Rosenblatt withdrew into the airplane and was replaced by Fred Howard.

I squeezed up against the wall and held my breath.

Hushed conversation ripped back and forth among the three men. I could not hear what they were saying until Fred Howard left the plane and drew Po toward the building. Through the seam in the doorjamb, I could make out the following words: "You're sure."

"Yeah, sure, she's here. I seen her this afternoon pokin' her nose about out at the ranch, just like I said on the phone."

"And she's still here."

"Yeah! Look there! Her plane's still tied down, like I told ya. I saw the sticker on her car, called the agency, asked around, and that's the story. There are no secrets in a town this size. She flew that there plane here from Denver, and as you can see for yourself, it's still here."

"Then you don't know where she's staying."

"Nope! I tell ya, I checked every motel and hotel in town, but no car. She's a sly little thing, kind of slips in and out, thinks no one sees her." Po laughed, as if it was a good joke. The sound sliced through the air.

There was a pause, a scuffing of shoes on pavement. "Don't let her leave," said Fred Howard.

"What? No, a'course not."

"No, I don't think you understand."

"Well—"

I heard a cough in the crisp air. Across the floor of the room, I saw a play of shadows as another man emerged from the lighted aircraft and moved toward the building. He was large and broad-shouldered, and he threw a shadow the size of a truck. As he neared the doorway, I heard Fred Howard say, "Hugh, you stay here with this man. He'll point her out. You do the rest," and then, in heavy disgust, he added, "Our friend Po here doesn't have the stomach."

I heard Po say, "But—"

"You want to make yourself as unpopular as Hansen? It's your ball-game, shithead." After a moment, footfalls whispered away toward the plane, and Fred Howard's shadow came careening through the empty lounge.

As the twin fired its engines for takeoff, I heard the new man ask, "There a man here during business hours?" His voice was easy, matter-of-fact.

"Yes," said Po. "You're not really gonna—"

"I don't like this setup. Too out in the open."

Suddenly, the doorknob rattled. I stopped breathing altogether.

The man said, "Locked. And that hangar door is buttoned down tight. How 'bout this entrance road? There more than the one way in here?"

Po's voice came smaller, tighter. "No. She'd have to come this way."

"Then we'll set up down there."

As the sound of their feet crunching on the pavement receded toward the parking lot, I slid to the floor and buried my head in my arms.

♦

THE WEAK GLOW from the numbers on my wristwatch counted out the hours and minutes. I had pulled my sleeping bag out of the car, and now I sat huddled behind a stack of boxes on the cold concrete floor at one corner of the hangar, waiting, listening. I thought of finding the telephone in the darkness, of calling the Sheriff's Department, but that guaranteed nothing. The big man might just as easily shoot me through the door of a police cruiser as through the window of my car or the plane, and what if he heard me placing the call? I had certainly heard him easily enough. No, I would wait until dawn, when I could see where he was hiding, and then call the Sheriff's Department. Duluth would take pleasure in rousting Po out of his stakeout, I told myself, and I would have a chance to get away by air.

In those long, cramped hours of fear, I had oceans of time to contemplate each fact and dark trail that led outward from the scene of Miriam's killing, and I faced the fact that I had no real confidence in Sheriff Duluth. Po Bradley was up to his eye sockets in the trouble that swarmed all around me, but that didn't mean he had killed Miriam Menken. What had the sheriff been doing before he answered Cecelia's call?

As the long minutes stretched into hours, I formulated one detailed plan of escape after another, but none seemed safer than staying where I was. I could unchain the airplane and fly away, but I had no experience flying in the dark, had no flashlight with me in case I lost the cabin lights and could not read the dash. Depths and distances read differently in the dark from altitude, Peggy had told me, and it was easy to misgage how far away a lighted city or even the end of a runway was. I could try instead to drive like hell with my headlights off and hope that the element of surprise worked in my favor, but I knew from having watched the airport attendant raise and lower the enormous hangar door to put in my car that anyone within a mile of the place would hear it and have plenty of time to notice my car leaving the building. Or I could try to take the road on foot, but I had no idea from which direction I must conceal myself.

I dreamed of calling Sergeant Ortega. I would admit my foolishness and say good-bye, hear a kind and trusted voice before I died. As fear and fatigue danced and multiplied, I resolved finally to proceed as planned. I would wait until the attendant returned at seven. He would distract the men who waited for me while I unchained the plane from the tie-down apron, and I'd be off. They wouldn't know where I was going. They couldn't follow. I would be away. All I had to do was get the plane off the ground without winning a bullet through the gas tanks.

With the first glimmerings of daylight, I heard a truck engine boom to life at the far corner of the parking lot. So they had been there all night, waiting, only a breath away. Po's truck moved stealthily away from the building and purred into the distance, its sound quickly swallowed by those of other cars and trucks passing on the highway beyond the entrance road. Where were they now? Had they gone only as far as the nearest cover and parked again? Tears burning anew, I pulled the sleeping bag up over my ears and allowed myself the luxury of a groan.

At 6:45, I heard the sound of a car arriving, then a key scratching in a lock beyond the service counter. Then I heard whistling.

I fairly slid out from behind the stack of boxes behind which I had been hiding. Gathering up my sleeping bag, I staggered toward the door into the lounge. "Good morning," I said quietly.

The airport attendant turned. "Oh, there you are!" he said.

I put a finger to my lips.

The man's brow wrinkled, but he lowered his voice. "What's going on?"

"Did you see a couple of men sitting in a truck out there somewhere?" I whispered.

"Nope. Can't see much of anything. Take a look." He pointed to the windows that looked over the runway.

Outside, there was nothing but a dim milk white fog.

"You aren't going nowhere till that burns off," he said.

"No." And they were out there somewhere, hiding in the fog.

The attendant stared at me, his hands fisted on his fatherly hips. "Someone got a fear in you?" he asked.

I nodded. "I just want to get my plane off the ground without being seen. Then I'll be okay."

"Need me to call the sheriff?"

"No. Thanks." No, I would stay gone until the men in suits could jail these men who wanted me gone. At liberty, I would do what I could to unravel the last of the connections, and hasten their incarceration. It was foolish, I knew, a cowboy's lonesome stance, but I did not know how long it would take to wrap up the case, and I could not picture a life of hiding.

The man nodded and walked away.

I took up a position from which I could watch the windows unseen and settled in to wait.

Fog. It was rare, although not surprising, once I thought about it. Moist air had pooled along the Platte River, condensing into a ground-hugging shroud. It was my fate to wait until it lifted and dispersed. It was a simple fact that a pilot had to be able to see where she was going in order to take off. *It can't be too long before it burns off,* I told myself. *Soon as the sun heats it up, this fog will fry like bacon. I'll be in the sky by seven-thirty, eight. No problem.*

I jumped as the outside speaker of the unicom radio burst into life, booming a pilot's voice across the tarmac: "Douglas unicom, this is Beechcraft eight six three two hotel. I'm ten miles southeast, and all I see is fog. Request airport advisory."

Was it the twin coming back?

The attendant's voice came back, "Roger that. We got pea soup here, dead calm. Your guess is as good as mine."

"Three two hotel."

I looked hopefully at the service attendant. "How long does this usually take?" I asked.

"Got me," he said. "This doesn't happen more'n so often. Prolly hour or two. Maybe more. You know the adage, 'Time to spare? Go by air.'"

An hour, I told myself. I thanked the man, slithered through the lounge to the bathroom, swilled some water from the water fountain by the bathroom hallway, bought a cup of coffee, and crept back into my hiding place.

An hour later, overhead traffic was still asking when the fog might lift. "I can see the tops of the trees along the Platte," one pilot reported, "but I can't see you. You got an update?" I could hear his unseen engine grind overhead, describing a wide, lazy circle.

"I can hear your engines, but that's all."

"Well then, I'm running on up to Casper, rent a car. You call my wife and tell her I'm gonna be late?"

A car. How I would prefer to simply get into that car and slip away. To where? To Chandler Jennings? *Isn't that like jumping out of the frying pan and into the fire?* I froze. Until that moment, I had not owned up to the other end of the plan: I would proceed to Jackson. I would find Chandler Jennings. I wanted to argue, explain to myself how wide the sky was, how many different directions I could fly in that little plane with its full tanks of gasoline, but Jackson pulled like a magnet. Somehow, he had swollen in my mind into the key to ending things, the guide who was going to show me the way out of this hell. *Or farther into it,* I told myself grimly.

I waited.

At 9:15, the air suddenly began to move, and the fog melted, first into long furrows of cotton and then into wispy ghosts. I asked the man at the counter to take a look out the back way for Po's truck. He came back with the report that no vehicles were visible between the hangar and the highway except his.

"Thank you," I said. Sprinting to the plane, I unchained its wings and tail, fired the engine, taxied to the east end of the runway, punched the throttle to the dashboard, and took off.

I heard no shots fired. No holes appeared in the wings, no abrupt drop in the fuel gages. My plan had worked. I was free.

The cottonwood trees along the riverbank dwindled to a brown haze, fell away below me. The prairie opened up, melting into smooth contours on a lion's back, resolving into to an abstraction of the ground I used to walk. The robust rampart of the Laramie Range, high and proud, began to shrink, drop away, reveal the far sweep of open spaces. I was aloft, a tiny gnat disappearing over the horizon.

I was flying along the north side of Casper Mountain before I remembered to radio Casper Flight Service to open my flight plan. I considered omitting this step, flying completely without surveillance, but my enemies couldn't possibly get into FAA records and track me, could they? No, they can't, I told myself jubilantly, my spirits rising with the plane; all thoughts to that effect were simple paranoia. Hunching with the chill of the high, cool air through which I flew, I keyed the microphone and identified not myself, but the plane, and activated the plan.

Casper acknowledged and wished me a nice trip, then gave the frequency for Denver Center should I wish to be tracked on their radar. "Thanks, six two foxtrot out," I told them, and reset the dial for Denver Center, fumbling a little with my stiff, chilled fingers. "Denver Center, this is Piper two two six two foxtrot over Casper for Jackson Hole via Big Piney. Request flight following if able." It felt good to talk to someone who thought I was nothing but a normal, everyday pilot headed westward. I was going to make it.

"Six two foxtrot, what is your planned cruising altitude?"

"Six two foxtrot is at eight thousand five hundred for ten thousand five hundred."

"Roger six two foxtrot, squawk and ident four three one seven."

I reached over to the transponder and dialed in the four digits, my mind growing calmer as I settled into the routine of flying. I pushed the button that would flash my position on Denver Center's radar screen, moving smoothly through the motions. "Four three one seven for six two foxtrot, squawk and ident completed."

The radio crackled.

"Denver Center, six two foxtrot; say again?" I said.

"Six [crackle] trot, cycle and try [crackle]."

I took that to mean that my transponder had failed to pop me on their radar screen, so I repeated the job. "Six two foxtrot."

With the vagary of radio communications, Denver Center suddenly came in loud and clear. "Six two foxtrot, we don't see you. You're probably shadowed by mountains. You'll be in range of Salt Lake Center soon. Suggest you try them a little way down the line."

"Thank you. Six two foxtrot out."

"Nice while it lasted. Denver out."

I smiled wanly. Denver had had a nice voice.

I stretched and yawned. I had whole hours before me in which I could stand down my guard and relax. Below me, the Platte River curved south-westward toward its high mountain source. I pressed the throttle forward and eased back on the yoke, retrimming the aircraft for the climb to 10,500 feet. VFR flight rules stated that if flying westward, I should select an altitude of an even number of thousands of feet plus five hundred, which meant that either 8,500 or 10,500 was good until I needed to clear South Pass and traverse the high valley around Big Piney. Either way, the higher altitude would probably be preferable, having less turbulence. Un-fortunately, the air would be less dense there, and one needed air in order to burn fuel. And to breathe.

I followed my course along the air chart, reckoning airspeed into dis-tance traveled, matching bends in the river with the winding blue line on the chart. It occurred to me that I was following the trace of the Oregon Trail, on which 350,000 people had walked and driven creaking Con-estoga wagons a century and a half before. I looked down upon the trace, feeling a strange kinship with the risk they had taken in their westward journey, wondering if mine would end less tragically than had so many of theirs. They had inched along, wearing away shoe leather with every step, making twenty miles a day if they were lucky. Or making no miles if they succumbed to the smallpox and cholera that swept through the tired trains of pioneers as they bent to drink from waters fouled by those who had gone before them. Staggering numbers had perished. Their bones lay below me now, crumbling to dust in shallow graves, their names forgot-ten. Some had left the trail right here and built a life for themselves, toil-ing hard under the unrelenting sun of summer and through the freezing winds of winter, carving a home out of the wilderness with nothing but strong backs and willing hearts. Their bones lay also in the shadows of my wings.

I peered southward toward Saratoga, where other bones now whitened beneath pastures turned into playgrounds for the rich and ruthless. I sent them hatred through my eyes.

Then I laughed a dry, ironical laugh. Here I was, a child of the ranching era, bemoaning the wreckage brought by the advent of the boys with money. What was I thinking of? The lives of my ancestors had not been without impact. The advent of European peoples had ripped into the lives of the Indian tribes, the Oregon Trail emigrants creating a fine legacy of wagon ruts, grass eaten to the roots, wood scavenged to the last twig, and game hunted out and driven away across a path fifty miles wide. I would see no herds of buffalo in my transit today. Those once-mighty grazers, whose countless numbers would have blackened the ground below me, were gone, having been hunted carelessly by the builders of the railroads, all but extinct in the wild, their few remaining descendants eating protected grass in the national parks, or penned up to be raised for meat that would bring a high price in Tokyo. And the ancestors of the Indians—hadn't they hunted the woolly mammoth to extinction?

Yes, time and circumstances changed, and change often came harshly and with terrible loss. But I told myself that this newest wave of change was worse. This wave brought a new disease, the poison of a new piracy. These pirates of industry built nothing—not schools, not homes, not ranches, no herds of animals that would feed the nation. These men brought only greed. They gobbled up companies, pillaged retirement funds to cover their leveraging, sold off the sustaining assets, and left, leaving only bones where businesses once had grown. And these hobby ranches? These happy weekend hideaways? What would become of them when the people who knew how to tend the grasses and the herds had all given up and moved to the festering cities?

I looked down across the buckskin-colored sea of prairie with a heart tight with pain. *I'll be back,* I promised myself. *I may be running for years or decades, but I'll be back.*

Far below and to the south, I spotted Alcova and Pathfinder reservoirs, the confluence of the Platte and the Sweetwater rivers. Beyond these, I picked out the sweet knobs of the Granite Mountains and Devil's Gate, that harsh notch in a fin of naked rock where the Platte sawed down through Seminoe Mountain. I passed Independence Rock, the broad dome the emigrants hoped to see by Independence Day if they were to make it into Oregon before the snow flew in autumn. I checked my position on the chart, back-calculated to reckon my airspeed. I was behind my estimate. The needle on the instrument panel registered ninety-seven knots, but I was only making eighty over the ground. The head winds were stronger than I had expected.

Calculating forward again, I revised my estimated time of arrival into Jackson: 1:20. An extra half hour in transit would cut deeper into my emergency fuel ration, but I was still within required limits. I stared at the instrument panel, willing it to tell me something new.

I had been under way for over an hour now, grinding westward over the Sweetwater, now certain where I was, now momentarily lost as the markings on the chart blended into one another, one twist in the river beginning to look like another. I was in a wide, lonely part of the back of nowhere, where the roads were far apart and the ranches few. I could see the Wind River Mountains up ahead and to the right, a high, wide ridge of white. I could make out vaguely on the horizon the low saddle that was South Pass.

I checked the altimeter. I had not made 10,500 feet, not by nearly a thousand. Once again, I pushed in the already-maximized throttle and eased back on the yoke, but the plane became more sluggish and would not climb. Conscious that I was at an altitude for eastbound flights, I scanned the horizon, searching for oncoming traffic. I was alone.

It then occurred to me that I had not heard a radio call since my final contact with Denver Center. Flipping the upper radio to Salt Lake Center, I keyed the microphone and gave them a call. "Salt Lake Center, this is Piper two two six two foxtrot. Request flight following if possible."

Nothing. I heard no reply.

Giving the dashboard around the radio a good Peggy-sized slam with the heel of my hand, I flicked the power switch off and on and tried again. Nothing. Peggy had warned me about this, right? She had told me this so I wouldn't panic if the radio cut out on me. So I wouldn't do something stupid, like forget that flying the damned airplane was my first priority. Fine.

I shrugged off gathering fatigue and jiggled the dial, then reset the radio on 122.8, the frequency for Big Piney, and left it on standby. And reminded myself that I would be over South Pass before I could hear them.

An hour later, I skimmed over South Pass, hove northwestward toward Bondurant, and tried Salt Lake Center again. No answer, only static. I switched to the radio for Big Piney and got nothing at all.

Well, this is not uncommon, I assured myself, but a worry began to bloom in the back of my mind: had that man not been content to wait for me on the ground? What if he had picked the lock on this plane and sabotaged the radios? I had no way of knowing, had I? Perhaps he had taken the precaution of putting a tracking device on one of them, something that transmitted whatever I was saying directly to Saratoga, and it had fouled the wires. After all, I had not so much as checked the fuel tanks in my hurry to take off, let alone do my pilot's walk-around or check underneath the dash for fresh wiring.

I spun the dial and reset it for Big Piney.

Static.

"Do your job," I said aloud. "Remember what Peggy told you about times like this? Aviate first, then navigate, then communicate. See? Talking to people while you fly is your third priority, not your first."

But I was talking to myself. Not a good sign. I forced myself to concentrate, to reason through my fears. If that man had decided to do something to this plane, he would simply have wired a bomb to it, or more simply drained the fuel out of the tanks. What was I thinking of, thinking he would waste energy rewiring my radios? I was simply letting my imagination get away from me, that was all. . . .

"I'm okay; I'm fine," I said aloud. But then the plane suddenly shook with a new level of turbulence, and I felt my buttocks tighten just as if they belonged to someone else.

Some cowgirl I am, trying to hold on to the saddle with my butt. And what the fuck are you doing, rushing off in search of Chandler?

I realized that I didn't have a good answer.

I tried to distract myself with the spectacular view I was getting of the

Wind River Range. This was a long, straight range, an upraised block of stone glazed with snow and ice standing proud of the surrounding low-lands like the ridgepole of a house. The snow sat thicker in pockets carved by the mountain glaciers that had moved like serpents down toward the lowlands, pushing great piles of rubble before them. I could see those piles now—terminal moraines, geologists called them. I could see more of them now, great U-shaped valleys laid out one next to the other with neat heaps of rubble kicked up at their feet, much as if a colossal mountain lion had dragged her claws along the ramparts. The glacial valleys were long and wide and beautiful, and filled with high mountain lakes dammed by the moraines.

With the next heavy buffeting, I rechecked my position. I was not making good time, there were no two ways about it. As I noted that, I remembered, belatedly, to switch to the second wing tank. What had I been thinking of? No wonder the plane had begun to feel a little heavy on the left aileron and rudder: the right wing tank was almost empty, increasing its lift. I had been compensating right along, slowly taking up the slack.

The buffeting increased. I took a slow turn to the right to check the horizon. The once-clear skies, which had begun to look hazy over South Pass, were now dark with clouds. I reset my course and tried to relax, reminding myself to breathe deeply and go with the turbulence. For an instant, I wished the little plane had an autopilot, so I could rest my arms and legs, but then I remembered that an autopilot would not manage turbulence this strong. I began to curse my bladder, which had long since filled with the coffee I had drunk in Douglas and begun to scream for relief.

I looked to the west. The sky was darkening.

A half hour of hard turbulence and myriad course corrections later, I was nearing Bondurant, Jackson's Little Hole, the high meadow surrounded by mountains on four sides and hills on the fourth where the mountains squeezed together around Hoback Canyon, and I saw something that turned my heart cold.

A tongue of dark rain-filled cloud had crested the mountains to the west and filled the canyon to its bottom.

My hands rigid on the control wheel, I banked quickly to the left to head back toward Big Piney, only to find that the storm had swung even faster around the south end of the Wyoming Range and consumed ground and sky to the south. I was trapped.

I clutched the chart to the control wheel, refolding the paper twice to make it fit, as the plane now bounced harder and harder in a wide, slow circle. I reduced the throttle, bringing my airspeed down so the plane wouldn't rip apart in the turbulence. I noted Wenz Field over by Pinedale. *Maybe that's still clear,* I thought. Turning, I looked out over the hills to southeast and across the mesas to the Wind River Range. I counted lake-filled glacial valleys, north to south. Wenz would be at the foot of the fourth or fifth.

I saw only two.

I looked north. Mountains—high, impassable mountains as far as I could see. I was in a valley no more than four or five miles across at its widest place, an infinite space for turning in an automobile, but little comfort to the aviator, who must maintain an airspeed of at least fifty-five knots to maneuver without falling out of the sky. I kept turning, circling over the meadow.

With every turn, the storm swept closer, moving faster now. I felt the chill of coming moisture seep into the tiny cockpit of the plane. I twisted on more heat, a frail creature huddling toward the fire.

Resetting the radio once more just in case a jostling would make it work, I called the larger of the two airports. "Big Piney, this is Piper two two six two foxtrot. I am over Bondurant for Jackson Hole."

I released the microphone, waited, but got no response.

Pressing the key again, I said, "Big Piney, I am circling and getting low on fuel. Hoback is way below minimums and I sure can't see you. If anybody's out there, I sure could use some suggestions about now."

Nothing.

I looked hungrily below at the narrow strip of highway that wound up over the rising ground and into the blackness of the clouds. Here and there, it was gray with clods of leftover ice and snow. What had I been thinking of, flying this plane instead of driving?

Wait, can I land this thing on that strip of pavement?

Pressing the control wheel forward, I began to descend. I would find the straightest stretch, I told myself, then fly up and down it a few hundred feet up, see how flat it was, gage how bad the patches of snow and ice might be. Then, if the clouds didn't lift, or, worse yet, continued to loom closer—as they were—or my fuel got too low to make Big Piney or Wenz even if the clouds did rise, I would declare an emergency and set her down.

Emergency—why hadn't I thought of that before?

I reset the radio to the international emergency frequency, took a breath, and announced, "Mayday, Mayday, Mayday. This is Piper two two six two foxtrot. I am a student pilot over Bondurant, and I'm losing minimums. Please come back if you hear me."

No one answered.

Leaning forward, I looked out overhead through the windshield. The clouds were reaching over me now. No time to climb and see if I could fly over them. I descended lower.

I was four hundred feet over the ground now, six hundred feet under the safe minimum altitude I was supposed to maintain, dangerously low in this sea of unexpected downdrafts. The clouds roiled down toward me, closing, the angry air beginning to bounce me harder and harder, a spattering of drops now greasing the windshield. In an instant, the windshield was streaming with water and the highway below had turned black with rain. I thanked what thin luck I had that the moisture was coming as rain and not a sheet of ice that would quickly coat my wings and drop me like a rock. I scanned the roadway hungrily. With a sinking feeling, I realized that even if I found a section I liked for a landing, I would be hard-pressed in this amount of wet and turbulence to set the plane down without flipping it over its propeller or at least spinning it around to one side and breaking a wing. *But any landing I can walk away from,* I prayed silently. *Any landing I can . . .*

Up ahead, in the mouth of the canyon, the clouds had risen.

I lengthened my carousel turns, bringing me closer to the mouth of the canyon. At three or four hundred feet above the ground, I could see a half mile in. Underneath those clouds, it was not yet raining.

Quickly recalculating my position, I checked my airspeed indicator, set the controls for eighty knots, and reckoned times and bearings I would have to travel at that speed to thread my way through the canyon. At that speed, I would fly one and a third nautical miles per minute, or four every three minutes, barely easy enough for my panicked brain to reckon in this hurry. I ran my thumb along the line that marked the river on the chart, checking to see how tight the canyon was at four or five hundred feet above the water. Tight, but it meant staying aloft longer, maybe even flying through to one of the private airstrips marked on the chart where the canyon turned a right angle before the final pitch into Jackson. "Any port in a storm," I muttered aloud, setting my watch to beep at me in six minutes. "To hell with you stuck-up rich boys. I'll land this sucker right across your patio if I have to."

Calling my intentions out over the silent radio, I turned over Bondurant once more, glanced at the course that set on the compass, and headed into the muck.

I skimmed along over the river, now three hundred feet up, now four, groping to keep sight of the ground without flying too close to it, gritting my teeth with the hope that I met no cliffs where the river dropped suddenly over a waterfall. Looking more closely at the cataracts below me, I realized with relief that the I had crossed a divide just east of Bondurant; this water was flowing west, toward the Snake River. "Point to Em," I muttered bitterly. "Now, how about a little more sky?"

I glanced at my watch, checked airspeed. Tried to relax. Flicked my eyes left and right, watching the canyon walls. And saw a wall of cloud and slashing rain, black all the way to the river.

I looked left. I looked right. Enough room to turn back, but what would I find there? Pressing the control wheel forward one more time, I turned toward the right side of the canyon to give myself room to turn around to the left, eased off the throttle, and eyed the road hungrily. *Yes, there, up there, I can put it down there, start your turn . . .* I eased off the throttle farther, set a notch of flaps.

A semitractor pulling a heavy load loomed out of the murk, its headlights burning against the gloom.

I slapped the throttle forward. Released the flaps. Straightened my course. Pulled back the control wheel. Cursed. And flew up into the cloud.

I could see nothing. The windscreen streamed with water, but beyond it was only darkness.

I glanced at my watch. How much time had I lost slowing down for the aborted landing? How much distance gained speeding up? How would I know when to turn, flying completely blind? I felt moisture on my cheeks and realized that I was crying.

Not now, I told myself. *First get yourself out of this jam, and then cry.*

Staring into the gray nothing, my head swam with vertigo. Pressing my cheek against the cold glass of the window beside me to keep my head clear, I rested my eyes on the artificial horizon instrument, made quick glances toward the dials that indicated altitude and rate of decent, and forced myself to make only tiny movements with the controls.

Suddenly, the clouds parted, and I saw only rock, a sheer face, the ugly shoulder of a mountain directly ahead. I banked left. The clouds closed, opened again. Closed. *You idiot!* a voice screamed. *What were you thinking of? Where did you think you were passing through to this time?* I glanced left and right, trying to spot the mouth that spoke, and realized that I was alone, and that the voice howled from inside my head.

I flew onward, climbing, praying. I corrected my course to the northwest. Gave it ten endless minutes more, straining my senses for each small glimpse of the river down below me, saw finally a confluence with another, glanced at the chart to make certain there were no creeks that size coming into the one I was following before the canyon turned, grabbed myself by my heart, and rolled right to zero compass bearing. Held my breath, waiting for the blinding flash that would be the last thing I saw. And flew out into brilliant sunshine.

Light, blessed light danced on the waters of the Snake River as I flew up the long glacial outwash valley that led me north into Jackson Hole. Tears streamed down my cheeks. I felt alive and newborn, each sight, sound, and smell around me brilliant, sharp, and richly perfumed.

Ten minutes later, I slipped the tiny plane into the downwind line of landing aircraft traffic between a Delta Airlines jet and a Beechcraft Baron, not even bothering to call the unicom frequency. *What the heck,* I told myself. *My radio doesn't work, this ain't no control-tower airport, and I can sure see better'n I could twenty minutes ago.*

I banked left and left again, turning base and final, running out the flaps. I slowed to sixty, then fifty-five, dropped the little plane gently onto the numbers at the end of the runway, rolled a third of the way down the strip until the first exit onto the taxiway, pulled off, set the brake, and bawled.

36

I stood on the walkway in front of the Rambling Rose Bed-and-Breakfast Inn, my knees still weak, my hands trembling slightly even though thrust deep into my pockets. I felt poised on the threshold between heaven and hell, no longer sure which way was which. I needed to be near people in this aftermath of almost dying, to step resolutely back into a world of normalcy, where I could walk up the steps of a harmless-looking inn and in fact find no harm there.

It was, after all, just a quaint Victorian house painted yellow, no doubt a fitting backdrop to the vigorous climbing roses whose winter-naked canes twined through dark green trellises along the front. In my heightened sense of nerves, I imagined the blaze of color that would greet visitors in the summertime, could almost smell the perfume that would fill the air when the last snows had melted off the slopes and the leaves and buds had burst forth for another season's luring of the bees.

My mind dwelt in the shadows, hopelessly removed from the bucolic image it beheld. And found something next to this in that place of shadows, a deep and basic need, a motivation to rebel against nature. It urged me to break even further away from the sanity and safety of the herd, to move down into the coldness and mystery of the night, to be the woman I was at last.

Inside this house waited a man who knew about the dark.

Ortega was but a distant memory, a sentinel left behind on the surface. I was underground, bedeviled by the illusion of daylight.

I thought of Miriam, who loved to be touched. What had she learned in her hours of ecstasy?

A distant voice tried to remind me that the man inside this house was a monster, a predator who preyed on women and even girls like a cougar stalked sick sheep.

So what am I, asked a voice within me that knew a new candor, *healthy?*

With resignation, I moved my feet down that walkway toward the inn.

THE FRONT DOOR stood open to the fresh-smelling breeze that had followed the rain. With a sigh, I let myself in, and found myself confronted immediately with the temptation of the registration calendar, which lay open on an antique desk. Reaching out a hand, I flipped through it, discovering that it went back only to the first of the year. I needed further back. Crossing fingers that still wobbled slightly from the stresses I now raced to escape, I silently eased open the drawer beneath it.

"What you lookin' for, darlin'?" asked a hearty female voice, the voice I had heard the day before on the phone. I didn't even jump. There wasn't enough adrenaline left in me. Instead, I just felt slightly dizzy. Looking up, I found myself confronted by the smiling but curious innkeeper. She was a middle-aged woman, dressed that day in soft gabardine slacks and a loose white tab-collared shirt, its tails hanging out underneath a long vest, the better to artistically drape a spreading waist. She was petite and had dark curly hair cut close to her face.

"Uh, trying to see if a friend of mine was here last August."

"August what?"

"Oh, around the third."

She laughed. "No one here but me and your friend Chandler," she said. When my eyes flew wide in surprise, she added, "I recognize your voice. And that's an easy date to remember. It was my birthday. Right in the middle of the tourist season, but I always close that day, or at least for guests who don't stay as long as he does. Chandler's in the parlor," she added, and disappeared into the dining room.

I looked sharply into the space where she had stood. Even through my mental fog, I could hear that the alibi had come quickly, easily. Could I believe it?

I turned and pushed the French doors, which opened to my left. It was time to find out.

❖

I FOUND CHANDLER as a blind person locates the fireplace in a cold room—following the heat. The jittery sense of exhaustion I felt now rose, gripping my throat. My heart began to cannon. *Over there . . . closer . . .* I turned toward the windows, excitement ripping at me like the flood that races suddenly down a dry creek bed carrying mud and the artillery of stones.

I saw his legs first—long, well-muscled and limber, like an athlete's, and enshrouded in corduroy trousers that draped just so. They were crossed lazily one over the other, sprawling lavishly off the front of an overstuffed chair sumptuously upholstered in cabbage roses. His long feet were dressed in gray woolly socks and a well-worn pair of deck shoes, even though he was about as far from an ocean as one can get in the United States. The rest of him, save for his large, broad fingertips, was screened from my view by the newspaper he was reading. But it had to be him.

The newspaper folded and snapped shut as he laid it across his lap and lengthened his gaze to take me in, just as if he'd been waiting for me to arrive. He smiled, a wolfish, half-crazy glow lighting his broad-boned face as the skin at the corners of his eyes crinkled with the quickness of the easily merry.

The eyes themselves were a pale greenish gray, like the mist that spins across a lake just before morning. But unlike the dawn lake, they were not calm, but crazy. Totally mad. Alive in some other universe. And looking straight at and inside me, as if I were a cage and the mouse he wanted to catch was in there hiding.

His lips moved beneath his rich brush mustache. "Who might you be?" he asked.

"Em," I said foolishly.

"Great."

"Hansen."

"Better yet."

I looked down quickly at my hands. They were trembling again, visibly. I was certain he could see it even from across the room. I forced myself to look him in the eye. "I've been looking for you."

His eyebrows flicked upward in ardent surprise, like a hungry gourmet finding that the wayside restaurant is not only open but serving delicacies. He got up from the chair, rising as a slow series of unwinding S curves, dropping the newspaper on the floor, stretching his arms above his head until his shirttail pulled free a bit at the waist, revealing a finely muscled abdomen covered with soft, smooth skin dappled with golden brown hairs. Exalting for a moment in the pleasure of his stretch, he closed his eyes and sighed. Lowered his arms, let them swing at his sides, totally relaxed. "Mmmm," he purred, "looks like you've found me."

"I—"

"Want something to drink, Em Hansen? The house stocks tea and coffee, but I know where they keep the beer."

"No. I—"

He strode past me, brushing my arm as he did so, and I had to rock my head back to take in his height. Six four at least, a good two hundred pounds of muscle and grace. When he was almost out of reach, he swung an arm backward almost as an afterthought and caught my hand, spinning me around to follow him, and murmured, "This way to the goodies."

I stumbled awkwardly behind him through a catchment of narrowing hallways and into the kitchen. We settled at either side of a round oak table, he swilling a beer, I chewing nervously at a date from the dish that rested invitingly in the middle of a lace doily between us. "So, Em Hansen," he purred. "You've found me. Now tell me: was I lost?"

I was just about to launch into some stupid explanation of how no, he was right where he was, I was sure, when I realized that the wide-eyed gaze he had fixed on me was his version of a playful grin. "No, I don't suppose so."

"Then perhaps it's you who were lost."

"I—" Huh? "Sure," I volleyed, going along with the insanity of his speech. As fear melted into the relative peace of confusion, I thought, *When in Rome, right?* "Yeah, I've been totally lost for about a year now," I said, more candidly than I'd intended, "and it's been the pits."

"Tell me more."

"Me?"

"Who else?"

I stared into his eyes. They were hypnotic, yes, but what fascinated me was the particular elements that conspired to make them so: I had the sense that whatever lived behind them was both hurtling toward me and escaping me at the same instant. *This is what makes charisma,* I thought dully, and without meaning to, I began to speak again. "It's the usual story, I suppose. Out of work, father died last summer, mom took over the ranch— *but what in hell am I telling you this for!*" I jumped up from the table, started to back away into the common room nearer the front door.

Chandler calmly took another swig of his beer, then put it down on the lace doily in the center of the table and rose to his feet. "Of course. You're tired. Long trip? How far did you come today?"

How the hell did he know I didn't live in Jackson? I didn't answer.

"No matter," he said soothingly, looking away so that the intensity of his gaze no longer disturbed me. "We'll take my car. It's parked out back here. Just let me get my coat." As he started to move out of the kitchen, he spun quickly back, looking on me with anxiety stitching his brow. "Don't go away. Really. My car's out back there. It's the—"

"Gold BMW. Needs a tune-up."

His invasive grin returned. "Yeah."

I braced myself against the doorjamb, trying to sort out what it was I thought I was going to get from his human whirlwind.

He didn't leave me time to think. He was gone just an instant, returning with a dark brown suede jacket draped softly over one broad shoulder. Planting one enormous hand against the small of my back, he steered me out the back door to his car. What flashed through my mind was: *Don't let him out of your sight. The boys from Saratoga might not know where to find him, but let's not give him a chance to tell them where to find me.*

"Can't we walk?" I asked, my mind focusing enough to remind me not to get into a car with this man. Better off on Jackson's still-icy sidewalks, in broad daylight in the middle of the town, where I could call for help if needed.

"Anything you say, Em Hansen."

We walked (I almost running to keep up with his enormous strides) about half a mile to a pub run by the Snake River Brewery. It was a two-story deconstructionist modern job with all sorts of metal beams and glass and most of the ground floor open clear to the roof. Chandler rocked his head back to appraise the balcony seating, then showed me to a table up there. From this lofty perch, we looked inward to the brewing vats and downward onto the heads of the assembled swells, who sat sipping their porters and ales and munching on succulent-looking appetizers. Everyone seemed too relaxed, too unaware that I had so recently been awash in the fetid breath of eternity. Couldn't they smell it on my skin? I felt lost and confused, relieved to have gotten there alive but uncertain where I now was. The subtle aromas of someone's dinner met my nostrils, and I began to shake. It hit me all at once that I hadn't eaten since dawn.

Chandler ordered us each a Snake River ale, recommended the pasta special as "Always the way to go," and settled down to filter foam through his mustache. He waited for me to speak.

"Listen," I began, trying to sip at my water rather than swill my beer on an empty stomach, "I came here to ask you about someone we know . . . ah, knew in common. Or at least, I think *you* knew her. I only just met her—" I stopped, realizing what little sense I was making. "I'm talking about Miriam Menken."

Chandler's eyes went blank, the way a cat's do when it realizes you're playing for keeps. For a moment, I was afraid he'd get up and leave, or that he was already in some sense gone. "Miriam . . ." He whispered her name as if trying to remember the melody to a half-forgotten song.

"Yeah, Miriam Menken. I guess you, ah, knew her in college as Miriam Benner," I said, trying as always to be diplomatic.

"Yes, of course." He glanced right and left, then back at me, his eyes shining with moisture.

Embarrassed at the sight of such obvious emotion in a grown man, I said, "Well, you see, I'm a friend of the family's, and I've been trying to learn some things about her, and—"

Chandler suddenly leaned toward me across the table, almost a lunge, and grabbed my nearest hand. "No. First you have to tell me about *you*."

Me? I almost squeaked, my mouth sagging open. *You want to know about me? I'm Em Hansen, this totally confused lost child from Chugwater who's out tilting at windmills. I'm supposed to be a geologist, see, and—*I forced my mouth to make words. "Ah, what do you want to know?"

"Why do you care?" It was almost a plea.

"About what? About Miriam?"

"Yes, about Miriam. About living. About whatever." *Save me from this sadness, his eyes said.*

"Well, ah . . ." Looking into his crazy, mourning, deeply intelligent eyes, I made one of those snap decisions that go like this: tell the truth. But then I had to hurry to catch up with him, as I suddenly wasn't at all sure that the truth I'd been holding on to so fiercely—whatever that was—was in fact *the* truth. Or more than a partial truth. Or a limited truth. In short, I was a mess. I took a breath. I opened my mouth. I began to speak. "Her husband asked me to do this, to look into her death. He used to be my boss. He's even crazier than you are, but in a different way. Hell, I didn't know any better; I was in the middle of hiding out on my folks' ranch out there in Chugwater when he found me. Like I said, I hadn't worked—or not as a geologist—in over a year. Hadn't wanted to. Yeah, I was hiding. And like I said, Dad died awhile—after I got unemployed, but before—and anyway, yeah. To tell the truth, I'd hoped Mom would totally auger in and leave the ranch to me and I could hide out there forever. But no, she's feeling much better now, and the calves had all dropped, and there you have it: I had to go. And just then Menken comes along and reaches out his big hook and says he can find me a job and gets me snarled up in all of this." Once I'd gotten rolling, the words came easily. It's amazing what you can say to a madman.

"And did he find you a job?"

"Yes. Or no, that's not being altogether honest, either. I started reading Miriam's journals, you see, and I just got hooked on, well, her life. The only problem was, she didn't have any more of it, being dead now, and I just couldn't reconcile that. Is this making any sense to you?"

"Perfect." Chandler kept leaning toward me as the waiter served his salad, forcing the man to set it to one side. I stared numbly as mine was placed in front of my hands.

"I liked her," I said miserably.

"So did I," he said huskily.

"Yeah, well, that's what her journals kind of said. That you—" What? Ate her, the way a fire consumes oxygen? "That you showed her a pretty good time." I felt immediate remorse for the understatement, and for saying that I knew anything about their intimacy. What was I thinking of, launching into such a naked conversation with a man like this? Was *I* crazy, too? "I mean, God, man, didn't you care what you were doing to her? Didn't you care about her?"

Those eyes now consumed me. "I *worship* women," he whispered. His words licked past my ears like a hot wind from the desert as he reached out one large hand and wrapped it around both of mine. His was warm and dry, like my father's. I wanted to cry. I looked up at him, the tears brimming, fury rising in my breast. This was wrong; totally, absolutely wrong. What I had felt for my father was sacred, a daughter's love. What was this man thinking, stealing feelings from me like this? Worship women? What kind of a religion was that, to put women on an altar? Wasn't he confusing his idol with his object of sacrifice? And he wasn't my father; he was an animal, a sexual predator—

I jerked my hand away.

His hand followed, braked my escape, drew mine back, now with infinite tenderness. "I'm sorry," he said softly.

My whole chest constricted with the tenderness of his words, his voice. I clenched my teeth, willing myself to escape the raging hell of my feelings.

"Look at me," he whispered.

I looked. In his eyes, I knew he meant it. He was sorry. Sorry for things he had never even done. Sorry for not knowing me sooner. Sorry that the storm had almost eaten me.

Glancing miserably away, I looked around the room, at the hanging sculptures of eagles, at the wall-mounted TV sets that were broadcasting a sporting event full of gaudily clad athletes and flying sweat, at the heads of the diners down below. The weight and terror of the day, the week, and all the weeks that had come before it loaded in on me, and I felt like I was floating. Hovering over a sea of darkness. Could I trust this man with this level of feeling? And was trusting him the issue? For a moment, I gazed inward at that dark expanse of water, and realized that some days when you fly that far out over the ocean, you have to dive in.

"I read about you in her journals," I whispered.

Chandler wrapped his other hand around mine, looked into my eyes with a gentleness I hadn't seen in a man's eyes since I'd left Frank, and said, "Em Hansen, if there's anything I know that can help you, it's yours for the asking."

Okay, there it was—I had to ask for something, but what? What was it I wanted so badly that I was willing to fly hell bent in bad weather across Wyoming, risking a mountain passage when I didn't know yet how to fly one safely, and walk right into the lair of the lion? I didn't know what I was going to ask, but when I opened my mouth, I said, "Did you kill her?"

Chandler dropped my hands and rose halfway from his seat. *"What?"* He loomed over the table, eyes aflame.

I started to cringe, but something in his action made me wonder if he was acting, not reacting. Something different in his eyes. Something . . . sane. "Well, hell, man, she died of an overdose of cocaine. What am I supposed to think?"

The crazy, lost look returned to Chandler's eyes. He dropped back into his seat. "Cocaine?"

"That surprises you?"

"Well, yeah."

"Why?"

"Because she didn't do drugs. Never did. Even back in college, when everybody did. A little alcohol, maybe, but . . . well . . ."

"But what?"

"Shit! I was wondering where that packet went."

"What packet?"

He gave a dismissive wave with one hand. "Nothing. Just a business matter."

"You came back from visiting her one delivery short?"

Chandler looked at me out of one eye, feigned indignance. "Mind your own business."

We didn't say anything to each other for a while, each thinking our own thoughts. I picked up my fork, tried to eat a little more, then gave up. I realized his eyes were on me once again. "Penny for your thoughts," he said.

My thoughts. What were my thoughts? "Why'd she have to die?" I said, and in so saying, I noticed that this was the question that had brought me here. Not how, but why. Why Miriam, who was just beginning to discover life?

He sat back, his chest caving. "I don't know." He shook his head, as if scolding himself. "No, that's not good enough. No, the thing is, I don't know *who* killed her. And while I think I might know *why* . . ." His eyes suddenly shifted, flicking inward toward an internal anger. His shoulders tensed for the first time since I'd met him.

"Then *why*? Don't run away! You said you'd tell me anything!"

Chandler's mustache stiffened. "Listen, I'm sorry, but I guess I lied. This is something I can't tell you. At least not yet. But don't worry." He patted my hand resolutely, his eyes focused somewhere toward the middle of his inner space.

I stared at him, wondering where he'd gone. Suddenly, his eyes flicked back toward me, a quick glance, gauging me. Then he gave me that look again, the hungry lion asking me to distinguish myself from prey, and said, "Ask me more."

Ask a madman for the answer to the riddle of the stars, and sometimes all you get is stardust. "What about Cecelia?" I said.

"Cecelia Menken?"

"Yes, damn it! Cecelia the underaged kid with the problems."

He knit his brow, thought. "I'm not sure what you mean."

"What did you think were you doing, visiting her? She's a child!" My heart turned in my breast. I had almost said *my* child.

Chandler looked somewhat affronted. "I take it you're talking about the times I'd run into her around the neighborhood."

"Yeah, *sure*. You 'ran into her' at the stables. A bit off your track, aren't they? What were you *thinking* of?"

Chandler took a long, visible breath in and let it out. "I'm afraid this borders on those things I can't tell you about."

"What the—"

"Okay, then I'll say this: I did go to those stables, and yes, fairly often, but it wasn't to meet Cecelia." He gave me a look, one of those "read between the lines and shut up" looks.

"Oh. Mrs. Wentworth."

His eyes flew wide open in bemused surprise. "You *have* been busy."

"And the others."

Chandler's look now held irritation. "Mind your own business."

"Cecelia *is* my business. Looks to me like you paid her a little more than passing attention."

"Why not? She's an interesting girl. Besides, she's—"

"Her mother's daughter," I said, finishing his sentence for him. "A way to keep tabs on Miriam."

"That, too." Chandler nodded, smiling, one warrior saluting another. "Smart kid, aren't you?" Then his eyes clouded. "But think also, here's this kid who *needed* some attention."

"The hell. She didn't need drugs."

Chandler knit his brow, affronted. "You're accusing me of giving that child drugs?"

"Yes. Maybe you didn't do it directly, but you brought them into the neighborhood. You think you can mess with the mothers without messing up the daughters? Who did you think was going to be left to care for them? Or be a good example for them?" I seethed. "So maybe you didn't turn her on to cocaine, but let's talk about marijuana. Or some other downer."

"No."

"You had them in your car, didn't you?"

He just looked at me.

"Well?"

Chandler managed to look almost hurt. "Cecelia is a very nice girl."

Ignoring this, I said, "You've just said you had at least one delivery go missing. Nice uncut cocaine, the hot stuff, the kind you only get when you deal direct. You think those nicely reared girls knew to stay out of your stash when you left your car parked by that barn unlocked?" I was guessing, spinning a surmise, but he wasn't answering, which meant that maybe I was right. Cecelia and what's-her-name Wentworth, lighting up behind the barn while mommy gets the hard stuff up in the hayloft.

All he said in his own defense was a cryptic and matter-of-fact "I can see you don't understand the true nature of my business."

"Perhaps you're right," I replied, parrying his parry. "So why don't you just explain it to me?"

We ate our salads in silence. Mine was good—something classy with tiny olives and walnuts. His disappeared into his mouth like nectar, each merciful morsel lacing his tongue with ecstasy.

My mind bogged down with fatigue. *This is not the mastermind who killed Miriam,* it told me. *This is just a mad errand boy who thinks he is a businessman.*

Our pastas came. The sun set. The lights of the brew pub shifted to a nighttime radiance. A water skier on the television crashed horribly in competition. I ate. Chandler ate. My brain spun along in neutral, stunned, exhausted.

When we were done, we divvied up the bill, I insisting and he arguing just enough to indicate that he had manners. Somehow I knew he was the type who would pay his own way only, and maybe. I put a large-denomination bill on the salver, knowing also that Chandler would wait for the change and pocket the excess from a reasonable tip, giving me time to slip off to the women's room. By the bathrooms, I found a telephone and called Sergeant Ortega.

"You disappeared off the radar!" he said, barging across my greeting.

"Radar?"

"I had them tracking you, like you said. You disappeared." It was an accusation. Carlos was hurt.

"I'm sorry. No, wait; I did try to stay in touch. Listen, flying is not simple. Surely they told you that I just fell into the radar shadow." Why was I arguing this?

"You are where now?" he continued huffily.

"Jackson, Wyoming. I found Chandler."

"You what?"

"He's right here in the restaurant with me. He's—"

"What!"

"And I'm, um, trying to figure out what to do next." It sounded just as foolish to me as it must have sounded to Ortega.

" 'Do'?" he said, his voice softer and more deadly than I had ever heard it. "You are asking my advice?"

"Well, like as in how do we get an arrest warrant?"

"For what? Murder? Trafficking? Shall I choose?"

"Trafficking will do nicely. I really don't think he killed her, Carlos."

The phone line filled with choice Spanish insults, all directed to enhance his sense of self-pity. I let him rave onward, get it out of his system. When he was done, he said simply, "Give me the particulars."

I told him where I was, and where Chandler was staying. "We walked over here. I'll walk back there with him. I'll stall as long as I can before leaving here, give you time to move some local guys into position, or whatever it is you guys do."

"Ai-yi-yi!"

"Okay? I really think I'm safe here, or as safe as I am anywhere these days. When I get back to my car, I'll just leave and drive somewhere else, call you when I get a room. I'm tired, Carlos."

"You crying on my shoulder? You think I slept last night?"

All I could think to say was, "I'm sorry." It never occurred to me to tell him about Po and the hired killer. That was too far away, and in another reality.

CHANDLER AND I wandered up the streets of Jackson through the cold breath of snow that still flowed down off the ski slopes, passing all the chichi shops jammed in cheek by jowl next to T-shirt emporia and postcard dens, turned left past the park with the arches made of elk horn all covered with twinkly lights, threading our way between the few stray clusters of upscale tourists who had wandered into town between seasons, posing as health nuts and athletes while they dripped with windbreakers and Rolexes purchased in Los Angeles, Chicago, Houston, and points overseas. As we neared the Rambling Rose, a sadness swept over me. Sadness mixed with another wave of the jitteriness that had followed me into town from the tiny airplane that now sat mute and cold, chained down in a row between rich people's wings, waiting like an unspoken accusation for me to pull myself together and fly it home.

I felt let down. What was I doing here? What had I learned, and what more had I neglected to ask? I had chased this man all over the universe, or my known universe at least, and here I was next to him without the wit or the know-how to lure his precious information from him. I considered leaving him there, parting company on the square and just sneaking back to fetch my car later, after I'd arranged a room in some lonely motel where I could rest my screaming bones for the night, but I did not. I rationalized that I had to keep him in sight until Ortega communicated with the local authorities and got their men into position. The truth was that I wasn't ready to let him go.

As if he sensed this, he let his near hand drop from his hip pocket, then reached out and drew me close, just as if we'd been friends forever and had always wandered thus of an evening. I stopped, confused by the sudden closeness, and he turned fully toward me and put his other arm around me.

There was something incredibly tender in his embrace, a softness, and gentle curiosity, all mixed up with the potent seduction of some need of his own. The last cynical cell in my brain asked giddily, *Why stop him? He is so good at this.*

He sighed, squeezed my back and shoulders with his enormous hands, like a cat working its paws while you stroke its fur.

"Did you ever see any of Miriam's journals?" I asked the warmth of his chest. *Do you know what you do to people?*

He nodded dreamily, his hand now sliding cozily down my spine.

The last journal. How I needed it now, needed to climb down into the warmth of its candor. What would Miriam have done just now? What *had* she done?

"What about it?" he murmured, his warm breath seeping into my hair. "Do you have it?"

"No."

Looking into the scene as in a dream, I said, "Did you see one at her rented ranch house the afternoon before she died? That was you, wasn't it, who visited?"

He nodded again, the strong angle of his jaw massaging the crown of my head.

Yes, he had visited, or yes, he had seen her journal there that afternoon? "That last volume is missing," I whispered.

He shook his head. Taking this for commiseration, I sighed again. Perhaps I would never see that volume. Perhaps the sheriff had it, and read it greedily in the evenings, when he wasn't rubbing salve on his private parts. Or worse yet, when he was. The thought drifted away from me as the anger around it melted into sadness. "How'd you know she had gone ahead and rented the Broken Spoke Ranch?" I asked, asking anything to make the intimacy of the moment last. "Was it Po Bradley told you?"

"No. Cindey Howard."

Click. "Cindey. She didn't *like* Miriam very much, *did* she?"

Chandler tipped his head to look down into my face. He shrugged. "The Cindeys of the world have no balls. I guess they envy the women who do." He smiled lazily, making the comment into a comparison, a compliment.

I smiled back. I couldn't help it. It was just too rich and heady an experience to be so near to this man, to share these easy confidences. I felt clever, as if I was winning him with my mind. "Why'd she tell you where Miriam was? I thought the whole idea was that Miriam was hiding Cecelia from you."

"I guess she just wanted me to know."

"Had you just told her you were on your way down to see Po?" I asked, now bouyed on a cloud of arrogance that said I was so clever that it was *I* who was seducing *him*.

Chandler's cheek muscles twisted into a wry smile that bunched his mustache. He lifted one hand, drew a lock of hair from my forehead. "I don't think I go around telling Cindey Howard my plans, Em Hansen."

"Well, if—"

Chandler pulled me up close to his body again with both hands. Smiled at me without showing any teeth. Put an index finger over my lips. "Enough questions," he said firmly. "Let's enjoy what's left of this fine evening."

So we walked, and soon we reached the front steps of the inn. I paused next to my rental car, but he tightened his grip on my waist and drew me up the steps. Ever so softly, he said, "We're not done here yet."

A boost of warm adrenaline swept through my system, half fear and half anticipation. I looked quickly around, saw a middle-aged man sitting on the steps of a porch across the street, beyond Chandler's back. The man raised one index finger in a brief salute, a quick motion that let me know he was watching. *Ortega has been busy,* I realized, half-glad and half-disappointed that this meeting was almost at an end. *The sentinels are in place. They'll move in soon, probably just waiting for a warrant, a final signal. I'm supposed to keep him in sight.* To Chandler, I said, "Lead on."

37

THERE WAS NO CHAIR IN HIS ROOM. ONLY THE BED, A BIG QUEEN-sized fantasy done up with wrought-iron head and foot, mountains of pillows, and an enormous soft goose-down duvet decked in lace. Chandler reached up under the pillows, grasped the top of the comforter and the crisp white top sheet underneath, and pulled them down to the foot of the bed. Then he knocked a few of the fluffy pillows off onto the floor, selected two that looked more like they were meant to be slept on, and plumped them down at the head of the bed. He swept me up into his arms and arranged me on the mattress, placing me so that my head landed squarely on one of the pillows. Trading hugs on the town square was one thing, but being thrown around like a doll in the silence of his lair unleashed another layer of fear. I tried to sit up again, but he placed one wide hand firmly on my abdomen and held me down while he kicked off his shoes. "Hey!" I squealed, trying to pass off uncertainty in a cloud of humor. "Don't I even get kissed?"

Chandler smiled appreciatively at my joke. "That's not what this is about, Em Hansen. Now you just relax and let the Chandler do his job."

Job?

I started to thrash, unwilling to be found naked with this man when the authorities moved in for the collar. But Chandler now had my feet in his hands, raised above mattress level. He lifted them a little farther and expertly swiveled himself underneath them, so that he wound up sitting at the foot of the bed with my feet in his lap. None too sensuously, he removed my shoes, and then my socks, and then, lest I worry about whether my feet were clean, he pulled off his socks, too, and pulled his feet up under him cross-legged. And began to massage the soles of my feet.

I love being massaged. Backs are great, legs and arms wonderful, heads terrific, but feet are the nectar of the gods. I was in heaven. He probed deeply with his two great thumbs, bracing his fingers along the tops of my feet, digging, bursting at tension, nudging, cajoling. . . .

"I'm in love," I mumbled idiotically, some tiny part of my brain still wondering what I was doing on this man's bed.

"Good."

"More!" I said, deciding that I didn't care what happened, that I knew exactly what I was doing, that—

"There's no rush. You just relax, lady."

And I did. I closed my eyes and slid slowly into a narcotic syrup of comfort, sank past the last tearful barriers that broke away like screaming timbers, sank through layers of tension that broke like shining bubbles touched by children. My mind wandered onward through mountains and across the prairies of my youth, hovering like a kestrel, gliding like an eagle. Chandler searched my feet with authority, seeking out each cramp and tightness, now pressing, now warming, now caressing with his great broad hands. And by and by, a tiny gem of light caught my mind's eye, and I hovered downward, circling, trying to find the facet that had shattered the sky. I felt myself falling. Falling through the afternoon's roiling clouds, stuck endlessly in the cockpit of that airplane, the angry clouds now parting, revealing a terrifying wall of rock and another and another, again and again, with no relief, the end looming but never quite coming.

Forcing the dreadful fantasy to a conclusion, I imagined that I rammed the little plane into the cliff, engulfing my own tiny spark in a ball of flames.

From flames, I fell into a pool of darkness. The darkness held a seed, half made of light and half of darkness. I moved toward it and found, to my sadness, my own self, all curled up tightly like an embryo in an egg. As I watched, I grew and uncurled, becoming now a child, now a young woman, and now . . . With horror, I stared into my own eyes and saw that they had become my mother's.

I gasped.

"What is it?" Chandler's voice asked, as if from far away.

"I'm afraid!" I cried.

"Dive through it!"

I did. My mother's face vanished, leaving only an ache that spun like a wheel, now turning with a terrible strength. The strength hurled me into the darkness, and I was alone, yet still a wheel myself, turning, an endless carousel of life.

I saw myself then, in all my fear and vanity, wisdom and foolishness, pride and nakedness. And I began to cry.

Quick as that, Chandler was next to me, his great long body wrapped around me, holding me tightly as the first strangled sobs grew into a torrent. He held me and rocked me, the male strength of his body drawing the tears out fiercely. Tears of anger. Tears of sadness. Tears of loss. As my eyes leaked and grew wet, I blubbered something into his ear, in the confused, selfish madness of grief: "All I get is hugs? Miriam got sex!"

Chandler squeezed me harder. "That's what she needed," he whispered hotly into my ear. "She hadn't reached as far as you."

In the fullness of my grief, I roared onward, crying out each hurt and loss in the mad safety of Chandler's arms. And as my eyes dried, I fell asleep.

38

I woke to the smells of black coffee and crisp bacon wafting up the stairs from the dining room.

I felt around under the covers. I was still clothed, and Chandler was gone.

My eyes shot open. The brilliant sunlight of a rare cloudless Jackson spring morning was streaming through the fussy lace curtains, spilling onto the bed. I threw back the covers, yanked on my shoes, and hurried downstairs.

In the dining room, I found a table laid for one. Steam rose encouragingly from a coffee urn beyond the plate. Uncertain how to proceed, I stopped, grasping the back of the pressed-wood chair.

"Ready for some waffles?" came a voice behind me. I turned, saw the innkeeper coming in from the kitchen. She offered me a preliminary smile as she peered at me through her sharp blue eyes.

"Waffles. Ah—"

"Chandler left me a note asking me to hold his breakfast for you. He said you'd probably sleep pretty late." She laughed. "The rest of the guests ate an hour ago."

"Chandler. Where—"

"He's gone, darlin'. Gone, gone, gone. Caught a flight with a friend in a private jet to L.A. at midnight, I hear, and he's on his way to Hong Kong by now."

"Hong Kong?" I asked, completely flabbergasted.

"Or maybe they were really on their way to New York, and he'll be seen in Paris next."

"Paris?" My voice came out high and weepy.

"It's the nature of the beast, dearie. Easy come, easy go. The nice thing is, he always pays in cash."

"Do you think—"

"Someone's after him? Oh, probably. Like those nice sheriff's deputies who came by here a couple hours ago? They asked after you. I told them you were still upstairs sawing logs, but they insisted on taking a peek. Friends of yours? They said to tell you—let me make sure I get this right—'Ortega says the coast is clear.' "

I shook my head slowly, dazed. Was the coast clear? In my rush, what had I failed to tell him? Ortega didn't know about the man waiting with Po Bradley in Douglas. Would he just fold his tent and vanish if his boss was behind bars?

Reading my expression, she said, "Let it go, honey. If it wasn't the law that chased Chandler away, it would be someone who wants him to pay a debt for some bigger frog in the pond, if you know what I mean. Boys like him can't seem to stay out of trouble. Or was it *you* who scared him off?" she asked, bowing her head slightly, so that she was looking at me through her eyebrows.

"Shit."

"Oh, relax. If anyone knows how to survive out there in the big bad world, it's our Chandler. Now about your breakfast: you want yogurt and berries on those waffles, or are you strictly a butter and maple syrup type?"

❖

AN HOUR LATER, I was full past my eyebrows with freshly squeezed orange juice, herbed sausage, waffles, some truly great black coffee, and, why not, a muffin or two; I had luxuriated just a bit in the claw-foot tub down the hall from Chandler's room, had wrestled a clean shirt and underwear out of the bag in my rental car, and was standing by the front door, trying to figure out what one says in farewell to an innkeeper like that one, when a middle-aged man came shambling out of what I presumed to be the innkeeper's living quarters beyond the kitchen. He was a gray kind of man, quiet in his manner, one of those types who don't seem to take up much room in the world, personality-wise. Shrugging his way into a heavy plaid shirt, he shuffled up to the innkeeper, kissed her sweetly on the cheek, and said, "Be back in a coupla days."

"Have a good run, Tom."

"Right. See you then, cupcake." The man exited back through the kitchen, and a moment later I heard the deep growl of a diesel tractor starting up.

"My husband," the innkeeper said. "He drives an eighteen-wheeler."

"Seemed like a nice guy," I said. The words flew out of my mouth before I thought, and I was immediately sorry, as they sounded as condescending as I felt. Couldn't or hadn't a woman who had the moxie to run as fine a place as this do better than that?

The innkeeper answered my unspoken question with her eyes. They said, Back down, sister.

I looked at the floor. My overcurious mind was on the way to giving me a sad comedown from the night's relief and the more solitary pleasures of the morning. Uncertain what to say, I just stood there staring at my feet.

"You look to me like a woman who needs just one more cup of coffee," she said.

I grinned. "Ain't that the truth."

The innkeeper took me into the inner sanctum of her kitchen and poured me another cup of her wonderful brew. When she was settled back with a cup of her own and had drawn a good strong draft from its depths, she leaned back and stared out the window toward her husband's semitractor, which was now warmed up and ready to roll. He tooted a horn and she gave him a cheery wave. He shifted the truck into gear and it started to roll. "Chandler's note said you were one of his Don Quixote types. What is it you're trying to find out?"

"Ma'am?"

"Come on! You're no ingenue. You know and I know that the Chandlers of the world have a whole string of women."

"Listen here!"

The innkeeper waved a hand at me. "Simmer down, darlin'; *this* girl hasn't a whole lot of room to go judging you."

I looked out the window toward the spot where her husband's truck had sat only moments before.

"Exactly," she said. "Tom's a good man, let there be no doubt. I will wash his clothes and keep his brand of beer in the fridge until the day one or both of us dies. But honey baby, that beer can go a little flat."

There was nothing to say, so I just smiled that smile you offer someone who's just told you this kind of thing about herself.

"The world needs more men like Chandler Jennings," she went on. "He expects so little, and gives so much in return. What other kind of guy will sleep upstairs like a good boy when your husband's home and clap him on the back and say 'Hey there, buddy' like they're long-lost friends and then—" She broke off, stared a while into her coffee, then took another draft.

"Has he been coming here a long time?" I asked.

"Chandler? A few years."

"I'm, ah, curious about him. I mean, I don't really know him, past last night anyway. Aw hell, that's the first time I ever met the guy—who am I kidding?"

"Not me, darling." The innkeeper gazed at me, waiting. Clearly it was still my turn to speak.

I thought about telling her how I'd come to know about him and how and why I'd followed him here, but I couldn't see the point. Much better just to ask, and let this woman celebrate her secret passion on her own terms and in her own time. "I got the feeling he's here a lot, like he uses this place as a base of operations."

"Operations? That's as good a word as any other. God knows what our boy is up to. He's forty-nine and doesn't do any regular work that *I* know about. He shows up here on his own schedule, sometimes here for a week or maybe two, sometimes gone for months on end." She shifted her gaze to the window, a look of forced patience, of endless waiting settling into her lovely face. "I store his car in the garage out back and he pays me for it, bless his heart, though I'd do it for free, even though it would get Tom to wondering. No one's ever called him here except you, so he must get his messages somewhere else, though this is a small town and I've yet to figure out who he uses."

It occurred to me that this woman, whose name I did not even know, was telling me things she did not tell other people. But then, I was not her usual type of guest. I was an interloper, a hunter who had flushed her fancy man out of her nest, and she knew it. He might not ever return. It was my job therefore to listen, to ask questions, to keep her company while she made her adjustment to the empty seasons that would follow. I didn't know what to think of her, but my heart was full of fear. I knew only that I did not want to end up like her, eking out an ounce of gratification while the world passed by her table.

"Has anyone else ever tracked him here?" I asked. "I mean, other than me calling?"

The innkeeper inclined her head. "You mean other women? No. Chandler's a gentleman, you know? He has men friends about town, and they drop by now and then. Or you can find him at the brew pub, or half a dozen other places, and I'm sure he's a regular visitor out with the golf course set."

I thought of Saratoga and of the imposingly large houses I'd seen surrounding the golf course on the plain south of the Jackson Hole Airport, recalibrating Chandler in my mind, adding the word *chameleon* to his list of virtues. For this woman, he had formed himself into a gentle has-been, a dilettante with an appetite for gin, no doubt. There was within his madness a gift for empathy and the odd flash of healing. He could tower up with the eyes of the hunter, or roll over and look like prey, easy to love, in a small way, and easy to discount if one needed to. It was all a matter of what one needed at the moment, as he had so simply explained to me. This woman didn't know the Chandler who delivered powdered dreams of invulnerability to aging suburban housewives, or to ranch owners with dwindling resources and a taste for the wild side.

I wiped a red-and-white-checked napkin across my mouth and resolved to leave this one woman within the limits of her knowledge. "How about men? Any men come looking for him? Other than this morning, I mean."

"Just that sheriff from Converse County."

My eyebrows flew up. "Duluth? Duluth was here?"

"Guy that looks like he has a rash on his private parts? Yep, that's our boy."

"When?"

"Clear last August. He asked the same questions you did. Like where was Chandler the night of August third."

"And you told him?"

The innkeeper turned toward me. "I told him the *truth*. Chandler pulled in here about eleven o'clock that night. Like I say, I was closed for everyone except him."

"And you told this to Duluth."

"I confirmed that he had arrived here at eleven o'clock, and that to the best of my knowledge, he was here the rest of the night. After all," she said saucily, "a girl can sleep rather hard after heavy exercise."

Eleven o'clock. About when Miriam was being killed. I dragged a napkin across my lips, my business there finished. "You've been very kind to me," I said.

"It's nothing," she said.

"I want you to know that Chandler and I . . . I mean, last night, we . . . nothing ah—"

"I know. If he had, I'd have broken his balls."

TEN MINUTES LATER, I was pulling on my jacket to leave. "Thanks again," I said.

"Come by anytime," the innkeeper said automatically. Her sharp blue eyes had taken on a dreamy quality, and I was having trouble telling which way she was looking, given the reflection off her rimless glasses. "You going far today?"

I groaned. "Just to Douglas. By light plane." How was I going to do this? Getting back on a horse after a fall was one thing, but horses didn't fly so far off the ground.

"Perfect flying weather, or such as we get around here. Not too often we have sunshine this time of the year here in Jackson."

I gave her a rueful smile. This I now certainly knew.

"No, really, I used to take a turn at the yoke myself. I caught a weather report this morning, and you've got a nice high-pressure system from Oregon to Nebraska." When I didn't say anything, she asked, "How many hours you got?"

I looked at my feet.

"You even licensed yet?"

"Student," I said miserably.

"And you flew in here yesterday?"

I nodded.

"Goll, woman, get yourself a good scare maybe? That weather was for shits."

This time, my head wouldn't even move.

"That bad, huh?"

In a small voice, I said, "I'm not so sure I want to fly anymore."

"Aw hell. Scares are good. They teach you a lot. Like the saying goes, There are old pilots and bold pilots, but no old bold pilots. Give yourself a break. You're less bold today than you were yesterday."

I muttered something like, "Maybe."

"Would you do again today what you did yesterday?"

"No."

"Okay, then. You ask for John Hendrix out at the airport. He's the fool who taught me. You tell him I sent you, and he'll go over your flight plan with you and make sure you know what you're doing.

"My radio doesn't work."

"Go see John. He'll take a look at your gear, and if he thinks you shouldn't be airborne, he'll tell you so, and you come on back here."

"Yes, ma'am."

"Good. Now go out there and fly that plane. But first, you're going to let me make you a sandwich."

I let her, hungry as I was for any token that might bring me courage. She bustled about her kitchen, throwing together luncheon meats and cheeses, spreading special mustards on thick slabs of chewy bread. Inserting a crisp layer of red-leaf lettuce, she slapped down the top slice, cut the sandwich in two, and wrapped it carefully in plastic. She put it in a bag, added an apple and a paper napkin, and handed it to me.

I started toward the street again, my feet numbly taking me forward. As I swung the door open, the innkeeper stared through it, waiting to see what life brought her next. Suddenly, her gaze stopped drifting and her eyes snapped my way. "Wait—I almost forgot!" she said, and hurried back out of the room. On her return, she handed me a thin, flat package wrapped up in brown paper and sealed with fiberglass-filament packaging tape. It didn't take any great intuition to decide it was a book. She said, "Our boy said to give this to you. Something about lightening his load, or maybe it was that you needed this more than he did. I forget which."

Quickly thanking her, I hurried out the door, down the steps, and around to my car, already shifting the handles of my bag so that I could pick at the tape on Chandler's package.

In the car, I got a thumb underneath the edge of the paper and tore. Sure enough, as the paper yielded, it revealed a journal with a pasteboard cover decorated in marbled black and white to look like leather.

39

I drove north of Jackson toward the airport, but turned right instead of left, following the banks of the Gros Ventre River. I felt the need to be completely alone when I read Miriam's last entries, away from any prying or insensitive eyes.

The Park Service campground a few miles up along the river was closed, but I parked the car near the gate and took Miriam's last journal through the trees until I could see that jumble of half-melted ice and freezing water and hear nothing but its call. Kicking aside a thatch of frozen leaves and cuddling down against the roots of a pine tree, I placed the volume on my lap and smoothed the cover with one hand. There was only one date inscribed there, the day she had begun writing in it. The date she had finished, her hand could write no more. I held it sadly, knowing there would be no completion, and no farewell.

I began to read, skimming along for those entries that held answers for me:

September 7

Things are getting difficult with Cecelia. Her moods are growing worse and worse, and she doesn't look after herself. Her hair hangs like a filthy mop. It's so hard to remember that this was my little darling, the one I thought glowed with the light of the angels. Right now, I'd say she was getting her ideas from downstairs.

September 22

I'm trying to remember the last time Joe and I had sex. I won't call it lovemaking anymore. I'm just talking about getting laid. Last night, I brought the subject up again and in no time at all it was a fight, with me using any words I could think of to try to get him riled so I'd at least see some feeling. In the end, I felt like I'd been begging him for sex again. I hate that, and I can see in his face that it just pushes him farther away. I know my anger toward him is just making things worse. I wouldn't like someone coming at me like that, so why should he?

I read faster and faster, lines jumping out at me.

October 14

Cecelia is seeing someone she doesn't want to tell me about.

November 17

Joe and I had sex last night, the first time in months. A Saturday, of course. It just didn't do much for me. I tried thinking sexy thoughts about someone else, like I used to, but that just made me feel like I was losing my mind.

January 22

I'm taking a night course on storytelling. Our assignment for tonight is to write an outline for a story so we can learn what goes into story structure. I hope the teacher's broad-minded, because mine is a sizzler. I'm going to write about a woman who finds the perfect man. He's mature but has the body of a young man, he takes pleasure in cleaning up the kitchen after the woman messes it up, and, best of all, his greatest pleasure is to bring her pleasure. He gets into bed at night ready to give her a back rub if that's what she wants, hold her tenderly and listen to her innermost thoughts if that's what she wants, and, best of the best, give her truly fantastic sex. Oh, and he's genetically engineered so that his hormones resonate off of hers, and so his arousal depends upon and follows hers. He never comes too quickly.

January 23

The teacher read my story outline and wanted to know where the next page was! She used it as an example of what doesn't work. I was shocked! She explained that as the story core for a novel, my story wouldn't make it, because nothing happens. I argued that lots happens, he cleans up the kitchen, massages her back, and gives her great sex, what did she want? She said it needed tension, action, learning. My characters are the same at the end of the novel as they are in the beginning. Then she read a few love scenes from books where the characters are in complete harmony and she was right, they were boring. It wasn't even titillating.

January 25

Still thinking about the storytelling class. I'm beginning to see something from this, like the message is that if Joe indulged me in every little thing and knew what I wanted without my telling him, I wouldn't learn anything. And I clearly have a lot to learn.

February 16

My therapist suggested that I look at the places where I'm angry with Joe and see what that tells me about me, instead of him. In a flash, I saw that I've really needed him to be safe, just like he is. But this same thing—his very safeness—drives me nuts. For the first time, I feel kind of grateful to him. And when I think of things in this light, I realize that we've been together so long, and I know him so well, that if I had to start over with somebody else, it would take me many years to get to this stage of knowing him, and then I'd have to continue on from there. And maybe I'd make all the same mistakes again, and wind up with someone just as inflexible. I guess I'm so wobbly that I need someone to be that inflexible, just so I know where and who I am. Am I realizing that I truly love Joe, at least in the nonromantic sense?

February 28

I'm reading back my most recent entries and something just hit me: it's not sex I want at all; it's sensuality. I realized a while ago that Joe can be sexual, but he doesn't know how to be sensual. That's what C was, just a creature of the senses, with no substance. Is it so much to ask to have both qualities in one man? And now that I know this, can Joe be taught? I don't think so. Or is he capable, but just holding it back behind that incredible wall of his? I'm not sure I want to think about the possibility that some people are born asensual. That would be a terrible handicap. Or do they just suffer less?

April 26

Cecelia's behavior has taken a real downturn. I thought she was doing so much better, even though she hardly talks to me, just glares, but I had a call today from the headmistress of her school saying she's been cutting classes in the afternoons. I confronted her and asked if she was sneaking off with some boy, and she said what if she was? and sneered at me. I suggested she bring the boy home to meet us. She just started to laugh. I didn't like the sound of it.

May 5

I had Joe talk to Cecelia about the boy. She wouldn't speak, didn't even listen. He's worried, too. Her moods are atrocious.

May 14

I can hardly bear to write this, but I must. I came home early from the gym today and found Cecelia hiding out behind the horse barn, talking to Chandler Jennings. I was so furious I ran at him, screaming. He looked at me with those crazy eyes of his and said nothing. Cecelia was hitting at me and shrieking, telling me I had no right to run him off like that. Good God, she's not even sixteen; please help her! I'd have the son of a bitch arrested, but he's disappeared like a mist. Cecelia was hysterical, saying that if he couldn't meet her there how was she going to find him? I asked her point blank if she was sleeping with him, and she came at me clawing and

scratching, totally incoherent. It's all my fault for ever having anything to do with that monster. I don't know what to tell Joe.

May 16

I've decided to take Cecelia away with me for the summer. I can
take her to school myself until then, and pick her up each day, instead of letting her ride with Heather or any of the other girls, but
after school lets out, I can't be vigilant every day. I need to get her
away somewhere I can keep her safe from him. I don't have the
courage to tell Joe. Just when I'm realizing there's something worth
having in our marriage, my mistakes come back to haunt me.

May 20

I told Julia I wanted to get Cecelia away from a man that was paying her too much attention, and she suggested I take Cecelia to a
dude ranch. There would be horses there to distract her. She was all
for protecting her from older men.

May 29

Julia called back today and said she had just the place for me, a
small ranch in the middle of nowhere up in Wyoming with horse
barns and everything. Who of all people but Cindey Howard
knows the landowner, some rancher she met during her weekends
up in Saratoga. I guess old Cindey can be helpful once in awhile
after all.

Joe agreed to the price of the rental and I've explained to everyone that we want a quiet hideaway summer, as in don't tell anyone
where we are. It's close enough to Denver that Joe will come up Friday evenings and return on Sunday afternoons, God bless his pre-
dictability. Maybe we'll be like a family again. And what the hell,
he'll be with me Saturday nights.

June 13

School's out today. We're off tomorrow, pulling our horse trailer
like a couple of ranch women. Cecelia doesn't seem too horrified

at being taken away from her friends, just her usual moping. I'm beginning to feel very hopeful about this.

June 22

It's beautiful here. The ranch sits near the north end of the
Laramie Range, and the meadows are full of wildflowers. The horses
are kicking up their heels.

Cecelia sleeps late each day, but I suppose that's normal for an
adolescent.

Po Bradley, the foolish man who owns this ranch, dropped by
again today. He seems to think himself the ladies' man. I think he's
very sweet, but he ought to get a life. He told me to watch out for
the local sheriff, a man called Elwin Duluth, of all corn-fed names.
Po says Elwin has a crush on me. He said it in all seriousness. What
a joke.

July 15

Cecelia's 16th birthday. My little girl is a woman now. How
I wish I could spare her some of the confusion that comes with
all those hormones. As Cecelia slept late this morning, I danced
around the meadow outside remembering her birth, wishing her a
better, wiser adulthood than I've had. It's nice to dance again. Why
has it taken me this long to realize that for some pleasures, I don't
need a partner?

July 18

I was dancing in the meadow again this morning and found Po
Bradley watching me from a thicket of willows up by the irrigation
ditch. He brought me a handful of wildflowers and said I was the
most beautiful thing he'd seen around "these parts" in years. I felt vi-
olated. This is supposed to be our safe place.

July 27

Joe just left to drive back to Denver for the week. Last night as
we lay in bed here talking about this and that, where Cecelia might

go to college and what travels we might like to take together someday when we have the time, I had a glimpse of how nice it is for
some couples who have been married for fifty or sixty years and
have all those years together. They're old and maybe sex doesn't
mean much anymore and all those things they've been through together have grown up into a garden of memory and shared importance for them. I guess I'm finally realizing that while Joe isn't the
intimate I've always dreamed of, he is the one who's been along for
this ride, and while he hasn't been a source of joy and stimulation
exactly, he hasn't beaten me or played around. He's not the exten-
sion of myself and fountain of gratification I've always wished he
was, but he's my constant, my rock. And he said something really
sweet: he said that it was important to have me next to him at night,
just to reach out and touch if he awakens.

July 31

Joe called this evening as usual and told me the most wretched
news. Fred Howard's company is being bought out by someone or
other, but Fred "borrowed" a lot of money from the company retirement fund to cover his and Cindey's expensive habits. Not just
his money, everybody's money! That's theft! He came to Joe asking
for a loan to cover it so no one would find him out when they ran
the audit. Fred claims he had always banked on an upturn in oil
prices that would make his stock worth more so he could cover the
"loans" his company was "making" for him. I said I guessed they'd
have to stay home from Saratoga once in a while and quit eating
such expensive steak and drinking such fancy wine as if it were
water. Joe said he didn't think that leopard was going to change his
spots. Joe sounded really disgusted. I was proud of him. I asked if he
was going to give Fred the money and he said no, that it was a lot,
and besides, what kind of banker makes unsecured loans to spenders
who keep on spending? I said I agreed, that I didn't think it was a
good idea to bail people out from such activities.

This is going to kill Cindey. She always was too proud for words.
I feel lucky, because Joe's always been so smart about his invest-

ments. Julia would say that I shouldn't be relying on a man to look after me, but I say that one way or another, the bare bones of existence need to be maintained and that past a certain point it doesn't matter whether each person is out there working separately or whether people have an old-fashioned division of labor like Joe and I have.

Joe will be up tomorrow night and I'm truly looking forward to seeing him. It's nice to feel this homey old warmth growing up between us.

August 3

Joe just left. He went over the back way so he could stop in Saratoga on the way home. Even though he isn't going to loan him money, he wants to hold Fred's hand through this merger.

We had a really nice weekend. Cecelia was her usual morose self, but Joe and I went for a long ride together up into the hills by the Laramie Range and it was just plain pleasant. I guess before I was always worried about getting my own needs met, but now that I'm being a grown-up and really giving to others with all my heart, I find that my own needs are met more strongly than ever. What an irony. Oddly, the needs that are being met are not the needs I thought needed meeting.

There are the same old adult things I will always want and need, but I see now that I really want them from Joe. Maybe he'll remain forever tone-deaf as a lover, but he's *my* lover. True, he still shuts down whenever I let him know how much all these years of living with a stone just plain hurts, but maybe I'm strong enough now just to let that go.

Right, fat chance. Heaven knows, I've tried and tried to let go of that hurt, tried to rationalize it away a hundred thousand ways, but it still just plain hurts. Maybe like my therapist says, everyone has one or two needs that can't be met, but they're legitimate needs just the same.

It's hard to stay conscious of the hurt—much easier to rage about it or hide out in a depression—but I'm learning to hold on to the hurt. I ram it like a thorn through my hand to keep me conscious, honoring it as the uncontrollable force that it is. It humbles me, and humble feels good and sturdy and sane. So here it is: I offer my pain as a daily act of contrition. I offer it to God, or to the great whatever that gives me enough heart even to wonder if there is a God. And as I stop asking Joe to be God for me, I find I love him more and more for being just a man.

Perhaps I'm finally growing up.

On the morning of Tuesday, August 3, Miriam began her last entry.

August 3

It's another beautiful day in paradise. I'm sitting out here on the front porch writing in you, my old pal journal, and enjoying the way the breeze plays through the tall grasses, nothing more.

It's almost noon, time to try to get Cecelia to go for a ride with me. If I can even get her out of bed! How that girl can sleep!

Later—

Joe just called. He says he wants to come up this evening. He says he needs to discuss something with me but that he can't talk about it over the phone. How unlike him.

Cecelia wouldn't get up. Cursed at me. I'll just sit here and write.

All right, I'm worried. What if after all this, Joe found out about good old you know who?

I'll just think about something else.

There's somebody coming. I'm getting to be a real ranch woman, sitting here watching the dust kick up on the road as someone approaches. I wonder who it could be? The mailman? Po, with another one of his pretty nosegays? His snarling wife? I'm getting good at judging whether it's a pickup truck or a sedan, even before the dust clears enough to see. This one's a sedan, a noisy gold BMW, just like

And that was all. A harsh line of ink stretched away from the last word, an uncontrolled mark left by a woman afraid.

40

I RAN UP THROUGH THE TREES TOWARD THE TELEPHONES I HAD seen by the gate to the campground. It took two calls to find Sergeant Ortega. The operator at the police switchboard directed me to his mother's home, where I found him having a second breakfast.

"Em," he said tiredly.

"I'm okay, Carlos."

"Okay? Just okay?"

"Yeah. 'Just okay' will have to do for now. I've got the last volume of the journal. Get J.C. and Cecelia in a car, and meet me in Douglas."

He snorted. "Just like that?"

"Please, Carlos. I'm on the way to the airport." Yes, I was going to drive to the airport, pull myself together, climb into that plane, fire its engine, and fly the hell back down that canyon. "It'll take you four hours' road time to Douglas, plus whatever to round up the Menkens. I've got to dump my rental car, get some provisions, and find a man named John. Lay out a flight plan—carefully. Talk to the guys that fly out of here all the time." I stopped myself, realizing that I was babbling. "So what I'm saying is, I have to fly from here to there, so I'm guessing about the travel time, you see, give or take an hour. I'll make sure the radio is working, trust me on this, and stay in touch with Flight Following and Casper Flight Service. Please just meet me at the Douglas Airport as soon as you can."

I heard the sound of chewing from Carlos's end of the line.

"Please," I urged. And then realized what I had forgotten to say. "I have it narrowed down to just a few people who could have killed Miriam, but I need your help to narrow it to one. And to protect me from Po Bradley." I explained, finally, and with great contrition, that he had been right.

I heard lips smacking, fingers being licked. "I'll have you know Mama made fritters. And the boys in suits have been digging through Mr. Howard's books for hours now while Mr. Howard and his friends enjoy the Fed's very finest hospitality. A regular fiesta. You leave Mr. Bradley to me."

Laughing almost giddily, I replaced the phone in its cradle, knowing that my friend would come through for me once again.

41

Six hours of instruction, preparation, prayer, and intense concentration later, I touched down smoothly at Douglas, again scattering the small herd of pronghorn antelope and a few jackrabbits away from the end of the strip. The little plane's engine hummed smoothly as I taxied around the near side of the blue hangar, and as I shut down the engine and climbed wearily from the door over the wing, Carlos Ortega climbed out of his sedan. The grease spots of his morning meal were still evident on his pressed white broadcloth shirt. A second door of his car opened, and J.C. Menken swung a foot free, levered out his greater height, and stood up. He appeared anxious but he smiled, ever optimistic. In the backseat of the car I could see a dark tangle of hair: Cecelia.

I gave Carlos an affectionate half hug and shook J.C.'s hand stiffly. His face was tight, and his usually shallow eyes had gone deep with anxiety. "Good flight?" Carlos asked.

"Uneventful, I'm glad to tell you. I waited to take off until I was damned sure I could make it without—" I stopped short, embarrassed.

He nodded. "We been here only a little while."

Making sure we were not overheard, I asked, "What about the flights to Casper?"

He closed his eyes and shook his head. "That wasn't how it was done."

I set my lips in frustration. "Damn. Well, we'll have to pry it out of her, then."

After locking and tying down the Piper and ordering its tanks topped up, I checked to make certain my rental car was still in the hangar. When we were done with our errand, I would fetch it and drive into Douglas, check into the LaBonte, and sleep until I could sleep no more.

But first things first. I followed Carlos over to his sedan, and climbed in next to Cecelia. "Nice to see you," I told her soberly.

She made brief, gloomy eye contact, but then quickly looked away. Taking her hands in both of mine, I murmured, "We'll have this all cleared up in just awhile now, Cecelia. You just stick with me."

Carlos started the engine of the sedan and pulled away from the apron. "Where to?" he asked.

"Head back out like you're returning to the interstate, but just past the McDonald's turn left on Riverbend and then right on the Cold Springs Road. I'm sure J.C. knows the way."

Menken turned around in his seat to look at me. "Are you sure this is a good idea, Emily? I mean, I'm all for anything that can help Cecelia, but . . ."

All I could say was an uncertain "Don't worry, J.C."

The air was soft and warm and dry. I watched the back of Sergeant Ortega's head as he drove along the now-familiar stretch of the Cold Springs Road as it wound along through lengthening afternoon shadows past this ranch and that, past the reservoir, and along La Prele Creek. "Turn in there," I said when I spied the approach to the old homestead.

Po Bradley and Sheriff Duluth were waiting for us at the ranch house, Po standing on the front porch with his arms folded nervously across his chest, and Sheriff Duluth sitting insolently in his prowl car, sipping coffee from a Styrofoam cup. The two men studiously ignored each other. "You called Duluth?" I asked Ortega.

He nodded. "Professional courtesy," he said. "And suggested that Mr. Bradley join us also. I figured it would save Sheriff Duluth some driving around after you finish swearing out your complaints."

I thought delicately of foolish old Po cooling his heels in jail, and smiled even as I wanted to cry. This was not how old ranch families were supposed to wind up. He seemed righteously nervous, and when he saw me there, he avoided meeting my eyes.

Duluth heaved himself out of his car as we drove up. He fixed a look of irritation on me, as if he'd finally found the source of his rash, but he addressed himself to Sergeant Ortega. "A bit out of your jurisdiction, ain't it, Sergeant?"

Ortega gave him his patent cheery "Who, me?" smile and climbed up out of his sedan. "I'm here as a friend of the Menkens', Sheriff. I appreciate your turning out to assist us." Then he turned to Po. "You Mr. Bradley? I'm Carlos Ortega. Nice ranch you have here. My family comes from the San Luis Valley in southern Colorado, and we had a place like this once. Only it was adobe. But very open." He held out a hand, palm up, and surveyed the scene as if we had gathered for a picnic.

Po extended a quizzical hand. "You a cop?" he asked.

"De-tec-tive," Carlos sang.

"Well, let's get on with it," Duluth said, stomping up onto the wooden boards of the porch.

"Hold it!" We all turned. J.C. Menken stood next to Cecelia's door in Ortega's sedan, holding it closed. "Gentlemen, Emily, we need to get something straight right now. I will not put Cecelia through any more trauma. I've watched her all the way up here, and I can tell you this is not good. I agreed to come, but now we need a little explanation."

Duluth opened his mouth to say something sour, but I spoke first. "You're right, J.C., we need to take this by increments. Po, could you please unlock the door, and all the rest of you, I'd like you to stay outside for a while so we can ease Cecelia along."

Menken wasn't going to be led that easily. "Are you absolutely certain she even needs to go inside?"

"Yes."

"Perhaps just you and I should go first, make sure there's no sign of—"

"I've already checked, Joe." I reached out a hand to urge him toward me. "Please. I've thought this through carefully. This may hurt worse at first, but she needs to face it if she's ever going to heal."

Menken set his jaw, looked each person in the eye, and at last opened the door for his daughter. "Come on, sweetheart," he said gently. "We've come this far. Let's do this now, and then we can go home."

◆

CECELIA STOOD IN the middle of the living room with her back to the door. Menken stood behind her, his hands extended around her but not touching her, as if guarding a porcelain vase that might at any moment fall. After checking to make certain that the door was latched shut against the prying ears and eyes of the three men who waited on the porch, I walked around toward the fireplace and looked into her face. It was as blank as uncut stone. I stepped closer and took her hand in mine. Its palm was damp and cool.

Menken shot me an anxious look.

I addressed myself to Cecelia. "Let's go into your mother's room," I said, attempting to draw her toward the passageway.

Cecelia stood frozen to the floor.

Menken spoke quickly. "This isn't good, Em. I think we'd better take her back outside."

"No, J.C., there's something we can discover here."

"But Em—"

"Be quiet, please, J.C. I think Cecelia needs to speak for herself."

Cecelia's eyes grew glassy. Her hand went stiff in mine. Impulsively, I shifted my grip to her wrist, held the back of her hand to my cheek. Her pulse was fast and faint.

"Now, Cecelia," I began again, "let's start earlier in the day, back before the part you forget."

Cecelia's gaze moved toward me and back, a quick flick.

"You had slept late," I continued. "Your mother had tried to waken you, but you went back to sleep, or pretended you had. But certainly you heard the phone ring when your father here called from Denver."

Joe's eyes widened.

"Yes, Cecelia," I said softly. "You heard the phone ring, and not long after that, you heard a car coming in from the road—a familiar-sounding car. It was Chandler's car, wasn't it?"

Out of the corner of my eye, I saw Menken stiffen, but my gaze was intent on Cecelia, watching for even the slightest change in her bearing. At the mention of Chandler's name, a dark cloud swept across her face, crimping the softness of her cheeks and jaw first into pain and then into the stiffness of hatred. I could see her teeth now, but no words slipped between them.

"Yes, that angers you, doesn't it, Cecelia?"

Joe said, "Em, I can't see what—"

"Yes," I pressed, "you heard his car, and your heart leapt. But then he got to where your mother stood, and he stopped. You thought he'd come to see *you*. But no, it was your *mother* he wanted to see; you didn't know that. Until then, you had thought it was only Heather's mother that he visited, that it was some other man your mother had gone away with. How *could* he?"

Cecelia's eyes boiled with feeling.

Menken put his hands on his daughter's shoulders and leaned his forehead down to rest on the back of her head. "You don't have to say anything, Cecelia," he whispered anxiously. "I can take you home now. Em, that's enough. She's too young."

Ignoring his words, I said, "All those times he came to see you at the stables, you thought it was for you. And now here he was, right out there on the porch, wasn't he? But *she* was there. She stopped him. He stopped for *her*. Yes, he came at least that close; I know that, Cecelia, because he took your mother's journal with him when he left. Think about it, Cecelia: was he just in the neighborhood to exchange a little powder for information? To ask more of his questions? Questions about the oil business, about test holes and the exchange of money, very large amounts of money." I turned my eyes toward Menken. Were my words finding their mark? "Or maybe he really just came to see Miriam."

Menken's hands slackened their grip on Cecelia's shoulders.

Cecelia's chest began to move, breath rising and falling in her with the return of feeling. But still she said nothing.

"What did she do, Cecelia? Did she run in here and lock the door, closing him out of your life? And what happened then? Did he knock on that door? Pound on it? Call out to her? To *her*, Cecelia? But then he left. Left without seeing you. Turned and drove back down that driveway like you didn't even exist."

Cecelia's eyes had grown enormous, whether with fear or anger, I could not discern.

I said, "You and your mother fought about it, didn't you? It must have been terrible, because she had a temper, *didn't* she? Or perhaps you ran away outside somewhere. Did you go see Po? Or did you see him out by the willows, watching your mother dance? Did she dance that day? I bet she didn't. I bet she was afraid. Afraid for *you*, Cecelia. Afraid of what he might do. Afraid of what he might have done already. She loved you so much that she was *afraid*."

Cecelia's eyes slid shut. Far beyond her shoulder, I could see Po Bradley's face pressed anxiously to the window, his hands cupped to either side to cut the glare from the glass, his eyes hot with worry. To the other side of the door, I could see the sheriff and, ever faithful, Sergeant Ortega.

Menken's eyes flew open with understanding. His mouth began to open.

I leaned forward and grabbed Cecelia's face in both my hands. "Then what, Cecelia? What happened *then*? What happened after it got dark?"

Cecelia began to shake, her hands balled into fists.

Menken's voice came as a whisper first. "Em, you are a clever girl, as always." He straightened, looked into my eyes, commanding my attention. I saw a J.C. Menken I'd never seen before: cold and hard as ice. He tipped his head toward the men who waited outside the door. "But did you have to bring all of *them*? How are we going to get past them?" He let go of his daughter and smiled, stepped around in front of her so I'd have to look at him and not her. He shifted his weight onto one hip, a parody of the old jaunty J.C. returning, but with eyes as dark and wild as the storm I'd almost died in. "No problem, we can manage this. We'll just say you were wrong about a supposition, or better, we'll say your shock treatment didn't work."

I met his gaze. "Tell me more."

"What more is there to tell? Darling Em, you did your job well, as always, except for one thing: you weren't supposed to bring the law into this."

"Oh, no?"

He patted Cecelia's shoulders. "I had something gentler in mind when

I asked your help with this. Yes, we need to help her out of her melancholy, but your methods are entirely too brash. Cecelia, dear, why don't you wait outside on the porch?"

Cecelia promptly turned and started for the door.

"No," I said firmly, trying to keep my voice down so the men with their faces to the glass wouldn't hear me. "Cecelia stays here, or I call them in right now."

She froze.

Menken bunched his lips in frustration. "This wasn't what I had in mind," he repeated.

"Oh? Just what *did* you have in mind?"

Menken advanced toward me. "Emily, silly girl, how else was I going to make certain you could marry me?"

"Do *what*?"

He was talking very quickly now. "I'll admit that I was a bit hasty the other night after that dinner with the Howards, but you can't blame a fellow. You see, I *know* you, Em. I know you need everything settled, each detail tucked in where it belongs, and—"

"You cut this shit right now!" I said.

"You see?" he said to Cecelia, taking her in his fatherly grasp once again, "Em understands. I couldn't have her marrying me without knowing. She's a person who must know the truth about things. Has been as long as I've known her." Then, almost plaintively, he added, "It's what draws me to her, actually. Strange, isn't it?"

"Joe, you can't—"

Words continued to tumble from his mouth. "But Cecelia, darling, Em also knows that truth is one thing, and justice another. She understands that I *had* to do what I did to your mother, and, knowing that I was only protecting you, she'll be content now, and marry me, and then we'll be a complete family again. Isn't that right, Em?"

Cecelia opened her eyes. She began to reel, as one drunk.

"No, Joe," I whispered, "it's not that simple."

"Why, sure it is. It—"

"*No!* You're right about me: I like the truth. And this lie can kill you both. Maybe not right away, but little by little, as you warp the entire universe around this one fact you can't stand to notice. Just look what that's done to your daughter." Softly, I said to Cecelia, "Chandler is a monster with a pretty face, Cecelia. I wish I could have spared you the kind of lessons he deals out, but if you've got to have them, then for God's sake, *learn* from them. *Speak*, Cecelia. There was no one else in the house with you. There was no man, not Chandler, not Po, and not your father. Because after Chandler came, your mother was so scared and upset she called your father back and told him not to come that day, didn't she?"

Tears formed in Menken's eyes as he drank in his daughter's face, knowing that the ease with which he touched her now might at any instant be taken from him.

"Joe," I whispered sadly, "you'll have to let her go now."

Sorrow spilled past his eyelashes and down his face. His lips moved, mouthing the words: *Please, Em, she's all I've got,* and then, finding his voice, he said, "*Please,* Em. Right, she was cheating on me, and I couldn't let her do that. I struck her. I . . ." His voice trailed off miserably, uncertain, ashamed.

I reached out and took her hand. "Don't let your father do this, Cecelia," I said softly. "He's a good man, a decent man. Don't make him go to jail for you." I touched her hair, that tousled halo of a fallen angel. A strand clung to my finger, holding me an instant longer, just as her need of me always had, and for that instant, I gave myself to Menken's tender dream that we could save her from what she'd done. "Men don't kill with poison, do they, Cecelia? No, that's a woman's trick, even a woman who's still a child."

Cecelia stood quietly for a long time, staring at some point on the far wall near the floor. Then she turned to her weeping father, her face crumpling up like a little girl's, and said, "I'm sorry, Daddy. I only meant her to be dead for a little while."

42

IT TOOK NO SMALL FEAT OF ENGINEERING TO GET J.C. MENKEN, Cindey Howard, and Julia Richards all in the lobby of the Brown Palace Hotel at the same moment. In fact, it took the assistance of a slowly recovering Mrs. Wentworth and a couple of lies, but it was worth it.

"You!" Cindey wheezed when she saw me. She turned to Mrs. Wentworth. "You said we were meeting—"

Mrs. Wentworth smiled. "I said diddly. Suck it up, Cindey."

Cindey wheeled next on Julia. "What are *you* doing here?" she burbled, as if Julia had no right to frequent a public place.

"I'm here to find out who killed Miriam," Julia said flatly. "Or at least that's what Em said."

Cindey spun around to face J.C. Menken, seething. "*You* know the answer to *that*," she spat.

Menken had turned gray underneath his tan. He looked warily at me. He had been the most difficult to persuade to come. It had been less than forty-eight hours since I had extracted his daughter's confession, and it would be a great many years before we would be friends again, if ever. He had not wanted to see me. He had insisted angrily that he must stay near the phone, in case Cecelia needed him and was able to call from the juvenile psychiatric center where she was being held while the courts of Wyoming and Colorado decided her fate. Menken twitched, looked ready to bolt.

I said, "This is for you, Joe."

Cindey began to bray, her voice louder than I had ever heard it. "I'll tell you who killed Miriam, Julia! It was this man's precious little darling! Yes! That's true, isn't it, Joe?"

Menken drew himself up with glacial dignity. "That is no secret, Cindey."

"Hah! She won't be allowed back in that fancy school of hers, ever!" Cindey retorted.

"Joe! Tell me this isn't true!" Julia gasped, but Joe did not pause to answer her. His attention was focused on Cindey.

I said, "It is true, but it wasn't her idea, was it, Cindey? You were the one who told her that cocaine could kill. You even suggested the hot chocolate, didn't you?"

Cindey's eyes glittered with triumph. "I may have told her to put some of Chandler's powder in her mother's cocoa if she wanted her to go away again. . . . But I only meant it as a *jest*. You can't hang anything on *me*!"

Joe's eyes had gone black as soot. They seemed to bore into Cindey. He said, very slowly and distinctly, "You are the sickest woman I have ever met."

"Me?" squealed Cindey. "Me! I'm a faithful wife! I—"

I was about to say, No one gives you the opportunity to be otherwise, but just then, with the most exquisite timing I could have hope for, a flood of middle-aged and elderly women spewed out of a meeting room onto the second floor balcony. Betty Bloom and I had planned the event carefully, selecting the moment when the women's society that supported the local symphony would be convening for their monthly tea. On cue, the party was just breaking up, and all those opinionated, gossip-hungry dowagers now sluiced down the grand staircase into the lobby, washing all around us like a tide of deadly jelly fish. Bringing up the rear, I saw Betty, flushing the stragglers ahead of her. She winked, clearly enjoying herself.

Joe's eyes locked on Cindey's. He thundered with anger, oblivious to the sea of nosy women who now churned around us. "What do you know of faith? You have no virtue! You're a bitter, flesh-eating wart on humanity! You've envied my wife as long as I've known you. You're a sad sight, Cindey. You couldn't have the man you wanted in college, so you married Fred. You couldn't have children of your own to manipulate, so you tried to poison my daughter's feelings toward her mother. You—"

Cindey's face turned a mottled bluish red. Her eyes rolled left and right, and her lips opened and closed like a fish sucking air. "So what if I did? She deserved it, hanging around with that—"

"That man who wouldn't have you!" I said, pitching my voice toward the growing crowd.

Cindey spun in horror, taking in the faces of the women around her. "Lisa! Hilary! Don't let these people . . ."

"Let us what?" I said. "Call a spade a spade? Hey, you're the wife of a felon now. Oh, sure, you've been lucky so far; your husband's arrest in Wyoming hasn't made the *Denver Post* yet, but it will. And when it does, there will be detailed reporting about his embezzlement, his drug trafficking, and his blatant rip-off of investor's funds. I'll bet some of the women in this lobby had money in some of his spurious wells, didn't you, ladies?"

Glances flew back and forth. Jaws began to flap, and a low rumble of unhappy murmurs grew into a yelping chorus.

"You can't say that!" Cindey spat. "That's libel!"

I tipped my head to one side and said, "So sue me. Madam, I've tried my best to feel sorry for you, but I'm just not that big."

"Righteous!" caroled Mrs. Wentworth, who was finding her sense of humor as she warmed to the performance. "It's about time we shook a little reality into this community!"

Gasping, Cindey turned to Joe, squinched her face up into a pathetic approximation of a pout, and whined, "Joe, how can you let them do this to me?"

J.C. Menken opened his mouth, and said simply, "Cindey Howard, I used to pity you. Now I hold you beneath contempt." And with that, he turned on his heel and marched out the main exit from the hotel and onto the street.

I grabbed Julia by the elbow and dashed after him. We caught him at the corner of Seventeenth Street and Broadway, and then only because he had to break stride for a light. "Joe!" I hollered over the roar of accelerating traffic. "Joe, listen! Julia wants to tell you something!"

"I do?" said Julia.

Menken turned and glared at me.

I said, "Yes, Julia, you do. Okay, I told you I'd let you know who killed Miriam. Yes, it was Cecelia. It was Cecelia, but it wasn't. That was what that whole scene was for in there, a chance to let Joe name just a little bit of the damage that Cindey has done to him and his family. Yeah, Miriam screwed up; she had an affair and she ran off to heal herself, but she came back when she'd grown up enough to love this man. This man here, Julia. This man who can quietly find it in his heart to love a woman who's done all of that. Think about it, Julia."

Julia's eyes were on Menken. She was thinking.

I took a breath. "But even more, think about Cecelia. She's made a mistake that will follow her all the days of her life, and no relationship she can ever have will be the same—not with her friends, her teachers, her lovers, or even her father here. She's just a girl, and she's all but ruined her life. But she can learn from her mistake, and hope to heal into a worthy woman, *if* there's someone there for her, someone tough enough, mature enough, and smart enough to stand by her and guide her without being sucked into all her games. I'm thinking that someone might be you, Julia."

Julia's lips parted. Her eyes searched Menken's face. His eyes had widened with naked pain, and hope.

I nodded. "You see? Joe can't trust me anymore, not ever, and I never was the right companion for him. I'm too young, too full of my own problems, but you two go way back. I'm not saying you have to fall in love, but you can love each other as only two people who share this much can, and keep each other company while you help each other help Cecelia, y'know?"

43

IN HANDS THAT COULDN'T GROW WARM, I CRADLED THE CUP OF tea Tina Schwartz had given me. Steam rose in curling columns, soothing my eyes from the biting Denver smog. "How did you know?" she asked.

"It was when I heard the nine-one-one tape. Or not exactly then, but I kept thinking about it, wondering what seemed to be missing."

"And that was?"

"The voice of Miriam's attacker. I couldn't hear it. That's because no one was there. You see, the sheriff withheld the true cause of death so he would know when he found a true eyewitness. That gave everyone the impression that someone strong enough to rough up a grown woman had pinned her down and forced her to consume enough cocaine to kill her. I'd always wondered about that. It's terribly toxic stuff, but still, it's damned difficult to force that much into someone who is fighting you. But Sheriff Duluth misunderstood the tape; he thought the killer was a big, fully enraged man. After all, there were signs of a struggle, and bruises all over her, indicating that she had in fact been pinned."

"Then what did she die of?"

"Asphyxiation. She suffocated when she began to vomit while lying on her back."

"Then it wasn't really murder?"

"Only the original intent had been to kill."

What I didn't tell Tina just then was that as I lay in Chandler's arms, I had finally faced how angry I was at my own mother, and in facing that, I had made room for seeing how right she was that I was frittering away my life. I'd had to see that by throwing me out on my own, she was doing me a favor, forcing me to grow up and take responsibility for myself at last. In facing my own capacity to simultaneously hate and cling to my mother, I had come to see what might have happened.

I said, "I love Cecelia, or I loved to think that I was her one true friend, the one in all the world who understood her. I wanted my love to heal her, to have her grow up in my own image, another little incurable romantic like myself, another sojourner after the truth."

Tina smiled. "There are worse things to want for someone."

"Yeah? What about a dose of reality? Wouldn't it have been better for Cecelia if I had been a little tougher on her right along, maybe looked behind her manipulations and tried to see what was making her so angry? The kid was a mess, but I didn't like to see that. I just wanted to feel good and noble about *myself*, for Pete's sake."

"Oh, I see. Now you're a specialist on teenage behavior and addictions."

"No, but . . ."

"Yeah, psychotherapists do this to themselves, too. Want to take responsibility for the failures of their patients."

"But she was just a kid."

"Right. A kid with a damned hard head and one hell of a temper. So let it go, if you can. Stay at it with good intentions, and keep the courage it takes to care about people, and you'll learn what you're really responsible for, and what you're not."

"Maybe." I glowered. "Maybe I'll just move to Alaska and mind my own business. I've had enough of other people's problems." I was getting tired of thinking about responsibility, and I let the conversation lag, wondering once more if it had been quite right for me to keep Cecelia's appointment. I had told myself I was doing it for Tina's sake, to let her know what had become of her almost client, but I knew in my heart of hearts that in fact I had just needed someone safe to tell the whole awful story to. "Wouldn't it have tasted funny?" I asked.

"What?"

"The chocolate. I've never taken drugs."

"Funny? It would have anesthetized her mouth in an instant." Tina put a hand over her mouth in shock. "Then the poor woman knew what her daughter had done to her."

"No, she didn't know *exactly*. Like both Julia and Chandler told me, she was one of the great holdouts in college. She didn't take drugs. She was hypersensitive. And that was the problem, really. There was a lot of cocaine in the chocolate, but she didn't drink that much of it, only enough to get a ferocious buzz, Carlos tells me. What killed her was . . ." I buried my own face in my hands. "You can hear her on the tape, screaming, begging. She begged Cecelia. She begged God. She said, 'Oh, God, please stop him.' And yes, there was a commotion, as if someone was assaulting her. But that was *her*—Miriam. Throwing things. Banging into things. All her work to know herself, and in her last moment, she threw another fit!"

"Maybe it was just a reaction to the drug. So Miriam took a swallow of the laced chocolate and it was not enough to kill her, but enough to send her flying. Then what happened?"

I shook my head. "She begged her daughter to phone for help."

"But the ambulance didn't get there soon enough."

"It's a twenty-minute run even at top speed with sirens blaring."

"And Miriam was having an unusually strong reaction."

"Yes. She tried to vomit. She was so wound up that she hit her head on the headboard, hard. She fell back across the bed and started to thrash."

Aghast, Tina said, "And Cecelia didn't move to *help* her?"

I hung my head. "Cecelia thought her mother was having a seizure. She didn't know what to do, so she just got up on the bed and held her down. I guess the vomit finally came, but she got it in her lungs and suffocated." Tears burned my eyes. "The poor girl thought she was helping."

"She made that call."

"Yes, she called all right. And she washed and dried the cup she'd put the chocolate in. And burned what was left of Chandler's little 'packet.' It hurts. It hurts to know that the little girl I cared so much about could be so cold." I fought back tears, unwilling to cry in front of a stranger.

"Anger isn't cold, Em."

"I suppose she even faked the whole memory loss thing," I said bitterly.

Tina looked at her hands. "Em, kids don't feel things the same way adults do. And kids like Cecelia . . . well, we really don't know *what* they feel, and in what sense they remember things. You'd be amazed how easily the mind amends things, rearranges them, attaches them to something else. Tells us we weren't responsible. Tells us someone else did what we can't bear to remember. And then there's the matter of feelings. Cecelia may have been so busy not getting blamed for what she'd done that she's never faced her guilt or loss."

That struck a chord.

We sat together quietly for a while, I with my face in my hands. There seemed to be no hurry; I'd paid for a full hour, even though I wasn't going to include it or any of the other expenses I'd run up when I paid Joe back his thousand dollars. It just didn't seem fair, or clean. Finally, I said, "I want to blame that idiot Po for lifting that packet of coke out of Chandler's car and then leaving it in his truck where Celia could find it. Or that monster Chandler for—"

Tina shifted in her seat, her manner changing ever so subtly from an interested acquaintance to a trained listener beginning to steer the conversation. "Tell me more about that monster Chandler."

Tears rained down through my fingers. "Tina, why did I go to that man! I mean—what, am I tired of living? I wasn't sure he wasn't the one who killed Miriam, not really! Do I have that little regard for myself? Am I crazy?"

"Define crazy."

"Someone who doesn't listen to her own best sense."

"Then we're all crazy most of the time."

"But this is more extreme."

"Yes."

"What am I supposed to do? Forgive myself? Write it off as a walk on the wild side? The man is, after all, a criminal!"

"Nothing bad happened."

"Nothing? Oh, sure, I got lucky this time, is that what you mean? I fly hell-bent into a storm, but no matter, I landed safely and got a nice foot massage," I said bitterly.

"Weren't you running from some pretty bad men?"

"To another? Hell, I could have gone anywhere else!" I gave in for a while to my tears, but at last I said the thing that so heavily weighted my soul: "How am I supposed to trust myself in the future?"

Tina leaned back and stared out the window. "Em, you ask so much of yourself. You want to know the answers to some of life's toughest questions. You want to slay *all* the dragons. *And* you don't want to take risks. Tell me what is wrong with this picture."

"But other people aren't this *reckless.*"

"No. But you kept your head and landed the plane. Then you had dinner in a public place, you phoned your friend in Denver for a backup, and, even if you were beginning to hope for something else in that man's room, you had a good cry and then just had a good night's sleep. Sounds like you needed both."

Pitifully, I said, "No, that's not all."

"What, then?"

I squeezed my fingertips into my face until I saw lights on the backs of my eyelids. "Sure, I finally felt all that pain I'd been holding back, but also I felt . . . I felt this raw, oozing sore where my heart should be. It's like I can't love anyone, and I *hate* my mother. Or feel like I don't even have a mother. Or like I do, but I can't let myself open to her. I'm scared *shitless* of her; it's as if I think she's going to take me down by the cottonwood trees and drown me in the creek. And I . . . I told Chandler. He got it out of me. I don't really feel like that, do I?"

"Don't you?"

I felt numb.

Tina said nothing for a long while. At last, she spoke slowly and carefully, making sure I understood her. "It's the great surprise, to find that even when we're grown, we still need our parents; that deep inside, we're still only children. You're right, Em, most people live a more careful life, but perhaps they never learn what you have. Perhaps they aren't willing, as you are, to walk through their own personal underworlds. Hell's a scary place, Em, and even when we want to go there, clear out the demons and reclaim our own darkness, it's damned hard to take that first step down the stairs. For that, sometimes we need to find someone as crazy as Chandler to seduce us into going." She looked away. "Count yourself lucky, Em; some people's Chandlers aren't such gentlemen."

"Like Cecelia's," I said bitterly.

"Like Cecelia's. He screwed up that time, didn't he? She was too damned young and confused to deal with him. It wasn't the first time he'd blown it, and it won't be the last. But then, sociopaths don't really care, do they? It's all a game to them."

I thought of Chandler's tender young bride, who had gone home sick, a wreck. That bullet, Miriam had dodged. She had waited until she was much older and stronger to visit hell.

Tina was still talking. "Isn't it awful when people make mistakes? But you're smart and twice Cecelia's age, and you are going to learn from this experience."

"Don't make me sorry I told you this stuff."

"Em, I don't want to take your sorrow away from you. But I must say this: little children cling to their mothers, or to the mothers they wish their mothers were. Part of growing up is learning to step out on your own. To fight your own fights."

In rising fury, I said, "You're suggesting I don't know how to fight?"

"I'm suggesting that deep inside of each and every one of us is a little girl who wishes that mommy and daddy would magically take care of her forever. We're vulnerable. We can fight tooth and nail to learn all there is to learn, and grow as strong as we can, but we're still just human beings, still vulnerable to our feelings and our needs. And we can do everything perfectly, right all our wrongs, and still be killed. It's *painful* realizing that on our best days, we're only flesh and bones."

I pondered that one for about a minute, which, as she was saying, was about all I could stand. Then I set it aside, making a bitter joke. "So you're saying that messing around with psychopaths is all part of growing up."

"You think you'd do it again?"

"No," I said, a bit too quickly. But even as I said it, the memory of another trip to hell with another man-devil crowded my mind. What was it going to take for me to learn?

Tina gave me a wry smile. "Well, even if you do, you're normal. It's not human to learn quickly. We like to try something a couple times at least, just to make certain we didn't miss the shortcut that lets us get away with eating nothing but sugar, or which makes the house clean itself. But learning from our mistakes and growing up are kind of the same thing, don't you think? So you get to choose: are you going to sweep your fears and failings under the rug like Cecelia, pity yourself and blame them on someone else like Cindey, or get down there and face them?"

"I don't know *how.*"

"Then let someone help." Tina sat up and put her hands on her knees with a little pat. "Well. Thanks for coming in. I appreciate knowing what happened."

I dug my hand into my pocket and pulled out my beleaguered checkbook. It would be a while before the ebbing tide of my finances began to flow again, but I had resolved that morning that I would, sooner or later, find another job as a geologist.

Tina said, "Put it away. This visit's on the house." She stood up and began getting ready to go out, picking up her coat and her purse. "I'll walk out with you. Got to pick my daughter up from school."

As I watched her preparations, I felt a rising panic at the thought of walking out the door myself. "Tina," I began.

"Yes?"

"You got another minute or two?"

"Sure."

I wasn't sure what I wanted to say. Tina stood expectantly by the door.

Well, what the hell, I thought. "You're right: this Chandler thing has me thinking. Um, why do women find men like that attractive? I mean in the real world, not this underworld stuff."

"Why a bad man instead of a good one?"

"Yeah. It seems every time I meet a good man, I push him away. Like this guy Jim Erikson. I look at what happened between us and I know damned well I set that meeting up for failure. I pushed him away." I stopped, awash in longing. "And hell, someday I might even like to have a kid or two—I don't know—but it seems important to have a decent relationship first, one that can last. And then there's this itch I have to have a job. No, a career. I . . . I'm having trouble sorting all this out."

Tina smiled. "That's it? That's all the underworld you've got to walk through?"

I smiled back in spite of myself. "Well, that's the easy stuff on the top steps."

"I see. And you're thinking maybe it would be nice to have company along the way?"

"Something like that. But not a psychologist. Not a 'Sit down on the couch and I'll tell you what's the matter with your head.' No offense, but I've met a few lately, and I was thinking of someone more like an . . . assistant. Or a teacher. Or a guide."

Tina cocked her head to one side. "I don't know about leading you anywhere I haven't been myself, but I do have a good flashlight." She thought for a while. "Yeah, I think we could make it work, and I'd be glad to walk with you as far as you'd like to have my company."

"That would be nice," I said. "Some light for my darkness."

Postscript

There is usually an author's note at the end of an Em Hansen mystery, but this time Miriam gets the last word. We found another volume of her journal. It was written on the clouds above the wide Wyoming prairie:

Date? The no time infinite time!

I am one now, and touch my finger to the non-linear journal of eternity. In my wildest moments among the living, I had no idea how fine. I spent so much time when there was time and in time running from the dark being half of one and all to another, now I am all of us and none. Ha ha! Darkness and light are one.